KARIN SLAUGHTER

KISSCUT

D0210186

HARPER

An Imprint of HarperCollinsPublishers

This is a work of fiction. Names, characters, places, and incidents are products of the author's imagination or are used fictitiously and are not to be construed as real. Any resemblance to actual events, locales, organizations, or persons, living or dead, is entirely coincidental.

HARPER

An Imprint of HarperCollins*Publishers*
10 East 53rd Street
New York, New York 10022-5299

Copyright © 2002 by Karin Slaughter
Excerpts from *Blindsighted, Kisscut, A Faint Cold Fear,* and *Indelible*
© 2001, 2002, 2003, 2004 by Karin Slaughter
ISBN 978-0-06-053404-2

First Harper paperback printing: July 2008
First HarperTorch paperback printing: October 2003
First William Morrow hardcover printing: October 2002

HarperCollins® and Harper® are registered trademarks of HarperCollins Publishers.

Printed in the United States of America

Visit Harper paperbacks on the World Wide Web
at www.harpercollins.com

20 19 18 17

For Doris Smart
who loved Auburn football
and reading—in that order

KISSCUT

Saturday

1

"Dancing Queen," Sara Linton mumbled with the music as she made her way around the skating rink. "Young and sweet, only seventeen."

She heard a furious clicking of wheels to her left and turned just in time to catch a small child before he crashed into her.

"Justin?" she asked, recognizing the seven year old. She held him up by the back of his shirt as his ankles wobbled over his in-line skates.

"Hey, Dr. Linton," Justin managed around gasps for breath. His helmet was too big for his head, and he pushed it back several times as he tried to look up at her.

Sara returned his smile, trying not to laugh. "Hello, Justin."

"I guess you like this music, huh? My mom likes it, too." He stared at her openly, his lips slightly parted. Like most of Sara's patients, Justin seemed a bit shocked to see her outside of the clinic. Sometimes she wondered if they thought she lived in the basement there, waiting for them to get colds or fevers so she could see them.

"Anyway," Justin pushed back his helmet again, knocking himself in the nose with his elbow pad. "I saw you singing it."

"Here," Sara offered, leaning down to adjust the chin strap. The music in the rink was so loud that Sara could feel the bass vibrating through the plastic buckle as she tightened it under his chin.

"Thanks," Justin yelled, then for some reason he put both his hands on top of the helmet, as if to rest them. The motion threw him off balance, and he stumbled, clamping on to Sara's leg.

Sara grabbed his shirt again and led them both over to the safety railing lining the rink. After trying on a pair of in-line skates herself, Sara had asked for the old four-wheel kind, not wanting to fall on her ass in front of half the town.

"Wow." Justin giggled, throwing his arms over the railing for support. He was looking down at her skates. "Your feet are so huge!"

Sara looked down at her skates, feeling a flush of embarrassment. She had been teased about her large feet since she was seven years old. After nearly thirty years of hearing it, Sara still felt the urge to hide under the bed with a bowl of chocolate-fudge ice cream.

"You're wearing boy's skates!" Justin screeched, letting go of the rail so that he could point at her black skates. Sara caught him just before he hit the ground.

"Sweety," Sara whispered politely into his ear. "Remember this when you're due for your booster shots."

Justin managed a smile for his pediatrician. "I think my mom wants me," he mumbled, edging along the rail, hand over hand, casting a wary eye over his shoulder to make sure Sara was not following him.

She crossed her arms, leaning against the railing as she watched him go. Sara loved kids, a characteristic most pediatricians shared, but there was something to be said for not spending her Saturday night surrounded by them.

"That your date?" Tessa asked, coming to a stop beside her.

Sara gave her sister a hard look. "Remind me how I got roped into this."

Tessa tried to smile. "Because you love me?"

"Right," Sara returned caustically. Across the rink, Sara picked out Devon Lockwood, Tessa's latest boyfriend, who also worked in the Linton family's plumbing business. Devon was leading his nephew around the kiddy rink while his brother watched.

"His mother hates me," Tessa mumbled. "She gives me nasty looks every time I get near him."

"Daddy's the same way about us," Sara reminded her.

Devon noticed them staring and waved.

"He's good with children," Sara noted, returning his wave.

"He's good with his hands," Tessa said in a low voice, almost to herself. She turned back to Sara. "Speaking of which, where's Jeffrey?"

Sara looked back at the front entrance, wondering that herself. Wondering, too, why she cared whether or not her ex-husband showed up. "I don't know," she answered. "When did this place get so packed?"

"It's Saturday night and football season hasn't started; what else are people going to do?" Tessa asked, but did not let Sara change the subject. "Where's Jeffrey?"

"Maybe he won't come."

Tessa smiled in a way that let Sara know she was holding back a snide comment.

"Go ahead and say it."

"I wasn't going to say anything," Tessa said, and Sara could not tell if she was lying or not.

"We're just dating." Sara paused, wondering whom she was trying to convince, Tessa or herself. She added, "It's not even serious."

"I know."

"We've barely even kissed."

Tessa held up her palms in resignation. "I know," she repeated, a smirk on her lips.

"Just a few dates. That's all."

"You don't have to convince me."

Sara groaned as she leaned back against the railing. She felt stupid, like a teenager instead of a grown woman. She had divorced Jeffrey two years ago after catching him with the woman who owned the sign shop in town. Why she had started seeing him again was as much a mystery to Sara as it was to her family.

A ballad came on, and the lights dimmed. Sara watched the mirrored ball drop down from the ceiling, scattering little squares of light all over the rink.

"I need to go to the bathroom," Sara told her sister. "Will you keep an eye out for Jeff?"

Tessa glanced over Sara's shoulder. "Somebody just went in."

"There are two stalls now." Sara turned toward the women's rest room just in time to see a large teenage girl go in. Sara recognized the girl as Jenny Weaver, one of her patients. She waved, but the girl didn't see her.

Tessa muttered, "Hope you can wait."

Sara frowned, watching another teenager she did not recognize follow Jenny into the rest room. At this rate, Sara would go into renal failure before Jeffrey arrived.

Tessa tilted her head toward the front door. "Speaking of tall, dark, and handsome."

Sara felt a foolish smile come to her lips as she watched Jeffrey make his way toward the rink. He was still dressed for work in a charcoal-gray suit with a burgundy tie. As chief of police for Grant County, he knew most of the people in the room. He glanced around, looking for Sara, she supposed, stopping here and there to shake hands. She refused to do anything that would get his attention as he walked through the crowd. At this point in their relationship, Sara was content to let Jeffrey do all of the work.

Sara had met Jeffrey on one of her earlier cases as town coroner. She had taken the helm of the medical examiner's office as a way to earn extra money to buy out her retiring partner at the Heartsdale Children's Clinic. Even though she had paid off Dr. Barney years ago, Sara still kept the job. She liked the challenge of pathology. Twelve years ago, Sara had done her residency in the emergency room of Atlanta's Grady Hospital. Going from such a fast-paced, life-and-death job to tummy aches and sinus infections at the clinic had been a shock to her system. The coroner's job was a challenge that helped keep her mind sharp.

Jeffrey finally caught sight of her. He stopped in the middle of shaking Betty Reynolds's hand, the corners of his mouth rising slowly, then dipping into a frown as he was pulled back into conversation with the owner of the town's five-and-dime.

Sara could guess what Betty was talking about. The store had been broken into twice in the last three months. Betty's posture was adversarial, and even though Jeffrey's attention was obviously elsewhere, she continued to speak to him.

Finally, Jeffrey nodded, giving Betty a pat on the back as he shook her hand, probably making an appointment to talk with her tomorrow. He extricated himself, then walked toward Sara, a sly smile on his face.

"Hey," Jeffrey said. Before she could stop herself, Sara was shaking his hand the way almost everyone else in the rink had.

"Hello, Jeffrey," Tessa interrupted, her tone uncharacteristically sharp. It was usually Eddie, their father, who was rude to Jeffrey.

Jeffrey gave a puzzled smile. "Hey, Tessie."

"Uh-huh," Tessa mumbled, pushing off from the rail. She skated away, tossing Sara a knowing look over her shoulder.

Jeffrey asked, "What was that about?"

Sara pulled back her hand, but Jeffrey held on to her fingers just long enough to let her know it was his choice to release her. He was so damn sure of himself. More than anything else, this quality appealed to Sara at a very base level.

She crossed her arms, saying, "You're late."

"I had trouble getting away."

"Is her husband out of town?"

He gave her the same look he gave witnesses he knew were lying. "I was talking to Frank," he said, naming the lead detective on the Grant County squad. "I told him that he's in charge tonight. I don't want anything to interrupt us."

"Interrupt what?"

The same smile tugged at the corner of his lips. "Oh, I thought I'd seduce you tonight."

She laughed, backing up as he leaned in to kiss her.

"Kissing usually works better when the lips touch," he suggested.

"Not in front of half my practice," she countered.

"Come here, then."

Despite her better judgment, Sara ducked under the railing and took his hand. He rolled her into the back of the rink by the bathroom, tucking them into a corner and out of sight.

"This better?" he asked.

"Yeah," Sara answered, looking down at Jeffrey, because with the skates on she was a couple inches taller. "Much better. I really need to use the bathroom."

She started to move, but he stopped her, putting his hands on her waist.

"Jeff," she said, aware her tone was far from threatening.

"You are so beautiful, Sara."

She rolled her eyes like a teenager.

He laughed, trying, "I thought about kissing you all last night."

"Yeah?"

"I miss the way you taste."

She tried to sound bored. "It's still Colgate."

"That's not the taste I was talking about."

Her mouth opened in surprise, and he smiled, obviously pleased with her reaction. Sara felt something stir deep inside her and was about to say something—she had no idea what—when his pager went off.

He kept staring at her as if he didn't hear the beeping.

Sara cleared her throat, asking, "Shouldn't you answer that?"

He finally looked down at the pager clipped to his belt, muttering, "Shit," at what he saw.

"What?"

"Break-in," he answered curtly.

"I thought Frank was on call."

"He is for the little things. I've got to use the pay phone."

"Where's your cell phone?"

"Dead battery." Jeffrey seemed to get his irritation under control enough to offer her a reassuring smile. "Nothing is going to ruin tonight, Sara." He put his hand to her cheek. "Nothing is more important to me than tonight."

"Got a hot date after our dinner?" she teased. "Because we can cancel if you need to."

He narrowed his eyes at her before turning away.

Sara watched him go, letting a "Jesus Christ" hiss out between her lips as she leaned back against the wall. She could not believe that in less than three minutes he had managed to turn her into a blithering idiot.

She jumped as the bathroom door banged shut. Jenny Weaver stood there, looking out at the rink as if she was contemplating something. The teenager's skin looked pasty next to the black long sleeved T-shirt she was wearing. She held a dark red backpack in her hand, which she swung over her shoulder as Sara rolled toward her. The bag brushed against Sara's chest in a wide arc.

"Whoa," Sara said, backing up.

Jenny blinked, recognizing her pediatrician. She mumbled a soft, "Sorry," averting her eyes.

"It's okay," Sara returned, thinking to start a conversation; the girl seemed troubled. "How about you?" Sara asked. "Are you okay?"

"Yes, ma'am," Jenny said, clutching the bag to her chest.

Before Sara could say anything else, Jenny walked away.

Sara watched the teenager retreat into a crowd of kids near the video game room. The light from the screens gave Jenny's body a green cast as she disappeared into the corner. Sara sensed something was wrong, but it wasn't like she could chase the girl down and demand to know what was going on. At that age, everything was a drama. Knowing teenage girls, there was probably a boy involved.

The lights came up as the ballad ended, and another old rock song blared over the speakers, the bass resonating in Sara's chest. She watched the skaters in the rink pick up the tempo, wondering if she had ever been that agile. While Skatie's had changed ownership several times since Sara was a teenager, it was still the hot spot for Grant County's teens. Sara had spent many a weekend night in the back of this very building, necking with Steve Mann, her first serious boyfriend. Their relationship had not been so much passionate as an alliance, both of them united in one cause: to get out of Grant. Steve's father had been struck down by a heart attack their senior year and Steve had been running the family hardware store ever since. Now he was married with kids. Sara had escaped to Atlanta, but returned a few years later.

And here she was tonight, back at Skatie's, necking with Jeffrey Tolliver. Or at least trying to.

Sara shrugged it off as she turned toward the bathroom. She put her hand on the doorknob, then jerked it back as she felt something sticky. The light was still low in this part of the rink, and Sara had to hold her hand close to her face in order to see what was on it. She caught the scent before she recognized the texture. She looked down at her shirt where Jenny Weaver's backpack had brushed against her.

A narrow streak of blood arced across her chest.

2

Jeffrey tried not to rip the pay phone off the wall, but that was exactly what his hands were itching to do. He took a calming breath, dialed the number to the station, and patiently waited through the rings.

Marla Simms, his secretary and the station's part-time dispatcher, answered, "Good evening, Grant County Police Department, could you hold please?" then clicked him onto hold without waiting for an answer.

He took another deep breath, trying not to let his irritation get the best of him. Jeffrey thought about Sara back in the skating rink, probably talking herself out of their date tonight. Every step he took toward her, Sara took two steps back. He understood her reasons, but that did not mean he had to like them.

Jeffrey leaned against the wall, feeling the sweat start to drip down his back. August was coming on full force, making the record-breaking highs Georgia had seen in June and July look like winter weather. Some days, going outside, he felt as if he was breathing through a wet washrag. He loosened his tie and undid the top button of his shirt to let some air in.

A short bark of laughter came from the front of the building, and Jeffrey peered around the corner, to get a clear view of the parking lot. There was a small group of boys hanging out beside a beat-up old Camaro, passing a cigarette between them. The pay phone was to the side of the building, so Jeffrey was shadowed by the bright green-and-yellow canopy. He thought he caught a whiff of pot, but wasn't sure. The kids had the stance of boys up to no good. Jeffrey recognized this not just because he was a cop but because he had hung out with a similar group at that age.

He was debating whether or not to approach them when Marla clicked onto the line.

"Good evening, Grant County Police Department, thanks for holding. Can I help you?"

"Marla, it's Jeffrey."

"Oh, hey, Chief," she said. "Sorry to bother you. It was a false alarm down at one of the stores."

"Which one?" he asked, remembering the earful he had just gotten from Betty Reynolds, who owned the five-and-dime downtown.

"Cleaners," she said. "Old man Burgess accidentally set it off."

Jeffrey wondered at Marla, who was well into her seventies, calling Bill Burgess an old man, but he let that slide. He asked, "Anything else?"

"There was something at the diner Brad called in, but they didn't find anything."

"What'd he call in?"

"Just said he thought he saw something, is all. You know how Brad is, calls in his own shadow." She gave a small chuckle. Brad was somewhat of a mascot around the station house, a twenty-one-year-old man whose round face and wispy blond hair made him look more like a boy. It was a joke among the senior squad to steal Brad's hat and hide it around various landmarks in town. Jeffrey had seen it resting on top of the statue of General Lee in front of the high school just last week.

Jeffrey thought of Sara. "Frank is in charge tonight. Don't page me unless someone's dead."

"Two birds with one stone," Marla chuckled again. "The coroner and the chief in one call."

He tried to remind himself that he had moved from Birmingham to Grant because he wanted to be in a small town where everyone knew their neighbor. Everyone knowing his own personal business was one of the few tradeoffs. Jeffrey was about to say something innocuous to Marla, but stopped when he heard a loud shriek from the parking lot.

He leaned around the corner to take a look just as a girl's voice yelled, "Fuck you, you fucking bastard."

Marla said, "Chief?"

"Hold on," he whispered, feeling his gut clench at the anger in the girl's voice. He knew from experience that a ticked-off young girl was the worst thing to have to deal with in a parking lot on a Saturday night. Boys he could handle, it was all a pissing contest and, for the most part, any young man wanted to be stopped from getting into an actual fight. Young girls tended to take a lot to get riled up and a hell of a lot more to get calmed back down. An angry teenage girl was something to fear, especially when she had a gun in her hand.

"I'm going to kill you, you fucking bastard," she yelled at one of the boys. His friends quickly peeled off into a semicircle, and the young man stood alone, the gun pointed at his chest. The girl was no more than four feet away from her target, and as Jeffrey watched, she took a step closer, narrowing the gap.

"Shit," Jeffrey hissed, then, remembering he had the phone in his hand, he ordered, "Get Frank and Matt over to Skatie's right now."

"They're over in Madison."

"Lena and Brad, then," he said. "Silent approach. There's a girl with a gun in the front parking lot."

Jeffrey slipped the phone back into its cradle, feeling his body tense. His throat was tight, and his carotid artery felt like a pulsating snake inside his throat. A thousand things went through his mind in the course of a few seconds, but he pushed these thoughts away as he took off his suit jacket and slid his paddle holster behind his back. Jeffrey held his arms out to the side as he walked into the parking lot. The young girl glanced his way as he came into her line of sight, but she still kept the gun leveled at the boy. The muzzle was pointing down toward the boy's gut and as Jeffrey drew closer he could see that her hand was shaking. Thankfully, her finger was not yet tucked around the trigger.

Jeffrey positioned himself so that he was parallel to the building. The girl's back was to the rink, the parking lot and highway in front of her. He hoped that Lena had the sense to make Brad come in from the side of the building. There was no telling what the girl would do if she felt crowded. One stupid mistake could end up killing a lot of people.

When Jeffrey was about twenty feet from the scene, he said, "Hey," loudly enough to get everyone's attention.

The girl startled, even though she had noticed his approach. Her finger slipped around the trigger. The weapon was a Beretta .32, a so-called mousegun, which was certainly not a man-stopper but could do plenty of damage up close. She had eight chances to kill somebody with that gun. If she was a good shot, and even a monkey would be at such close range, she was holding eight lives in the palm of her hand.

"Y'all get back," Jeffrey told the young men standing around. There was some hesitation before this sunk in, and the group finally moved toward the front of the parking lot. The smell of pot was pungent even at this distance, and Jeffrey could tell from the way the intended victim was swaying that he had smoked a great deal before the girl had surprised him.

"Go away," the girl ordered Jeffrey. She was dressed in black, the sleeves of her T-shirt pushed up past her elbows, probably to fight the heat. She was barely a teenager, and her voice was soft, but she managed to project it well.

She repeated her order. "I said go away."

Jeffrey stood his ground, and she turned her gaze back to the boy and said, "I'm gonna kill him."

Jeffrey held his hands out, asking, "Why?"

She seemed surprised by his question, which was why he had asked it. People with guns don't tend to do a lot of thinking when they're holding them. The nose of the gun tilted down slightly as she addressed Jeffrey.

"To stop him," she said.

"Stop him from what?"

She seemed to mull this over in her mind. "That's nobody's business."

"No?" Jeffrey asked, taking a step closer, then another. He stopped at around fifteen feet from the girl, close enough to see what was going on, but not enough to threaten her.

"No, sir," the girl answered, and her good manners put him a little more at ease. Girls who said "sir" did not shoot people.

"Listen," Jeffrey began, trying to think of something to say. "Do you know who I am?"

"Yes, sir," she answered. "You're Chief Tolliver."

"That's right," he told her. "What do I call you? What's your name?"

She ignored the question, but the boy stirred, as if his pot-altered brain had just clicked in to what was going on. He said, "Jenny. It's Jenny."

"Jenny?" Jeffrey asked her. "That's a pretty name."

"Yeah, w-well," Jenny stammered, obviously taken aback. She recovered quickly, though, saying, "Please just be quiet. I don't want to talk to you."

"Maybe you do," Jeffrey said. "Seems to me like you've got a lot on your mind here."

She seemed to debate this, then raised the gun back to the boy's chest. Her hand still shook. "Go away or I'll kill him."

"With that gun?" Jeffrey asked. "Do you know what it's like to kill someone with a gun? Do you know what that feels like?" He watched her digest this, knowing immediately that she did not have it in her.

Jenny was a large girl, probably fifty pounds overweight. Dressed totally in black, she had the appearance of one of those girls who blends in with the scenery as a way of life. The boy she was aiming the gun at was a good-looking kid, probably the object of an unrequited crush. In Jeffrey's day, she would have left a nasty note in his locker. Today, she was pointing a gun.

"Jenny," Jeffrey began, wondering if the gun was even loaded. "Let's work this out. This guy's not worth getting into trouble over."

"Go away," Jenny repeated, though her voice was not as firm. She used her free hand to wipe her face. He realized that she was crying.

"Jenny, I don't think—" He stopped as she disengaged

the safety. The metallic click was like a knife in his ear. He reached around to his back, putting his hand on his weapon but not drawing.

Jeffrey tried to keep his voice calm and reasonable. "What's happening here, Jenny? Why don't we talk this through? It can't be that bad."

She wiped her face again. "Yes, sir," she said. "It is."

Her voice was so cold that Jeffrey felt a chill on his neck. He suppressed a shiver as he slid his gun out of its holster. Jeffrey hated guns because, as a cop, he saw what kind of damage they could do. Carrying one was something he did because he had to, not because he wanted to. In his twenty years on the police force, Jeffrey had drawn his weapon on a suspect only a handful of times. Of those times, he had fired it twice, but never directly at a human being.

"Jenny," he tried, putting some authority in his voice. "Look at me."

She kept her gaze on the boy in front of her for what seemed like forever. Jeffrey was silent, letting her have her sense of control. Slowly, she let her eyes turn toward Jeffrey. She let her gaze settle low, until she found the nine millimeter he held at his side.

She licked her lips nervously, obviously assessing the threat. The same dead tone rang in his ears when she said, "Shoot me."

He thought he had heard wrong. This was far from the answer he had been expecting.

She repeated, "Shoot me now or I'm gonna shoot him." With that, she lifted the Beretta toward the boy's head. Jeffrey watched as she spread her feet apart to a shoulder-width stance and cupped the butt of the gun with her free hand. Her posture was that of a young woman who knew how to hold a weapon. Her hands were steady now, and she kept her eyes locked on the boy's.

The boy whined, "Oh, shit," and there was a spattering sound on the asphalt as he urinated.

Jeffrey raised his gun as she fired, but her shot went wide over the boy's head, splitting pieces of the plastic sign and canopy off the building.

"What was that?" Jeffrey hissed, knowing that the only reason Jenny was still standing was that his gut had stopped his own finger from pulling the trigger. She had hit the center of the dot on the "i" in Skatie's. Jeffrey doubted most of his cops on the force could shoot with that much precision, under this much pressure.

"It was a warning," Jenny said, though he had not expected her to answer. "Shoot me," the girl repeated. "Shoot me or I swear to God I'm gonna blow his brains out right here." She licked her lips again. "I can do it. I know how to use this." She jerked the gun slightly, indicating what she meant. "You know I can do it," she said, again taking a wide stance to counteract the Beretta's recoil. She turned the muzzle slightly and blasted out the apostrophe on the sign. People in the parking lot might have scattered or yelled, but Jeffrey did not notice. All he could see was the smoke coming off the muzzle of her gun.

When he could breathe again, Jeffrey said, "There's a big difference between a sign and a human being."

She mumbled, and he strained to hear her say, "He's not a human being."

Jeffrey caught movement out of the corner of his eye. He recognized Sara instantly. She had taken off her skates and her white socks stood stark against the black asphalt.

"Honey?" Sara called, her voice pitched up in fear. "Jenny?" she said.

"Go away," Jenny snapped, but her tone was petulant, more like the child she was than the monster she had been just a few seconds earlier. "Please."

"She's okay," Sara said. "I just found her inside, and she's fine."

The gun faltered, then Jenny's resolve seemed to kick in as she raised it back, pointing the weapon squarely between the boy's eyes. The same dead voice came back with her resolve, and she said, "You're lying."

Jeffrey took one look at Sara and knew that the girl was right. Sara was not a practiced liar, so she was easy to read. Discounting that, even from this distance Jeffrey could see the blood covering the front of Sara's shirt and jeans. Someone inside the rink had obviously been injured and was possibly, probably, dead. He looked back at Jenny, finally able to reconcile the soft, little girl's face with the threat that she had become.

With a start, he realized that the safety was still engaged on his gun. He clicked it off, giving Sara a look of warning to stay back.

"Jenny?" Sara's throat made a visible swallow. Jeffrey did not recognize the singsong voice she used; she had never talked down to children. Obviously, whatever violence Jenny had wreaked inside the rink had altered Sara. Jeffrey did not know what to make of it. There hadn't been any gunfire in the rink, and Buell Parker, the rink's rent-a-cop, had said everything was fine when Jeffrey had checked in with him. Where was Buell, Jeffrey wondered. Was he inside, securing a crime scene, not letting anyone out? What had Jenny done inside the rink? Jeffrey would have given anything at that moment in time to pause the scene in front of him and find out exactly what had happened.

Jeffrey chambered a round into the nine-mil. Sara's head snapped around at the sound, and she held her hand out to him, palm down, as if to say, No, calm down. Don't do this. He looked past her shoulder at the rink entrance. He expected to see a group of spectators with their noses pressed to the glass, but the doorway was empty. What had happened inside that was more interesting than the scene playing out in front of him?

Sara tried again, saying, "She's fine, Jenny. Come see."

"Dr. Linton," Jenny said, her voice wavering, "please don't talk to me."

"Sweety," Sara answered, her tone as shaky as Jenny's. "Look at me. Please just look at me." When the girl did not respond, Sara said, "She's fine. I promise you she's fine."

"You're lying," Jenny answered. "You're all liars." She turned her attention back to the boy. "And you're the worst liar of all," she told him. "You're going to burn in hell for what you did, you bastard."

The boy spoke in a fit of rage, spittle flying from his mouth. "I'll see you there, bitch."

Jenny's voice took on a calmness. Something seemed to pass between her and the boy, and when she answered, her voice was childlike. "I know you will."

Out of the corner of his eye, Jeffrey saw Sara step forward. He watched as Jenny sighted down the barrel of the short-nosed gun, lining it up to the boy's head. The girl stood there, stock-still, waiting. Her hands did not shake, her lip did not tremble, and her hand did not falter. She seemed more resigned to the task in front of her than Jeffrey did.

"Jenny . . . ," Jeffrey began, trying to see some way out of this. He was not going to shoot a little girl. There was no way he could shoot this kid.

Jenny looked over her shoulder and Jeffrey followed her gaze. A police car had finally pulled up, and Lena Adams and Brad stepped out, weapons drawn. They were in a textbook triangle formation, with Jeffrey at the top.

"Shoot me," Jenny said, keeping her gun steady on the boy.

"Stand down," Jeffrey told the officers. Brad followed

orders, but he saw Lena hesitate. He gave her a hard look, about to repeat his order, but finally she lowered her weapon.

"I'll do it," Jenny mumbled. She stood impossibly still, making Jeffrey wonder what was inside the girl that she could approach this situation with such resignation.

Jenny cleared her throat and said, "I'll do it. I've done it before."

Jeffrey looked to Sara for confirmation, but her attention was focused on the little girl with the gun.

"I've done it before," Jenny repeated. "Shoot me, or I'll kill him and then shoot myself anyway."

For the first time that night, Jeffrey assessed his shot. He tried to force his brain to accept that she represented a clear danger to the boy in front of her, no matter what her age was. If he hit her in the leg or shoulder, she would have enough time to pull the trigger. Even if Jeffrey went for her torso, there was still the chance that she would squeeze off a shot before she went down. At the level Jenny was pointing the gun, the boy would be dead before she hit the ground.

"Men are so weak," Jenny hissed, sighting the weapon. "You never do the right thing. You say you will, but you never do."

"Jenny . . . ," Sara pleaded.

"I'll give you to five," Jenny told him. "One."

Jeffrey swallowed hard. His heart was pounding so loudly in his ears that he saw rather than heard the girl as she counted.

"Two."

"Jenny, please." Sara clasped her hands in front of her as if in prayer. They were dark, almost black with blood.

"Three."

Jeffrey took aim. She wouldn't do this. There was no way she would do this. She could not have been more than thirteen. Thirteen-year-old girls did not shoot people. This was suicide.

"Four."

Jeffrey watched the young woman's finger tighten on the trigger, watched the muscles along her forearm work in slow motion as she moved to tighten her finger.

"Five!" she screamed, the veins in her neck standing out. She ordered, "Shoot me, goddamn it!" as she braced herself for the Beretta's recoil. He saw her arm tense and her wrist lock. Time moved so slowly that he could see her muscles engaging along her forearm as her finger tightened on the trigger.

She gave him one last chance, yelling, "Shoot me!"

And he did.

3

At twenty-eight weeks old, Jenny Weaver's child might have been viable outside the womb had its mother not tried to flush it down the toilet. The fetus was well-developed and well-nourished. The brain stem was intact and, with medical intervention, the lungs would have matured over time. The hands would have learned to grasp, the feet to flex, the eyes to blink. Eventually, the mouth would have learned to speak of something other than the horrors it spoke of to Sara now. The lungs had taken breath, the mouth gasped for life. And then it had been killed.

For the past three-and-a-half hours, Sara had tried to re-assemble the baby from the parts Jenny Weaver had left in the bathroom and in the red book bag they found in the trash by the video game room. Using tiny sutures instead of the usual baseball stitches, Sara had sewn the paper-thin flesh back together into the semblance of a child. Her hands shook, and Sara had redone some of the knots because her fingers were not nimble enough on the first try.

Still, it was not enough. Working on the child, tying the tiny sutures, was like pulling a thread on a sweater. For every area repaired, there was another that could not be concealed. There was no disguising the trauma the child had been through. In the end, Sara had finally accepted that her self-appointed task was an exercise in futility. The baby would go to the grave looking much the way she had looked the last time her mother had seen her.

Sara took a deep breath, reviewing her report again before signing off on her findings. She had not waited for Jeffrey or Frank to begin the autopsy. There had been no witnesses to the cutting and dissecting and reassembling Sara had performed. She had excluded them on purpose, because she did not think she could do this job while other people watched.

A large window separated Sara's office from the outer morgue, and she sat back in her chair, staring at the black body bag resting on the autopsy table. Her mind wandered, and she saw an alternative to the death she had been assessing. Sara saw a life of laughing and crying and loving and being loved, and then she saw the truth: Jenny's baby would never have these things. Jenny herself had barely had these things.

Since an ectopic pregnancy several years ago, Sara had been unable to have children. This had been hard news to bear at the time, but over the years the loss had dulled itself with other things, and Sara had learned to stop wanting what she knew she would never have. Yet there was something about the unwanted child on the table, the child whose own mother had taken her life, that stirred up these emotions in Sara again.

Sara's job was taking care of children. She held them in her arms, cradled them, and cooed at them the way she would never be able to with her own child. Sitting in the morgue, staring at the black bag, that longing to carry a baby came back with startling clarity, and with it came an emptiness that made her chest feel hollow.

There were footsteps on the stairs, and Sara sat up, wiping her eyes, trying to collect herself. She pushed her palms against the top of her desk and forced herself to stand as Jeffrey walked into the morgue. Sara was looking for her glasses, trying to compose herself, when she noticed that Jeffrey had not come directly into her office, as he normally did. Through the glass, she could see that he had stopped in front of the black bag. If he saw Sara, Jeffrey did not acknowledge her. Instead, he leaned over the table, his hands behind his back. Sara wondered what he was thinking, wondered if he was considering the life the baby could have had. Wondered, too, if Jeffrey was considering the fact that Sara could never give him children.

Sara cleared her throat as she walked into the room, holding the autopsy report to her chest. She slid the chart onto the edge of the table and stood across from Jeffrey, the baby between them. The bag was too large for the baby and it gaped open around the body like a blanket because Sara had not had the emotional strength to zip the child into more darkness and place her on a shelf in the freezer.

There was nothing she could think to say, so Sara was quiet. She tucked her hand into the pocket of her lab coat, surprised to find her glasses there. She was putting them on when Jeffrey finally spoke.

"So," he said, his voice gravelly and low as if he had not used it much lately. "This is what happens when you try to flush a baby down the toilet."

She felt her heart stop at his callousness, and did not know how to respond to it. She slipped off her glasses and rubbed the lenses with the tail of her shirt to give herself something to do.

Jeffrey took a deep breath and let it go slowly. She leaned in closer, thinking she smelled alcohol, knowing this could not be the case because Jeffrey seldom drank more than the occasional beer while watching Saturday college football.

"Tiny feet," he mumbled, his eyes still on the body. "Are they always that small?"

Again, Sara did not answer. She looked at the feet, the ten toes, the wrinkled skin on the soles. These were the kind of feet a mother would kiss. These toes were the kind of toes a mother would count each day the way a gardener counts blooms on a rose bush.

Sara bit her lip, trying not to let herself go again. The emptiness in her chest was almost overwhelming, and she put her hand over her heart without thinking.

When Sara was finally able to look up, Jeffrey was staring at her. His eyes were bloodshot, tiny red lines shooting out from his irises. He seemed to be having trouble holding himself up. She did not know if this was from alcohol or grief.

"I thought you didn't drink," she said, aware there was an accusatory tone to her voice.

"I thought I didn't shoot children, either," he said, staring somewhere over her shoulder.

Sara wanted to help him, but she felt paralyzed by her own grief.

"Frank," Jeffrey said. "He gave me a shot of whiskey."

"Did it help?"

His eyes watered, and she watched him fighting this. His jaw worked and he gave a humorless smile.

"Jeffrey—"

He shook off her concern, asking, "Did you find anything?"

"No."

"I don't—" He stopped, looking down, but not at the child. His eyes were focused on the tiled floor. "I don't know how to behave," he finally said. "I don't know what I should be doing."

Something in his tone cut Sara deep down. To see him broken like this hurt her more than the pain she was experiencing herself. She walked around the table and put her hand on his shoulder, but he would not turn toward her.

He asked, "Did you think she was going to shoot him?"

Sara felt a lump in her throat, because she had not let herself consider this question up until now. Jenny's back had been to Sara. Only Jeffrey, Lena, and Brad had a clear view of the scene.

"Sara?"

The way Jeffrey was looking at her, Sara knew that now was not the time for equivocation.

"Yes," she answered, making her voice firm. "It was a clean shot, Jeffrey. You had to take it."

Jeffrey walked away from her. He turned and leaned his back against the wall, asking, "Mark is probably the father, right?" He rested his head against the wall. "The boy she was going to shoot?"

Sara put her hands in her pockets, made her feet stay flat on the ground so that she would not walk over to him. She said, "It would make sense."

"His parents won't let us interview him until tomorrow. Did you know that?"

She shook her head slowly side to side. Mark wasn't under suspicion for anything. It wasn't as if Jeffrey could arrest the kid for having a gun pointed at his chest.

"They say he's been through enough." Jeffrey let his head drop down. "What would make her do something like that? What has she been through that would make her think . . . ?" His voice trailed off as he looked back up at Sara. "She was one of yours, right?"

"They moved here about three years ago." Sara paused, trying to shift gears. She knew that it would help Jeffrey more to talk this through like any other case rather than to dwell on the horror of his involvement. At this moment in time, it was irrelevant that this wasn't what *she* needed.

He asked, "Where from?"

"I think they were from up North somewhere. Her mother moved down here after what sounded like a nasty divorce."

"How do you know this?"

"Parents tell me things." She paused. "I didn't know Jenny was pregnant. I don't think she's been in for at least six months, maybe more." Sara put her hand to her chest. "She was such a sweet kid. I never would have imagined that she'd do something like this."

He nodded, rubbing his eyes. "Tessa's not sure she can I.D. anybody from the restroom. Brad's gonna take over one of the yearbooks from the school, see if anybody looks familiar. I want you to look, too."

"Of course."

"It was so packed," he said, obviously meaning the skating rink. "People left before giving statements. I don't know if we'll be able to track everyone down."

"Did you get anything?"

He shook his head no. "You're sure only two people went into the bathroom? Jenny and one other?"

"That's all I saw," Sara answered, though after tonight she did not know how she could ever be sure of anything again. "I didn't see her. I suppose if she was in my practice I would have recognized her. I guess." Sara stopped, trying to remember, but nothing new popped into her head. "She was tall, maybe wearing a baseball cap."

He looked up at this. "You remember the color?"

"It was dark, Jeffrey," Sara answered, knowing she was letting him down. She understood now why so many witnesses willingly gave false testimony. She felt stupid and useless for not knowing who the other girl was. Her mind tried to compensate for this by throwing out random bits of information that could or could not be real memories.

Sara said, "I'm not even sure if it was a baseball cap, now that I'm thinking about it. I wasn't paying attention." She tried to smile. "I was looking for you."

He did not smile back. Instead, he said, "I talked to her mother."

"What did you say?"

His flippant tone was back. " 'I shot your daughter, Mrs. Weaver. Sorry about that.' "

Sara chewed her bottom lip. In a larger county, Jeffrey would not have been in charge of notification; he would be off the job pending an investigation. Of course, Grant County was far from large. All the responsibility rested squarely on his shoulders.

"She didn't want the autopsy," he said. "I had to explain to her that she didn't really have a choice. She said it was . . ." He paused. "She said it was killing her twice."

Sara felt guilt settle into the pit of her stomach.

"She called me a baby killer," he said. "I'm a baby killer now."

Sara shook her head no. "You didn't have a choice," she said, knowing this was true. She had made love to this man, shared her life with him. There was no way he had misjudged.

Sara said, "You followed procedure."

He gave a derisive laugh.

"Jeff—"

"You think she would have done it?" he asked again. "I don't think she would have, Sara. I'm thinking back on it, and maybe she would have walked away. Maybe she would have—"

"Look at this," Sara interrupted, indicating the table. "She killed her own child, Jeffrey. Do you think she wouldn't have killed the father, too?"

"We'll never know, will we?"

Silence came like a thick cloud. The morgue was in the basement of the hospital, a tiled room with an institutional feel. The compressor on the freezer was the only noise, and it turned off with a loud click that echoed against the walls.

"Was the baby alive?" Jeffrey asked. "When she was born, was she alive?"

"She wouldn't have survived long without medical help," Sara said, not answering his question. For some reason, she wanted to protect Jenny.

"Was the baby alive?" he repeated.

"She was very small," she said. "I don't think she would have . . ."

Jeffrey walked back to the table. He tucked his hands into his pockets as he stared at the baby. "I want . . . ," he began. "I want to go home. I want you to go home with me."

"Okay," she answered, hearing his words but not sure she understood what he wanted.

He said, "I want to make love to you."

Sara's eyes must have registered her shock.

"I want to—" He stopped himself midsentence.

Sara stared at him, a sinking feeling in her chest. "You want to make a baby."

The look in his eyes told her this had been the last thing on his mind. Sara felt a flush of humiliation. Her heart jumped into her throat, and she could not speak.

He shook his head, "That's not what I was going to say."

Sara turned away from him, her cheeks burning. She could not think of words to cover what she had already said.

He said, "I know you can't—"

"Forget about it."

"It's just that I—"

She was mad at herself, not Jeffrey, but when she spoke to him, her tone was sharp. "I said forget about it."

Jeffrey waited a few beats, obviously looking for the right thing to say. When he finally spoke, his tone was plaintive and sad. "I want to go back about five hours, okay?" He waited for her to turn around. "I want to be back in that stupid fucking skating rink with you, and when my pager goes off, I want to throw it in the fucking trash."

Sara stared at him, not trusting herself to speak.

"That's what I want, Sara," he repeated. "I wasn't thinking about the other. What you said—"

She stopped him, holding up her hand. There were footsteps on the stairs, two sets of them. Sara walked into her office, drying her eyes as she went. She tugged a Kleenex out of the box on her desk and blew her nose, then counted to a slow five, bracing herself, swallowing back the humiliation she felt.

When she turned around, detective Lena Adams and Brad Stephens were in the morgue, standing by Jeffrey, who by his look had managed to mask his emotions much as Sara had. All three of them had their hands clasped behind their backs the way cops do when they're at a scene so they won't accidentally contaminate anything. In that moment, Sara hated them all, even Brad Stephens, who was as harmless as a fly.

"Hey, Dr. Linton," Brad said, taking off his hat as she walked into the room. His face was paler than usual and there were tears in his eyes.

"Will you . . . ?" Sara began, then had to stop. She cleared her throat. "Will you please go upstairs and get some sheets for me?" she asked. "Bed sheets. About four of them." Sara did not need the sheets, but Brad had been one of her patients. She still felt the need to protect him.

Brad gave her a smile, obviously glad to have something to do. "Yes, ma'am."

After he had left, Lena asked in a matter-of-fact way, "Have y'all already done the baby?"

Jeffrey answered, "Yes," even though he had not been there. He noticed the chart at the end of the table and picked it up. Sara did not say anything as he took his pen out of his breast pocket and scribbled his signature along the bottom of the autopsy report. Technically, Sara had violated several laws by performing the autopsy without at least one witness.

"Is the girl in the freezer?" Lena asked, walking toward the door. There was a cavalier bounce to her walk, as if what Lena was seeing was a common occurrence. Sara knew Lena had been through a lot recently, but she still felt angry at the other woman's attitude.

"Here?" Lena prompted, her hand on the freezer door.

Sara nodded, not moving. Jeffrey walked over to help Lena, and Sara zipped the bag closed around the baby before she could stop herself. Her heart was pounding like a drum in her chest by the time Lena and Jeffrey rolled the gurney containing Jenny Weaver's body into the room. They both braked the wheels by the table, waiting for Sara to move the bag. Finally, Jeffrey scooped the large black bag into his arms. Sara looked away as he cradled what was obviously the head with his hand. The loose ends of the bag dragged the floor as he walked toward the freezer.

Lena made a point of looking at her watch. Sara wanted to slap her, but instead she walked over to the metal supply cabinet beside the sinks. She opened a sterile pack and slipped on a gown, glancing over her shoulder at the freezer, wondering what was taking Jeffrey so long. Sara was helping Lena move the body onto the table when he finally emerged.

"Here," he said, taking Lena's place as they maneuvered the body of Jenny Weaver onto the white porcelain table. Weaver was a large girl, and the hoses at the head of the table rattled as they moved her into place.

Sara propped the head up on a black block, trying to think of herself as a coroner rather than the girl's pediatrician. In her ten years as Grant's medical examiner, there had been only four cases where Sara had known the deceased. Jenny Weaver was the first victim who had also been a patient at the clinic.

Sara rolled over a fresh tray with clean instruments, making sure she had everything that she needed. The two hoses at the head of the table were used to evacuate the body during examination. Over this was a large scale for weighing organs. At the foot was a tray for dissecting. The table itself was concave in shape, with high sides to keep matter from spilling over and a pronounced downward slant toward a large brass drain.

Carlos, Sara's assistant at the morgue, had placed a white sheet over Jenny Weaver's body. A medium-sized red dot spread out over the part that covered her throat. Sara had let Carlos take care of Jenny while she worked on the child. He had taken the X rays and prepared Jenny for autopsy while Sara had tried in vain to do something right for the baby. If Carlos was surprised when Sara told him to go home when he was finished with Jenny, he did not say.

Sara folded back the sheet, stopping just above the girl's chest. The wound was far from clean and most of the right side of her neck dangled like pieces of raw meat. Cartilage and bone stood out from the black blood that had clotted around the wound.

Sara walked over to the light box on the wall and turned it on. The light flickered, then showed the X rays Carlos had taken of Jenny Weaver.

She studied the films carefully, at first not understanding what she was seeing. She checked the name on the chart again before calling out her findings. "You can see here there are faded lines of a fracture to the left humerus, which I would date at less than a year old. It's not a typical fracture, especially for someone who was not athletic, so I'm assuming it came from some kind of abuse."

"Did you treat her for this?" Jeffrey asked.

"Of course not," Sara answered. "I would have reported it. Any doctor would have reported it."

"Okay," Jeffrey said, holding up his hands. Her tone must have been sharper than Sara realized, because Lena seemed to be taking a sudden interest in the floor.

Sara turned back to the X ray. "There's also evidence of trauma around the costal cartilage, which is here in the rib." She pointed to the chest film. "Up here, near the sternum, there's bruising that's consistent with a hard push or shove, moving posteriorly. That's to the back." She let this sink in, wondering if Jenny had seen another doctor for this. A first-year resident would recognize something was not right with this kind of injury.

Sara said, "I would guess the person who did this was taller than her. It's recent, too."

Sara popped a new X ray into the light box. She crossed her arms over her chest, studying the film. "This is the pelvic girdle," she explained. "Note the fade line here against the ischium. This would indicate traumatic pressure to the pubis. It's what's commonly referred to as a stress fracture."

"Stress from what?" Jeffrey asked.

Sara was surprised when Lena provided the answer to Jeffrey.

"She was raped," Lena said, the same way she might say the girl's eyes were blue. "Raped hard. Right?"

Sara nodded, and was about to say something else when she heard footsteps on the stairs again. She guessed from the sloppy lope that Brad had returned.

"Here you go," Brad said, walking backward through the door. He held an armful of sheets, his hat dangling from his hand.

Sara stopped him, asking, "Did you get pillowcases?"

"Oh," Brad said, surprised. He shook his head. "Sorry, no."

"I think they're on the top floor," Sara said. "Could you get at least four?"

"Yes, ma'am," he answered, setting the sheets down on a table by the door.

Lena crossed her arms as he left. "He's not twelve," she said.

Jeffrey spoke to Lena for the first time since she had entered the morgue, giving her an uncharacteristic, "Shut up."

Lena colored, but she was silent; also out of character.

"The bruising on her chest couldn't really be treated with anything other than Tylenol," Sara continued. "The pelvic fracture could heal on its own. It might explain why she had weight gain recently. It would be hard for her to get around."

Jeffrey asked, "You think the boyfriend was abusing her?"

"Someone was," Sara said, looking over the films again,

trying to see if she had missed anything. All the times she had seen Jenny Weaver, Sara had never suspected child abuse. How the child had kept it hidden, and why, Sara did not know. Of course, it wasn't as if Sara ordered X rays for sore throats, Jenny *didn't* take off her clothes, evidently and Jenny had never taken off her clothes for an examination. Teenage girls were very sensitive about their bodies, and Sara had always slipped her stethoscope under Jenny's shirt to listen to her chest and lungs so the girl would not be embarrassed.

Sara walked over to the table to resume the preliminary examination. Her hands shook slightly as she pulled back the sheet, and Sara was so absorbed in trying to get her hands to stop shaking that she did not notice what she was uncovering.

"Holy shit," Lena said, giving another low whistle.

Jeffrey did not reprimand her this time, though, and Sara understood why. There were small cuts across the girl's body, specifically on her arms and legs. The wounds were at various stages of healing, but some of them looked as recent as the last few days.

"What happened?" Jeffrey asked. "Was she trying to kill herself?"

Sara looked at the slices marking the skin. None of them was across the wrist or in places that would be apparent to anyone who was not looking for something specific. This would at least explain why the girl was wearing a long-sleeved shirt in the middle of summer. Thin rows of very deep cuts lined Jenny's left forearm, starting about three inches from the wrist and where the sleeve might have rolled up. Dark scars indicated that the injuries were a common occurrence. The leg cuts were much deeper, and seemed to have a crisscross pattern to them. Sara could guess from the scarring that the deeper cuts radiated from the knee to the thigh. The girl had done this to herself.

"What is this?" Jeffrey asked, though he must have known.

"Cutting," Lena provided.

"Self-injuring," Sara corrected her, as if that made it any better. "I've seen it at the clinic before."

"Why?" Jeffrey asked. "Why would someone do this?"

"Stupidity, for the most part," Sara told him, feeling anger well into her stomach. How many times had she seen this girl? How many signs had Sara missed? "Sometimes they just want to know what it feels like. Usually they're just acting out, not thinking about the consequences. This, though," she stopped, staring at the deep cuts along Jenny's left thigh. "This is something else. She hid them, she didn't want people to know."

"Why?" Jeffrey repeated. "Why would she do this?"

"Control," Lena answered him, and Sara did not like the look she was giving the child. It was almost respectful.

"It's a deep psychosis," Sara countered. "Usually bulimics or anorexics do it. It's a form of self-loathing." She gave Lena a purposeful look. "Usually something sets it off. Abuse or rape, for instance."

Lena held her gaze for just a second before looking away.

Sara continued, "There are other things that can lead to it, too. Substance abuse, mental illness, problems at school or at home."

Sara walked over to the supply cabinet and took out a plastic speculum. After slipping on a second pair of gloves, she unwrapped the speculum and clicked it open. Lena cringed slightly at the sound, and Sara was thankful that the detective was capable of showing a little emotion.

Sara walked down to the foot of the body and propped the feet apart. She stopped suddenly, her mind not accepting what her eyes saw. She dropped the speculum on the table.

Lena asked, "What is it?"

Sara did not answer. She had thought that after tonight nothing could shock her. She had been so wrong.

"What is it?" Lena repeated.

"She hasn't given birth to a child," Sara answered. "Any child."

Jeffrey indicated the unused speculum. "How can you be sure without completely examining her?"

Sara stared at them both, not sure how to say this. "Her vagina has been sewn shut," she finally told them. "From the rate of healing, I'd say it's been that way for at least six months."

Sunday

4

Lena ran her tongue along her front teeth as she stared out the car window. She could not get used to the fake feeling of the temporary partials. In three weeks, she would be fitted with four permanent replacements that would screw into her gums like tiny lightbulbs. She could not imagine how that would feel. For now, they served as a constant reminder of what had happened to her four months ago.

She tried to block out the memory as she watched the scenery go by. Grant County was a small town, but not as small as Reece, where Lena and Sibyl, her twin sister, had grown up. Their father had been killed in the line of duty eight months before they were born and their mother had died giving birth to them. The task of raising the girls had fallen to their uncle Hank Norton, an admitted speed freak and alcoholic, who had struggled with both addictions well into the girls' childhood. One sunny afternoon, a drunk Hank had backed his car down the driveway and slammed into Sibyl. Lena had always blamed him for blinding her sister. She would never forgive Hank for his role in the accident, and his response to her hatred was a seemingly insurmountable wall of anger. They had a past, the two of them, that prevented each from reaching out to the other. Even now, with Sibyl dead and Lena just as good as, Lena could not see Hank Norton as anything but a necessary evil in her life.

"Hot outside," Hank mumbled as he patted the back of his neck with a worn-looking handkerchief. Lena could barely hear him over the roar of the air-conditioning. Hank's old Mercedes sedan was a tank of a car, and everything inside the cab seemed overdone. The seats were too big. There was enough legroom to accommodate a horse. The controls on the dash were large and obvious, their design intended to impress more than elucidate. Still, it was comforting being inside something so solid. Even on the gravel road down from Lena's house, the car seemed to float across the ground.

"Sure is hot," Hank repeated. The older he got, the more he did this, as if repeating phrases made up for the fact that he didn't have much to say.

"Yeah," Lena agreed, staring back out the window. She could feel Hank looking at her, probably contemplating small talk. After a few beats, he seemed to give up on this, and turned on the radio instead.

Lena leaned her head back against the seat, closing her eyes. She had agreed to go to church with her uncle one Sunday shortly after she had gotten home from the hospital, and her attendance had turned into a habit over the ensuing months. Lena tagged along more because she was afraid to stay alone in her own home than because she wanted absolution. In her mind, Lena would never need forgiveness for anything ever again. She had paid her dues to God or whomever was keeping track of things four months ago, raped and drugged into a nightmare world of pain and false transcendence.

Hank interrupted her again. "You doin' okay, baby?"

What a stupid question, Lena thought. What a stupid fucking question.

"Lee?"

"Yes," she answered, conscious that the word hissed through her temporary teeth.

"Nan called again," he told her.

"I know," Lena said. Nan Thomas, Sibyl's lover at the time of her death, had been calling off and on for the last month.

"She's got some of Sibby's stuff," Hank said, though surely he knew Lena was aware of this. "She just wants to give it to you."

"Why doesn't she give it to you?" Lena countered. There was no reason she needed to see that woman, and Hank knew it. Still, he kept forcing the issue.

Hank changed the subject. "That girl last night," he began, turning down the radio. "You were there, huh?"

"Yes," she said, making the same hissing sound. Lena clenched her jaw, willing herself not to cry. Would she ever talk normally again? Would even the sound of her voice be a constant reminder of what *he* did to her?

He, Lena thought, unable to let her mind use his name. Her hands rested in her lap, and she looked down, staring at the matching scars on the back of her hands. If Hank had not been there, she would have turned them over, looked at the palms where the nails had pierced through as they were hammered into the floor. The same scars were on her feet, midway between her toes and ankles. Two months of physical therapy had returned the normal use of her hands and she could now walk without cringing, but the scars would always be there.

Lena had only a few sharp memories of what had happened to her body while she was abducted. Only the scars and her chart at the hospital told the entire story. All she remembered were the moments when the drugs wore off and *he* came to her, sitting by her on the floor as if they were at Bible camp, telling stories about his childhood and his life as if they were lovers, just getting to know each other.

Lena's mind was filled with the details of his life: his first kiss, his first time making love, his hopes and dreams, his sick obsessions. They came to her now as easily as memories from her own past. Had she told him similar stories about herself? She could not remember, and this scarred her more deeply than the physical aspects of the attack. At times, Lena thought of the scars as inconsequential compared to the intimate conversations she had with her abuser. He had manipulated Lena so that she was no longer in control of her own thoughts. He had not just raped her body, but her mind as well.

Even now, his memories constantly mingled with her own, until she was uncertain whether or not something had happened to her or to him. Sibyl, the one person who could settle this, the one person who could give Lena back her life, her childhood, had been taken by him as well.

"Lee?" Hank interrupted her thoughts, holding out a pack of gum. She shook her head no, watching him try to hold the wheel and retrieve a stick of Juicy Fruit. The sleeves of his dress shirt were rolled up, and she could see the track marks lining his pasty white forearms. They were hideous, these scars, and they reminded Lena of Jenny Weaver. Last night, Jeffrey had kept asking why anyone would purposefully cut herself, but Lena understood how pain could be a comfort. About six weeks after being released from the hospital, Lena had accidentally slammed her fingers in the door of her car. Searing hot pain had radiated up her arm, and for the briefest moment, Lena had caught herself enjoying it, thinking, *This is what it's like to feel again.*

She closed her eyes, clasping her hands in her lap. As usual, her fingers found the scars and she traced the circumference of one, then the other. There had been no pain when it had happened. The drug had convinced her that she was floating on the ocean, that she was safe. Her mind had created an alternate reality from the one her rapist created. When he touched her, Lena's mind had told her it was Greg Mitchell, her old boyfriend, inside of her. Lena's body had responded to Greg, not *him.*

Yet, the few times since then that Lena had been able to sleep long enough to dream, she had dreamed of her rapist touching her, not Greg. It was *his* hands on her breasts. It was *him* inside of her. And when she awakened, startled and scared, it was not Greg that she looked for in her dark, empty room.

Lena clenched her fists when the sickly sweet smell of Hank's chewing gum hit her. Without warning, her stomach pitched.

"Pull over," she managed, using one hand to cover her mouth, grabbing the door handle with the other. Hank abruptly swerved the car to the side of the road just as Lena lost it. She had only had a cup of coffee for breakfast, but that and more came up quickly. Soon, she was dry heaving, her stomach clenching. Tears came to her eyes from the exertion, and her body shook hard as she tried to hold herself up.

After what seemed like several minutes, the nausea finally passed. Lena wiped her mouth with the back of her hand just as Hank tapped her on the shoulder, offering his handkerchief. The cloth was warm and smelled of his sweat, but she used it anyway.

"Your gum," she mumbled, grasping the dashboard as she tried to sit up. "I don't know why—"

"It's okay," he answered abruptly. The window sucked down at the press of a button, and he spit out the gum before pulling onto the road again. Hank stared straight ahead, his jaw a straight line.

"I'm sorry," she said, not knowing why she was apologizing even as she said the words. Hank seemed angry, but she knew his animosity was directed toward himself for not knowing how to help, not at Lena. It was a familiar scene that had played out every day since she had come home from the hospital.

Lena reached around to retrieve her purse from the back seat. There were Pepto Bismol tablets and Altoids in there for this very occasion. She hated her days off from work. When she was on the job, she was too busy to allow the luxury of these episodes. There were reports to fill out, and calls to make. She knew who she was at the station, and riding around with Brad, an assignment she had balked at initially, made her feel competent and safe.

It wasn't that she was throwing herself into her job because being a cop was the only thing keeping her alive. Lena knew better than that. She would feel the same way if she were a cashier at the hardware store or a janitor at the high school. Crime and criminals had as much meaning to her as giving out the correct change would, or getting a stain off the cafeteria floor. What her job gave her these days was structure. She had to show up at eight in the morning. Certain tasks were expected of her. Brad needed direction. At noon, they had lunch, or, rather, Brad did. Lena did not have an appetite lately. Around three, they stopped for coffee at the Donut King over in Madison. They were back at the station by six and Lena's world fell apart until it was time to go back to work the next day. On the rare nights— nights like last night—when Jeffrey allowed her to take overtime, she nearly wept with relief.

Hank asked, "You okay now?" the accusatory tone still in his voice.

She gave it right back to him. "Just drop it."

"Yeah, okay," he answered, thumping the turning signal down as he stopped behind a line of cars in front of the church. They were both silent as the car inched closer to the parking lot.

Lena looked up at the small white building, resenting it for being there. She had never liked church and had even been thrown out of Sunday school at the age of twelve for ripping out the pages of a Bible. When Hank had confronted her, she had told him she had done it out of boredom, but the truth was that even then Lena had resented rules. She hated being told what to do. She could not follow an authority that had not proven itself to her. The only reason she was good at being a cop was she had a certain degree of autonomy in the field, and everyone had to listen to *her* when she told them to.

"That girl," Hank said, picking up the conversation as if the last ten minutes had not happened. "It's a sad thing, what she did."

"Yeah," Lena shrugged, not really wanting to think about it.

"People get lost along the way, I guess," Hank said. "Don't ask nobody for help until it's too late." He paused, then, "Not until it's too late."

She knew what he was doing, making a comparison between the dead girl and herself. Some bullshit A.A. pamphlet probably had the directions for doing this on the back, right beside a little space where you could fill in your sponsor's name and phone number.

Lena snapped, "If I was going to kill myself, I would have done it my first day home."

"I wasn't talking about you," Hank shot back.

"Bullshit," she hissed. She waited a beat, then said, "I thought you were going home soon."

"I am," he answered.

"Good," she told him, and for the moment, she really meant it. Hank had been living with her since she came home from the hospital, and Lena was over having him pry into every part of her life.

"I got a business to run," he told her, as if the dilapidated bar he owned on the outskirts of Reece was IBM. "I need to get back to it. I'll leave tonight if you want me to."

"Fine," she said, but her heart started pounding at the thought of being alone at night. Lena did not want Hank in her home, but she knew that she would never feel safe if he left. Even during the daytime when she was working and Hank went to check on his bar, she felt an aching fear that he would get into a car accident or just decide not to come back at all, and Lena would have to come home to a dark, empty house. Hank was not just an unwanted house guest. He was her shield.

He told her, "I got better things I could be doing."

She was quiet, though in her mind, she repeated her mantra—please don't leave me, please don't leave me. Her throat was closing up with the need to say it out loud.

The car jerked as Hank accelerated, taking a parking space close to the chapel. He slammed the gear into park and the old sedan rocked back and forth several times before it settled.

He glanced at her, and she could tell that he knew he had her. "You want me to go? Tell me to go, then. You never had a hard time telling me to leave before."

She bit her lip hard, wanting to taste blood. Instead of her flesh giving, her front teeth moved, and she put her hand to her mouth, startled by the reminder.

"What? You can't talk now?"

Lena choked a sob, overcome with emotion.

Hank looked away from her, waiting for her to get hold of herself. She knew that he could listen to a room full of strangers whine about wanting needles in their arms or double shots of whiskey, but could not handle Lena's tears. Part of her also knew that he hated Lena for crying. Sibyl had been his baby, the one he had taken care of. Lena was the strong one who didn't need anybody. The role reversal had knocked him on his ass.

"You gotta go to that therapist," Hank barked at her, still angry. "Your chief told you that. It's a requirement, and you're not doing it."

She shook her head side to side in a violent arc, her hand still at her mouth.

"You don't run anymore. You don't work out," he began, as if this was part of an indictment against her. "You go to bed at nine and don't get up until late as you can the next morning," he continued. "You don't take care of yourself anymore."

"I take care of myself," she mumbled.

"You go see a therapist or I'm leaving today, Lee." He put his hand over hers, forcing her to turn her head. "I am serious as a fucking heart attack, child."

Suddenly, his expression changed, and the hard lines around his face softened. He pushed back her hair with his fingers, his touch light against her skin. Hank was trying to be paternal with her, but the soft way he touched her was a sickening reminder of the way *he* had touched her before. The tenderness had been the worst part: the soft strokes, the delicate way he used his tongue and fingers to soothe and stimulate her, the agonizingly slow way he had fucked her, as if he were making love to her instead of raping her.

Lena started to shake. She could not stop herself. Hank moved his hand away quickly, as if he had just realized he was touching something dead. Lena jerked back, her head banging into the window.

"Don't ever do that again," she warned, but there was only fear in her voice. "Don't touch me. Don't ever touch me like that. Do you hear me?" She panted, trying to swallow the bile that came up her throat.

"I know," he said, holding his hand close to her back but not touching her. "I know that. I'm sorry."

Lena grabbed for the door handle, missing it several times because her hands were shaking so hard. She stepped out of the car, taking gulps of air into her lungs. The heat enveloped her, and she squeezed her eyes shut, trying not to make the connection between the heat and her dreams of floating on the ocean.

She heard a familiar friendly voice behind her. "Hey there, Hank," Dave Fine, the pastor of the church, said.

"Good morning, sir," Hank returned, his voice kinder than it ever was when he spoke to Lena. She had heard Hank use that tone before, but only with Sibyl. For Lena, there had always been nothing but sharp words of criticism.

Lena concentrated on getting her breathing back under control before she turned around. She could not smile, but she felt the corners of her mouth rise slightly in what must have seemed like a pained grimace to the pastor.

"Good morning, detective," Dave Fine said, the preacher-compassion in his voice getting under her skin worse than anything Hank had said in the car. For the last four months, Hank had been pushing Dave Fine on Lena, trying to get her to talk to the preacher. Pastor Fine was also a psychologist, or so he said, and saw patients in the evenings. Lena did not want to talk to the man about the weather, let alone what had happened to her. It wasn't that Fine was the Antichrist, it was that of all the people Lena could possibly talk to, a preacher would be the last one she would pick. It was like Hank had forgotten exactly what had happened to her in that dark room.

She gave him a curt "Pastor," walking past him, her purse tight to her chest like an old lady at a rummage sale.

She could feel his eyes on her back, hear Hank make his apologies as she walked away from them. Lena felt a flush of shame for being rude to Fine. It wasn't his fault—he was a nice enough man—but there was really nothing she could say to make them understand.

She quickened her step, her eyes staring straight ahead as she walked toward the church. A crowd of people milling around the entrance parted for her as she took the steps one at a time, forcing herself to move slowly and not run into the church like her body ached to do. Everyone except for Brad Stephens, who grinned at her like a puppy, found something better to do as she ascended the stairs. Matt Hogan, who was Frank Wallace's partner now that Lena had been assigned to patrol, focused on lighting his cigarette as if he were attempting nuclear fusion in the palm of his hand.

Lena kept her chin raised, her eyes averted so that no one would talk to her. Still, she could feel them staring at her, and she knew they would start whispering as soon as they thought she was out of earshot.

The people were the worst part about going to church. The whole town knew what had happened to her. They knew she had been kidnapped and raped. They had read every detail of the assault in the paper. They had followed her recovery and return home from the hospital the way they followed their soap operas and football games. Lena could not go to the store without someone trying to look at the scars on her hands. She could not walk through a crowded room without someone casting a sad, pathetic look her way. As if they could understand what she had been through. As if they knew what it was like to be strong and invincible one day and completely powerless the next. And the next.

The doors to the church were closed to keep the cold air in and the heat out. Lena reached for the handle just as one of the deacons did, and their hands brushed. She jerked back as if she had touched fire, waiting for the door to open, keeping her eyes cast down. Walking through the foyer and then into the chapel, she stared at the red carpet, the white molding trimming out the bottom of the pews lining the large room, so that no one would think to talk to her.

Inside, the church was simple by Baptist standards, and small considering the size of the town. Most of the older residents attended the Primitive Baptist on Stokes Street, their tithes going with them. Crescent Baptist Church was about thirty years old, and they hosted singles parties and divorce recovery groups and Parents Without Partners get-togethers in the basement of the small chapel. Crescent was not about a vengeful God. Sermons were about forgiveness and love, charity and peace. Pastor Fine would never admonish his congregation for their sins or threaten them with hell and brimstone. This was a place of joy, or so the church bulletin said. Lena was not surprised at all that Hank had chosen it. His A.A. meetings were held in the basement, right beside the parenting class for teens.

Lena took a pew close to the front, knowing Hank would want to be close to the pastor for his usual Sunday dose of forgiveness. Dave Fine's wife and two kids were in front of her, but thankfully they didn't turn around. Lena crossed her legs, smoothing out her pants until she felt the woman down at the other end of the pew staring at her hands. Lena crossed her arms and looked up at the stage. The pulpit sat in the center, large velvet-covered chairs fanning out from it on either side. Behind this was the choir loft, the organ to the side. Its pipes climbed the walls like a vertical rib cage on either side of the baptismal. In the center of it all was Jesus, his arms spread out, his feet crossed one over the other.

Lena made herself look away as Hank slid into the pew beside her. She checked her watch. The nine-thirty service would start soon. It would last an hour, then Sunday school would be another half hour. They would leave around eleven, then go to the Waffle House off Route 2 where Hank would eat lunch and Lena would nurse a cup of coffee. They would be home by noon. Lena would clean the house then work on a couple of reports. At one-thirty, she was expected at the station to go over the Jenny Weaver case. The briefing would take about three hours if she was lucky, then it would be time to come home and get ready for the Sunday potluck and the evening service. After that, there was some kind of choir concert that would last until around nine-thirty. By the time they got home, it would be well past time for Lena to go to bed.

She exhaled slowly as she thought this through, inordinately relieved to know that today, at least, she had things to do. Her hours were spoken for.

"About to start," Hank whispered. He took a hymnal out of the rack in front of them as the organ music started. He fidgeted with the book, then said, "Pastor Fine says you can come by tomorrow after work."

Lena pretended not to hear him, but her mental clock made a note of the appointment; at least it would be something to do. At least in agreeing to see him it would keep Hank in town a little longer.

"Lee?" he tried. Finally, he gave up as the choir started its hymn.

Lena stood with the crowd, Hank's baritone vibrating in her ear as he sang "Nearer My God to Thee." Lena did not bother to mouth the words. She traced her tongue along her front teeth, following Hank's finger along the page as he kept his place in the song. Finally, she looked back at the cross. Lena felt a lightness, an eerie kind of peace, staring at the crucifixion. As much as she wanted to deny it, there was something comforting about its familiarity.

5

Sara kept her dark green BMW Z3 in second gear as she drove through downtown Heartsdale. The car had been an impulse buy insofar as any purchase that ran over thirty thousand dollars could be considered impulsive. At the time Sara bought it, the ink was just drying on her divorce papers, and she had wanted something impractical and a little flashy. The Z3 more than fit the bill. Unfortunately, as soon as she drove the thing back from the Macon dealership, Sara realized that a car was not going to make her feel better. As a matter of fact, she had felt conspicuous and silly, especially when her family was through with her. Two years later, Sara still sometimes felt a tinge of embarrassment when she saw the car parked in her driveway.

Billy, one of her two greyhounds, rode in the passenger's seat, his head ducked down because the clearance in the small sports car was too low for him. He licked his lips occasionally, but was quiet for the most part, keeping his eyes closed as the cold air from the vents pushed back his

pointy ears. His lips tugged up a bit at the edges, as if he
was smiling, enjoying the ride. Sara watched him out of the
corner of her eye, wishing life could just once be that simple for her.

Main Street was fairly empty, since none of the shops
stayed open on Sunday. Except for the hardware store and
the five-and-dime, most of them were closed by noon on
Saturday. Sara had been born here, right down the street at
the Grant Medical Center back when it was the only hospital in the region. She knew every part of this street like a favorite book.

Sara made a slow turn at the college gates and coasted
into her parking space in front of the Heartsdale Children's
Clinic. Despite the fact that she had the air on high, the back
of her legs stuck to the leather car seat as she opened the
door. She braced herself for the heat, but it was still overwhelming. Even Billy paused before jumping out of the car.
He looked around the parking lot, probably regretting that
he had come along with Sara instead of staying in the cool
house with Bob.

Sara used the back of her hand to wipe her forehead. She
had thrown on a pair of cutoff jeans, a sleeveless undershirt,
and one of Jeffrey's old dress shirts this morning, but nothing could keep the heat and humidity at bay. Rain, when it
deigned to come, was about as useless as throwing water on
a grease fire. Some days, it was hard for Sara to remember
what it was like to be cold.

"Come on," Sara told the dog, tugging at his retractable
leash.

As usual, Billy ignored her. She let the leash out and he
showed her his skinny behind as he loped toward the back
of the building. There were scars on his hind legs and rear
end from where the gates had popped him one too many

times at the racetrack. It broke Sara's heart every time she saw them.

Billy took his time doing his business, lazily lifting his leg against the tree closest to the building. The college owned the property behind the clinic, and they kept it heavily forested. There were trails back there that the students jogged along when it was not too hot to breathe. Sara had watched the Savannah news this morning and learned that they were advising people not to go outside in the heat unless they absolutely had to.

Sara checked her key ring and found the one for the back door. By the time she had it open, sweat was trickling down her neck and back. There was a bowl by the door, and she used the outside hose to fill it while Billy scratched his back on the grass.

Inside the clinic was just as hot as out, mostly because Dr. Barney, who had been a better pediatrician than architect, had insisted on lining the south-facing front wall of the building with heat-trapping glass brick. Sara could not imagine what the temperature must be in the waiting room. The back of the building seemed hot enough to boil water.

Sara did not have enough saliva left to whistle. She held the door open, waiting for Billy to amble in. After a long drink of water, he finally came. Sara watched as he stopped in the middle of the hallway, glanced around, then fell onto the floor with a snort. Looking at the lazy animal, it was hard to imagine the years he had spent racing at the track over in Ebro. Sara leaned down to pet him and remove his leash before heading back to her office.

The layout at the clinic was typical of most pediatricians' offices. A long L-shaped hallway lined the length of the building, with three exam rooms on either side. Two exam rooms were at the back of the L, though one of them was used for storage. In the center of the hallway was a nurses' station that served as the central brain of the clinic. There was a computer that held current patient information and a row of floor-to-ceiling filing cabinets where current charts were kept. There was another chart room behind the waiting room that was filled with information on patients dating back to 1969. One day, they would have to be purged, but Sara did not have that kind of time and she could not bring herself to ask the staff to do something she herself was not prepared to do.

Sara's tennis shoes snicked as she walked across the clean tile floor. She did not bother to turn on the lights. Sara knew this place in the dark, but that was not the only reason she left them off. The flickering of a fluorescent light, the click of brightness as the tubes came to life, would seem intrusive considering the task ahead.

By the time she reached her office across from the nurses' station she had already unbuttoned her overshirt and tied it around her waist. She wasn't wearing a bra, but she did not expect to run into anyone who would care.

Pictures of patients lined her office walls. Initially, a grateful mother had given Sara a school snapshot of a child. Sara had stuck it on the wall, then a day later another photo had come, and she had taped it beside the first. Twelve years had passed since then and now photographs spilled into the hallway and the staff bathroom. Sara could remember them all: their runny noses and earaches, their school crushes and family problems. Brad Stephens's senior picture was somewhere near the shower in the bathroom. The photo of a boy named Jimmy Powell, a patient who just a few months ago had been diagnosed with leukemia, had been moved by Sara's phone so that she could remember him every day. He was in the hospital now, and Sara knew in her gut that within the next few months another patient of hers would be put into the ground.

Jenny Weaver's picture was not on the wall. Her mother had never brought one in. Sara only had the girl's chart to help reconstruct their history together.

The filing cabinet drawer groaned as Sara yanked it open. The unit was as old as Dr. Barney and just as difficult. No amount of WD-40 would fix it.

"Crap," Sara hissed as the cabinet tilted forward. The top drawer was full to overflowing, and she had to use her free hand to keep the whole cabinet from falling.

Quickly, Sara ran her fingers along the file tabs, reading off Weaver on her second run through. She pushed the cabinet back, slamming the drawer into the unit. The sound was loud in the small office. Sara was tempted to open it and slam it again, just to make some noise.

She snapped on her desk lamp as she sat, her sweaty legs skidding on the vinyl seat. Probably it would have been wiser to take the chart home. At the very least, it would be more comfortable. Sara did not want comfort, though. She considered it a small penance to sit in the heat and try to find what she had missed over the last three years.

Her wire-rimmed reading glasses were in the breast pocket of her shirt, and Sara felt a moment of panic, thinking she had broken them when she sat down. They were bent, but otherwise fine. She slipped on her glasses, took a deep breath, and opened the chart.

Jenny Weaver had first come to the clinic three years ago. At ten years old, the child's weight had been within normal ranges in relation to her height. Her first ailment had been a persistent sore throat that a round of antibiotics had evidently cured. There was a follow-up notation in the chart, and from what Sara could barely decipher from her own handwriting, Dottie Weaver had been contacted a week later by phone to make sure Jenny was responding to treatment. She had been.

About two years ago, Jenny had started to put on weight. Unfortunately, this was not uncommon these days, especially for girls like Jenny, who had gotten her first menstrual period shortly after her eleventh birthday. Their lives were more sedentary, and fast food was more readily available than it should be. Hormones in meat and dairy products helped the process along. Case studies in some of the journals Sara read were already dealing with ways to treat girls who entered puberty as early as eight years old.

Sara continued reading through Jenny's chart. Shortly after the weight gain began, Jenny had been diagnosed with a urinary tract infection. Three months later, the girl had come in with a yeast infection. According to Sara's notes, there was nothing suspicious about this at the time. In retrospect, Sara questioned her judgment. The infections could have been the beginning of a pattern. She turned to the next page, noting the date. Jenny had come in a year later with another urinary tract infection. A year was a long time, but Sara pulled out a sheet of paper and made notes of the dates, as well as the two other visits Jenny had made after, both for sore throats. Perhaps Jenny's parents shared custody. They could trace the dates to see if they corresponded with visits to her father.

Sara set down her pen, trying to recall what she knew about Jenny Weaver's father. Mothers were more likely to bring their children into the clinic, and as far as Sara could remember she had never met Jenny's father. Some women, especially women who were recently divorced, would volunteer information about their husbands as if their children were not in the room. Sara was always uncomfortable when this happened, and she usually managed to cut it off before it could really start, but some women talked over her, bringing up the kind of personal information that a child should never know about either parent. Dottie Weaver had never done this. She was talkative enough, even chatty, but Dottie had never disparaged her ex-husband at the clinic, even though Sara had gathered from the sporadic way the single mother paid her insurance balance that money was tight.

Sara's glasses slipped up as she rubbed her eyes. She glanced at the clock on the wall. Sunday lunch at her parents' was at eleven, then Jeffrey was expecting her at the station around one-thirty.

Sara shook her head, skipping over any thoughts of Jeffrey. A headache had settled into the base of her neck and the dull throbbing made it difficult to concentrate. She took off her glasses and cleaned them with her shirttail, hoping this might help her see things more clearly.

"Hello?" Sara called, throwing open the door to her parents' house. The cold air inside brought welcome goose bumps to her clammy skin.

"In here," her mother said from the kitchen.

Sara dropped her briefcase by the door and kicked off her tennis shoes before walking to the back of the house. Billy trotted in front of her, giving Sara a hard look, as if to ask why they had spent all that time in the hot clinic when they could have been here in the air-conditioning. To punctuate his displeasure, he collapsed onto his side halfway down the hallway so that Sara had to step over him to get to the back of the house.

When Sara walked into the kitchen, Cathy was standing at the stove frying chicken. Her mother was still dressed in her church clothes, but had taken off her shoes and pantyhose. A white apron that read DON'T MESS WITH THE CHEF was tied loosely around her waist.

"Hey, Mama," Sara offered, kissing her cheek. Sara was the tallest person in her family, and she could rest her chin on her mother's head without straining her neck. Tessa had inherited Cathy Linton's petite build and blonde hair. Sara had inherited her pragmatism.

Cathy gave Sara a disapproving look. "Did you forget to put on a bra this morning?"

Sara felt her face redden as she untied the shirt she was wearing around her waist. She slipped it on over her T-shirt, offering, "I was in the clinic. I didn't think I'd be there long enough to turn on the air."

"It's too hot to be frying," Cathy countered. "But your father wanted chicken."

Sara got the lesson on sacrificing things for your family, but answered instead, "You should have told him to go to Chick's."

"He doesn't need to eat that trash."

Sara let this go, sighing much as Billy had. She buttoned the shirt to the top, giving her mother a tight smile as she asked, "Better?"

Cathy nodded, taking a paper napkin off the counter and wiping her forehead. "It's not even noon and it's already ninety degrees out."

"I know," Sara answered, tucking a foot underneath her as she sat on the kitchen stool. She watched her mother move around the kitchen, glad for the normalcy. Cathy was wearing a linen dress with thin, vertical green stripes. Her blonde hair, which was only slightly streaked with gray, was pulled up behind her head in a loose ponytail, much the same way Sara wore hers.

Cathy blew her nose into the napkin, then threw it in the

trash. "Tell me about last night," she said, returning to the stove.

Sara shrugged. "Jeffrey didn't have a choice."

"I never doubted that. I want to know how you're holding up."

Sara considered the question. The truth was, she was not holding up well at all.

Cathy seemed to sense this. She slipped a fresh piece of battered chicken into the hot oil and turned to face her daughter. "I called you last night to check in with you."

Sara stared at her mother, forcing herself not to look away. "I was at Jeffrey's."

"I figured that, but your father drove by his house just to make sure."

"Daddy did?" Sara asked, surprised. "Why?"

"We thought you would come here," Cathy answered. "When you weren't at home, that was the obvious place to check."

Sara crossed her arms. "Don't you think that's a little intrusive?"

"Not nearly as intrusive as childbirth," Cathy snapped, pointing at Sara with her fork. "Next time, call."

After almost forty years, Cathy could still make Sara feel like a child. Sara looked out the window, feeling as if she had been caught doing something wrong.

"Sara?"

Sara mumbled a quiet, "Yes, ma'am."

"I worry about you."

"I know, Mama."

"Is everything okay?"

Sara felt her color rise again, but for a different reason. "Where's Tessa?"

"She's not down yet."

Tessa lived over the garage of their parents' home. Sara's house was just a mile down the road, but that was far enough to give her some sense of independence. Tessa did not seem to mind the closeness. She worked with Eddie, their father, in the family's plumbing business, so it was easier for her to walk down the stairs and report for work every morning. Besides, part of Tessa was still a teenage girl. It had not hit her yet that one day she would want a house of her own. Maybe it never would.

Cathy flipped the chicken, tapping her fork on the edge of the pan. She slipped it into the spoon rest, then turned to Sara, her arms crossed. "What's going on?"

"Nothing," Sara answered. "I mean, other than last night with the girl. And the baby. I guess you heard about the baby."

"It was all over the church before we even walked through the doors."

"Well"—Sara shrugged—"it was very hard."

"I can't even imagine how you do that job, baby."

"Sometimes, I can't either."

Cathy stood, waiting for the rest. "And?" she prompted.

Sara rubbed the back of her neck. "At Jeffrey's . . . ," she began. "It just didn't work out."

"Didn't work out?" her mother asked.

"I mean, didn't work out as in . . ." Sara gestured with her hands, encouraging her mother to fill in the rest.

"Oh," Cathy finally said. "Physically?"

Sara blushed again, which was answer enough.

"Well, that's not a complete surprise, is it? After what happened?"

"He was so . . ." Sara looked for the right words. "He was . . . abrupt. I mean, I tried. . . ." Again, she left out the details.

"Is this the first time that's happened?"

Sara shrugged. It was the first time it had happened with her, but who knew about Jeffrey's other conquests. "The part that was awful . . . ," Sara began, then stopped. "As long as I've known him, I have never seen him that mad. He was furious. I thought he was going to hit something."

"I remember once when your father couldn't—"

"Mama," Sara stopped her. It was hard enough talking to her mother about this without bringing Eddie into the picture. Not to mention that Jeffrey would kill Sara if he knew that she had told anyone his performance had been less than stellar. Jeffrey's sexual prowess was as important to him as his reputation as a good cop.

"You brought it up," Cathy reminded her, turning back to the chicken. She snatched a paper towel off the roll and lined a plate to put the chicken on.

"Okay," Sara answered. "What should I do?"

"Do whatever he wants," Cathy said. "Or nothing at all." She picked up another piece of chicken. "Are you sure you even want to bother at this point?"

"Meaning what?"

"Meaning, do you want to be with him or not? Maybe that's what it boils down to. You've been dancing around this thing with Jeffrey since the divorce." She tapped the fork on the pan. "As your father would say, it's time for you either to shit or get off the pot."

The front door opened, then banged shut, and Sara heard two thumping noises as Tessa kicked off her shoes.

Tessa yelled, "Mama?"

"In the kitchen," Cathy answered. She gave Sara a pointed look. "You know what I mean?"

"Yes, ma'am."

Tessa stomped her way down the hall, mumbling, "Stupid dog," as she obviously stepped over Billy. The kitchen door bumped open, and Tessa came into the kitchen with an irritated expression on her face. She was wearing an old pink bathrobe with a green T-shirt and a pair of boxer shorts underneath. Her face was pale, and she looked a bit sickly.

Cathy asked, "Tessie?"

Tessa shook her head as she walked to the refrigerator and opened the freezer door, saying, "I just need coffee."

Cathy ignored this, and kissed her on the forehead to take her temperature. "You feel warm."

"It's a hundred freaking degrees outside," Tessa whined, standing as close to the freezer as she could without actually getting in. "Of course I'm warm." As if to reinforce this, she flapped her robe open and closed several times to generate some cool air. "Jesus, I'm moving somewhere where they get real seasons. I swear I am. I don't care how funny they talk or that they don't know how to make grits. There has got to be a better alternative."

"Is that all that's wrong?" Sara asked, putting her hand on Tessa's forehead. As a doctor, Sara knew this was about as effective a gauge for a fever as Cathy's kiss, but Tessa was her baby sister. She had to do something.

Tessa pulled away. "I'm premenstrual, I'm hot, and I need chocolate." She stuck out her chin. "Do you see this?" she asked, pointing to a large pimple.

"I don't see how we could miss it," Cathy said, closing the refrigerator door.

Sara laughed, and Tessa popped her on the arm.

"Wonder what Daddy's gonna call it?" Sara teased, slapping her back. When his daughters were teenagers, Eddie had taken great delight in drawing attention to their facial blemishes. Sara still felt a flush of shame when she remembered the time her father had introduced her to one of his friends as his oldest daughter Sara, and Bobo, her new pimple.

Tessa was phrasing a response when the phone rang. She picked it up on the first ring.

Two seconds passed before Tessa hissed a curse and yelled, "I got it, Dad," as Eddie obviously picked up the extension upstairs.

Sara smiled, thinking this could have been any Sunday from the last twenty years. All that was missing was their father walking in, making some silly comment about how happy he was to see all three of his girls barefoot and in the kitchen.

Tessa said, "Hold on," then put her hand over the mouth of the receiver. She turned to Sara. "Are you here?"

"Who is it?" Sara asked, but she could guess the answer.

"Who do you think?" Tessa snapped. She did not wait for a response. Instead, she said into the phone, "Hold on, Jeffrey. Here she is."

6

Ben Walker, Grant County's chief of police before Jeffrey, had kept his office just off the briefing room in the back of the station. Every day, Ben had settled himself behind the large desk that almost filled the entire room, and anyone who wanted to talk to him had to sit on the other side of this mammoth hunk of wood, their knees grazing the desk, their backs firm to the wall. In the mornings, the men—and they were all men then—on the senior squad were called in to hear their assignments for the day, then they left and the chief shut his door. Nobody saw him again until quitting time, when Ben got in his car and drove two blocks up the street to the diner where he ate his supper.

The first thing Jeffrey did when he took over the station was throw out Ben's desk. The oak monstrosity had to be disassembled to get it through the door. Jeffrey made Ben's old office the storage room, and took the small office at the front of the squad room as his own. One quiet weekend, Jeffrey installed a picture window so he could look out on the squad and, more important, so they could see him. There were blinds on the window, but he seldom closed them. Jeffrey made a point of leaving his office door open whenever possible.

He stared out at the empty squad room, wondering what his people would make of Jenny Weaver's shooting. Jeffrey felt an overwhelming sense of guilt for what he had done, even though his mind kept telling him he had not been given a choice. Every time he thought about it Jeffrey felt like he couldn't breathe right, like not enough air was getting to his lungs. He could not let go of the obvious questions in his mind: Had he made the right decision? Would Jenny have really killed that kid in cold blood? Sara seemed to think so. Last night, she had said something about having two dead teenagers today instead of one if Jeffrey had not stopped the girl. Of course, Sara had said a lot of other things last night that had not exactly been a comfort.

Jeffrey pressed his hands together in front of his face, leaning his head against his thumbs as he thought about Sara. Sometimes, she could be too analytical for her own good. One of the sexiest things about Sara was her mouth. Too bad she didn't know when to shut up and use it for something more helpful to Jeffrey than talking.

"Chief?" Frank Wallace knocked on the door.

"Come in," Jeffrey answered.

"Hot outside," Frank said, as if to explain why he wasn't wearing a tie. He was dressed in a dark black suit that had a cheap shine to it. The top button of his dress shirt was undone, and Jeffrey could see his yellowed white undershirt underneath. As usual, Frank reeked of cigarette smoke. He had probably been outside, smoking by the back door, giving Jeffrey some time before he came in for their meeting. Why anyone would voluntarily hold a burning cigarette in this kind of heat, Jeffrey would never know.

Frank could have had Ben Walker's job if he had asked. Of course, the old cop was too smart for that. Frank had worked in Grant County his entire career, and he had seen the way the cities were changing. Once, Frank had told Jeffrey that being chief of police was a young man's job, but Jeffrey had thought then as he did now that what Frank meant was it was a foolish man's job. During Jeffrey's first year in Grant, he had figured out that no one in his right mind would sign up for this kind of pressure. By then, it had been too late. He had already met Sara.

"Busy weekend," Frank said, handing Jeffrey a weekend status report. The file was thicker than usual.

"Yeah." Jeffrey indicated a chair for the man to sit down.

"Alleged break-in at the cleaners. Marla told you about that one? Then there's a couple or three DUIs, usual shit at the college, drunk and disorderly. Couple of domestic situations, no charges filed."

Jeffrey listened half-heartedly as Frank ran down the list. It was long, and daunting. There was no telling what a larger city dealt with this weekend if Grant had been hit so hard. Usually, things were much quieter. Of course, the heat brought out violence in people. Jeffrey had known that as long as he had been a cop.

"So . . ." Frank wrapped it up: "That's about it."

"Good," Jeffrey answered, taking the report. He tapped his finger on the papers, then with little fanfare slid Jenny Weaver's file across the desk. It sat there like a white elephant.

Frank gave the file the same skeptical look he would give an astrology report, then reluctantly picked it up and started to read. Frank had been on the job long enough to think he had seen everything. The shocked expression on his face belied this as he examined the photographs Sara had taken.

"Mother of God," Frank mumbled, reaching into his coat pocket. He pulled out his cigarettes, then, probably remembering where he was, put them back. He closed the file without finishing it.

Jeffrey said, "She didn't give birth to the child."

"Yeah." Frank cleared his throat, crossing his legs uncomfortably. He was fifty-eight years old and had already put in enough time to retire with a nice pension. Why he kept working the job was a mystery. Cases like this must make Frank wonder why he kept showing up every day, too.

"What is this?" Frank asked. "Good Lord in heaven."

"Female Genital Mutilation," Jeffrey told him. "It's an African or Middle Eastern thing." He held up his hand, stopping Frank's next question. "I know what you're thinking. They're Southern Baptist, not Islamic."

"Where'd she get the idea, then?"

"That's what we're going to find out."

Frank shook his head, like he was trying to erase the image from his mind.

Jeffrey said, "Dr. Linton is on her way in to do the briefing," feeling foolish for using Sara's title even as he said it. Frank played poker with Eddie Linton. He had watched Sara grow up.

"The kid gonna be here, too?" Frank asked, meaning Lena.

"Of course," Jeffrey answered, meeting him squarely in the eye. Frank frowned, making it obvious that he did not approve.

For everything Frank was—sexist, probably racist, certainly ageist—he cared for Lena. He had a daughter about Lena's age, and from the moment Jeffrey had partnered her with Frank, the old cop had protested. Every week Frank had come in, asking for a change in assignment, and every week Jeffrey had told him to get used to it. Part of the reason the city had brought in Jeffrey, an outsider, was to drag the force out of the Stone Age. Jeffrey had handpicked Lena Adams from the police academy and groomed her from day one to be the first female detective on the squad.

Jeffrey did not know what to do with her now. He had put Lena with Brad Stephens on a temporary basis until her hands healed, hoping the downtime would help her ease back into her job. Just last month she had gotten a clearance from her doctor to return to active duty, but Lena had yet to ask for her old assignment back. For Frank's part, he could not even look her in the eye when she said hello to him. Jeffrey had heard Frank say a million times that women did not belong on the force, and Frank seemed to take Lena's attack as confirmation of this.

Logically, Jeffrey did not agree with Frank's assessment. Women cops were good for the force. Ideally, the makeup of the force should reflect that of the community. Lena had brought a thoughtfulness to the job. She was better with certain types of perpetrators and knew how to handle female victims of crime, something that had been missing in the senior squad prior to her promotion. What's more, having a female detective had encouraged other women to join the ranks. There were fifteen women on patrol now. When Ben Walker had left the force, the only women in its employ had been secretaries. Despite all of this progress, when Jeffrey thought about what Lena had gone through, what had been done to her, he wanted to lock her up in her house and stand outside with a shotgun in case anyone ever tried to hurt her again.

Frank interrupted his thoughts, asking, "There gonna be some kind of internal investigation on this thing?" He paused, picking at the corner of the case file. "The Weaver shooting, I mean."

Jeffrey nodded, sitting back in his chair. "I talked to the mayor this morning. I want you to take Brad and Lena's statements. Buddy Conford's the city attorney on this one."

"He's a public defender," Frank pointed out.

"Yeah, well, not on this one," Jeffrey told him. "There's some concern about the girl's mother. The city has an insurance policy for this kind of thing. Maybe they'll settle it out of court. I dunno." Jeffrey shrugged. "She was threatening someone with a gun and all. It's just kind of tricky, you know?"

"Yeah," Frank answered. "I know." He waited a few beats, then asked, "You okay with this, Chief?"

Jeffrey felt some of his resolve falter. The sinking, lost feeling he had experienced last night with Sara came back, and he felt a heaviness in his chest. He had never shot anyone, let alone killed a little girl. His mind kept playing back the scene with Jenny, picking apart the clock, trying to find the place where his negotiations had gone sour. There had to be something else he could have said or done that would have made her put down that gun. There had to be an alternative.

"Chief?" Frank said. "For what it's worth, Brad and Lena will back you a hundred percent. You know that, right?"

"Yeah," Jeffrey answered, not taking comfort in Frank's words because he knew that Brad and Lena would back him even if they did not think what Jeffrey had done was right. There were gray areas in law enforcement, but when it came down to the wire, cops always backed cops. Brad would do this because at some level he worshipped Jeffrey. Lena would do it because she felt she owed Jeffrey something for letting her back on the job.

For Jeffrey, this was hardly a consolation.

Both men were silent. Jeffrey turned his head, looking at the shelves lining the far wall of his office. Shooting trophies were there, awarded for his marksmanship. An old football from when he played for Auburn was on the bottom shelf. Pictures of guys he had worked with on the job in Grant as well as back in Birmingham were alongside a couple of snapshots of Sara he had taken on their honeymoon. He had put these up recently, when they started dating again. Now, he wasn't so sure about wanting the pictures in his office, let alone wanting Sara in his life. Jeffrey still could not get over how distant she had been last night, tensing up when he touched her, telling him what to do. Like he didn't know how to do what he was doing. Like he hadn't done it hundreds of times before with other women who were a hell of a lot more receptive than Sara had been.

Frank turned around in his chair when the half-doors separating the squad room from the reception area clapped open. Sara walked through, her briefcase in one hand. She was dressed in a light blue dress that looked like a long T-shirt. Jeffrey could see she had decided to go with tennis shoes without socks to complete the ensemble. She probably hadn't even shaved her legs.

Both men watched as Sara made her way to the office. Her hair was a mess and Jeffrey wondered if she had even bothered to comb it. Sara had never been the kind of woman who was interested in high fashion and she seldom wore makeup. Sometimes this was sexy, sometimes it made her look sloppy, like she was more interested in being a doctor than being a woman. As she got closer to them, he could see that her glasses were crooked on her face. For some reason, this irritated him more than anything else.

Frank stood when she entered the room, so Jeffrey followed suit.

"Hi," she said, smiling nervously. Jeffrey was glad she was uncomfortable.

"Hey there," Frank said, buttoning his jacket.

Sara smiled at Frank, then said, "I've called Nick Shelton," referring to Grant County's Georgia Bureau of Investigations field agent. "I asked him to track any cases involving this kind of mutilation. He said he'd have something Wednesday at the latest."

When Jeffrey did not address this, Frank supplied, "Good thinking."

"And," Sara continued, "I called around to the hospitals. Nobody came in last night seeking postlabor treatment. I left the number here at the station in case they get someone in."

Frank pulled at the collar of his shirt. "So, you think there's any way the girl could have done this to herself? This circumcision thing?"

"God, no." Sara seemed to bristle at this. "And, it's not circumcision," she told him. "This is tantamount to castration. Her clitoris and labia minora were completely scraped away, then what was left was sewn together with thread."

"Oh," Frank said, obviously uncomfortable with this information.

Sara pursed her lips. "It's the same as cutting off a man's penis."

Frank looked uncomfortably from Jeffrey to Sara, then back again.

"Anyway." Sara gestured to her briefcase. "I'm ready to start the briefing."

"That's been postponed," Jeffrey said, hearing the hard tone to his voice but unable to do anything about it. When he had called to ask Sara to come in early, he had not mentioned why. He told her, "Dottie Weaver will be here in about fifteen minutes. I want to get her out of here as soon as I can."

"Oh," she said, surprised. "Okay. I guess I can do some paperwork at the clinic. You think a couple of hours will do it?"

He shook his head no. "I want you to sit in on the interview."

Sara gave him a careful look. "I'm not a cop."

"Lena is," he told her. "She'll be leading the interview. I want you there because she knows you."

She tucked her hand into her hip. "Lena or Dottie?"

Frank cleared his throat. "I got some calls to make," he said, giving Sara a polite nod before leaving the room.

After he was gone, Sara turned to Jeffrey, giving him a questioning look.

He asked, "Is that a nightgown?"

"What?"

"What you're wearing," he said, indicating her dress. "It looks like a nightgown."

Sara laughed uncomfortably. "No," she said, as if he was leaving out some part of the joke.

"You could have worn something more professional," he said, thinking about what she had worn last night. Her sweat pants and a ratty old T-shirt didn't exactly help the situation. And her legs had felt hairier than his.

He asked, "Would it kill you to dress up a little bit?"

Sara lowered her voice, the way she did when she got angry. "Is there some reason you're talking to me like you're my mother?"

He felt a flash of anger that was so intense he knew not to open his mouth and say what wanted to come out.

"Jeff," Sara said, "what is going on?"

He walked past her and slammed the door shut. "Would it kill you to do me this one favor?"

"Favor?" She shook her head, as if he had started talking gibberish.

"Sit in on the interview," he reminded her. "With Weaver."

Sara exhaled sharply. "What could I possibly say to her?"

"Never mind," he answered. To give himself something to do, he closed the blinds. "Just forget about it."

"Just tell me what you want me to do," she said, her voice irritatingly reasonable. "Do you want me to go home and change? Do you want me to leave you alone?"

He turned around, saying, "I want you to stop breaking my balls, is what I want you to do."

Sara tucked in her chin. It seemed to be her turn to hold back something she wanted to say.

He raised his eyebrows, prompting her to speak. "What?" he demanded, knowing he was pushing her, wanting a fight to release some of the anger he felt.

Sara took a deep breath, letting it out slowly. "I don't understand why you're so angry at me."

Jeffrey did not answer.

She smoothed down his tie with the back of her fingers, then put her palm to his chest. "Jeff, please. Just tell me what you want me to do."

Words failed him. He turned away from her and then, because there was nothing else for him to do, he twisted the wand to open the blinds again. He felt Sara's hand on his shoulder.

She said, "It's all right."

"I know that," he snapped, but he didn't. He felt like his brain was on fire, and every time he blinked all he could see was Jenny Weaver's head jerking back as the bullet cut through her neck.

Sara put her arms around him, then pressed her lips against the back of his neck. "It's okay," she whispered against his neck, and he felt the coolness of her breath calming him. She kissed his neck again, holding her lips there for what seemed like a long time. His body started to relax, and Jeffrey wondered why she hadn't done this last night. Then he remembered that she had.

She told him again, "It's all right."

He felt calm for the first time that morning, like he could breathe again. It felt so good that for just a second he thought he might do something really stupid, like cry or, worse, tell Sara that he loved her.

He asked, "You gonna sit in on the interview or not?"

She let her hands drop, and he could tell this was not the reaction she had been hoping for. He looked at her, trying to think of something to say. Nothing came to mind.

Finally, she nodded once, telling him, "I'll do whatever you want me to do."

Jeffrey stood in the observation room, watching through the one-way mirror as Sara comforted Dottie Weaver. He had never been able to stay mad at Sara for long, mostly because Sara would not allow it.

Dottie Weaver was a largeish woman with dark brown hair and olive colored skin. Her hair looked long, but she kept it in a neat bun on top of her head. The style was a bit dated, but it seemed to suit her. She had what Jeffrey thought of as an older face, the kind where the person looks the same at ten as she does at forty. Her cheeks were more jowls, and she carried about twenty pounds more on her than she should have. There were deep creases in her forehead above her nose, which gave her a stern look, even when she was crying.

Jeffrey glanced at Lena, who was standing beside him with her arms crossed over her chest. She was watching Sara and Dottie with her usual focused intensity. Here they were, the two most emotionally raw people in the station, responsible for finding out what had happened the night before. Jeffrey knew then that he had asked Sara to do this for selfish reasons. She would act as his sanity.

Jeffrey turned to Lena, telling her, "I'm using you."

She did not react, but that was hardly uncommon. Six months ago, Lena Adams would have been rabid for this interview. She would have strutted through the station, flaunting the fact that she had been chosen by the chief. Now, she just nodded

"Because you're a woman," he clarified. "And because of what happened to you."

She looked at him, and there was an emptiness to her eyes that struck him to his core. Ten years ago, at the training academy in Macon, Jeffrey had watched Lena fly through the obstacle course like a bat out of hell. At five-four and around a hundred twenty pounds, she was the smallest recruit in her group, but she made up for it by sheer force of will. Her tenacity and drive had caught his attention that day. Looking at her now, he wondered if that Lena would ever show herself again.

Lena broke eye contact, staring back at Sara. "Yeah, I guess she'll feel sorry for me," she said, her tone flat. It unnerved him the way she did not seem to feel anything. He even preferred her intense anger to the automaton Lena seemed to be lately.

"Go slowly," he advised, handing her the case file. "We need as much information as we can get."

"Anything else?" she asked. They could have been discussing the weather.

Jeffrey told her no and she left without another word. He turned back to the mirror, waiting for Lena to enter the interview room. When the young detective had returned to her job, Jeffrey had told her she would have to get some kind of therapy to deal with what had happened. As far as he knew, Lena had not. He should ask her about this. Jeffrey knew that. He just did not know how.

The door creaked as Lena opened it. She walked into the room, her hands tucked into the pockets of her dress slacks. She was wearing tan chinos with a dark blue button-down dress shirt. Her shoulder-length brown hair was tucked back neatly behind her ears. At thirty-three years old, she had finally grown into her face. Lena had always been attractive, but in the last couple of years she had developed a womanliness that was not lost on the senior squad.

Jeffrey looked away, uncomfortable with these thoughts. After what she had been through, it felt wrong for him to be considering Lena this way.

"Mrs. Weaver?" Lena asked. She extended her hand, and Jeffrey cringed along with Dottie Weaver as they both stared at Lena's open palm. The scar in the center was horrible to see. Sara was the only one who did not seem to react.

Lena withdrew her hand, clenching it by her side as if she was embarrassed. "I'm Detective Lena Adams. I can't tell you how sorry I am for your loss."

"Thank you," Dottie managed, her Midwestern twang a sharp contrast to Lena's soft drawl.

Lena sat opposite Sara and Dottie at the table. She clasped her hands in front of her, drawing attention to her scars again. Jeffrey half expected her to take off her shoes and put her feet on the table.

"I'm sorry . . . ," Dottie began, then stopped. "I mean, for what happened with you."

Lena nodded her head once, staring down as if she needed to collect herself. One of the first interrogation tricks Jeffrey had taught the young detective was that silence is a cop's best friend. Normal people do not like silence, and invariably they try to fill it. Most of the time, they do this without letting their brain enter the equation.

"And your sister," Dottie continued. "She was a lovely person. I knew her from the science fair. Jenny loved science. She was . . ."

Lena's chest rose and fell as she took a deep breath, but that was all the reaction she gave. "Sibyl was a teacher," Lena supplied. "She loved teaching kids."

The room was silent again, and Jeffrey found himself staring at Sara. Strands of her dark red hair had fallen loose from her ponytail and were sticking to her neck. Her glasses were no longer crooked on her nose, they were crooked on the top of her head. She was staring at Lena the way she might stare at a snake, trying to decide whether or not it was poisonous.

Lena asked, "Do we need to contact your husband, Mrs. Weaver?"

"Dottie," the mother answered. "I've already told him."

"Will he be coming down for the funeral?"

Dottie was quiet, and she fidgeted with a thin silver bracelet on her wrist. When she spoke, she directed her words to Sara. "You cut her open, didn't you?"

Sara opened her mouth as if to respond, but Lena answered the question.

"Yes, ma'am," Lena said. "Dr. Linton performed the autopsy. I attended the procedure. We wanted to do everything we could to make sure Jenny was taken care of."

Dottie stared from Lena to Sara, then back again. Suddenly, she leaned over the table, her shoulders stooped as if she had been punched in the gut. "She was my only child," she sobbed. "She was my baby."

Sara reached out to touch the grieving woman on the back, but Lena stopped her with a look. She leaned forward herself and took Dottie's hand in her own. Lena told the woman, "I know what it's like to lose someone. I really do."

Dottie squeezed Lena's hands. "I know you do. I know."

Jeffrey realized he had been holding his breath, waiting for this moment. Lena had broken through.

Lena asked, "What happened with her father?"

"Oh." Dottie took a tissue out of her purse. "You know. We weren't getting along. He wanted to do more with his life. He ended up running away with his secretary." She turned to Sara. "You know how men are."

Jeffrey felt mildly irritated, because she was obviously referring to Jeffrey's infidelities. Such was the nature of a small town.

"He never married her, though," Dottie finished. "The secretary." Her lips curved in a slight, triumphant smile.

"My best friend in high school went through this," Lena began, making the bridge between her and Dottie Weaver more solid. "Her father did the same thing to them. He just picked up one day and never looked back. They never saw him again."

"Oh, no. Samuel wasn't like that," Dottie provided. "Not in the beginning, anyway. He saw Jenny once a month until he got transferred to Spokane. That's in Washington." Lena nodded and Dottie continued, "I think the last time he saw her was over a year ago."

"What was his response when you told him last night?"

"He cried," she said, and tears rolled down her own cheeks. She turned to Sara, perhaps because Sara had known Jenny. "She was so sweet. She had such a gentle heart."

Sara nodded, but Jeffrey could tell she was uncomfortable with the way Lena was handling the interview. He wondered what Sara had expected after her physical findings last night.

Dottie blew her nose, and when she spoke her words were more punctuated. "She just got mixed up in this crowd. And that Patterson boy."

"Mark Patterson?" Lena asked, referring to the boy Jenny had threatened to kill.

"Yes, Mark."

"Was she seeing him? Dating him?"

Dottie shrugged. "I can't tell you. They did things in groups, and Jenny was friends with his sister, Lacey."

"Lacey?" Sara asked. She seemed to realize she'd interrupted the flow, and nodded for Dottie to continue.

"Jenny and I were so close after her father left, more like friends than mother and daughter. She was my anchor through everything that happened. Maybe I was too close to her. Maybe I should have given her more independence." Dottie paused again. "It's just that Mark seemed so harmless. He used to cut our grass in the summer. He did odd jobs around the house to earn extra money." She laughed without a trace of humor. "I thought he was a good kid. I thought I could trust him."

Lena did not let her go on this tangent for long. "When did Jenny start hanging around with Lacey?"

"About a year ago, I guess. They were all in the church together. I thought it was good, but these kids . . . I don't know. You would think that a church would be a safe place for your child, but . . ." She shook her head. "I didn't know," she said. "I didn't even know she had ever been with a boy, let alone . . ."

Lena gave Sara an almost imperceptible nod. Jeffrey saw Sara brace herself as she prepared to deliver the news. "Dottie, I did examine Jenny last night."

Dottie pressed her lips tightly together as she waited.

Lena said, "Jenny wasn't pregnant. That wasn't her baby in the skating rink."

The mother stared openly from Sara to Lena, then back again. She seemed too shocked to show anything but disbelief.

Sara clarified. "Lena's right. She wasn't pregnant, though I can tell you that she was sexually active prior to six months ago."

Dottie's mouth worked, but no words came. She smiled, finally, interpreting this as good news. "So, she didn't do it? She didn't hurt the baby?"

Lena answered, "We don't really know what happened with that yet." She paused, looking at her hands, this time not for effect. After a few beats, she looked back up at Dottie. When she spoke, her voice was low, her eyes locked on the mother as if Sara were no longer in the room. "This is just my opinion, ma'am, but from everything I've learned about your daughter, I can't see her doing what she's been accused of."

The mother's shoulders dropped in obvious relief. She began to cry again, putting a tissue to her nose. "She was so gentle," she said. "There's no way she would ever do this kind of thing." She turned to Sara for confirmation. "She was such a good girl."

Sara nodded again, her smile weak.

"She talked about being a doctor one day," Dottie told Sara. "She said she wanted to help kids just like you do."

Sara's smile wavered, and Jeffrey could see the guilt flash in her eyes.

Lena cut through the moment, asking, "Jenny and this group she was with, the Patterson children?"

"Yes, Mark and Lacey."

"She was still going to church with them? Still active?"

"Until about eight months ago," Dottie answered. "She stopped going. I can't tell you why. She just said she didn't want to go anymore."

"This would have been in January?"

"I suppose."

"Right after Christmas?"

Dottie nodded. "Thereabouts."

"Did anything happen during that time? Maybe a falling out? Did she get angry at anyone? Maybe have a fight with Mark Patterson?"

"No," Dottie answered firmly. "As a matter of fact, she went on a youth retreat with the church the week after Christmas. They all went to Gatlinburg to go skiing. I didn't want her out of the house around the holidays, but she had her heart set on it, and she had brought her grades up in school, so . . ." She let her voice trail off.

"So, she was gone a week?"

"Yes, a week, but then I had to go to my sister's in Ohio because she wasn't feeling well." Dottie pressed her lips together. "Eunice, my sister, was diagnosed with emphysema a couple of months prior to that. She's doing better now, but it was a really difficult time."

"Jenny was alone in the house then?"

"Oh, no," Dottie shook her head. "Of course not. She stayed with the Pattersons for three or four days, then I came back."

"That was normal, for her to stay with the Pattersons?"

"Yes, then it was," Dottie provided. "Every weekend Lacey would stay over or Jenny would go to the Pattersons'."

"You know the Pattersons well?"

"Teddy and Grace?" She nodded. "Oh, yes, they both go to the church. I'm not too crazy about Teddy," she said, lowering her voice a little. "You can see where Mark gets it, I'll tell you that."

"How's that?"

"He's just kind of . . ." Dottie began, then shrugged. "I don't know. If you ever meet him, you'll see what I mean."

"So," Lena summed it up. "At Christmas, Jenny was on the church retreat, then she stayed with the Pattersons, then she stopped going to church and stopped talking to the Pattersons?"

"Well," Dottie seemed to go over this in her mind. "Yes, I guess so. I mean, it seems that way now. Before, when it was happening, I didn't make a connection."

"Did you ever suspect your daughter of using drugs?"

"Oh, no, she was adamantly against them," Dottie answered. "She didn't even drink caffeine, and just recently she cut out all sugar."

"For her weight?"

"For her health, she said. She wanted to make her body pure."

" 'Pure,' " Lena repeated. "Did that have something to do with the church, do you think?"

"She had stopped going by then," Dottie reminded her. "I don't know why she did it. We were driving home from school one day, and she just said it: 'I don't want to eat anything with sugar in it anymore. I want my body to be pure.' "

"This didn't strike you as odd?"

"At the time, no," Dottie said. "I mean, maybe it did, but she had been acting so strange lately. Not strange like you would notice, but strange like she stopped drinking Co-Colas when she got home from school, and she started concentrating more on her homework. It was like she was trying to do better. She was more like her old self."

"Her old self before she started hanging out with the Patterson children?"

"Yes, I guess you could say that." Dottie pursed her lips. "It was very strange, because Lacey was a cheerleader, and very popular, and from the day Jenny walked through the school doors Lacey tortured her."

Sara asked, "Tortured her how?"

"Just mean," Dottie answered. "Teasing her about her weight. And this was back when she was just a little chubby. Not like she's been lately."

"You don't think Lacey or Mark ever hit her?"

Dottie seemed surprised. "Heavens no. I would have called the police." She patted her eyes with the tissue. "They just teased her is all. Nothing physical. Like I said, they became friends."

Lena said, "Why did that change?"

"I don't really know. Maybe when they all went from the middle school to the senior high. It's a big adjustment. I think Lacey didn't make the cheerleading team, and she kind of dropped in the pecking order. You know how kids are. They want to belong. Now that I think about it, the sugar thing was probably Lacey's idea."

"Lacey's?" Lena asked.

"Oh, yes. She was always coming up with things for them to do. What kind of clothes they would wear to school, where they would go for the weekend. They spent hours on the telephone talking about it."

Lena smiled. "My sister and I used to do the same thing," she said. Then, "Was it some kind of religious thing, you think?"

"What's that?" Dottie asked, caught off guard.

"The sugar. The caffeine. It sounds kind of religious."

"You don't think . . . ?" Dottie stopped herself. "No, I don't think it's religious. She was very happy with the church. I think it must have been those Patterson children. Mark has some kind of criminal record for stealing things." She shook her head in a slow arc. "I didn't know what to do. Should I have told her she couldn't see him? That would have made her want to spend even more time with him."

"That's generally the case with young girls," Lena agreed. "You still go to church, right?"

"Oh, of course," Dottie answered, nodding her head. "It's a great consolation to me."

"Have you made arrangements yet? I guess they'll do the service?"

Dottie sighed. "I don't know. I just . . ." She stopped, blowing her nose on a tissue. "I think she liked Preacher Fine. He came by the house to talk to her. So did Brad Stephens. He's the youth minister at the church."

"That so?" Lena asked.

"Oh, yes, Brad is very active in the community."

"Did Pastor Fine come by after Jenny stopped going to church?"

"Yes," she nodded, and she seemed glad to be able to remember something that might be important. "He came by after she had missed a couple of Sundays."

"Did you hear what she said to him?"

"No," Dottie answered. "They were in the den, and I wanted to give them some privacy." She seemed to remember something. "He did call back a week later on the telephone, but she told me to say she wasn't in. That must have been a Saturday, because I was home during the daytime. And I remember that she got a couple more calls that day, and didn't take those, either."

"Was this odd?"

"Not by then," she said. "This must have been around February. I remember I was kind of relieved that she didn't want to talk to Mark anymore."

"Did she have some kind of argument with him?"

Dottie shrugged. "All I know is that she hated him. She went from spending most of her time with him to absolutely hating him."

"Hating him the way a girl hates a guy who won't ask her out?"

Dottie sat back, giving Lena a hard look of appraisal. She finally seemed to realize that this interview was being conducted to establish Jenny's guilt, not clear her name.

Lena repeated her question. "She hated Mark because he didn't want to go out with her anymore?"

"No," Dottie snapped, her nasally twang back. "Of course not."

"You're certain?"

"He was arrested around that time," Dottie told her, obviously more comfortable putting Mark in the criminal role. "For assault. He attacked his sister."

Jeffrey cursed himself for not having checked this before. He picked up the phone in the interview room and punched Marla's extension.

"Yep?" Marla asked.

"Pull a file for me," he said, keeping his voice low. "Mark Patterson."

"Kid from last night?"

"Yes."

"Sure thing," she answered, ringing off.

When Jeffrey turned his attention back to the room, the climate had changed drastically. Dottie Weaver sat in her chair, her jaw set in an angry line.

Lena asked, "Would you like something to drink?"

"No, thank you."

"Did you know your daughter's arm was fractured last year?"

Dottie seemed surprised. She asked Sara, "Did she come see you without me?"

"No," Sara answered, not elaborating. She seemed angry, but not at Dottie Weaver.

Lena pressed on. "Was your daughter interested in African or Middle Eastern culture?"

Dottie shook her head, not understanding. "Of course not. Why? What does that have to do with anything?"

Sara asked, "Dottie, do you want to take a break?"

Lena shifted in her seat, keeping the questioning up. "Your daughter also had a stress fracture in her pelvis, Mrs. Weaver. Did you know this?"

Dottie's mouth worked, but she did not answer.

Lena said, "She was probably raped." She paused, then without emotion added the word, "Brutally."

"I don't . . ." Dottie turned to Sara, then back to Lena. "I don't understand."

"What about the scarring on her arms and legs?" Lena demanded. "What happened there? Why was your daughter cutting herself?"

"Cutting herself?" Dottie demanded. "What are you talking about?"

"There were cuts all over her body. Self-inflicted, from the looks of them. You want to tell me how she could do this without you knowing?"

"She was secretive," Dottie countered. "She covered herself up with her clothes. I never—"

Lena interrupted, "Did you know that she'd had surgery in the last six months?"

"Surgery?" Dottie repeated. "What are you talking about?"

"Not surgery," Sara interrupted, putting her hand on Dottie's arm. She said, "Dottie, when I examined Jenny—"

Lena opened the case file. She tossed a picture across the table, then another. From his position, Jeffrey could not make out which ones, but he knew by the expression on Dottie's face exactly what the mother was looking at.

"Oh, my God, my baby." She put her hand to her mouth.

"Lena," Sara warned, putting her hand over the pictures. She tried to move them away, but Dottie stopped her. They struggled for a few seconds with one of the photos before Sara reluctantly let go.

"W-what?" Dottie stuttered. Her hand shook as she held the photo close to her face.

Lena looked smug as she sat back in her chair, crossing her arms over her chest. She actually turned to the mirror, to Jeffrey, and raised her eyebrows in a sort of triumph.

Sara put her hand to Dottie's back. "Let me have this," she said, trying to take away the photo.

"My God, my God," the woman muttered, sobbing openly. "My baby. Who did this to my baby?"

Sara shot a look at Lena, and Jeffrey could feel the heat from her stare. Lena shrugged, as if to say, "What did you expect?"

"Oh, God, oh, God," Dottie whispered, then stopped abruptly. Her body went limp, and Sara softened the woman's fall as she fainted to the floor.

Jeffrey stood in the hallway outside the briefing room, talking to Lena.

"We'll need to get to the Patterson boy right away," Jeffrey told her. "Sara can do the autopsy briefing by herself."

Lena looked over his shoulder toward the back door. Sara had walked Dottie to her car to make sure the woman was okay, but not before giving a taut warning to Lena that she would be back.

Jeffrey said, "Marla is pulling his address right now. There may be something more to his involvement in this. Hopefully, we'll catch his sister at home, too."

Lena nodded, crossing her arms. "You want me to take the sister and you can do Mark?"

"Let's see how it goes," Jeffrey answered. "I also want to get a look at this preacher."

Something flickered in Lena's eyes. She said, "He's at my church. Well, not *my* church, but it's where Hank goes, and I go along with him sometimes." She shrugged. "You know, for something to do. I'm not religious like that or anything."

"Yeah," Jeffrey answered, a little startled that she had offered this information. It was as close to chatty as Lena had gotten since her attack. He thought maybe it was doing her some good to be involved in the case, and Jeffrey was pleased with that.

"I'm gonna call Brad in off patrol," Jeffrey said. "I want to talk to him as soon as I can and see what he says about Fine."

"You think Fine's the one who did this to Jenny?"

Jeffrey tucked his hands into his pockets. He could not imagine anyone harming a child, but the fact remained that someone had. "We need to find out if Fine was on that retreat during Christmas."

"Maybe I could—" Lena stopped as the back door was thrown open with a loud bang.

Jeffrey turned just as Sara closed the door. He could tell from the way she walked up the hall that she was angry as hell.

About ten feet away from them, Sara demanded, "What were you doing in there? How could you do that to her?"

Lena dropped her hands to her side. Jeffrey saw her fists clench as Sara shortened the distance between them.

Lena moved away, so that her back was against the wall. She kept her hands clenched and her voice was strong when she said, "I was doing my job."

"Your job?" Sara shot back, getting in Lena's face. Sara had a good six inches on Lena, and she was using them to her advantage. "Is it your job to torture a woman who's just lost her kid? Is it your job to show her those pictures?"

Sara's voice cracked on this last word. "How could you do that to her, Lena? How could you make those pictures the last memory she'll ever have of her daughter?"

Jeffrey said, "Sara—" just as Sara leaned in and whispered something in Lena's ear. He could not hear what she had said, but Lena's reaction was immediate. Her shoulders dropped, and she reminded Jeffrey of a kitten that had been picked up by the scruff of its neck.

Sara saw this, and he could see the immediate guilt on her face. She put her hand over her mouth, as if she could keep the words in. "I'm sorry," she said to Lena. "I am so sorry."

Lena cleared her throat, looking down at the floor. "It's okay," she said, though clearly it was not.

Sara must have realized that she was still crowding Lena, because she stepped back. "Lena, I'm sorry," she repeated. "I had no right to say that."

Lena held up her hand to stop Sara. She took a breath, but did not let it go. Instead, she said, "I'll be in the car when you want to go."

The comment was meant for Jeffrey, he realized, and he told Lena, "Okay. Good." He fumbled for his keys and held them out to her, but she did not take them. Instead, she extended her hand, palm up, waiting for him to drop them.

"Okay," Lena said, holding the keys in her fist. She did not look at Jeffrey or Sara again. She stared at the floor, even as she walked down the hallway. Her posture was still slack, and she had an air of being completely defeated about her. Whatever Sara had said to the woman had cut to the bone.

Jeffrey turned to Sara, not understanding what had just happened, or why. He asked, "What the hell did you just say to her?"

Sara shook her head, putting her hand over her eyes. "Oh, Jeff," she said, still shaking her head. "The wrong thing. The completely wrong thing."

7

Lena sat in Jeffrey's Lincoln town car, her body tight as a drum. Her breathing came in pants, and she felt slightly light-headed, as if she might pass out. She was sweating, and not just from being trapped in the hot car. Her whole body felt lit up, as if she had touched a live electrical wire.

"Bitch," she breathed, thinking of Sara Linton. "Stupid bitch," she repeated, as if calling her this would take away what had been said.

Sara's words still echoed in Lena's head: *Now you know what it's like to hurt somebody*.

Hurt, Sara had said, but Lena knew what she had meant. Now you know what it's like to rape somebody.

"Goddamn it!" Lena screamed as loud as she could, trying to replace the sound. She slammed her hand against the dashboard, cursing Sara Linton, cursing this stupid job.

Back in the interrogation room, drilling Dottie Weaver like that, for the first time in forever, Lena had started to feel human again, and Sara had taken that away with one simple sentence.

"Dammit!" Lena screamed again, her voice hoarse from the effort. She wanted to cry, but there were no tears left, just a seething anger. Every muscle in her body was tense, and she felt like she could lift the car up and flip it over if she wanted to.

"Stop it, stop it, stop it," Lena told herself, trying to calm down. She had to be okay with this when Jeffrey got to the car, because he would tell Sara—he was fucking her, for God's sake—and Lena did not want Sara Linton to know her words had struck so deep.

Lena snorted a laugh at the thought of Sara's lame apology. As if that made a difference. Sara had said exactly what she meant. The only reason she apologized was she felt bad for saying it out loud. On top of being a bitch, she was a coward.

She took another deep breath, trying to get herself together. "It's okay," Lena whispered to herself. "It doesn't matter. Nothing matters."

After a couple of minutes, Lena felt better. Her heart was not beating so hard, and her stomach seemed to unclench. She kept reminding herself that she was strong, that she had been through worse than this and survived. What Sara Linton thought did not matter in the big scheme of things. What mattered was that Lena could do her job. She *had* done her job. They had gotten some solid leads to follow in that interview, something that would not have happened if Sara Linton had been in charge.

Lena looked at her watch, then did a double take. She had not realized what time it was. Hank would be wondering what was taking her so long. There was no way she could go to church with him now.

Jeffrey's car had a cell phone mounted into the console,

and Lena leaned over, cranking the engine so she could use the phone. She turned on the air conditioner and cracked the window to let some of the heat out of the car. The phone took its time powering up, and she glanced at the station, this time to make sure Jeffrey was not coming out.

Hank picked up on the first ring. "Hello?"

"It's me," she said. There was a pause from his end, and she realized what her voice must sound like. There was a rawness to it, and the edge from her confrontation with Sara was still there. Thankfully, Hank did not ask her what was wrong.

She said, "I'm not going to be able to make it to church."

"Oh?" he said, but did not go further.

"I've got to do an interview with Jeffrey," she told him, even though she did not owe Hank Norton an explanation. "We're going to be a while, probably. You should go without me." Lena's voice went down on the last part of her sentence as she thought about going home and being by herself.

"Lee?" Hank asked, obviously sensing her fear. "I can stay here for you if you want. You know, just until you get home."

"Don't be stupid," she said, aware that her tone wasn't very convincing. "I'm not a three year old."

"You could come after, you know," Hank said, hesitancy in his voice. "I mean, to hear the choir sing."

Lena experienced a sinking feeling as she remembered the concert. It would be dark outside by the time Hank got home. Inside the house would be darker, no matter how many lights Lena turned on.

"I gotta get up early to go check on the bar, anyway," Hank offered. "I could come home after the service."

"Hank," Lena said, trying not to let on that her heart was about to explode in her chest. "Listen, go to the fucking concert, okay? I don't need you baby-sitting me all the time. I mean, for fuck's sake."

Sunlight flashed off the back door as Jeffrey came out of the building. Marla Simms was right behind him, holding a file folder out to the chief.

Hank asked, "You're sure?"

"Yeah," she answered before she could think about it. "Listen, I've gotta go. I'll see you when you get home."

She hung up the phone before Hank could respond.

"Jesus," Jeffrey said as soon as he opened the car door. "Is the air on?" he asked, throwing her the file Marla had handed him.

"Yeah," Lena mumbled, shifting in her seat as he got in. Without thinking about it, she had moved away from him, as close to the door as she could get. If he noticed this, Jeffrey did not comment.

Jeffrey threw his suit jacket into the back seat. "I got a call," he said, obviously preoccupied. "My mother's had an accident. I've got to go to Alabama tonight."

"Now?" Lena asked, putting her hand on the door handle, thinking she could call Hank from her car and tell him to wait for her.

"No," Jeffrey told her, making a point of looking at her hand. "Tonight."

"Okay," she said, keeping her fingers on the handle, as if she was resting them there.

"It's gonna be a pain in the ass to leave in the middle of this. Maybe Mark Patterson can straighten things out."

"What do you mean, like it was a lover's tiff or something?" Lena asked.

"Maybe he can tell us who the other girls were, who the mother is."

She nodded, but did not think it was likely.

"I talked to Brad. Fine wasn't on the Ski Retreat." Jeffrey frowned. "I'll call Brad again after we talk to Mark and see if I can push him to remember anything else." He paused. "I'm sure he would have said if something bad happened."

"Yeah," Lena agreed. Brad was the kind of cop who would turn in his own mother for jaywalking.

"First thing tomorrow, I want you and Brad to talk to Jenny Weaver's teachers and see what kind of kid she was, maybe find out if there was somebody she was hanging around with. Also, talk to the girls who went on the retreat with Jenny and Lacey. They probably all go to the same school."

"Okay."

"I can't get out of going to Alabama or I'd do this myself."

"Sure," she said, wondering why he kept making excuses. Technically, he was in charge. Besides, it wasn't like there was much Jeffrey could do on the case right now. Unless Mark pointed the finger at someone, they didn't have very much to go on.

He said, "I also want you to interview Fine as soon as possible." He looked at his watch. "Tomorrow morning. Take Frank with you for that one, not Brad."

She repeated, "Okay."

"You said you know him, the preacher," Jeffrey began, putting the car into reverse. "You think he's got this in him?"

"This?" Lena said, then remembered why they were here. "No," she answered. "He's not a bad guy. I just don't get along with him is all."

Jeffrey gave her a look that said she didn't seem to get along with anybody.

Lena offered, "Actually, I've kind of got an appointment with him tomorrow evening."

"An appointment?"

Lena looked at the dashboard. "Like you said before.

What you wanted me to do," she prompted, but he did not pick up on it. "Talk to somebody," she supplied.

"Well, maybe you shouldn't be the one to—"

"No," she insisted. "I want to do it." She tried to smile, but it felt fake, even to her. "It'll surprise him, right? Thinking that I'm there for a session or whatever, but turning it around and asking him about Jenny and the Pattersons."

Jeffrey frowned as he turned the car out of the parking lot. "I'm not sure I like that."

"You always said that the best time to interview somebody is when you catch him off guard," she reminded him, trying to keep the desperation out of her voice. "Besides, Hank set it up. It's not like I would talk to him about . . ." Lena looked for a word, but could not find one. "I wouldn't talk to him, okay? He's a freak. I don't trust him."

"Why?"

"I just don't," she said. "I just have a feeling about him."

"But you don't think he did this?"

She shrugged, trying to find a way to backpedal. How could she explain to Jeffrey that the main reason she did not like Dave Fine, did not trust him, was that he was a pastor? Jeffrey was being just as stupid about it as Hank. How anyone could not make the connection between Lena's being assaulted by a religious fanatic and her not wanting to talk to a preacher about it was beyond her.

She said, "I dunno, maybe he's got it in him."

The lie seemed to swing Jeffrey. "Okay. But, take Frank with you."

"Sure."

"This isn't an interrogation. We're just trying to find out if he knows anything. Don't go in there and piss him off for no good reason."

"I know."

"And set something else up," he said. "Something with

somebody else." He paused. "That was a condition, Lena. The only reason I let you come back so early was because you promised you would talk to somebody about what happened."

"Yeah," she nodded. "I'll set something up with somebody else, first thing."

He stared at her, as if he could figure her out just from looking.

She tried to sound casual as she changed the subject, asking, "She okay? Your mom, I mean."

"Yeah," he answered. "Are you all right?"

She tried not to sound glib. "I'm fine."

"That thing with Sara—"

"I'm fine," she reassured him, using a tone that would have shut up Hank in two seconds flat.

Jeffrey, of course, was not Hank Norton. He persisted, "You're sure?"

"Yeah." Then, to prove it, she asked, "What was that thing in the interview? Dr. Linton sounded surprised when the mother mentioned Lacey Patterson."

"She was a patient of Sara's at the clinic," Jeffrey told her. Then, almost to himself, he said, "You know how Sara feels about her kids."

Lena didn't, and she looked down at the file, not answering him. Mark Patterson's name was on the tab, and she flipped it open to see what he had been up to. The top sheet had his vitals on it, including his address. "They live in Morningside?" she asked, referring to a shady part of Madison.

"I'm thinking it's that trailer park. The one with the green awning over the sign?"

"The Kudzu Arms," Lena supplied. She and Brad had been called out to the Kudzu on several occasions over the course of the last few months. The hotter the weather, the hotter the tempers.

"Anyway," Jeffrey said, moving things along. "What's he got on his sheet?"

Lena thumbed through the pages. "Two B and Es when he was ten, both of them at the Kudzu Arms. Most recently, he beat up his sister pretty bad. His father called us out, we got there, they wouldn't press charges." She stopped reading, providing, " 'We' means Deacon and Percy," she supplied, referring to two beat cops. "They pulled this one, not me and Brad."

Jeffrey scratched his chin, seeming to think this through. "I don't even remember when it happened."

"Just after Thanksgiving," Lena told him. "Then, around Christmas time, Deacon and Percy were called back. It was the father again, and he asked for them specifically." She skimmed the report Deacon had written. "This time, charges were filed. They took him down to the pokey for a couple of days. Mark was supposed to take some anger management classes in exchange for time served." She snorted a laugh. "Buddy Conford was his lawyer."

"Buddy's not that bad," Jeffrey said.

Lena closed the file, giving him an incredulous look. "He's a whore. He puts addicts and murderers back on the streets."

"He's doing his job, just like we are."

"His job screws our job," Lena insisted.

Jeffrey shook his head. "He's gunna be talking to you about the Weaver situation," he told her. "The shooting."

Lena snorted a laugh. "He's working for Dottie Weaver?"

"The city," he told her. "I guess he's doing it as a favor to the mayor." Jeffrey shrugged. "Anyway, work it out with him. Tell him what happened."

"It was a clean shot," Lena told him, because if there was one truth in her life right now, it was that Jeffrey had taken the only option given to him. She said, "Brad will say the same thing."

Jeffrey was quiet, and he seemed to drop the subject, but after a few minutes he pulled the car over to the side of the road. Lena felt a sense of déjà vu, and her stomach lurched as she thought about being in the car with Hank that morning, and how she had embarrassed herself. There was no question in her mind now that Lena would not have the same problem with Jeffrey. She could be stronger around Jeffrey because he did not see her the way that Hank did. Hank still thought of Lena as a teenage girl because that was the only way he had ever really known her.

Lena waited as Jeffrey put the car in park and turned toward her. She felt the hair on the back of her neck rise, and thought she might be in trouble or something.

"Between you and me . . . ," Jeffrey said, then stopped. He waited until she looked him in the eye and repeated himself. "Between you and me," he said.

"Yeah," Lena nodded, not liking the serious tone in his voice. Her stomach sank in her gut as she realized he was going to say something about Sara.

He surprised her, saying instead, "The shot."

She nodded for him to continue.

"With Weaver," he said, as if he needed to narrow it down. She could see how upset he was. For the first time, she understood what it meant to read someone like a book. She saw the kind of pain in his eyes that she would never expect to see in Jeffrey Tolliver.

"Tell me the truth," he said, a begging quality to his voice. "You were there. You saw what happened."

"I did," she agreed, feeling a startling need coming off of him.

"Tell me," he said, begging more openly this time. Lena

felt a kind of rush from his desperation. Jeffrey needed something from her. Jeffrey Tolliver, who had seen her naked, nailed down to the floor, bruised and bleeding, needed something from Lena.

She let the moment linger, savoring the power more than anything else. "Yeah," she finally said, though with little conviction.

He continued to stare, and she could see the doubt in his eyes. For a moment, she thought he might even tear up.

"It was a clean shot," she told him. He kept staring straight at her, as if he could see into her. Lena knew that her tone wasn't confident, and that he had picked up on this. She knew, also, that she had not made it clear that she trusted his judgment. Her response had been purposefully ambiguous. Lena had no idea why she had done this, but she felt the thrill of it for a long while, even as Jeffrey put the car back into gear and drove down the road.

Grant County was made up of three cities: Heartsdale, Madison, and Avondale. Like Avondale, Madison was poorer than Heartsdale, and there were plenty of trailer parks around because it was cheap housing. This did not necessarily mean that the people occupying the trailers were cheap. There were some better parks with community centers and swimming pools and neighborhood watches, just as there were some that festered with domestic violence and drunken brawls. The Kudzu Arms fell into this second category. It was about as far from a neighborhood as a place could get without falling off the map. Trailers in various states of dilapidation fanned out from a single dirt road. Some of the residents had tried to plant gardens to no avail. Even without the drought, which had put all of Georgia on water restrictions, the heat would have killed the flowers. The heat was enough to kill people. The plants did not have a chance.

"Depressing," Jeffrey noted, tapping his fingers on the steering wheel. It was a nervous habit she had never seen in him, and Lena felt the guilt come back like a strong under-tow, pulling her the wrong way. She should have been more adamant about the shooting. She should have looked him right in the eye and told him the truth, that killing the teenager was the only thing he could have done. Lena could not think how to make it better. A thousand adamant yeses would never erase her initial reticence and the impact it had made. What had she been thinking?

Jeffrey asked, "What's the address?"

Lena flipped the file open, tracing her finger to the address. "Three-ten," she said, looking up at the trailers. "These are all twos."

"Yeah," Jeffrey agreed. He looked over his shoulder across the road from the park. "There it is."

Lena turned as he backed out of the park. A large mobile home, she guessed a doublewide, was on the other side of the road. Unlike the ones in the park across from it, this trailer looked more like a house. There was something like landscaping in the front yard, and a cinder block foundation covered the bottom portion. Someone had painted the con-crete blocks black to offset the white trailer, and a large covered deck served as a front porch. To the side was a car-port, and beside this was a large diesel semi.

"He's a truck driver?" Jeffrey asked.

Lena thumbed down to the proper space on the form. "Long hauler," she told him. "Probably owns his own rig."

"Looks like he makes some money from it."

"I think you can if you own your own truck," Lena told him, still skimming Mark Patterson's file. "Oh, wait," she said. "Patterson owns the Kudzu, too. He put it up as collateral when he bailed out Mark."

Jeffrey parked in front of the Patterson trailer. "Sure doesn't take good care of it. The park, I mean."

"No," Lena answered, looking back across the road. The Patterson house was a stark contrast to the desolate-looking Kudzu Arms across the street. She wondered what this said about the father, that he would take such pride in his own home, yet let the people living less than thirty yards away live in such squalor. Not that it was Patterson's responsibility to help people out, but Lena would have thought the man would try to pick himself some nicer neighbors, especially with two kids in the house.

"Teddy," Lena told Jeffrey. "That's the father's name."

"Marla pulled his sheet back at the station," Jeffrey told her. "He's got a couple of assaults on him, but they go back about ten years. He did some time on one of them."

"Apple doesn't fall far from the tree."

A large man stepped from the trailer as Jeffrey and Lena got out of the car. Lena guessed this was Teddy Patterson, and she felt a momentary flash of panic because he was such a physically large man. Taller than Jeffrey by a couple of inches and at least thirty pounds heavier, Patterson looked as if he could pick up both of them in one hand and toss them across the road.

Lena felt angry that she even took note of his size. Before, Lena had felt like she could take on anybody. She was a strong woman, muscular from working out in the gym, and she had always been able to push herself to do whatever she wanted to do. Now, she had lost that feeling, and the sight of Patterson gave her a slight chill, even though he wasn't doing anything more threatening than wiping his hands on a dirty dish towel.

"You lost?" Patterson asked. He had that look about him that all cops learned to recognize: Teddy Patterson was a con, right down to the jailhouse tattoos clawing up his arms like chicken scratches. Lena and Jeffrey exchanged glances, which did not seem to be lost on Patterson.

"Mr. Patterson?" Jeffrey asked, taking out his badge. "Jeffrey Tolliver, Grant Police."

"I know who you are," Patterson shot back, tucking the dish towel into his pocket. Lena could see it was soiled with what looked like grease. She also took note of the fact that Patterson had not bothered to acknowledge her.

Lena opened her mouth to speak, to let him know that she was there, but nothing came out. The thought of him training his animosity on her brought a cold sweat.

"This is detective Lena Adams," Jeffrey said. If he noticed her fear, he did not seem to register it. "We're here to talk to Mark about what happened last night."

"Alright," Patterson said, running the words together like most people in Madison did, so that it came out more as *"Ahte."*

Patterson turned his back to them and walked toward the house. He stood in the doorway as Jeffrey passed, crowding him on purpose, and Lena could see that the man was a lot taller than she had thought from the car. Lena was not sure, but Patterson seemed to narrow the space between his stomach and the door jamb as Lena passed through. She turned slightly so that she would not be forced to touch him, but even then Lena could tell from the smile on his face that he knew she was feeling intimidated. She hated that she was so transparent.

"Have a seat," Patterson offered, indicating the couch. Neither Jeffrey nor Lena took him up on this. Patterson's arms were crossed over his barrel chest, and Lena noticed that his head was about three inches from the low ceiling. The room was large, but Patterson filled the space with his presence.

Lena looked around the trailer, trying to behave like a cop instead of a scared little girl. The place was orderly and clean, certainly not what she would have guessed if she had met Teddy Patterson in a bar somewhere. The room they stood in was long, a kitchen at one end, with a hallway to what she assumed was the rest of the trailer, then the room they stood in, which had a medium-sized fireplace and a big-screen television. A floral scent was in the air, probably from one of those plug-in air fresheners. The living room seemed feminine, too, the walls painted a light pink, the couch and two chairs covered in a light blue with a matching pink stripe. A quilt was over the couch, the pattern complementing the decor. On the coffee table, a bowl of fresh cut flowers was surrounded by women's magazines. There were some nice framed prints on the walls, and the furniture looked new. The carpet, too, was freshly vacuumed. Lena could see Patterson's footprints indenting the pile where he had walked.

"We just need to talk to Mark about what happened last night," Jeffrey told Patterson as Lena continued her survey of the room. She stopped midturn, seeing a picture of Jesus hanging over the fireplace. His pierced and bleeding hands were open in the classic "let's be pals" Jesus pose. Jeffrey seemed to notice the painting at the same time, too, because he was staring at Lena when she made herself look away. He raised his eyebrows, as if to ask if she was all right. Lena could feel rather than see Patterson assessing this exchange. Of course he had heard about what happened to Lena. She could only imagine what kind of pleasure Patterson was getting out of reviewing the details of her assault in his mind. The hold this gave Patterson over Lena was suffocating, and she made herself look the other man right in the eye. He held her gaze for just a second, then glanced down at her hands.

She knew exactly what he was looking for, and Lena was fighting the urge to tuck her hands into her pockets when a small woman with a ravaged look about her walked up the hallway, asking, "Teddy? Did you get my pills?"

She stopped when she saw Jeffrey and Lena, putting her hand to her neck. "What's this about?"

"Police," Patterson said, looking away quickly. Something like guilt flashed in his eyes, as if his wife might guess what he had been thinking about Lena a few seconds before.

"Well," she said, a wry look on her face. "Tell me something I don't know."

She was a small woman, probably no taller than Lena's own five-foot-four. Her dark blonde hair was thin, her scalp showing through in places. She looked almost emaciated, like pictures Lena had seen in history books of Holocaust survivors. There was strength to her, though, and Lena imagined this was the woman who was responsible for keeping the trailer so neat and organized. Underneath her sickly appearance, she had the stance of a person who knew how to take care of things.

"I knew you were coming," the woman said, "so I know I shouldn't feel surprised." Her hand stayed at her neck, nervously playing with a charm on her necklace. Lena guessed from the Jesus on the wall that it was a cross.

"Mrs. Patterson?" Jeffrey asked.

"Grace," she told him, holding out her hand. Jeffrey shook it, and Lena took the opportunity to let herself study Teddy Patterson. He watched his wife and Jeffrey with a

slack expression on his face. His shoulders stooped somewhat when his wife was in the room, and he did not seem so
threatening in her presence.

"We want to talk to Mark," Jeffrey told the woman. "Is
he around?"

Grace Patterson gave her husband a worried look.

Patterson told his wife, "Why don't you sit down, hon?"
Then, as if he needed to explain this to Jeffrey, he said,
"She's been sick lately."

"I'm sorry to hear that," Jeffrey said. He sat down by
Grace on the couch and nodded to Lena, indicating that she
should sit as well. Lena hesitated, but did as she was directed, sitting in one of the chairs.

The light coming through the window hit Grace Patterson just right, and Lena could see how pale she was. There
were dark circles under her eyes, and her lips were an un-
natural shade of pinkish blue. Lena realized the woman
matched the living room perfectly.

Grace spoke. "I appreciate your not interrogating Mark
last night, Chief Tolliver. He was very upset."

Jeffrey said, "It's understandable that he would need
some time to recover from what happened."

Teddy Patterson snorted at this. Lena was not surprised.
Men like Teddy Patterson did not think that people needed
to recover from things. He was actually more like Lena in
that regard. You dealt with it and you got over it. Or, at least
you tried and did not whine about it.

"Is his sister around?" Jeffrey asked. "We'd like to talk
to her, too."

"Lacey?" Grace said, putting her hand to her necklace
again. "She's at her grandmother's right now. We thought it
would be best."

Jeffrey asked, "Where was she last night?"

"Here," Grace answered. "She was taking care of me." She swallowed, looking down at her hands in her lap. "I don't usually ask her to stay with me, but I had a very bad night, and Teddy had to work." She gave him a weak smile. "Sometimes the pain gets to be too much for me. I like having my children around."

"But Mark wasn't here?" Jeffrey said, even though that much was obvious.

Her face clouded. "No, he wasn't. He's been a bit difficult to control lately."

"He smacked up his sister a while back," Patterson told them. "I guess you got that on his sheet. He's a real shit, that boy. Nothing good coming from him."

Grace did not make a sound, but her disapproval traveled through the room.

"Sorry," Patterson apologized. He actually looked contrite. Lena wondered at the hold Grace had over her husband. In the space of a few short minutes, she had subdued the man.

Patterson said, "I'll go fetch Mark," and left the room.

Lena caught herself running her tongue along the back of her teeth again. For some reason, she could not speak. There were questions to ask, and Lena knew that Jeffrey wanted them to come from Lena, but she was too preoccupied to focus. Her goal was to get out of this trailer and away from Teddy Patterson as quickly as possible. The truth was that even with his wife sitting three feet away, and Jeffrey right beside her, Lena felt scared. More than that, she felt threatened.

Lena tried to take her mind off the claustrophobia she was feeling. She stared off into the kitchen, which was roomy but not large. Strawberry wallpaper lined the walls, and there was even a clock with a strawberry on it over the kitchen table.

Grace cleared her throat. "Mark has had a bad time lately," she said, picking up where she had left off. "He's been in and out of trouble at school."

"I'm sorry to hear that, Mrs. Patterson," Jeffrey said. He sat up on the couch, probably to establish a sense of rapport. "How about Lacey?"

"Lacey has never been in trouble a day in her life," Grace told him. "And that's the God's truth. That child is an angel."

Jeffrey smiled, and Lena could guess what he was thinking. Usually the angels were the ones who committed the most heinous crimes. "Is she dating any boys?"

"She's thirteen," Grace told him, as if that answered it. "We don't even let boys call the house."

"She couldn't have been seeing anyone on the side?"

"I don't see how," Grace answered. "She's home from school every day when she's supposed to be. Whenever she goes out, it's always with a group of her girlfriends and she always comes back in time for her curfew."

Lena could sense Jeffrey trying to catch her eye, but she ignored him.

He asked, "What time is her curfew?"

"School nights we don't let her go out, of course. Fridays and Saturdays, nine o'clock."

"Does she ever sleep over with anybody?"

Grace looked as if she had just realized that Jeffrey's interest in Lacey was more calculated than she had originally thought. The look was similar to the one Dottie Weaver had given Lena just hours before, but there was far more menace in Grace Patterson than there had been in Dottie Weaver.

She demanded, "Why are you asking so many questions about my daughter? It was Mark that little girl pointed the gun at."

Jeffrey said, "Dottie told us that Lacey and Jenny were friends."

"Well . . . ," she began, the hesitancy still there as she obviously tried to think a step ahead of Jeffrey's questions. Finally, she said, "Yes, they were friends. Then something happened and they stopped hanging around each other." She shrugged. "I guess it's been a few months since that happened. We haven't seen Jenny around for a while, and I know Lacey hasn't gone over to her house."

"Did she tell you why?"

"I assumed it was some silly little disagreement."

"But you didn't ask her?"

Grace shrugged. "She's my daughter, Chief Tolliver, not my best friend. Little girls have their secrets. You can ask your ex-wife about that."

He nodded at this. "Sara said Lacey's a great kid. Very smart."

"She is," Grace agreed, and she seemed pleased to have her daughter complimented. "But, it's not my place to pry if she's not ready to talk about it."

"Maybe she wouldn't mind talking with someone else about it?"

"Meaning?"

"Do you mind if I talk to her?"

Grace gave him another sharp look. "She's a minor. If you don't have cause, you can't talk to her without my permission. Is that right?"

"We don't want to talk to her as a suspect, Mrs. Patterson. We just want to get some idea of what state of mind Jenny Weaver was in. We don't really need your permission for that."

"But, I've just told you that Lacey hasn't seen Jenny for a while—probably since Christmas. She wouldn't have any idea about this." Grace gave a polite but humorless smile. "I do not want my daughter interrogated, Chief Tolliver." She paused. "By you or by Dr. Linton."

"She's not suspected of any wrongdoing."

"I want to keep it that way," she said. "Do I need to call the school and tell them that she is not to talk to anyone without either her father or me in the room?"

Jeffrey paused, probably thinking that she knew a hell of a lot more about the law than they had initially suspected. Schools were very friendly with law enforcement, and since administrators served as in loco parentis while the kids were on campus, they could allow interviews.

Jeffrey said, "That's not necessary."

"Do I have your word on that?"

Jeffrey gave a quick nod. "All right," he said, and Lena could hear the disappointment in his voice.

"We'd still like to talk to her," Jeffrey said. "You're more than welcome to sit in on an interview."

"I'll have to talk to Teddy about that," she told him. "But we can both imagine what he'll say." She gave a slight almost-smile, ending the hostility. "You know about daddies and their little girls."

Jeffrey sighed, and nodded again. Lena knew that Teddy Patterson was more likely to slip on his wife's Sunday best than to let his daughter talk to a cop. Cons learned to distrust the police early on, and despite the fact that he had been out of prison for a good while, Teddy still seemed to be practicing this.

To his credit, Jeffrey did not completely give up. He asked, "She hasn't been sick lately, has she?"

"Lacey?" Grace asked, obviously surprised. "No, of course not. Ask Dr. Linton if you like." She put her hand to her chest self-consciously. "I'm the only one in the family who's ever been ill."

"She was going to church? Lacey was?"

"Yes," Grace told them. She smiled again, and Lena could see that her teeth were slightly gray. "Mark was, too.

For a while, anyway." She paused, looking at the fireplace. Lena thought she was looking at the painting, but then she noticed there were pictures of the family on the mantel. They were the kinds of snapshots every family had, kids and parents at the beach, at an amusement park, out camping in the woods. The Grace Patterson in these photos was a little heavier and not so sunken-looking. The kids looked younger, too. The boy who must have been Mark looked around ten or eleven years old, his sister around eight. They seemed like a happy family. Even Teddy Patterson smiled for the camera in the few shots that showed him.

"So," Jeffrey prompted, "they went to the Baptist?"

"Crescent Baptist," Grace answered, her voice animated for the first time. "Mark seemed very happy there for a while. Like some of his nervous energy was being directed, finally. He even started doing better in school."

"And then?"

"And then . . ." She shook her head slowly, her shoulders slumped. "I don't know. Around Christmas, he started to get bad again."

"Christmas this past year?" Jeffrey asked.

"Yes," she said. "I really don't know what happened, but the anger was back. He seemed so . . ." Again, she let her voice trail off. "We tried to get him into counseling, but he wouldn't show up. We couldn't make him go, though"— she looked down the hallway, as if to check to see if they were alone—"his father tried. Teddy thinks that people should be like him. Boys, that is. Or men, I should say. He has strong ideas about what's acceptable."

"There was a church retreat at Christmastime. Did Mark go on that?"

"No," she shook her head. "This was around the time he started to act up. He was grounded, and his father wouldn't let him go."

"Lacey went?"

"Yes," she smiled. "She'd never been skiing before. She had a wonderful time."

They fell silent, and Grace Patterson picked at some non-existent lint on her dress. Obviously, she had more to say.

"I'm very sick," she said, her voice low. "My doctors don't hold out much hope for me."

"I'm sorry to hear that," Jeffrey said, and he truly seemed to be.

"Breast cancer," Grace said, putting her hand to her chest. Lena noticed for the first time that the woman's chest was almost completely flat under her blouse. "Lacey will be fine. She always lands on her feet. I don't like to think what will happen to Mark when I'm gone. For all his posturing, he's a gentle boy."

"I'm sure he'll be okay," Jeffrey assured her, though even to Lena he did not seem confident. Short of a miracle, boys like Mark did not turn themselves around.

Grace picked up on the deception. She gave a small, knowing chuckle. "Oh, I'm no fool, Chief Tolliver, but I thank you all the same."

Teddy Patterson's footsteps were heavy in the hallway, and the trailer shifted slightly from his weight as he entered the room. His son was behind him, a stark contrast to the father. Patterson grabbed the boy's arm and pulled him into the room.

Lena's first impression of Mark Patterson was that he was incredibly handsome. Last night, she had not taken much notice of him because so much had been going on. In the trailer, she took her time assessing him. Mark's dark blond hair matched his mother's, but it was more full, and slightly shorter. His eyelashes were longer than any she had ever seen on a man, and his eyes were a piercing blue. Like most sixteen-year-old boys, he had the beginnings of a goatee on his chin and the semblance of a mustache over his full lips.

As Lena watched, he tucked his hair behind his ears with his fingers. She could not help but think there was something erotic in the gesture. There was also something about the way he walked and held his shoulders that gave him a certain sensuality. His faded jeans rested a little below his thin hips, and the tight white T-shirt he wore rode up a little, showing off the definition in his abs.

Despite all of this, there was a sexlessness to him. Mark Patterson was a sixteen-year-old child on the verge of becoming a man. He was boyish in that androgynous way that was now popular with teenagers. When Lena was in high school, boys had done everything possible to make themselves appear more masculine. Today, they were more comfortable with blurring the roles.

"Here he is," Patterson barked, pushing Mark farther into the room. The man seemed angry, even more so than before, and his hands were in tight fists like he wanted nothing more than to pummel his son. For some reason, Teddy Patterson reminded Lena of Hank. The gruff way he had pushed Mark and the nasty tone of his voice could have come from Hank twenty years ago.

"We'll go for a drive," Patterson told his wife. "Get your pills from the pharmacy."

"Teddy," Grace said, the word catching in her throat. Lena wondered, too, why a man with Teddy Patterson's innate distrust of the police would leave his only son alone with them. By law, Teddy could be in on the interview. He was effectively hanging his son out to dry.

Jeffrey obviously wanted to capitalize on this. "Mr. Patterson," he began. "Do you mind if we schedule an appointment with Mark tomorrow to get a blood sample from him?"

Patterson's eyebrow went up, but he nodded. "Just tell him when and he'll be there."

Grace said, "Teddy."

"Let's go," Patterson ordered his wife. "The pharmacy closes soon."

If Grace Patterson had power over her husband, she had learned when not to use it. She stood, offering her hand first to Jeffrey, then to Lena. Grace had not even talked to Lena the entire time, but the woman kept Lena's hand in hers for longer than just a polite good-bye.

"Take care," she told Lena.

Grace Patterson stopped in front of her son before she followed her husband out the door, giving him a kiss on the cheek. She was a couple of inches shorter than he was, and she had to rise up on her toes to do this.

"Good-bye," Grace told him, patting his shoulder.

Mark watched her leave, touching his fingers to his cheek where his mother had kissed him. He looked at his fingers, as if he might see the kiss on them.

"Mark?" Jeffrey asked, getting the boy's attention.

"Sir?" he said, drawing out the word. His body was too loose to stand still, and he swayed a bit.

Jeffrey asked, "You stoned?"

"Yes, sir," he answered, putting his hand on the back of a chair to steady himself. Lena saw a large gold class ring on his finger. The red stone caught the light, and she guessed there was an initial underneath.

Mark asked, "You wanna take me to jail?"

"No," Jeffrey told him. "I want to talk to you about what happened last night."

"What happened last night," he mimicked, his words slurring together. "I wanna thank you for shooting the right person."

Jeffrey took out his notebook, flipping it open to a blank page. As Lena watched, he took out his pen and wrote Mark's name at the top of the page, asking, "You think I did?"

Mark smiled lazily. He walked around the chair and sat down, blowing air out between his lips as he did. There was something sexual even in this movement, and rather than being repulsed, as Lena thought she would have been, she was intrigued. She had never met a grown man who seemed so comfortable with himself, let alone a teenage boy.

Jeffrey started out with a hard question. "Were you the father of that baby last night?"

Mark raised his eyebrow the same way his father had. "Nope," he said, his lips smacking on the word.

Jeffrey tried a different avenue, asking, "Was your sister with you last night?"

"Naw, man," Mark answered. "My mom, you know. She's not doing too well. Lace stayed home with her." He shrugged. "She don't ask often, you know? My mom likes to leave us out of the fact that she's fucking dying."

He swallowed visibly, turning his head to the side, looking out the window. He seemed to compose himself, because when he looked back at Jeffrey, the smile was there, teasing at his lips. There was something more to this kid than his looks. A shadow seemed to be hanging over him, and not just because of what happened last night. He had about him the air of being damaged, something Lena could relate to. He seemed fragile, but slightly dangerous at the same time. Not that he was threatening like his father. If anything, Mark Patterson seemed to be a danger only to himself.

Lena found her voice for the first time since they had gotten to the trailer. "You like your sister?" she asked.

"She's a saint," Mark said, twisting the ring on his finger. "Daddy's little girl."

"Has she been feeling okay lately?" Lena asked. "She hasn't been sick or anything, right?"

Mark stared openly at Lena. There was nothing hostile about the stare. He seemed curious about her and nothing more. He said, "She seemed fine this morning. You'd have to ask her."

Lena tried, "Why was Jenny Weaver so mad at you?"

He raised his shoulders, held them there for a while, then let them drop. Lena watched as he lifted up his shirt and absently started to stroke his flat stomach. "You know, lots of girls get mad at me."

Jeffrey asked, "Were you involved with her?"

"What, in a relationship?" He shook his head slowly side to side. "Nah. I mean, I did her a couple of times, but it was nothing serious." He held up his hand to stop the next question. "This was when I was fifteen, officer."

Lena told him, "There has to be at least a five-year age difference for statutory rape."

Jeffrey shifted on the couch, obviously not pleased that Lena had given Mark this information. He could have used this threat for leverage. Now he had to find something else.

Jeffrey asked, "When was the last time you had sex with her?"

"I dunno," Mark said, still stroking his belly. There was a small tattoo on the webbing between his thumb and forefinger. Lena could make out a black heart with an inverted white heart in the center of it. Mark had obviously done this himself, because the symbol looked as rudimentary as his father's jailhouse ballpoint ink tattoos.

Lena prompted, "You had sex with her a lot?"

Mark shrugged. "Often enough," he said, still stroking

his stomach. He started picking at the trail of hair between his navel and his pubis, giving Lena a sly look. She glanced at Jeffrey, wondering what he was making of this. Jeffrey was not looking, though. Instead, he was copying the tattoo into his notebook.

"Well," Jeffrey began, blacking in the heart. "Take a guess."

"Maybe a year or so ago?" Mark offered. "She wanted it, man. She begged me."

Jeffrey finished the drawing, looking up. "This isn't about nailing you for rape, Mark. I don't care if you've been banging goats in the backyard. You know what this is about."

"It's about her wanting to kill me," he said. "And why."

"Right," Lena said. "We just want to get to the bottom of this, Mark. This is about Jenny, and why she would do what she did."

Mark gave Lena a lazy smile. "Gosh, detective, you sure are pretty."

Lena felt embarrassed, and wondered what signals she had given the boy. Certainly, sex was the last thing on her mind, and she wasn't sure that she thought Mark Patterson was so much attractive as perfect. There was a cinema-idol quality to his appearance. He seemed too good-looking to be true. She was showing the same interest in him as she would a beautiful painting or an exquisite sculpture.

"You're pretty handsome yourself, Mark," she countered, making her words sharp. Teddy Patterson might be able to fuck with her, but she would be damned if his precious boy would. "Which is why I'm puzzled about Jenny. She wasn't exactly homecoming queen material. Couldn't you get any better than that?"

Her words hit him exactly where she had intended them to, in his ego.

"Trust me, detective, I've had a *lot* better than that."

"Yeah?" she asked. "What, you banged her out of the goodness of your heart?"

"I let her suck me off sometimes," he said, his fingers moving lower down his belly, his eyes on Lena as he obviously tried to gauge her reaction to him touching himself. His interest gave Lena some insight into the boy. She imagined that someone so attractive was used to trading on his looks. No wonder his father, a man who had the physical presence of a freight train, was so disgusted by his son.

Suddenly, she felt sorry for him. Lena shifted on the couch, feeling a bit unsettled. She had spent such a long time feeling sorry for herself that for a moment she did not know what to do with this new emotion.

Mark said, "She had this thing she did with her tongue, like a lollipop. No teeth. It was great."

Lena felt her heart rate accelerate, willing herself not to react to his words. Probably the boy had no idea who she was or what had happened to her.

She could sense Jeffrey about to step in, so she said the first thing that came to her mind to keep him from interfering. "So, you let her give you blow jobs?" she said, trying to be flippant. Still, she kept her tongue firmly against the back of her teeth as she waited for his answer.

A smile broke out on his lips, and he stared at her, his piercing blue eyes sparkling with humor. "Yeah."

"Here? In this house?"

Mark gave a light chuckle. "Right down the hall."

"With your mama in the house?"

He stopped, seeming more afraid than angry. "Don't bring my mama into this."

Lena smiled. "We have to, Mark, because that's where you've tripped yourself up. You wouldn't do that kind of thing in your mother's house."

He twisted his lips to the side, obviously thinking this through. "Maybe we did it in her house. Maybe we did it in the car."

"So, you went out with Jenny? Dated her?"

"Shit no," he countered. "I took her places with my sister." He shrugged, and thankfully his hand stopped. "The mall, the movies. Different places."

"This is when you let her do you? On these trips?"

He shrugged, meaning yes.

"And your sister was where? In the front seat?"

He paled slightly. Mark seemed to transition back and forth from a child to a teenager to a man. If someone had asked her how old Mark Patterson was, she would have guessed anywhere between ten and twenty.

Lena cleared her throat, then asked, "Where was Lacey when you were letting Jenny do you, Mark?"

Mark stared at the flower arrangement on the coffee table. He was very quiet for what seemed like a long time. Finally, he told them, "We met at the church, alright?" He said alright the same way his father did, running the words together.

"You were having sex with her in church," Lena said, not a question.

"The basement," he told them. "They don't check the windows. We sneaked out, okay?"

"That sounds pretty elaborate," Lena said.

"What does that mean?"

Lena thought about how to phrase her answer. "It's not opportune, Mark. You know what that means?"

"I'm not stupid."

"Taking her to the mall, maybe running her and your sister to the store," Lena paused, making sure she had his attention. "Those things sound like opportune times to me. She was there, you were there, it just kind of happened."

"Right," he said. "That's how it was."

"But the church," Lena countered. "The church seems more deliberate. These were not sudden opportunities. These were planned meetings."

Mark nodded, then stopped himself. He said, "So?"

"So," Lena picked up again, "if your relationship was casual, why were you arranging these late night meetings?"

Mark turned his head slightly, looking out the window. He was obviously trying to come up with an answer to the question, but unable to.

Lena said, "She's dead, Mark."

"I know that," he whispered, his eyes flickering toward Jeffrey, then back to the floor. "I saw it happen."

"Is this how you want to talk about her, like she was a whore?" Lena asked him. "Do you really want to tear her down like that?"

Mark's throat bobbed as he swallowed. After a couple of minutes, he mumbled something she could not understand.

"What?" Lena asked.

"She wasn't bad," he said, looking at her out of the corner of his eye. A tear slid down his cheek, and he turned his gaze back toward the window. "Okay?"

Lena nodded. "Okay."

"She listened to me," he began, his voice so low she had to strain to hear him. "She was smart, you know? She read and things, and she helped me with school, some."

Lena sat back on the couch, waiting for him to continue.

"People think things about me," he said, his tone more childish. "They think I'm a certain way, but maybe I'm not. Maybe there's more to me than that. Maybe I'm a human being."

"Of course you are," Lena told him, thinking that she probably understood Mark more than he thought. Every time she walked out in public, Lena felt like the person she really was had been erased. All she was now was the girl who had been raped. Sometimes, Lena wondered if she would not have been better off if she had died. At least then people would see her as tragic rather than as some kind of victim.

Mark rubbed his fingers along his goatee, pulling Lena back into the interview. He said, "There's things I did, okay? That maybe I didn't want to do and maybe she didn't want to do . . ." He shook his head, his eyes closed tightly. "Things she did . . ." His voice trailed off. "I know she was fat, okay? But she was more than that."

"What was she, Mark?"

He tapped his fingers on the arm of the chair. When he spoke, he seemed more sure of himself, back under control. "She listened to me. You know, about my mom." He gave a humorless laugh. "Like when my mom told us she didn't want fucking chemo this time, that she was just gonna let herself die. Jenny understood that." He found a thread on the arm of the chair and picked at it until it pulled. Mark's concentration was so focused on the string that Lena wondered if he had forgotten she and Jeffrey were there.

Lena let herself look at Jeffrey. He was sitting back on the couch, too. Both of them stared at Mark, waiting for him to finish.

"She tutored me in school, some," he said, twisting his ring. "She was younger than me, but she knew how to do things. She liked to read." He smiled, as if a distant memory had come back. He used the back of his hand to wipe under his nose. "She started hanging out with Lacey. I guess they had a lot in common. She was so nice to me." He shook his head, as if to clear it. "I just liked her because she was nice to me." His lips trembled. "When Mama got sick . . ." he started. Again he was quiet. "We thought she'd beat it, you know? And then it was back, and she was in and out of the hospital, and sick all the time. So sick she couldn't even walk sometimes. So sick Daddy had to help her stand up to take a shower, even." He paused, then, "And then she said she wasn't gonna do it anymore, couldn't take the chemo, couldn't take the being sick. Said we didn't need to see her like that, but how does she want us to see her, man? Dead?"

Mark put his hands over his eyes. "Jenny was just there, you know? She was there for me, not anybody else . . ." He paused. "She was so sweet, and she was interested in me, and talking to me, and she understood what I was going through, right? She wasn't about being a cheerleader or wearing my damn class ring. She was all about being there for me." He dropped his hands, staring at Lena. "It wasn't about Lacey, or about Dad. She thought I was good. She thought I was worth something." He dropped his head into his hands, obviously crying.

Lena became conscious of the clock on the wall. Its tick was loud, popping in her ears. Jeffrey was completely still beside her. He had a way of making himself seem part of the scenery, letting her take the lead in things. This was the old Lena and Jeffrey. This was Lena who knew how to do her job, Lena who was in charge of things. She took a deep breath, pulling her shoulders up, letting the air fill her lungs. In this moment, in this room right now, she was herself again. For the first time in months, she was Lena again.

She let a full minute pass before asking Mark, "Tell me what happened."

He shook his head. "It's so wrong," he said. "It all just went so wrong." He leaned forward, his chest almost to his knees, his face contorted in pain as if someone had kicked him. He covered his face with his hands and started to sob again.

Before she knew what she was doing, Lena was down on her knees beside the boy, holding one of his hands. She put her hand on his back, trying to comfort him. "It's okay," she told him, hushing him.

"I love her," he whispered. "Even after what she did, I still love her."

"I know you do," Lena told him, rubbing his back.

"She was so mad at me," Mark said, still sobbing. Lena pulled a Kleenex out of the box and gave it to him. He blew his nose, then whispered, "I told her we had to stop."

"Why did you have to stop?" Lena whispered back.

"I never thought she needed me, you know? I thought she was stronger than me. Stronger than everybody." His voice caught. "And she wasn't."

Lena stroked the back of his neck, trying to soothe him. "What happened, Mark? Why did she end up hating you?"

"You think she hates me?" he asked, his eyes searching hers. "You really think she hates me?"

"No, Mark," Lena said, pushing his hair back out of his face. He had switched to present tense, something people often did when they could not accept that a loved one had died. Lena had found herself doing the same thing with her sister. "Of course she doesn't hate you."

"I told her I wouldn't do it anymore."

"Do what?"

He shook his head no. "It's all so pointless," he said, still shaking his head.

"What's pointless?" Lena asked, trying to make him look up at her. He did, and for a shocking moment, she thought he might try to kiss her. Quickly, she moved back on her heels, catching herself on the arm of the chair so she wouldn't fall. Mark must have seen the shock in her expression because he turned away from her, taking another tissue. Mark looked at Jeffrey as he blew his nose. Lena looked at neither of them. All she could think was that she had somehow crossed a line, but what that line was and where it had been drawn she could not figure.

Mark spoke to Jeffrey, and his voice had more authority to it. The kid who had broken down moments ago was gone. The surly teenager was back. "What else?"

"Jenny liked to study?" Jeffrey asked.

Mark shrugged.

Lena said, "Was she interested in other cultures, other religions?"

"What the fuck for?" Mark countered angrily. "It's not like we're ever gonna get out of this fucking town."

"That's a no, then?" Lena asked.

Mark pursed his lips, almost as if he was going to blow a kiss, then said, "Nope."

Jeffrey crossed his arms over his chest, taking back over. "Around Christmas, you stopped being friends with Jenny. Why?"

"Got tired of her," he shrugged.

"Who else did Jenny hang around with?"

"Me," Mark said. "Lacey. That was it."

"She didn't have other friends?"

"No," Mark answered. "And we weren't really even her friends." He laughed lightly. "She was all alone, I guess. Isn't that sad, Chief Tolliver?"

Jeffrey stared at Mark, not answering.

"If you don't have any more questions," Mark began, "I'd like you to go now."

"Do you know Dr. Linton?" Jeffrey asked.

He shrugged. "Sure."

"I want you at the children's clinic tomorrow by ten o'clock to give that blood sample." Jeffrey pointed his finger at Mark. "Don't make me come looking for you."

Mark stood, wiping his palms on his pants. "Yeah, whatever." He looked down at Lena, who was still on the floor. She was at his crotch level, and he smiled, more like a sneer, when he noticed this.

Mark raised one eyebrow at her, his lips slightly parted in the same sly smile he had given her before, then left the room.

Monday

8

Around six o'clock in the morning, Jeffrey rolled out of bed and fell onto the floor. He sat up, groaning at the pain in his head as he tried to remember where he was. The trip to Sylacauga had taken him six long hours last night, and he had tumbled into the twin bed without even bothering to take off his clothes. His dress shirt was wrinkled, the sleeves pushed up well past his elbows. His pants were creased in four different places.

Jeffrey yawned as he looked around his boyhood room. His mother had not changed a thing since he had left for Auburn over twenty years ago. A poster of a cherry-red 1967 Mustang convertible with a white top was on the back of the door. Six pairs of worn-out sneakers were on the floor of the closet. His football jersey from Sylacauga High was tacked to the wall over the bed. A box of cassette tapes was stacked high under the room's only window.

He lifted the mattress and saw a stack of *Playboy*s that he had started stockpiling at the age of fourteen. A much-loved copy of *Penthouse*, purloined from the local store down the street, was still on the top. Jeffrey sat back on his heels, thumbing through the magazine. There had been a time in his life when he had known every page of the *Penthouse* by heart, from the cartoons to the articles to the lovely ladies in provocative poses that had been the focus of his sexual fantasies for months on end.

"Jesus," he sighed, thinking some of the women were probably old enough to be grandmothers now. Christ, some of them were probably eligible for social security.

Jeffrey groaned as he slid the mattress back into place, trying not to push the magazines out on the other side. He wondered if his mother had ever found his stash. Wondered, too, what she must have thought of it. Knowing May Tolliver, she had ignored them, or made up an excuse that allowed her to block out the fact that her son had enough pornography under his mattress to wallpaper the entire house. His mother was good at not seeing things she did not want to see, but then most mothers were.

Jeffrey thought about Dottie Weaver, and how she had missed all the signs with her daughter. He put his hand to his stomach, thinking about Jenny Weaver standing in the parking lot at Skatie's. The image was like a Polaroid etched into his eyelids, and he could see the little girl standing there, the gun in her hand trained on Mark Patterson. Mark was more defined in Jeffrey's memory now, and he could pick out details about the boy: the way he stood with his arms out to his sides, the way his knees bent a little as he stared at Jenny. The whole time, Mark had never really looked at Jeffrey. Even after Jeffrey had shot her, Mark had stood there, staring down at the ground where she lay.

Jeffrey rubbed his eyes, trying to push out this image. He let his gaze travel back to the Mustang, taking it in the way he had every morning of his teenage life. The car had represented so much to him when he was growing up, chief among these things being freedom. As a teenager, he had sometimes sat in bed, his eyes closed, imagining getting in that car and taking off across country. Jeffrey had wanted so much to get away, to leave Sylacauga and his mother's house, to be something other than his father's son.

Jimmy Tolliver had been a petty thief in every sense of the term. He never stole big, which was a point in his favor, because he always got caught. Jeffrey's mother liked to say that Jimmy couldn't break wind in a crowded building without getting caught. He just had that look of guilt about him, and he liked to talk. Jimmy's mouth was his biggest downfall; he couldn't stand not taking credit for the jobs he pulled. Jimmy Tolliver was the only person who was surprised when he had ended up dying in prison, serving out a life term for armed robbery.

By the time he was ten years old, Jeffrey knew practically every man on the Sylacauga police force by name, because at some time or another, one or all of them had come to the house, looking for Jimmy. To their credit, the patrol cops knew Jeffrey, too, and they always made a point of taking him aside whenever they saw him. At the time, being singled out by the police had annoyed Jeffrey. He had considered it harassment. Now, as a policeman himself, Jeffrey knew the cops had been taking time with him as insurance. They did not want to waste their time chasing down another Tolliver for stealing lawn mowers and weed whackers out of his neighbors' yards.

Jeffrey owed these cops a lot, not least of all his career. Watching the fear in his father's eyes that last time the cops had come to the house and slapped the cuffs on Jimmy, Jeffrey had known then and there that he wanted to be a cop.

Jimmy Tolliver had been a drunk, and a mean one at that. To the town, he was a bumbling crook and a sloppy drunk, to Jeffrey and his mother, he was a violent asshole who terrified his family.

Jeffrey stretched his hands up to the ceiling, his palms flat against the warm wood. As he padded to the bathroom, he noticed that even his socks were wrinkled. The heel had slid around sometime during the night. Jeffrey was balancing on one foot, trying to twist it back, when he heard his cell phone ringing in the other room.

"Dammit," he cursed, bumping his shoulder into the wall as he turned the corner to his room. The house seemed so much smaller now than it had when he was growing up.

He picked up the phone on the fourth ring, just before the voice mail came on. "Hello?"

"Jeff?" Sara asked, a bit of concern in her voice.

He let it linger in his ear before saying, "Hey, babe."

She laughed at the name. "Less than ten hours in Alabama and you're calling me 'babe'?" She waited a beat. "Are you alone?"

He felt irritated, because he knew part of her was not joking. "Of course I'm alone," he shot back. "Jesus Christ, Sara."

"I meant your mother," she told him, though he could tell from her lack of conviction that she was covering.

He let it pass. "No, they kept her overnight in the hospital." He sat on the bed, trying to get his sock to twist back into place. "She fell down somehow. Broke her foot."

"Did she fall at home?" Sara asked, something more than curiosity in her tone. He knew what she was getting at, and it was the same reason Jeffrey had come to Alabama himself in the middle of a case instead of just making a phone call. He wanted to see if his mother's drinking was finally getting out of hand. May Tolliver had always been what was politely called a functional alcoholic. If she had crossed the line into hopeless drunk, Jeffrey would have to do something. He had no idea what this would be, but knew instinctively that it would not be easy.

Jeffrey tried to redirect her interest. "I talked with the doctor. I haven't really seen her to find out what happened." He waited for her to get the message. "I'll see her today, see what's going on."

"She'll probably be on crutches," Sara told him. He could hear a tapping noise, and assumed she was at her office. He looked at his watch, wondering why she was there so early, but then he remembered the time change. Sara was an hour ahead of him.

"Ms. Harris across the street will look in on her," Jeffrey volunteered, knowing that Jean Harris would do whatever she could to help a neighbor. She worked as a dietician at the local hospital, and had often waved Jeffrey over after school to make sure he had a hot meal. Sitting at the table with her three lovely daughters had been a bit more enticing than Ms. Harris's chicken pot pie, but Jeffrey had appreciated both at the time.

Sara said, "You need to tell her to be very careful not to mix her pain meds with alcohol. Or tell her doctor that. Okay?"

He looked at his sock, realizing it was still backward. He twisted it the other way, asking, "Is that why you called?"

"I got your message about Mark Patterson. What am I pulling a sample for?"

"Paternity," he told her, not liking the image the word brought to his mind.

Sara was silent, then asked, "Are you sure?"

"No," he told her. "Not at all. I just thought I should look at everything I could."

"How'd you get a court order so fast?"

"No order. His father's sending him in voluntarily."

She was still incredulous. "Without a lawyer?"

Jeffrey sighed. "Sara, I left all of this on your machine last night. Is something going on?"

"No," she answered in a softer tone. Then, "Yes, actually."

He waited. "Yeah?"

"I wanted to make sure you were all right."

Sarcasm came, because that was all he could muster in light of her question. "Other than waking up knowing I killed a thirteen-year-old little girl, I guess I'm just peachy."

She was quiet, and he let the silence continue, not knowing what to say to her. Sara had not called him in a long time, not even for county-related matters. In the past, she had faxed him documents on cases, or sent Carlos, her assistant, over with sensitive information. Since the divorce, personal calls were out of the question, and even when they had started back kind of dating, Jeffrey had always been the one to pick up the phone.

"Jeff?" Sara asked.

"I was just thinking," he said, then, to change the subject, he asked, "Tell me a little bit more about Lacey."

"I told you yesterday. She's a good kid," Sara said, and he could hear something off in her tone. He knew she was feeling responsible for Jenny Weaver, but there was nothing he could do about it.

Sara continued, "She's bright, funny. Just like Jenny in a lot of ways."

"Were you close to her?"

"As close as you can be to a kid you only see a few times a year." Sara paused, then said, "Yeah. Some of them you connect with. I connected with Lacey. I think she has a little crush on me."

"That's weird," he said.

"Not really," Sara told him. "Lots of kids get crushes on adults. It's not a sexual thing, they just want to impress them, to make them laugh."

"I'm still not following."

"They get to be a certain age and their parents can't be cool anymore. Some kids, not all of them, can transfer their feelings onto another adult. It's perfectly natural. They just want someone to look up to, and at that point in their lives it can't be their parents."

"So, she looked up to you?"

"It felt that way," Sara said, and he could hear the sadness in her voice.

"You think she would've told you if something was going on?"

"Who knows?" Sara replied. "Something happens to them when they get into middle school. They get a lot more quiet."

"That's what Grace Patterson said. That they keep secrets."

"That's true," Sara agreed. "I just chalked up the change to puberty. All those hormones, all those new feelings. They've got a lot to think about, and the only thing they're certain of is that adults have no way of understanding what they're going through."

"Still," Jeffrey countered, "don't you think she would've talked to you if something was wrong?"

"I'd like to think so, but the truth is, she'd have to have her mother drive her here. I can't kick the mother out of the room without causing some suspicion."

"You think Grace would have been reluctant to leave y'all alone?"

"I think she would've been worried. She's a good mother. She takes an interest in her kids and what they're doing."

"That's what Brad said."

"What does Brad have to do with this?" Sara asked.

"He's the youth minister at Crescent Baptist."

"Oh, that's right," Sara said, making the connection. "He must've been on the retreat."

"Yeah," Jeffrey told her. "There were eight kids from the church: three boys, five girls."

"That doesn't sound like a lot of kids."

"It's a small church," Jeffrey reminded her. "Plus, skiing is expensive. Not a lot of people have that kind of money to begin with, especially around the holidays."

"That's true," she agreed. "But it was just Brad chaperoning?"

"The church secretary was supposed to help out with the girls, but she got sick at the last minute."

"Have you talked to her?"

"She had some kind of stroke. She was only fifty-eight years old," he said, thinking that when he had been a kid, fifty-eight had seemed ancient. "She moved down to Florida so her kids could take care of her."

"So, what did Brad say about Jenny and Lacey?"

"Nothing specific. He said Lacey and Jenny pretty much stayed by themselves while the rest of the kids were off skiing and having fun."

"That's not uncommon for girls that age. They tend to form tight little groups."

"Yeah," Jeffrey sighed, feeling yesterday's frustrations settling into his gut. "Brad went over to Jenny's house when she stopped coming to church. She pretty much burst into tears the minute she saw him and wouldn't talk."

"What'd he do?"

"Left with his hat in his hands. He asked Dave Fine to check in on her, but Dave got the same treatment."

"Did you talk to Dave about it?"

"Briefly. He was about to go into a therapy session." Jeffrey felt a flash of guilt, thinking about Lena. He should not have allowed her to use her therapy appointment to interview Fine. Jeffrey had given in too easily because it was convenient.

"Jeffrey?" Sara said, her tone indicating she had asked him a question and was waiting for an answer.

"Yeah, sorry," Jeffrey apologized.

"What did Fine say?"

"The same as Brad. He offered to come in tomorrow and talk some more, but neither one of them seem like they're going to be much help." Jeffrey rubbed his eyes, trying to think of any straw he could grasp. "What about Mark Patterson?" he finally asked. "Does he seem kind of weird to you?"

"Weird how?"

"Weird like . . ." Jeffrey tried to find the words. He did not really want to go into the Patterson interview with Sara, mostly because of what had happened with Lena. There had been something between her and the boy, something that set his teeth on edge. They both worked off each other somehow. "Weird like I don't know."

Sara laughed. "I don't think I can answer that."

"Sexual," he said, because that was a good word to describe Mark Patterson. "He seemed really sexual."

"Well," Sara began, and he could hear the confusion in her voice. "He's a good-looking kid. I imagine he's been sexually active for a very long time."

"He just turned sixteen."

"Jeffrey," Sara said, as if she were talking to an idiot. "I've got ten-year-old girls who haven't even started their periods asking me about birth control."

"Jesus," he sighed. "It's way too early in the morning to hear that kind of thing."

"Welcome to my world," she told him.

"Yeah." He stared at the jersey on his wall, trying to remember what it had felt like to be Mark Patterson's age and have the world in the palm of his hand. Though, Mark Patterson did not seem to feel that way.

Jeffrey did not like this helpless feeling. He should be back in Grant, trying to figure this out. At the very least, he should be keeping an eye on Lena. For a while Jeffrey had felt she was on the edge, but not until yesterday did he realize that she was closer to falling than keeping herself balanced.

"Jeff?" Sara asked. "What's wrong?"

"I'm worried about Lena," he told her, and the words felt familiar to him. He had been worried about Lena since he hired her ten years ago. First, he was worried that she was so aggressive on patrol, taking every collar like her life depended on it. Then, he had worried that she put herself in danger too often as a detective, pushing suspects to their breaking point, pushing herself to her own breaking point. And now he worried that she was about to lose it. There was no question in his mind that she would explode soon. It was just a matter of when. With a start, he realized this had been his fear from the beginning: When would Lena finally break in two?

"I think you should be worried about her," Sara said. "Why won't you take her off active duty?"

"Because it would kill her," he answered, and he knew this was true. Lena needed her job like other people needed air.

"Is there something else?"

Jeffrey thought about the conversation he'd had with Lena in the car. She had not been exactly sure of herself when she told him the shot was clean. "I, uh," he began, not knowing how to say this. "When I talked to Lena yesterday . . . ," he said.

"Yeah?"

"She didn't seem too sure about what had happened."

"About the shooting?" Sara demanded, obviously irritated. "What exactly did she say?"

"It wasn't what she said so much as how she said it."

Sara mumbled something that sounded like a curse. "She's just playing with you to get back at me."

"Lena's not like that."

"Of course she is," Sara shot back. "She's always been like that."

Jeffrey shook his head, not accepting this. "I think she's just not sure."

Sara mumbled a curse under her breath. "That's just great."

"Sara," Jeffrey said, trying to calm her down. "Don't say anything to her, okay? It'll only make it worse."

"Why would I say anything to her?"

"Sara . . ." He rubbed sleep from his eyes, thinking he did not want to talk about this now. "Listen, I was just fixin' to go to the hospital—"

"This really ticks me off."

"I know that," he said. "You've made it clear."

"I just—"

"Sara," he interrupted. "I really need to go."

"Actually," she said, moderating her tone, "I was calling for a reason, if you've got a minute?"

"Sure," he managed, feeling a sense of trepidation. "What's up?"

He heard her take a deep breath, as if she were about to jump off a cliff. "I was wondering if you'll be back tonight."

"Late, probably."

"Well, then, how about tomorrow night?"

"If I come back tonight, I won't have to come back to-morrow night."

"Are you being dense on purpose?"

He played back their conversation in his mind, smiling when he realized that Sara was trying to ask him over. Jeffrey wondered if she had ever done something like this in her life.

He said, "I've never been very bright."

"No," she agreed, but she was laughing.

"So?"

"So . . . ," Sara began, then she sighed. He heard her mumble, "Oh, this is so stupid."

"What's that?"

"I said," she started again, then stopped. "I'm not doing anything tomorrow night."

Jeffrey rubbed his whiskers, feeling the grin on his face. He wondered if there had ever been a time in this room when he had felt happier. Maybe the day he got the call from Auburn, saying he could go to college for free in exchange for getting the shit beaten out of him on the football field every Saturday.

He said, "Hey, me neither."

"So . . ." Sara was obviously hoping he would fill things in for her. Jeffrey sat back down on the bed, thinking hell would freeze over before he helped her out.

"Come over to my house," she finally said. "Around seven or so, okay?"

"Why?"

He could hear her chair squeak as she sat back. Jeffrey imagined she probably had her hand over her eyes.

"God, you are not going to make this easy, are you?"

"Why should I?"

"I want to see you," she told him. "Come at seven. I'll make supper."

"Wait a minute—"

She obviously anticipated his problem with this. Sara was not exactly a good cook. She offered, "I'll order something from Alfredo's."

Jeffrey smiled again. "I'll see you at seven."

As a boy, Jeffrey had done his share of stupid things. His two best friends from elementary school to high school had lived down the street from him, and between Jerry Long, a boy with a curiosity about fireworks, and Bobby Blankenship, a boy who liked to hear things explode, they had managed to risk their lives any number of times before puberty took hold and girls became more important than blowing things up.

At the age of eleven, the three had discovered the pleasure of exploding bottle rockets in a steel drum behind Jeffrey's house. By the time they were twelve, the drum was as dented and pockmarked as Bobby "Spot" Blankenship's face. By the time they were thirteen, Jerry Long had been given the name "Possum" because, when the drum had finally exploded, a piece of shrapnel had nearly sliced off the top of his head, and he had lain in Jeffrey's backyard like a possum until Jean Harris had called an ambulance to take him to the hospital, and the police to scare the bejesus out of Jeffrey and Spot.

Jeffrey had not earned his nickname until later, when he had started to notice girls and, more important, they had started to notice him. Like Possum and Spot, he was on the football team, and they were pretty popular in school because the team was winning that year. Jeffrey was the first of the trio to kiss a girl, the first to get to second base, and the first to finally lose his virginity. For these accomplishments, he was given the nickname "Slick."

The first time Jeffrey had taken Sara to Sylacauga, he had been so nervous that his hands would not stop sweating. They had just started dating, and Jeffrey had been under the impression that Sara was a little too socially elevated for Possum and Spot, and more than likely for ol' Slick as well. Sylacauga was the epitome of a small Southern town. Unlike Heartsdale, there was no college up the street, and no professors in town to add some diversity to the mix. Most of the people who lived here worked in some kind of industry, whether it was for the textile mill or the marble quarry. Jeffrey was not saying they were all backward, inbred hicks, but they were not the kind of people he thought Sara would be comfortable hanging around.

Sara wasn't just what the locals would call "book learned," but a medical doctor, and her family might have been blue collar, but Eddie Linton was the kind of man who knew how to manage a dollar. The family owned property up and down the lake, and even had some rental units in Florida. On top of that, Sara was sharp, and not just about books. She had a cutting wit, and wasn't the kind of woman who would have his slippers and a hot meal waiting for him when he got home from work. If anything, Sara would expect Jeffrey to have these things ready for her.

About six miles from the Tolliver house, there was a general store called Cat's that Jeffrey and everyone else had frequented growing up. It was the kind of place where you could buy milk, tobacco, gasoline, and bait. The floor was made from hand-hewn lumber and there were enough gashes and scars in it to trip you up if you did not watch where you were walking. The ceiling was low, and yellowed from nicotine and water stains. Freezers packed with ice and Coca-Colas lined the entranceway, and a large

Moon Pie display was up by the cash register. The gas pumps outside dinged with every gallon pumped.

While Jeffrey was at Auburn, Cat had passed away, and Possum, who worked at the store, had taken over for Cat's widow. Six years later, Possum had bought out the widow Cat, and changed the name to "Possum's Cat's." When Sara had first seen the sign over the dilapidated building, she had been delighted, and made reference to the Eliot poem. Jeffrey had fought the urge to crawl under the car and hide, but Sara had laughed when she found out the truth. As a matter of fact, she had enjoyed herself that weekend, and by the second day there, Sara was lying out by the pool with Possum and his wife, laughing at stories about Jeffrey's errant youth.

Now, Jeffrey could smile at the memory, though at the time he had been slightly annoyed to be the butt of their jokes. Sara was the first woman who had made fun of him like that, and, truth be told, that was probably the point at which she had hooked him. His mother liked to say that he liked a challenge.

Jeffrey was thinking about this, thinking that Sara Linton was, if anything, a challenge, as he turned into the parking lot of Possum's Cat's. The place had changed a lot since Cat had owned it, and even more since the last time Jeffrey had been in town. The only thing that remained the same was the big Auburn University emblem over the door. Alabama was a state divided by its two universities, Auburn and Alabama, and there was only one important question every native asked the other: "Who are you for?" Jeffrey had seen fights break out when someone gave the wrong answer in the wrong part of town.

A day care was to the right of the store, a new addition since the last time Jeffrey had visited. On the left was Madam Bell's, which was run by Possum's wife, Darnell.

Like Cat, Madam Bell had passed a long time ago. Jeffrey thought that Nell ran the place just to give her something to do while the kids were at school. He had dated Nell off and on in high school until Possum had gotten serious about her. Jeffrey could not imagine that same restless girl being happy with this kind of life, but stranger things have happened. Besides, Nell had been three months pregnant the week they all graduated from school. It wasn't like she had been given a lot of choices.

So he wouldn't take up one of the spaces in front of the store, Jeffrey let the car idle outside Bell's, Lynyrd Skynyrd's "Sweet Home Alabama" playing softly on the car's speakers. He had found the tape in the box under the window in his room, and experienced a bit of nostalgia when the first chords of what was one of his favorite songs reached his ears. It was odd how you could love something so much, but forget about it when it wasn't right under your nose. He felt that way about this town, and his friends here. Being around Possum and Nell again would be like nothing had changed in the last twenty years. Jeffrey did not know how he felt about that.

What he did know was that seeing his mother in the hospital ten minutes ago had made him want to get back to Grant as fast as he could. There was something suffocating about the way she held on to him when she hugged him, and the way she let her voice trail off, saying things by leaving them unsaid. May Tolliver had never been a happy woman, and part of Jeffrey thought his father had been such a bumbling crook so that he would get caught and taken off to jail, where his miserable wife could not nag him every day about what a disappointment he was. Like Jimmy, May was a mean drunk, and though she had never raised her hand to Jeffrey, she could cut him in two with her words faster than anyone he had ever met. Thankfully, she still seemed to be functioning, even with enough alcohol in her to fuel a tractor for sixty miles. If May could be believed, a feral cat from under the neighbor's house had startled her and she had fallen down the steps. Since Jeffrey had heard some cats over there this morning, he had to give his mother the benefit of the doubt. He did not want to admit to anyone, let alone to himself, how grateful he was that his mother did not need further intervention.

Jeffrey stepped out of the car, his foot sliding a little on the gravel drive. He had changed into jeans and a polo shirt back at his mother's house, and he felt odd being clothed so casually in the middle of the week. He had even considered wearing his dress shoes, but had changed his mind when he caught a glance of himself in the mirror. He slipped on his sunglasses, looking around as he walked toward Madam Bell's.

The fortune-teller's building was more like a shack, and the screen door groaned when Jeffrey opened it. He knocked on the front door, stepping into the small front parlor. The place looked just as it had when he was a boy. Spot had once dared Jeffrey to go in and have his palm read by Madam Bell. He had not liked what she had to say, and never stepped foot back in the place again.

Jeffrey craned his head around the door, looking into the shack's only other room. Nell sat at a table with a deck of tarot cards in front of her. The television was on low, or maybe the air conditioner in the window was drowning out the sound. She was knitting something as she watched her show, her body leaning forward as if to make sure she caught every word.

Jeffrey said, "Boo."

"Oh, my God." Nell jumped, dropping her knitting. She stood from the table, patting her palm against her chest. "Slick, you 'bout scared me half to death."

"Don't let that happen twice," he laughed, pulling her into a hug. She was a small woman, but nice and curvy through the hips. He stepped back to get a good look at her. Nell had not changed much since high school. Her black hair was the same, if not a little gray, straight and long enough to reach her waist, but pulled back in a ponytail, probably to fight the heat.

"You been over to Possum's?" she asked, sitting back down at the table. "What're you doing here? Is it about your mama?"

Jeffrey smiled, sitting across from her. Nell had always talked a hundred miles an hour. "No and yes."

"She was drunk," Nell said in her usual abrupt way. Her candor was one of the reasons Jeffrey had stopped dating her. She called things the way she saw them, and at eighteen Jeffrey had hardly been introspective.

Nell said, "Her liquor bills 'bout kept us afloat last winter."

"I know," Jeffrey answered, crossing his arms. He had paid his mother's utility bills for some time now just to keep her in liquor. It was pointless to argue with the old woman about it, and at least this way he knew she would stay at home and drink instead of going out to do something about it.

He said, "I just came from the hospital. They gave her a shot of vodka while I was standing there."

Nell picked up the cards and started to shuffle them. "Old biddy'd go into the DTs if they didn't."

Jeffrey shrugged. The doctor had said the same thing in the hospital.

"What're you lookin' at?" Nell asked him, and Jeffrey smiled, realizing that he had been staring at her. What he had been thinking was that it was easier to talk to Nell about his mother's alcoholism than it was to talk to Sara about it. He could not begin to understand why this was. Maybe it was because Nell had grown up with it. With Sara, Jeffrey tended to get embarrassed, then ashamed, then finally angry.

"How is it you get prettier every time I come see you?" he teased her.

"Slick, Slick, Slick," Nell said, clucking her tongue. She laid a couple of cards face up on the table, asking, "So, why'd Sara divorce you?"

Jeffrey startled, asking, "You see that in the cards?"

She smiled mischievously. "Christmas cards. Sara's had 'Linton' on the return address." She put another card down on the table. "What'd you do, cheat on her?"

He indicated the cards. "Why don't you tell me?"

She nodded, laying down a couple more. "I'd guess you cheated on her and got caught."

"What?"

Nell laughed. "Just 'cause she don't talk to you don't mean she don't talk to me."

He shook his head, not understanding.

"We've got a phone, too, puppy," she told him. "I talk to Sara every now and then, just to catch up."

"Well, then you must know I've been seeing her again," he said, aware he was sounding like the cocky old Slick he had been, but unable to stop it. "What do your cards say about that?"

She turned a couple more over and studied them for a few seconds, a frown tugging her lips down. Finally, she scooped the cards back into a deck. "These stupid things don't tell you nothing anyway," she mumbled. "Let's get over to Possum's. I'm sure he'll be glad to see you."

She held her hand out to him, and he hesitated, wondering if he should push her on the reading. Not that Jeffrey believed Nell had the gift, or that anyone did for that matter, but it set his teeth on edge that she would not at least make something up so that he would feel better.

"Come on," she said, tugging at his sleeve.

He acquiesced, letting her lead him out of the shack and back into the unrelenting Alabama heat. There were no trees in the gravel parking lot, and Jeffrey could feel the sun baking the top of his head as they crossed toward the gas station.

Nell looped her hand through his arm, saying, "I like Sara."

"I do, too," he told her.

"I mean, I really like her, Jeffrey."

He stopped, because she seldom called him "Jeffrey."

She said, "If she's giving you another chance, don't fuck it up."

"I don't plan to."

"I mean it, Slick," she said, tugging him toward the store. "She's too good for you, and God knows she's too smart." She waited at the door so he could open it. "Just don't fuck it up."

"Your faith in me is inspiring."

"I just don't want Little Jeffrey messing things up for you again."

" 'Little?' " he repeated, opening the door. "Your memory giving out on you?"

Jeffrey could tell she was going to answer him, but Possum's booming voice drowned out everything.

"That Slick?" Possum yelled as if Jeffrey had just gone out for a walk instead of been away for years. Jeffrey watched as the other man edged over the counter. His belly got in the way, but he landed on his feet despite the laws of physics.

"Damn," Jeffrey told him, rubbing the other man's large gut. "Nell, why didn't you tell me you got another one on the way?"

Possum laughed good naturedly, rubbing his belly. "We're gonna call it Bud if it's a boy, Dewars if it's a girl." He put his arm around Jeffrey, leading him into the store. "How you been, boy?"

Without thinking, Jeffrey delivered his standard response. "I ain't been a boy since I was your size."

Possum laughed, throwing back his head. "Wish we had Spot around. How long you gonna be in town?"

"Not long," Jeffrey told him. "I'm actually on my way out." He turned around to see that Nell had left them alone.

"Good woman," Possum said.

"I can't believe she's still with you."

"I take away her keys at night before I go to sleep," he told Jeffrey, giving him a wink. "Wanna beer?"

Jeffrey looked at the clock on the wall. "I usually don't drink until at least noon."

"Oh, right, right, right," he answered. "How about a Co-Cola?" He scooped a couple out of an ice chest without waiting for a response.

"Hot out," Jeffrey said.

"Yep," Possum agreed, popping the bottles open on the side of the chest. "I guess you dropped by to ask me to keep an eye on your mama."

"I've got a case back home," he said, and it felt good that home meant Grant now. "If you don't mind."

"Shit," he waved this off, handing Jeffrey a Coke. "Don't worry about that. She's still just right down the street."

"Thanks," Jeffrey said. He watched as Possum took a bag of peanuts off the rack and ripped it open with his teeth. He offered some to Jeffrey, but Jeffrey shook his head no.

"Damn shame her falling," Possum said, funneling some peanuts into the open neck of his Coke bottle. "Been real hot lately. Guess she just got dizzy in this heat."

Jeffrey took a swig of Coke. Possum was doing what he had always done, and that was covering for May Tolliver. Jerry Long didn't just get his nickname from playing dead that day in Jeffrey's backyard. If there was one thing Possum was good at, it was ignoring what was right in front of his face.

The heavy baseline from a rap song shook the front windows, and Jeffrey turned around in time to see a large burgundy colored pickup truck pull into a space in front of the store. Rap music blared, a cacophony of missed beats, before the engine was cut and a surly-looking teenager got out of the cab and walked into the store.

He was dressed in a shirt that matched the color of his truck, with the words ROLL TIDE emblazoned in white over a rampaging elephant. His hair was what got Jeffrey's immediate attention, though. It was corn rowed with little crimson colored barrettes at the end, and they snapped against each other as he walked. The boy was wearing black-and-gray camouflage pants that were cut off at the knee, but his socks and sneakers were colored the Crimson Tide. Jeffrey realized with a start that the kid was dressed head to toe in the colors of Alabama University.

"Hey, Dad," the boy said, meaning Possum.

Jeffrey exchanged a look with his friend, then turned back to the boy. "Jared?" he asked, certain this could not be Possum and Nell's sweet little kid. He looked like a motorcycle thug dressed for an Alabama gang.

"Hey, Uncle Slick," Jared mumbled, shuffling his feet across the floor. He walked right past Jeffrey and his father and into the room behind the counter.

"Man," Jeffrey said. "That has got to be embarrassing."

Possum nodded. "We're hoping he changes his mind." Possum shrugged. "He likes animals. Everybody knows Auburn's got a better vet school than Alabama."

Jeffrey kept his teeth clamped so he would not laugh.

"I'll be back," Possum said, going after the boy. "Help yourself to anything you want."

Jeffrey finished his Coke in one swallow, then walked to the back of the store to see what kind of bait Possum had stocked. There were wire-meshed cages with crickets chirping up a storm as well as a large plastic barrel filled with wet dirt that probably had a thousand or so worms in it. A small tank of minnows was over the cricket stands, with a net and some buckets in which to transport the bait. Sara liked to fish, and Jeffrey thought about getting her some worms before he considered what a hassle it would be, taking live bait back in his car. He would probably have to stop outside of Atlanta for something to eat, and it wasn't like Jeffrey could leave the worms to fry in the heat of his car. Besides, there were plenty of bait stands in Grant.

He dropped the empty Coke bottle into a box that looked like it was used for recycling and glanced out the window at the day-care center beside the store. Obviously, it was time for recess, and kids were running around, screaming their heads off. Jeffrey wondered if Jenny Weaver had ever felt that free. He could not imagine the overweight girl running around for any reason. She seemed more like the type to sit in the shade reading a book, waiting for the bell to ring so she could go back to class, where she felt more comfortable.

"You work here?" someone asked.

Jeffrey turned around, startled. A thirtyish-looking man was standing behind him at the bait display. He was what

Jeffrey always thought of as a typical redneck: skinny and soft-looking with razor burns from shaving too close. His arms seemed to be well-developed, probably from working construction. A cigarette dangled from his lips.

"No," Jeffrey said, feeling a little embarrassed to be caught staring so aimlessly out the window. "I was looking at the kids."

"Yeah," the man said, taking a step toward Jeffrey. "They're usually out this time of day."

"You got one over there?" Jeffrey asked.

The man gave him a strange look, as if to assess him. His hand went to his mouth, and he rubbed his chin thoughtfully. With a start, Jeffrey noticed a tattoo on the webbing between the man's thumb and index finger. It was the same tattoo Mark Patterson had on his hand.

Jeffrey turned away, trying to think this through. He stared out the window, and he could make out the man's partial reflection in the glass.

"Nice tattoo," Jeffrey said.

The man's voice was a low, conspiratorial whisper. "You got one?"

Jeffrey kept his lips pressed together, shaking his head no.

"Why not?" the man asked.

Jeffrey said, "Work," trying to keep his tone even. He had a bad feeling about this, like part of his mind was working something out, but not sharing it with him.

"Not many people know what it means," the man said, fisting his hand. He looked at the tattoo on the webbing, a slight smile at his lips.

"I've seen it on a kid," Jeffrey told him. "Not like them," he nodded toward the day care. "Older."

The man's smile broke out wider. "You like 'em older?"

Jeffrey looked back over the man's shoulder to see where Possum was.

"He won't come back for a while," the man assured him. "That boy of his gets hisself into trouble most every day."

"Yeah?"

"Yeah," the man said.

Jeffrey turned back to the window, looking at the children running around the yard in a different light. They no longer seemed young and carefree. They seemed vulnerable and in jeopardy.

The man took a step toward Jeffrey and used the hand with the tattoo to point out the window. "See that one there?" he asked. "Little one with the book?"

Jeffrey followed the man's direction and found a little girl sitting under the tree in the middle of the yard. She was reading a book, much the way Jeffrey had imagined Jenny Weaver would.

The man said, "That one's mine."

Jeffrey felt the hair on the back of his neck rise. The way the man said the words made it clear he was not referring to the girl as his daughter. There was something proprietary to his tone, and under that, something unmistakably sexual.

The man said, "You can't tell from this far, but up close, she's got herself the prettiest little mouth."

Jeffrey turned around slowly, trying to hide his disgust. He said, "Why don't we go somewhere else where we can talk about this?"

The man's eyes narrowed. "What's wrong with here?"

"Here makes me nervous," Jeffrey said, making himself smile.

The man stared at him for a long while, then gave an almost imperceptible nod. "Yeah, okay," he said, and he started walking toward the door, tossing a look over his shoulder about every five feet to make sure Jeffrey was still there.

Behind the building, the man started to turn, but Jeffrey

kicked him in the back of his knees so that he fell to the ground.

"Oh, Jesus," the man said, pulling himself into a ball.

"Shut up," Jeffrey ordered, raising his foot. He kicked the man in the thigh hard enough to let him know there was no use trying to stand.

The man just stayed there, curled into a ball, waiting for Jeffrey to beat him. There was something at once pathetic and disgusting about his behavior, as if he understood why someone might want to do this, and was accepting his punishment.

Jeffrey looked around, making sure no one could see him. He wanted to do this man some serious harm for threatening the child, but part of his resolve was lost when faced with the pathetic, whimpering lump lying on the ground in front of him. It was one thing to kick the shit out of somebody who fought back, quite another to harm what was basically a defenseless man.

"Stand up," Jeffrey said.

The man looked out between his crossed arms, trying to gauge if this was a trick. When Jeffrey took a step back, the man slowly uncurled himself and stood. Dust kicked up around them, and Jeffrey coughed to clear his throat.

"What do you want?" the man asked, taking a pack of cigarettes out of his shirt pocket. They were crushed, and the one he put in his mouth bent at an angle. His hands shook as he tried to light the tip.

Jeffrey fought the urge to slap the cigarette out of his mouth. "What's that tattoo for?"

The man shrugged, some surliness slipping into his posture.

Jeffrey asked, "Is that for some kind of club you're in?"

"Yeah, the freak club," the man said. "The club that likes little girls. That what you're going after?"

"So, other people have this?"

"I dunno," he said. "I don't got no names, if that's what you want. It's from the Internet. We're all anonymous."

Jeffrey hissed a sigh. Among other things, the Internet fed child molesters and pedophiles, linking them together to share stories, fantasies, and sometimes children. Jeffrey had taken a law enforcement class on this very thing. There had been some spectacular busts in recent history, but even the FBI could not work fast enough to track down these people.

"What does it stand for?" Jeffrey asked.

The man gave him a hard look. "What the fuck you think it stands for?"

"Tell me," Jeffrey said through clenched teeth, "unless you want to be back on that ground trying to figure out why your intestines are coming out of your asshole."

The man nodded, taking a drag on the cigarette. He blew smoke out through his mouth and nose in a slow stream.

"The heart," the man began, pointing to his hand. "The big heart is black."

Jeffrey nodded.

"But, inside, there's this little heart, right?" The man looked at the tattoo with something like love in his eyes. "The little heart is white. It's pure."

"Pure?" Jeffrey asked, remembering that word from somewhere. "What do you mean, pure?"

"Like a child is pure, man." He allowed a smile. "The white heart makes just a little part of the black heart pure, you know? It's love, man. It's nothing but love."

Jeffrey tried to do something with his hands other than beat the man into the ground. He held out his palm, saying, "Give me your wallet."

The man did not hesitate to do as he was told, nor did he protest when Jeffrey took a small spiral notebook out of his pocket and recorded the information.

"Here," Jeffrey said, throwing the wallet so hard at the man that it popped off his chest before he could catch it. "I've got your name now, and your address. You ever come back in this store again, or even think about hanging around that day care, my friend in there will beat the shit out of you." Jeffrey waited a beat. "You understand me?"

"Yes, sir," the man said, his eyes on the ground.

"What's this Web site?" he asked.

The man kept staring at the ground. Jeffrey started to take a step toward him, but the man backed up, holding up his hands.

"It's a girl-lovers newsgroup," he said. "It moves around sometimes. You gotta search for it."

Jeffrey wrote down the phrase, though he was familiar with it from the class.

The man took another drag on his cigarette, holding the smoke in for a second. He finally let it go, asking, "That all?"

"That kid," Jeffrey began, trying to keep his composure. "You ever hurt that kid . . ."

The man said, "I've never even been with one, okay? I just like looking." He kicked at a rock with his shoe. "They're just so sweet, you know? I mean, how could you hurt something that was so sweet?"

Without thinking, Jeffrey slammed his fist into the man's mouth. A tooth went flying, followed by a stream of blood. The man dropped to the ground again, prepared to take a beating.

Jeffrey walked back to the store, a sickening feeling washing over him.

9

Robert E. Lee High School was what locals called a "super school." This meant that the building was designed to house about fifteen hundred students from the three cities comprising Grant County. As it was, the school was still not large enough, and temporary classrooms—what other people called trailers—were in the back of the building, taking over the baseball field. Grades nine through twelve were offered here, while two middle schools served as feeders for Lee. There were four assistant principals and one principal, George Clay, a man who from all accounts spent most of his time behind his desk pushing paperwork for the governor's innovative new education program—a plan that made sure teachers spent more time filling out forms and attending certification classes than actually teaching kids.

Brad fiddled with his hat as they walked down the hallway, his police-issue sneakers thumping against the floor. Without thinking, Lena had started to count his steps as they walked up the locker-lined corridor. The place was institutional in its ambiguity, with its bright-white tile floor and muted cement-block walls. To match the school's colors, the lockers were painted a dark red, the walls a darker gray. There were posters cheering the Rebels to victory on every available blank space, but this served more to clutter than to encourage. Bulletin boards urged students to say no to drugs, cigarettes, and sex.

"It seems so small," Brad said, his voice a hushed whisper.

Lena did not roll her eyes at this, though it was hard. Since they had talked to George Clay, Brad had been acting like a high school freshman instead of a cop. Brad even looked the part, with his round face and wispy blond hair that seemed to fall into his eyes every three seconds.

"This is Miss Mac's room," he said, indicating a closed door. He glanced through the window as they passed by. "She taught me English," he said, pushing back his hair.

"Hmm," Lena answered, not looking.

All the doors on the hall were closed between classes, and all of them were locked. Like most rural schools, Lee had taken precautions against intruders. Teachers walked the hallways, and there were two officers, what Jeffrey called "deputy dogs," in the front office in case anything bad went down. As a patrolman, Lena had been called to the school more than her share of times to arrest drug dealers and brawlers. In her experience, perps picked up from school were a hell of a lot harder to deal with than their adult counterparts. Habitual juvenile offenders knew the laws governing their arrests better than most cops, and there was no fear in them anymore.

"Things have changed so much," Brad said, echoing her thoughts. "I don't know how the teachers do it."

"The same way we do," Lena snapped, wanting to cut off the conversation. She had never liked school and was not comfortable being here. Actually, since her interrogation of Mark Patterson, Lena had felt off. She was experiencing an odd mixture of self-assurance from being able to connect with the kid and an unsettling feeling that she had connected too closely. Worst of all, Jeffrey seemed to have picked up on this, too.

"Here we go," Brad said, stopping in front of Jenny Weaver's locker. He pulled a sheet of paper out of his pocket and started to unfold it, saying, "The combination is—" as Lena hooked her thumb under the latch and popped the locker open.

"How'd you do that?" Brad asked.

"Only geeks use the combinations."

Brad blushed, but covered for it by taking things out of Jenny Weaver's locker. "Three textbooks," he said, handing them to Lena so she could thumb through the pages. "A notebook," he continued. "Two pencils and a pack of gum."

Lena peered into the narrow cabinet, thinking that Jenny Weaver was a lot neater than she had been. There weren't even pictures taped on to the inside. "That's all?" she asked, even though she could see for herself.

"That's all," Brad answered, going through the books Lena had already checked.

Lena opened the notebook, which had a puppy on the cover. There were six colored tabs, one for each period, dividing the paper into sections. Almost every page was filled, but as far as she could tell there were only class notes. Jenny Weaver had not even doodled on the edges.

"She must've been a good student," Lena said.

"She was thirteen and in the ninth grade."

"Is that unusual?"

"Just means she skipped a grade," Brad told her, stacking the books back in the locker the way they had found them. He checked the packet of gum to make sure it was just gum. "She sure was neat."

"Yeah," Lena agreed, handing Brad the notebook. She waited while he thumbed through it, looking for something she might have missed.

"She wrote real neat," Brad said in a sad voice.

"What'd you think of her on the retreat?"

Brad pushed his hair out of his eyes. "She was quiet. I hate to say that I barely noticed her, but the girls pretty much kept to themselves. Mrs. Gray was supposed to be there to help out with them, but she got sick at the last minute. I didn't want to disappoint everybody, and the deposits were nonrefundable. . . ." He shook his head. "The boys were a handful. I had to spend most of my time looking after them."

"What about Jenny and Lacey?"

"Well . . ." Brad's forehead wrinkled as he thought. "They didn't do much, is the thing. The other kids skied and had fun. Jenny and Lacey kind of kept to themselves. They had their own room and I only really saw them around supper time."

"How'd they act?"

"Kind of like they had their own language. They'd look at me and giggle, you know, like girls do." He shifted uncomfortably, and Lena could see exactly why the girls had giggled. Brad probably knew as much about teenage girls as a goat did.

"They didn't act strange?"

"Stranger than giggling for no reason?"

"Brad . . . ," Lena said. She stopped herself before she told him why the girls were laughing at him. Telling him they probably thought he was a dork would only make him pout, and Lena did not want to deal with that for the rest of the day.

He stared at her openly, waiting for her to finish.

"Just . . . ," Lena began, then stopped again. "Did it seem like Jenny was sick?"

"That's what the chief asked," Brad said, and it seemed like he felt this was a compliment to Lena. "He asked a lot of questions about Jenny and how she looked, who she was hanging around with."

Lena closed the locker and indicated that they should continue walking. "So?"

"She didn't look sick to me," he said. "I mean, like I told you, they kept to themselves. They didn't seem to like the other kids. Honestly, I don't know why they went. They're not exactly part of that group."

"Meaning what?"

He shrugged. "Popular, I guess. I mean, Lacey could've been. She's real cute, like a cheerleader." He shook his head, as if he was still trying to figure it out. "Jenny definitely wasn't popular. I didn't catch anyone being mean to her—I would'a done something about that—but they didn't go out of their way to be nice to her, either."

"Weren't you supposed to be chaperoning them?"

He took this as it was meant, and immediately became defensive. "I watched them as best I could, but it was just me there, and the boys were getting into a lot more trouble than the girls."

Lena bit her tongue, wondering how someone as dense as Brad had gotten on the force.

"Here we go," Brad said, stopping in front of the library. He held the door open for Lena, something Brad's mama had taught him to do from an early age. Working with Frank, then Jeffrey, Lena was so used to men opening doors for her that she barely noticed it anymore.

The library was cool, yet friendly. Student projects were tacked up on the walls, and row after row of bookshelves were packed almost to overflowing. About twenty computer stations—another education initiative funded by Georgia's lottery—sat empty, their monitors dark because the school's electrical system was not equipped to handle the extra load. There was a second-level balcony with an open railing lining the back wall, and for just a moment Lena imagined that some kid had probably sat up in that second level, thinking about how easy it would be to open fire on his classmates.

Brad was staring at her, an expectant look on his face. "That's them," he said, indicating three girls and three boys sitting by the librarian's desk. Lena knew instantly what Brad had been talking about. These were the popular kids. There was something about the way they sat there, talking and laughing with each other. They were an attractive bunch, dressed in the latest fashions and with that casual air of entitlement that kids have who are worshipped by their peers.

"Let's get this over with," Lena told him, walking purposefully toward the table. She stood there for several seconds, but none of the kids acknowledged she was there. Lena gave Brad a wary look, then cleared her throat. When that didn't work, she rapped her knuckles on the table. The group started to quiet down, but two of the girls finished their conversation before looking up.

Lena said, "I'm detective Adams, this is Officer Stephens."

Two of the girls giggled as if they knew the best secret in the world. Lena was reminded of one of the many reasons she did not like kids, especially girls this age. There was nothing more vicious than a teenage girl. Maybe it was because boys were more capable of settling an argument with their fists, but girls at this age were much more conniving and torturous than anyone wanted to believe.

One of the giggling girls smacked her gum while the other said, "We know *Brad*."

Lena tried not to be hostile as Brad introduced the kids. "Heather, Brittany, and Shanna," he said, pointing them out. Then, indicating the boys, who were slouching so far into their chairs their butts were nearly touching the ground, "Carson, Rory, and Cooper." Lena wondered when parents had stopped giving their kids normal names. Probably around the time they stopped teaching them manners.

"Okay," Lena began, sitting opposite them. "Let's wrap this up quickly so y'all can go back to class."

"Why are we here?" Brittany demanded, her tone as hostile as her posture.

"You were on the ski retreat with Officer Stephens," Lena told them. "Jenny Weaver was there. You know what happened to her Saturday?"

"Yeah," Shanna said, smacking her gum. "Y'all shot her."

Lena took a deep breath and let it go. As shitty as she had been at this age, Lena would never have talked to a cop like this. She said, "We're just asking some routine questions about her, trying to figure out why she did what she did."

One of the boys spoke. Lena couldn't remember his name, but it was hardly relevant as they all looked alike. "Does my father know you're talking to me?"

"What's your name?" Lena asked.

"Carson."

"Carson," she repeated, returning the belligerent stare he gave her. His eyes were bloodshot, the pupils dilated.

"What?" he said, finally breaking the stare. He crossed his arms, looking around the room as if he was bored.

"One of your classmates is dead," Lena reminded him. "Are you not interested in helping us find out why?"

"The 'why' is because you shot her," Carson answered, picking up his backpack. "Can I go now?"

"Sure," Lena told him. "Why don't we get Dr. Clay to take a look in your bookbag?"

Carson smirked. "You don't have probable cause."

"No," Lena agreed. "But Dr. Clay doesn't need it."

Carson knew she was right. He dropped the bag onto the floor. "What do you want to know?"

Lena exhaled slowly. "Tell me about Jenny Weaver."

He waved his hand. "I didn't know her, okay? She was on the retreat and all, but she and Lacey didn't really socialize."

The other boys nodded. One of them said, "They didn't like to party."

Lena assumed that by "party" he meant get high. From what little she knew about Jenny Weaver, this was not surprising.

"She was younger than us," Carson added. "We don't hang around with babies."

Lena turned to the girls. "What about y'all?"

Brittany started first. Her posture was as poor as the others', and her backbone seemed pliable, molding her into the back of the chair like Silly Putty. She sounded just how Lena had imagined she would: whiny and put-upon. There was something wrong with a society that let children talk to adults this way.

Brittany said, "Jenny was weird."

Lena tried to stir them up, asking, "I thought y'all were friends."

"We most certainly weren't," Shanna toned in. "I for one couldn't stand her."

She said this as if she was proud of the fact.

"That so?" Lena asked.

Shanna's bravura dropped down a notch when she saw Lena was taking her seriously. She was considerably less confident when she said, "We weren't friends."

"None of us was really," Heather said, and she seemed to

be the logical one. She had uncrossed her arms, and Lena thought that, of the six, she was the only one who seemed to show any regret. Actually, Heather reminded Lena a little of herself at that age, on the periphery of things, more interested in sports than school gossip.

Heather said, "Jenny was quiet most of the time. Even back in middle school."

"You all went to the same school?"

They all nodded.

Heather indicated the other girls. "All of us live near her. We rode the bus together for a while."

Lena asked, "But you weren't friends?"

"She didn't really have a lot of friends." Heather was quiet for a few beats, then said, "When she first moved into the neighborhood, I tried to talk to her and all, but she liked to stay home and read a lot. I invited her to hang out a couple of times, but she didn't want to, then I just stopped trying."

"No one liked her," Brittany provided. "She was a real— what do you call it?—introvert."

Shanna laughed, covering her mouth with her hand. "Yeah, right," she said.

Lena pointed out, "She was friends with Lacey Patterson."

The girls exchanged a look.

"What?" Lena asked.

They shrugged in unison. The boys were either comatose or not interested.

Lena sighed, sitting back in her chair. "We'll sit here all night until you tell me what I need to know."

They seemed to believe her, even though Lena wanted nothing more than to leave this school.

Brittany spoke first. "Lacey was only friends with her because of Mark."

"Mark Patterson, Lacey's brother?"

"Okay," Shanna said, holding out her hand palm up, her voice excited, as if she'd just been cracked by Lena's tough interrogation and was now giddy to tell them all they needed to know. "She was a whore."

"Shanna," Heather gawked.

"You know it's true," Shanna countered. "She slept around, and not just with Mark."

Brad stirred in his seat, looking as uncomfortable as Lena had ever seen him, which was saying a lot.

"Who did she sleep with?" Lena asked, looking at the boys. None of them would meet her eye.

"I don't know for sure, other than Mark," Shanna said, as if she were talking with one of her girlfriends over the lunch table. "But there were all kinds of rumors that she'd blow guys—"

"Jeesh," Heather interrupted. "She's dead, okay? Why do you have to say all this?"

"Because it's the truth!" Shanna countered, her voice high and excited.

Heather seemed angry. "It was just rumors. Nobody knows if they were true or not."

Lena asked, "What were the rumors?"

Shanna was more than happy to supply this. "She was having sex with some of the guys behind the gym after fifth period."

"Intercourse or blow jobs?" Lena asked, still watching the guys.

Shanna shrugged, giving Heather a sideways glance. "I wasn't there."

"Heather was?"

"Heather doesn't like boys," Shanna provided.

"Shut up!" Heather ordered, alarmed.

Lena wondered if she looked just as shocked as Brad. It

was like having their very own *Jerry Springer* show right here in the school library.

"Okay," Lena said, holding up her hands, trying to rein this in. "What proof do you have that Jenny was sleeping around?"

The girls were silent, looking back and forth at each other.

"Nothing, right?" Lena asked. "You can't tell me any of the boys she was with?"

Carson stirred in his chair, but he didn't volunteer anything.

"Mark," Shanna said, shrugging. "But Mark was with, like, everybody."

"No kidding," Brittany muttered, with something like regret in her tone.

Lena sighed, rubbing the bridge of her nose. She was getting the kind of headache that would probably last for the rest of the day. "Okay, then who started the rumor?"

They all shrugged. This seemed to be the universal teenage response to any question. Lena wondered if they would later have rotator cuff problems.

"Pansy Davis told me," said Shanna.

"She told me she slept with Ron Wilson Thursday night," Brittany countered. "And you know Ron was at Frank's house that night."

"Frank said he sneaked out!" Shanna squealed.

"Stop, stop," Lena said, holding up her hands. It was like being nibbled to death by ducks. "None of y'all remembers where you heard the rumor?"

"It was just a known thing," Heather told Lena. "I mean, I don't remember who told me, but Jenny just acted weird, okay? She would go off with boys she didn't know. Boys, like, in twelfth grade."

"And you don't know their names?"

Heather shook her head. "They're seniors."

"Not popular seniors?" Lena asked.

"Some of them were skanky," Brittany provided. "Not seniors I would know. Not popular, okay? Sort of like Jenny."

"Did she ride the bus home with them?"

"They had cars," Heather said. "Seniors are allowed to drive."

"Do you remember any of the cars?"

Heather shook her head no, but Brittany snapped her fingers. "There's one I remember." She turned to Shanna. "Do you remember that cool black Thunderbird?"

"A new one or an old one?" Lena asked.

"The older kind that's really big in the back," Shanna said. "It was really loud, like something was wrong with the engine or something."

"Did the driver go to this school?"

They exchanged glances again. "Maybe," Brittany said.

"I don't think so," Shanna added.

Heather shrugged. "I don't pay attention to cars. It doesn't sound familiar."

Lena looked at the boys. "Do any of y'all recognize the car?"

They all shrugged or shook their heads.

Lena tried another line of questioning. "Do y'all have any idea why Jenny wanted to kill Mark?"

The girls were silent, then Brittany finally said, "We've all wanted to at least once."

Lena sat back, crossing her arms. She stared at the boys, guessing why they were being silent. "Okay," she said, and they all started to stand, but she stopped them. "Carson, Cory, Roper—"

"Rory and Cooper," Brad corrected.

"Right," Lena said. "Whatever. You guys stay. The girls can leave." She turned to Brad. "Why don't you get their phone numbers and addresses?"

Brad nodded. He knew she was getting rid of him, but didn't seem to mind.

Lena sat at the table across from the boys, silent until they started to squirm in their chairs.

"Well?" she said.

Carson spoke first. "Yeah, she was doing it."

The other boys nodded.

"All of you slept with her?"

They did not answer.

"Blow jobs? Hand jobs?" Lena asked.

"Sex," Carson clarified.

Lena felt her cheeks flush, but not from embarrassment. "When was this?"

"Mark brought her over to my house one time. We were all partying."

"I thought you said Jenny didn't party."

"No, she didn't," Carson said. "Not usually, but Mark told her to have something to take the edge off." He snorted a laugh. "She did whatever Mark told her to do."

"So," Lena said, trying to get all of this straight, "it was Mark, Jenny, and you three?"

They all nodded.

Carson said, "She got a little drunk and started coming on to us."

Lena pressed her lips together so she would not say anything.

"Mark said she'd do anything we wanted."

One of the boys smiled. "She sure did."

"You all had sex with her?" Lena asked.

Carson shrugged, smirking. "She was pretty drunk."

Lena looked down at the table, trying to compose herself. "So, she got drunk and you all had sex with her, Mark included?"

"Mark just watched," one of the boys said. "She let us do anything we wanted." His anger sparked like a brush fire. "She was a whore, okay? Why do you even care?"

Lena was startled by the hatred in his voice, as if it was Jenny's fault entirely that they had done this. She asked, "What was your name?"

He looked down, mumbling, "Rory."

"All right, Rory," Lena said. "Did she have sex with any of you on the retreat?"

"Fuck no." Carson crossed his arms angrily. "That was the thing. Why the fuck else would we go on that stupid retreat?"

"You were having sex with her then?" Lena asked.

"No," he said, still angry. "She wouldn't go near us. She was fine at the party. Couldn't get enough of it." He grabbed himself, as if Lena needed the visual aid. "But over Christmas she was tight as a drum. Wouldn't even talk to us." His lip curled. "The bitch."

Lena bit her tongue.

"She was a cock tease," Carson said. "She would've fucked a dog if Mark asked her to, but on the retreat it was like she was better than us."

"What do you think changed this?" Lena asked.

He shrugged. "Who the fuck cares?"

"Did you approach her on the retreat, or did she just ignore you?"

His lip curled. "It was this way, all right? We offered her a little something to help her relax, told her we all wanted to party, and she froze up."

"Exactly," Rory said. "It was like we weren't good enough for her all the sudden."

"Hell, yeah," Carson agreed. "She was pretending like it

didn't happen, and I said to her, 'Hey, you know what you did, you whore.'"

"Should've offered her money for it," Rory suggested.

"Should've offered *Mark* money for it."

"Right," Lena mumbled, trying to remember the third boy's name. He had been very quiet during all of this, not hostile like the others. "Cooper?" she guessed. He looked up, and she asked, "Did you ever wonder why a thirteen-year-old girl would do something like that in the first place?"

"She liked it," Cooper suggested, shrugging like they all shrugged. "I mean, why else would she do it?" He looked up at his friends and his whole demeanor changed. He was more adamant and just as hateful as his friends when he insisted, "She was a whore and she liked it."

"Yeah," Rory said, his tone filled with spite. "I mean, you could tell she liked it."

Lena suggested, "Even though she was drunk?"

They didn't answer her.

"How could you tell she liked it?"

"Hell, man," Rory said, "who knows? Her face was buried in the couch the whole time."

"Dude," Carson laughed, holding up his hand for a high-five.

Lightning fast, Lena reached out and grabbed his hand. She was holding on to his wrist tight enough to feel the bones, and he grimaced from the pain.

She said, "You think she enjoyed it, huh?"

"Hey," Carson said, looking around the room for help. "Come on, we were just having fun."

"Fun?" Lena asked, jerking his arm like she might rip it out of the socket. "Where I come from, we call that rape, you little shit." She let go of him because there was nothing else she could do short of taking out her gun and pistol-whipping him, which was tempting in light of the smirk that returned to his face when he sat back in his chair.

The bell rang for class changes, and Lena had to force herself not to jump at the loud sound. The boys had a Pavlovian response, gathering their bookbags, not waiting for Lena to release them.

She told them, "Give Officer Stephens your phone numbers and addresses in case we have any questions." She made sure she had their attention. "I'm going to make sure every cop at the station knows your name."

"Yeah," Rory said. "Whatever."

They started to shuffle away, but Carson stayed, asking, "You gonna tell Dr. Clay to search me or what?"

"I'm going to do every possible thing I can to make sure you're in jail before you're old enough to vote."

"Shit," he groaned, shuffling off.

Lena stood, wanting to get away from the table where she had heard their vile talk. She walked over to the computer area and rested her hand on the top of a monitor, feeling a cold sweat break out all over her body. It sickened her to know that boys this young were already learning to think this way about women. Lena could imagine *him* feeling the same way at that age, like girls were expendable. They all liked it. They were all whores.

"Lena?" Brad said, pulling her out of her thoughts. She looked back at the table and saw a couple of older women and one man taking their seats. "Jenny's teachers," Brad told her.

Lena put her hand to her chest, feeling claustrophobic. Brad was standing too close, and the room felt like it was getting smaller. "Why don't you start?" Lena suggested, thinking she needed to get out of here to catch her breath. She walked toward the doors, but he stopped her.

"By myself?" he asked, standing too close to her again.

She could smell his aftershave, and something that smelled like a strong breath mint. She could not lose it here. Lena knew if she got sick in front of Brad she wouldn't be able to go back to work again.

She indicated her cell phone as she took another step back. "I'll call back to the station and check on things there, maybe see if we can find out who owns a black Thunderbird in the area."

"I bet the principal would know," Brad suggested, stepping forward. "They keep logs on that, right? You can't park here unless you've got a parking pass."

"Good thinking," Lena said, taking another step back, aware that if she didn't get her breathing under control she would hyperventilate. "I'll check that out while you interview them. Be sure to ask about what the girls said."

He gave her a funny look. "Are you okay?"

"Yeah," she said. Suddenly, the room felt hot and unbearable, and she could feel her shirt starting to cling to her back. "Just get preliminary stuff, an impression of what she was like. I'll be back as soon as I make some calls."

He gave her a quick nod, his jaw tightening. "All right," he said, and she could tell he wanted to ask her again if she was okay.

She walked quickly into the hall, taking a deep breath to calm herself. She was still sweating, and took off her jacket. A kid jogged by. He slowed when he saw Lena's gun in her shoulder holster.

Lena slipped the jacket back on and leaned her head against the wall. She closed her eyes until the nausea passed. After a few deep breaths she felt better, if not a hundred percent.

Lena flipped open her cell phone to give herself something to do. She dialed the station and talked to Marla about the car, glad that Frank wasn't in. It was still hard for Lena to talk to Frank, and part of her felt that he blamed Lena for what had happened. That same part of her agreed with him. She had been so stupid.

Even though she was standing less than a hundred yards from the front office, Lena called the principal and asked him about the black car. He went through his records while she waited on the phone and gave her the answer she had assumed all along: No one in the school had registered a car fitting that description. Lena thanked the principal, then hung up, thinking it felt good to get some things done instead of just treading water. The more time that passed on this case, the more they seemed to be moving away from solving it. She should talk to Mark again and see what his reaction was to this latest information. Jeffrey probably wouldn't let her near Mark again after what happened last time.

Lena opened the phone again and dialed her voice mail at home. The first message was from the video store in town, telling her that her tapes were late. The second was from Nan Thomas, Sibyl's lover.

"Lena," Nan said, her low voice an irritated grumble. "I've still got this stuff, Sibby's stuff. If you want it, let me know. I don't . . ." She stopped, then, "It's just . . ."

Lena looked at her watch, wondering how much Nan's stuttering was costing her.

"I'll be at Suddy's tonight around eight," Nan said. "I'll have the boxes in my car if you want them. Meet me there if you . . . Otherwise, well . . ." Again, she stopped.

Lena fast forwarded, skipping the rest of the message. Suddy's was a gay bar on the outskirts of Heartsdale. There was no way in hell she was going to meet her sister's lover in a gay bar.

Lena's heart dropped into her stomach when she heard

the next message. Hank said, "Lee, Barry's sick. I gotta cover here tonight, maybe tomorrow."

She closed her eyes, leaning her back against the wall as Hank explained that it would be easier for him to stay in Reece because there was a beer delivery tomorrow morning. She felt panicked again, then angry, because he had taken the coward's way out, leaving the message instead of calling her cell phone to explain.

Lena walked over to the other side of the hallway, looking out the window. There was an atrium in the middle of the school, and across the way she could see the cafeteria staff setting up the tables. She was so absorbed in their movements that she missed part of the last message. She rewound it and listened again.

"This is Pastor Fine, Lena," the message began. "I apologize, but I'll have to cancel our appointment this evening. One of our parishioners has taken ill. I need to be with the family right now."

Lena snapped the phone closed as he asked for her to return his call so they could reschedule. She would let Jeffrey deal with that. She was not in the habit of letting herself think too far ahead, but the meeting with Fine had been something she had settled her mind on as something to do tonight. In a flash, she saw herself going back to her empty house, being alone. Panic enveloped her.

She put her hand to her chest, feeling her heart pounding against her rib cage. She was sweating, she noticed, and the back of her knees felt hot and sticky. She wanted to hear Hank's message again, to see if there was a nuance in his voice she had missed. Maybe he had left an opening. Maybe he was playing some kind of game to make her say that she wanted him there.

The final bell rang, a loud, piercing tone that vibrated in

Lena's ears. She looked around the empty hallway, forget-ting for a moment exactly where she was and why. As if out of a dream, she saw the image of a woman walking toward her. Lena's eyes felt like they blurred for a moment, then with a start she realized that she was in Jenny Weaver's school, and that Dottie Weaver was walking down the hall toward her.

"Shit," Lena mumbled, looking down at her cell phone, willing it to ring. She flipped it open like she might make a call, but it was too late. Dottie Weaver was less than ten feet away holding a heavy-looking textbook in her hands.

Weaver stopped in the hallway, her mouth an angry straight line. Her eyes were bloodshot, like she had been crying for the last year. Red splotches were all over her face.

"Mrs. Weaver," Lena said, flipping her phone closed.

Dottie shook her head, like she was too angry to say anything.

"We're just talking to some classmates and teachers to see if they can shed any light on—"

"Why can't you just leave her alone?" Dottie begged. "Why can't you just let her rest in peace?"

"I'm sorry," Lena told the woman, and she meant it.

"She was my baby."

"I know that," Lena answered, looking down at her phone.

"You're here raking her name over the coals, trying to make her out to be a bad person."

"That's not my goal."

"Liar!" Dottie screamed, throwing the book at Lena. Lena dropped her phone to catch it, but missed. The spine slammed into her stomach and she winced as it dropped to the floor.

"Mrs. Weaver," Lena began, stooping to retrieve the textbook.

"The school wanted her book back," Dottie said, her bottom lip trembling. "Take it. Take it and tell them all they can go to hell."

Lena tried to close the book without damaging the pages. She picked up her phone, which didn't seem to be broken.

Dottie dabbed her eyes with some tissue, then blew her nose. She did not leave, though, which Lena could not understand until she spoke again.

"Jenny loved this school," the mother said, wrapping her arms around her stomach as if it brought her pain to speak. "She loved being here."

Lena thought now was as good a time as any to get this out of the way. "Was she seeing anybody, Mrs. Weaver?"

Dottie shook her head. "A psychiatrist?" she asked.

"A boy," Lena clarified. "Was she seeing any boys?"

"No," Dottie snapped. "Of course not. She was just a child."

Lena nodded, feeling an encroaching dread. "Some of the girls said she was."

"Which girls?" Dottie asked, looking around as if they might be there.

"Just girls," Lena answered. "Friends from school."

"She didn't have friends," Dottie told her, narrowing her eyes, sensing some kind of trick. "What are they saying about my daughter?"

Lena tried to think of a way to say it. "That she . . ."

"That she what?" Dottie demanded.

Lena said, "That she saw a lot of boys. That she was with a lot of boys."

The slap came suddenly, and stung so much that after a few seconds the right side of Lena's face went numb. Before Lena could think to respond, let alone react, she was looking at the back of Dottie Weaver as the woman left the school.

The library door bumped open, and Brad stood there, holding the door for the group of teachers he had been interviewing. They looked tired, and a bit irritated, but this was pretty normal from Lena's recollection of teachers around lunchtime. One of them looked at Lena, and she could tell from the way the woman assessed her that she sensed something was wrong. The teacher raised an eyebrow as if to invite conversation, but Lena was too shocked to speak.

"Lena?" Brad prompted. She nodded that she was okay, wondering if her face was red where Dottie had slapped her.

Brad introduced all of the teachers, whose names Lena promptly forgot. He said, "They know about the rumor."

Lena blinked, not understanding.

"The rumor about Jenny," Brad clarified. "They said they had heard it."

"None of us believed it," one of the teachers said, her voice indicating that she had resigned herself a long time ago to the fact that there were things that went on in the school that no teacher would ever know about.

"She was a good student," another teacher said. "Very quiet, turned her work in on time. Her mother was involved."

The other teachers nodded, and Lena duplicated the gesture, still too shocked to offer anything of consequence.

"Thank you for your time," Brad said, moving things along. He shook hands with each of them in turn, and to the last one they gave him an encouraging look.

"I'm sorry we couldn't help more," one said.

Another told him, "If we think of anything, we'll call you."

The woman who had looked at Lena was last, and she told Brad, "You did an excellent job, Bradley. I'm very impressed."

Brad beamed. "Thank you, ma'am," he said, tucking his

head down like a happy puppy. He waited until the teachers were gone before asking Lena, "Whose book?"

"Jenny Weaver's," Lena provided, thumbing through the pages to see if any notes were tucked in. It was empty, just like the others.

"How'd you get it?"

Lena could not answer him. "Here," she said, handing him the book. "Take it to the front office, then meet me in the car."

The parking lot of Suddy's was pretty empty, even at eight o'clock. If Sibyl and Nan's life had been any indication, probably most of the lesbians in town were at home, watching sitcoms. Not that Sibyl could watch them, she was blind, but she liked to listen sometimes, and Nan would narrate what was happening.

Lena crossed her arms, thinking about Sibyl, and how she had looked the last time Lena had seen her; not the time in the morgue, but the day before she had died. As usual, Sibyl had been full of energy, and laughing at something that had happened in one of her classes. Above everything, Sibyl loved teaching, and she had taken great joy from being in front of a classroom. Maybe that was why Lena had had such a negative reaction to being at the school today.

Before she could stop herself, Lena got out of the car. Suddy's was nice by most bar standards. Compared to the Hut, Hank's bar over in Reece, it was a palace. Outside, the decor was spare, probably because a place like this would not want to draw attention to itself. Other than a Budweiser sign with a neon rainbow flag incorporated into the logo, the building was pretty nondescript.

The interior was more festive, but the lights were down low, making the room a little too intimate for Lena. Something soft played on the jukebox, and a spinning mirrored ball did a slow turn over what looked like the dance floor. Lena had always been uncomfortable with this side of Sibyl, and never understood how someone who was so pretty, who was so outgoing and energetic, could choose this kind of life for herself. Sibyl had always wanted children, always wanted to be taken care of and loved. Lena would not have predicted this kind of life for her sister in a million years.

When Sibyl had first come out to Lena fifteen years ago, Lena's response had been an emphatic, "No, you're not." Even after Sibyl moved in with Nan, Lena had still let herself believe that Sibyl was not gay. It sounded trite to say, but Lena could not help thinking in the back of her mind that it was just a phase, and that one day Sibyl would laugh about her confusion and settle down and have children. Being Sibyl's twin complicated matters, because Lena had always felt that a piece of herself was in Sibyl, and a piece of Sibyl was in Lena. It was unsettling to think that Lena might somewhere in her psyche share Sibyl's sexual leanings.

Lena dismissed this as she walked across the room. Two women at a corner table ignored her completely, seeming more intent upon pushing their tongues down each other's throat than seeing who had walked through the door. The bartender was reading a newspaper when Lena approached her, and she looked up, doing a startled double take.

The woman said, "You must be her sister."

Lena sat a couple of stools down from her. "I'm meeting someone here."

The woman closed the paper. She walked over and offered Lena her hand. "I'm Judy," she said.

Lena stared at the hand, then reluctantly shook it. The woman was tall, with long dark hair and a heart-shaped face. Her eyes were an intense hazel, which Lena noticed because the woman would not stop staring at her.

"Beer, please," Lena said, then, "make it a Jim Beam instead."

Judy paused, then walked over to the liquor display behind the bar. "Sibyl never drank," she said, as if by extension this meant that Lena, her twin, would not drink.

Lena pointed out, "She didn't fuck men, either."

Judy conceded the point. "Jim Beam?"

"Yeah," Lena answered, trying to sound bored as she took some money out of her front pocket. She had changed into jeans and a T-shirt at home before coming here, a decision she now regretted. She probably looked gayer than the women in the corner to these people.

Judy said, "She liked cranberry juice, though."

"Could you make that a double?" Lena asked, tossing a twenty-dollar bill onto the bar.

Judy glanced at her before filling the order. "We all really miss her."

"I'm sure you do," Lena told her, aware that she sounded glib. She stared at the dark liquid in her glass, remembering that the last time she had anything to drink was the night Sibyl had died. Lena did not like alcohol, because she hated the feeling of being out of control. Not that she had control of anything lately, anyway.

Lena looked at the clock over the bar. It was five till eight.

Judy asked, "Who you meeting here?"

Lena knocked the drink back in one swallow. "Jim Beam," she said, tapping the glass.

Judy gave her another look, but retrieved the bottle from the shelf.

To discourage conversation, Lena turned on the stool, looking out on the dance floor. A lone woman stood there, her eyes closed as she swayed to the beat. There was something familiar about her, but the light was bad, and Lena's memory did not want to work. Still, Lena watched her, wondering at the self-absorbed way the woman danced, as if no one else were in the room. As if nothing else mattered.

The song changed, and Lena recognized the tune before the lyrics to Beck's "Debra" came from the speakers. Mark Patterson popped into her mind again. There was something sensual and disturbing about the way the dancer moved that reminded her of the young man. She watched the dancer, wondering again what the hell had been going on with Jenny Weaver. What was Mark's hold over her? What was it about him that would make a thirteen-year-old kid prostitute herself? It did not make sense.

Lena wondered if this was the way Mark Patterson would dance, though she could not imagine the kid doing something so audacious as standing in the middle of an empty dance floor. The thought surprised her, because Lena was not aware that she had put herself in a position to make assumptions about Mark's personality. She knew so very little about him, yet somehow, her subconscious had assigned him certain traits.

Lena turned back around to break the spell. Judy was reading her paper, having left Lena's drink and her change on the bar. Lena was thinking about what to leave for a tip when she noticed her reflection in the mirror. For just a moment, she startled, and Lena imagined she looked much as Judy had when Lena had first walked into the room. In a split second, Sibyl was there, and Lena felt her heart jump at the sight.

Suddenly, shouting came from outside, and a crowd of people walked into the bar. They were laughing and raucous, all dressed in matching softball uniforms. The pants were black with white stripes up the sides, the shirts white with the word BUSHWHACKERS across the chest.

"Jesus Christ," Lena groaned, getting the reference. She stood up as she recognized Nan Thomas in the center of the group. The mousy librarian had a neon-pink athletic strap around her glasses and the front of her shirt was streaked with dirt as if she had slid across home plate. Unlike some of the others in the group, Nan showed no sign of mistaking Lena for her sister. As a matter of fact, she frowned.

Someone patted Lena on the back, and she turned around, surprised to see Hare Earnshaw standing beside her. He was dressed in jeans and a Bushwhacker T-shirt as well as a hat with a large B on it.

"How's it going, Lena?" Hare asked.

Maybe it was the alcohol, but Lena blurted out a surprised, "You're gay?" to him before she could stop herself. Hare was a doctor in town. Lena had actually seen him a couple of years ago for a cold that would not go away.

Hare laughed at her surprise. "I play on the team," he said, indicating his shirt. Then, he leaned closer, giving her a coy wink. "I'm the catcher."

Lena backed up right into Nan. There were people everywhere, though they seemed to be involved in their own conversations about the game they had just played. Lena pulled at the neck of her shirt, feeling claustrophobic. She moved away from the group, toward the front door.

"Lee?" Nan said, then corrected herself before Lena could, saying, "Lena."

"I told you not to call me that," Lena said, crossing her arms.

"I know," Nan held her hands up, palms out. "I'm sorry. It's just that Sibby always called you that."

Lena stopped her. "Can we get the stuff, please? I need to get home." Her voice went down on the word "home" as she thought about the empty house. Hank had not answered the phone when she called the Hut looking for him. The bastard was obviously ignoring her. It was so typical of him to leave her when she needed him most.

"It's out in the parking lot," Nan said, holding the door open for Lena. Lena stopped, waiting for Nan to go first. It was one thing to let Brad Stephens hold a door open for her; Lena would be damned if she would let some woman do it.

Nan talked as they walked out to the parking lot. "I tried to keep it the same way she had it," she said, a forced lightness to her voice. "You know how Sibby liked to keep things orderly."

"She had to," Lena shot back, thinking it was obvious that a blind person would have a system to things so that they would not be lost.

If Nan noticed Lena's biting tone, she ignored it.

"Here," Nan said, stopping in front of a white Toyota Camry. The driver's side window was down, and she reached in, popping the trunk.

"You should keep your doors locked," Lena told her.

"Why?" Nan asked, and she really seemed to be puzzled.

"You've got your car parked in front of a gay bar. I would think you might want to be a little more careful."

Nan tucked her hands into her waist. "Sibyl was killed in a diner in broad daylight. Do you really think locking my car door is going to protect me?"

She had a point, but Lena was not going to give it to her. "I wasn't saying you could get killed. Someone might vandalize the car or something."

"Well . . ." Nan shrugged, and for just a moment, she seemed exactly like Sibyl. Not that Nan was in any way similar to Sibyl in appearance, it was just her "whatever happens will happen" attitude.

"These are some of her tapes," Nan said, handing Lena a

box that was about eighteen inches square. "She labeled them in braille, but most of them have their own titles."

Lena took the box, surprised at how heavy it was.

"These are some photographs," Nan said, stacking another box on top of the first. "I don't know why she had them."

"I asked her to keep them for me," Lena provided, remembering the day she had brought the box of pictures to Sibyl. Greg Mitchell, Lena's last boyfriend, had just left her, and Lena did not want the photographs she had of him in the house.

"I'll get this one," Nan offered, picking up the last box. It was bigger than the other two, and she rested it on her knee to close the trunk. "This is just a bunch of stuff she had in the closet. A couple of awards from high school, a track ribbon I guess is yours."

Lena nodded, walking to her Celica.

"I found a picture of you two at the beach," Nan said, laughing. "Sibyl's got a sunburn. She looks miserable."

Because she was in front of Nan, Lena allowed a smile. She remembered the day, how Sibyl had insisted on staying outside even though Hank had warned her it was too hot. Sibyl's black glasses had shaded her eyes, and when she took them off, the only part of her face that was not beet red was where the glasses had been. She looked like a raccoon for days after.

". . . stop by Saturday to pick them up," Nan was saying.

"What?" Lena asked.

"I said that you can stop by Saturday to go through the other stuff. I'm donating her computer and equipment to the school for the blind over in Augusta."

"What other stuff?" Lena asked, thinking Nan meant to throw away Sibyl's things.

"Just some papers," Nan told her, setting the box down at her feet. "School stuff, mostly. Her dissertation, a couple of essays. That kind of thing."

"You're just going to throw them away?" Lena demanded.

"Give them away. They're not really valuable," Nan said, as if she were talking to a child.

"They were valuable to Sibyl," Lena countered, aware she was close to yelling. "How can you even think about giving them away?"

Nan looked down at the ground, then back at Lena. The patronizing tone was still there. "I told you that you're more than welcome to have them if you like. They're in braille. It's not like you can read them."

Lena snorted a laugh, setting the boxes on the ground. "Some lover you were."

"What the hell do you mean by that?"

"Obviously, it meant something to her or she wouldn't have kept it," Lena said. "But go ahead and give it away."

"Excuse me," Nan said, indicating the boxes. "How many times did I have to call you and beg you to take this stuff?"

"That's different," Lena said, digging in her pocket for her keys.

"Why?" Nan shot back. "Because you were in the hospital?"

Lena glanced back at the bar. "Lower your voice."

"Don't tell me what to do," Nan said, her tone louder. "You don't get to question me about whether or not I loved your sister. Do you get that?"

"I wasn't questioning you," Lena answered, wondering how this had escalated so quickly. She could not even remember what had started this, but Nan was obviously pissed.

"The hell you weren't," Nan barked. "You think you're the only one around here who loved Sibyl? I shared my life with her." Nan lowered her voice. "I shared my bed with her."

Lena winced. "I know that."

"Do you?" Nan said. "Because I'll tell you what, Lena, I am sick and tired of the way you treat me, as if I'm some sort of pariah."

"Hey," Lena stopped her. "I'm not the one playing softball for Suddy's."

"I don't know how she put up with this," Nan mumbled, almost to herself.

"Put up with what?"

"Your misogynistic cop bullshit, for one."

"Misogynistic?" Lena repeated. "You're calling me misogynistic?"

"And homophobic," Nan added.

"Homophobic?"

"Are you a parrot now?"

Lena felt her nostrils flare. "Don't fuck with me, Nan. You don't know how."

Nan didn't seem to catch the warning. "Why don't you go back into that bar and meet some of your sister's friends, Lee? Why don't you talk to the people who really knew her and cared about her?"

"You sound like Hank," Lena told her. "Oh, I see," she said, putting the pieces together. "You've been talking to Hank about me."

Nan pressed her lips together. "We're worried about you."

"That so?" Lena laughed. "Great, my speed freak uncle and my dead sister's dyke girlfriend are worried about me."

"Yes," Nan said, standing her ground. "We are."

"This is so fucking stupid," Lena said, trying to laugh it off. She slipped the key into the lock, opening the trunk.

"You wanna know what's stupid?" Nan said. "What's stupid is me giving a crap about what you do. What's stupid is my caring about the fact that you're throwing your life away."

"Nobody asked you to look after me, Nan."

"No," Nan agreed. "But it's what Sibyl would have wanted." Her tone was more moderate now. "If Sibyl were here right now, she would be saying the same thing."

Lena swallowed hard, trying not to let Nan's words get to her, mostly because they rang true. Sibyl was the only person who had ever really been able to get to Lena.

Nan said, "She would be saying that you need to deal with this. She would be worried about you."

Lena stared at the jack in the trunk of the car because it was the only thing she could focus on.

Nan said, "You're so angry."

Lena laughed again, but the sound was hollow even to her. "I think I have pretty damn good reason to be."

"Why? Because your sister was killed? Because you were raped?"

Lena reached out, holding on to the trunk of her car. If only it were that easy, Lena thought. She was not simply mourning the death of Sibyl, she was also mourning the death of herself. Lena did not know who she was anymore, or why she even got up in the morning. Everything Lena had been before the rape had been taken away from her. She no longer knew herself.

Nan spoke again, and when she did, she said *his* name. Lena watched Nan's lips forming the word, saw his name travel through the space between them like an airborne poison.

"Lee," Nan said. "Don't let him ruin your life."

Lena kept her grip on the car, certain her knees would buckle if she let go.

Nan used *his* name again, then said, "You've got to deal with it, Lena. You've got to deal with it now, or you'll never be able to move on."

Lena hissed, "Fuck off, Nan."

Nan stepped forward, like she might put her hand on Lena's shoulder.

"Get the fuck away from me," Lena warned.

Nan gave a long sigh, giving up. She turned and walked back to the bar without giving Lena a second glance.

Lena sat in the empty parking lot of the Grant Piggly Wiggly, sipping cheap whiskey straight from the bottle. She was past the harsh taste, and her throat was so numb from the alcohol that she could barely feel it going down. There was another bottle in the seat beside her, and she would probably go through that one, too, before the night was over. All Lena wanted to do was stay in her car in this empty parking lot and try to figure out what was happening in her life. Nan was right to some degree. Lena had to get over this, but that did not mean talking to some idiot like Dave Fine. What Lena needed to do was get her shit together and stop obsessing about stupid things. She just needed to get on with her life. She needed, Lena supposed, a night of self-pity, where she finally went through the motions of grieving and letting things go.

She listened to snippets of Sibyl's tapes, popping them one by one into the cassette player to see what was on them. She should label them, but she could not find a pen. Besides, it seemed wrong to write on Sibyl's things, even though Sibyl would not have minded. There were a few tapes that were already labeled, most of them Atlanta singers: Melanie Hammet, Indigo Girls, a couple more names Lena did not recognize. She ejected the last tape, which had been some kind of compilation of classical mu-

sic on one side and old Pretenders tunes on the other, and
tossed it in with the others.

Lena reached around to the back seat and pulled at the
last box. It was heavier than the others, and when she finally managed to get it to the front, pictures spilled onto the
seat beside her. Most of the photos were of Greg Mitchell
and Lena at various stages in their relationship. There were
some beach pictures, of course, as well as snapshots from
the time they went to Chattanooga to see the aquarium.
Lena blinked away tears, trying to remember what it had
been like that day, standing in line to see the exhibit, the
breeze coming off the Tennessee River so strong that Greg
had stood behind her to keep her warm. She had loved the
way her body felt when he put his arms around her waist,
rested his chin on her shoulder. It was the only time in her
life she could remember ever being truly content. Then, the
line had moved, and Greg had stepped back, and said something about the weather, or a story on the news, and Lena
had purposefully picked a fight with him for no reason
whatsoever.

Lena thumbed through another stack of pictures, sipping
the alcohol with deliberate care. She was beyond drunk
now, but not beyond caring. Looking at the photos, she
wondered how there had ever been a time when she wanted
a man's company, or felt like being alone with one, let
alone intimate. For all Lena had said when Greg left her,
she had still wanted him back.

Lena found the picture Nan had told her about. Sibyl did
look miserable, but she was still smiling for the camera.
They were both about seven in the photograph. At that age,
they had looked almost identical, though one of Sibyl's
front teeth was missing because she had tripped and
knocked it out on the front porch. The tooth that grew in to

replace it was snaggled, but it gave Sibyl's mouth some character. At least, that's what Hank had told her.

Lena smiled as she spotted a stack of pictures bound together with a rubber band. Hank had given her an instant camera for her fifteenth birthday, and Lena had used two boxes of film in one day, taking pictures of everything she could think of. Later, she had done her own editing, splicing some of the images together. There was one picture in particular she remembered, and Lena thumbed through the stack until she found it. Using a razor blade, she had made a kisscut over the image, scoring just the surface of the photograph but not cutting all the way through to the back, and excised Hank from the scene. Bonnie, their golden lab, had been glued in his place.

"Bonnie," Lena breathed, aware that she was crying openly now. This was one of the reasons Lena did not drink alcohol. The dog had been dead for ten years and here she was, crying over him like it was just yesterday.

Lena got out of the car, taking the bottles of liquor with her. She wanted to get them out of the car because she knew she would end up passed out if they stayed there. As she walked, she realized that she was closer to this than she had thought in the car. Her feet felt like they did not belong to her, and she tripped several times over nothing in particular. The store had been closed for hours, but she still checked the windows to make sure no one saw her stumbling across the parking lot. Lena pressed her palm against the side of the building as she walked around it, holding both bottles with her free hand. When she got to the back of the store and let go of the wall, she tumbled, her knees giving out from under her. Somehow, she caught herself with one hand and kept from falling, face first, onto the asphalt.

"Shit," she cursed, seeing rather than feeling the cut on

her palm. Lena stood, more determined now than ever to throw away the alcohol. She would sleep some of it off in her car and drive home when she could see straight.

Reeling back, she tossed the near empty bottle into the Dumpster. It made a rewarding crash as it broke against the metal wall inside the steel chamber. Lena picked up the other bottle and tossed it in. A couple of thunks later, and the bottle had not broken. She contemplated for just a moment going into the Dumpster and retrieving the bottle, but stopped herself before she did.

There was a stand of trees behind the building, and Lena walked over, her feet still feeling as if they were asleep. She bent over and made herself vomit. The alcohol was bitter coming up, and the taste made her sicker than she would have thought possible. By the end, she was on her knees, dry heaving, much as she had been in the car with Hank.

Hank, Lena thought, making herself stand. She was so angry with him that she thought just for a moment about driving into Reece, to the Hut, and confronting him. He had said four months ago that he would stay with Lena as long as she needed him. Where the hell was he now? Probably at some damn A.A. meeting talking about how worried he was about his niece, talking about how much he wanted to support her instead of actually being here and supporting her.

The Celica turned over with a rewarding purr, and Lena gassed the car, thinking just for a moment about letting off on the brake and smashing into the front windows of the Piggly Wiggly. The impulse was surprising, but not completely unexpected. A sense of worthlessness was taking over, and Lena was not fighting it. Even after throwing up the alcohol, her brain was still buzzing, and it was as if her barriers had been broken down, and her mind was letting her think about things that she did not really want to think about.

She was thinking about *him*.

The drive home was dicey, Lena crossing the yellow line more often than not. She nearly ran into the shed behind her house, the brakes squealing on the drive as she slammed them on at the last minute. She sat in the car, looking at the dark house. Hank had not even bothered to turn on the back porch light.

Lena reached over and unlocked the glove box. She pulled out her service revolver and chambered a round. The clicking sound from the bolt action was solid in her ears, and for some reason Lena found herself looking at the gun in a different light. She stared at the black metal casing, even sniffed the grip. Before she knew it, she had put the muzzle in her mouth, her finger resting on the trigger.

Lena had seen a girl do this before. The woman had put the gun right into her mouth and almost without hesitation pulled the trigger because she had seen this as the only way to get the memories out of her brain. The aftershock of the single shot to the head still reverberated to Lena, and what she remembered most of all from that day was that parts of the woman's brain and skull had actually dug into the Sheetrock on the wall behind her.

Lena sat in the car, breathing slowly, feeling the cold metal against her lips. She pressed her tongue against the barrel as she considered the situation. Who would find her? Would Hank come home early? Brad, she thought, because Brad was supposed to pick her up for work in the morning. What would he think, seeing Lena like this? What would that do to Brad to see Lena in her car with the back of her head blown out? Was he strong enough to handle it? Could Brad Stephens go on with his life, with his job, after finding Lena like that?

"No," Lena said. She ejected the clip and kicked out the chambered round, then locked all of it back in the glove box.

She got out of the car quickly, jogging up the stairs to the back porch. Her hands were steady as she unlocked the door and turned on the kitchen light. Lena walked through the house, turning on all the lights as she went. She took the steps upstairs two at a time, turning on more lights. By the time she was finished, the house was completely lit up.

Of course, with the lights on, anyone could look through the windows and see her. Lena reversed her steps, turning off the lights as she ran down the stairs. She could have pulled the curtains and closed the blinds, but there was something rewarding about moving, getting her heart pumping. She had not been to the gym in months, but her muscles remembered the movements.

When she had left the hospital, the doctors had given Lena enough pain medication to kill a horse. It was as if they wanted to give her as much medication as humanly possible to numb her. They had probably thought it would be easier on her to be medicated than to consider what had happened to her. The hospital shrink they had made Lena talk to even offered to give her Xanax.

Lena ran back upstairs and opened the medicine cabinet in her bathroom. Alongside the usual things were a half bottle of Darvocet and a full bottle of Flexeril. The Darvocet was for pain, but the Flexeril was a heavy-duty muscle relaxer that had knocked Lena on her ass the first time she had taken it. She had stopped taking them because at the time it was more important for her to stay alert than not to feel the pain.

Lena read the labels on the bottles, looking past the warnings to take the medications with food and not operate heavy machinery. There were at least twenty Darvocet and twice as many Flexeril. She turned on the faucet, letting the cold water run for a while. Her hand was perfectly steady as she took the cup out of its holder and filled it nearly to the brim.

"So," Lena mumbled, looking at the clear water, thinking she should say something important or poignant about her life. There was no one to hear her words, though, so it seemed silly to be talking to herself at this point. She had never really believed in God, so it wasn't as if Lena expected to meet up with Sibyl in the great hereafter. There would be no streets of gold for her to walk on. Not that Lena was well-versed in religious doctrine, but she was pretty sure that anyone who committed suicide, no matter what the religion, was pretty fucked as far as heaven was concerned.

Lena sat down on the toilet, considering this. For just a brief moment, she wondered whether or not she was still drunk. Certainly, she would not be contemplating such an act if she were sober. Would she?

Lena looked around the bathroom, which had never been her favorite room in the house. The tiles were orange with white grout, a popular color scheme when the house had been built in the seventies, but now was tacky. She had tried to compensate for the color by adding other colors: a dark-blue bathmat by the tub, a dark-green cover for the box of Kleenex on the back of the toilet. The towels tied the colors together, but not in a pleasing way. Nothing had helped the room. It seemed appropriate, then, that she would die here.

Lena opened the bottles and spread the pills out on the vanity. The Darvocet were large, but the Flexeril were more like little breath mints. Moving them around with her index finger, she alternated the big pills with the little pills, then moved them all back into their own separate piles. She sipped some of the water as she did this, and realized that to some degree she was playing.

"Okay," Lena said. "This one is for Sibby." She opened her mouth and popped in one of the Darvocets.

"To Hank," she said, chasing it with a Flexeril. Then, because they were small, she popped two more Flexeril, followed by two Darvocet. She did not swallow yet, though. Lena wanted to take them all at the same time, and there was one more person she felt the need to recognize.

Her mouth was so full that when she said his name, the sound was muffled.

"These are for you," she mumbled, scooping the remaining Flexeril into the palm of her hand. "These are for you, you fucking bastard."

She shoved the handful into her mouth, tilting back her head. She stopped midtilt, staring at Hank in the doorway. They were both quiet, their eyes locked on to each other's. He stood there with his arms crossed, his lips a firm line.

"Do it," he finally said.

Lena sat there on the toilet, holding the pills in her mouth. Some of them had started to break down, and she could taste an acrid, powdery paste forming at the back of her mouth.

"I won't call an ambulance, if that's what you're thinking." He gave a tight shrug. "Go ahead and do it if that's what you want to do."

Lena felt her tongue going numb.

"You scared?" Hank asked. "Too scared to pull the trigger, too scared to swallow the pills?"

Her eyes watered from the taste in her mouth, but she still did not swallow. Lena felt frozen. How long had he been watching her? Was this some kind of test she had failed?

"Go on!" Hank yelled, his voice so loud that it echoed against the tiles.

Lena's mouth opened, and she started to spit out the pills

into her hand but Hank stopped her. He crossed the small bathroom in two steps and clamped his hands around her head, one over her mouth, the other behind her so that she could not pull away. Lena dug her nails into his flesh, trying to pull his hand from her mouth, but he was too strong for her. She fell forward off the toilet, onto her knees, but he moved down with her, keeping her head locked between his hands.

"Swallow them," Hank ordered, his voice gravelly and low. "That's what you want to do, swallow them!"

She started to shake her head back and forth, trying to tell him no, that she did not want to do this, that she could not do this. Some of the pills started to slide down her throat, and she constricted the muscles in her neck to stop them. Her heart was beating so hard that she thought it might explode.

"No?" Hank demanded. "No?"

Lena kept shaking her head, digging at his hand to release her. He finally let go, and she fell back against the tub, her head popping against the edge.

Hank threw open the toilet lid and half grabbed, half dragged her toward it. He pushed her head down into the bowl and she finally opened her mouth, gagging, spitting the pills out. Retching sounds echoed back at her until her mouth was empty. She used her fingers to clean around her gums and then used her nails, scraping at her tongue to get the taste out.

Hank stood, and when she looked up at him she could tell that he was pissed as hell.

"You bastard," she hissed, wiping her mouth with the back of her hand.

His foot moved, and she thought he was going to kick her. Lena curled, anticipating the blow, but it did not come.

"Get cleaned up," Hank ordered. With an open palm, he

swept the remaining pills off the basin and onto the floor. "Clean up this shit."

Lena moved to do as she was told, walking on her hands and knees, collecting the Darvocet.

Hank leaned against the wall, his arms crossed over his chest. His voice was softer now, and she looked up at him, surprised to see that there were tears in his eyes. "If you ever do that again . . . ," he began, then looked away. He put his hand over his mouth as if to fight back the words. "You're all I got, baby."

Lena was crying now, too. She said, "I know, Hank."

"Don't . . . ," he began.

Lena asked, "Don't what?"

He slid down the wall, sitting on the floor with his hands to his side. He stared at her openly, his eyes searching hers for something. "Don't leave me," he whispered, his words hanging in the air above them like a dark cloud.

The distance between them was only a few feet, but to Lena it felt like an endless chasm. She could reach out to him. She could thank him. She could promise him that she would never try this again.

She could have done any or all of those things, but what Lena ended up doing was picking up the pills off the floor one by one and throwing them into the toilet.

Tuesday

10

"Hold on, Sam," Sara coaxed, struggling to hold a wriggling two year old in her lap so that she could listen to his chest.

"Be still for Dr. Linton, Sammy," his mother said in a singsong voice.

"Sara?" Elliott Felteau, who worked at the clinic for Sara, poked his head into the room. She had hired Elliott right out of his residency to help her out, but so far Sara had spent most of her time holding his hand. It was a trade-off, because an older doctor would have insisted on some kind of partnership, and Sara was not about to relinquish her control. She had worked too hard to get to where she was to start listening to someone else's opinions.

"Sorry," Elliott apologized to the mother, then said to Sara, "Did you tell Tara Collins that Pat could play football this weekend? She needs a medical release before the school will let him back on the team."

Sara stood, taking Sam with her. His legs wrapped

around Sara's waist, and she scooted him up on her hip as she lowered her voice, asking Elliott, "Why is this question coming from you?"

"She called and asked for me," he told her. "Said she didn't want to bug you."

Sara tried to unclench Sam's fist as he tugged her hair. "No, he can't play this weekend," she whispered. "I told her that on Friday."

"It's just an exhibition game."

"He has a concussion," Sara countered, the tone of her voice a warning to Elliot.

"Hmm," Elliott said, backing out of the room. "I guess she thought I'd be an easier target."

Sara took a deep, calming breath, then turned back around. "Sorry about that," she said, sitting down in the chair. Thankfully, Sam had stopped fidgeting, and she was able to listen to his chest.

"Pat Collins is their star quarterback," the mother said. "You're not going to let him play?"

Sara avoided the question. "His lungs seem clear," she told the woman. "Make sure he finishes his antibiotics, though."

She started to hand the child back to his mother, but stopped. Sara lifted up Sam's shirt and checked his chest, then his back.

"Is something wrong?"

Sara shook her head no. "He's fine," she told the woman, and the boy was. There was no reason to suspect abuse. Of course, Sara had thought the same thing with Jenny Weaver.

Sara walked to the pocket door and slid it open. Molly Stoddard, her nurse, was at the nurses' station writing out a lab request. Sara waited until she was finished, then dictated Sam's directions.

"Make sure I follow up," Sara told her.

Molly nodded, still writing. "You doing all right today?"

Sara thought about it, and decided that no, she was not doing all right. She was actually pretty on edge, and had been since her confrontation with Lena yesterday afternoon. She felt guilty, and ashamed of herself for letting her temper get the better of her. Lena had been doing her job, no matter what Sara thought about it. It was unprofessional to question the young detective, especially in front of Jeffrey. On top of that, what Sara had said was not only inexcusable, it was just plain mean. Sara was not the kind of person who liked to be mean. It was not in her nature to attack, and the more Sara thought about it, the more she believed that she *had* attacked Lena. Of all people, Sara should have known better.

"Hello?" Molly prompted. "Sara?"

"Yes?" Sara said, then, "Oh, I'm sorry. I'm just . . ." She nodded toward her office so that they could get out of the hallway.

Molly let Sara go first, then slid the door closed behind her. Molly Stoddard was a compact woman with what could be called a handsome face. In great contrast to Sara, the nurse was always neatly dressed, her white uniform starched to within an inch of its life. The only jewelry Molly wore was a thin silver necklace that she kept tucked into the collar of her uniform. The smartest thing Sara had ever done was hire Molly as her nurse, but some days Sara felt tempted to snatch off the woman's hat and ruffle her hair, or accidentally spill ink on her perfect uniform.

"You've got about five minutes before your next appointment," Molly told her. "What's wrong?"

Sara leaned her back against the wall, tucking her hands into her white lab coat. "Did we miss something?" she said, then amended, "Did *I* miss something?"

"Weaver?" Molly asked, though Sara could tell from her reaction that the other woman knew. "I've been asking myself that same question, and the answer is I don't know."

"Who would do that?" Sara asked, then realized Molly had no idea what she was talking about. The physical findings from the autopsy were hardly public, and even though Sara trusted Molly, she did not feel like she was in a position to share the details. Molly probably would not want to hear them.

"Kids are hard to explain," Molly provided.

"I feel responsible," Sara told the nurse. "I feel like I should have been there for her. Or paid more attention."

"We see thirty to forty kids a day, six days a week."

"You make it sound like an assembly line."

Molly shrugged. "Maybe it is," she said. "We do what we can do. We take care of them, we give them their medicine, we listen to their problems. What else is there?"

"Treat 'em and street 'em," Sara mumbled, remembering the phrase from her E.R. days.

Molly said, "It's what we do."

"I didn't come back here to work like this," Sara said. "I wanted to make a difference."

"And you do, Sara," Molly assured her. She stepped closer, putting her hand on Sara's arm. "Listen, honey, I know what you're going through, and I'm telling you that I see you here every day, putting your heart and soul into this job." She waited a beat. "You're forgetting what Dr. Barney was like. Now, there was an assembly line."

"He was always good to me," Sara countered.

"Because he liked you," Molly said. "And for every kid he liked, there were ten he couldn't stand, and toward the end he passed the ones he hated on to you."

Sara shook her head, not accepting this. "He didn't do that."

"Sara," Molly insisted, "ask Nelly. She's been here longer than I have."

"So, that's my standard? That I'm better than Dr. Barney?"

"Your standard is you treat all the kids the same. You don't play favorites." Molly indicated the pictures on the wall. "How many kids did Dr. Barney have on his walls?"

Sara shrugged, though she knew the answer to that. None.

"You're being too hard on yourself," Molly said. "And it's not going to accomplish anything."

"I just want to be more careful from now on," Sara told her. "Maybe we can cut the schedule so I can spend more time with each patient."

Molly snorted a laugh. "We barely have enough time in the day to see the appointments we have now. Between that and the morgue—"

Sara stopped her. "Maybe I should quit the morgue."

"Maybe you should hire another doctor?" Molly suggested.

Sara tapped her head against the wall, thinking. "I don't know."

The door shook as someone knocked on it.

"If that's Elliott . . . ," Sara began, but it was not. Nelly, the office manager at the clinic since before Sara was born, slid open the door.

"Nick Shelton's on the phone," Nelly said. "Want me to take a message?"

Sara shook her head. "I'll take it," she answered, then waited for Molly to leave before picking up the phone.

"Hello, sunshine," Nick said, his south Georgia drawl clear across the line.

Sara allowed a smile. "Hey, Nick."

"I wish I had time to flirt," he told her. "But I gotta meeting in about ten seconds. Real quick, though," he began, and she could hear him shuffling papers. "Nothing current came up on female castration, at least, not in the United States. But I'm sure you're not surprised to hear that."

"No," Sara agreed. Something so volatile would have certainly ended up in the press.

"A few years ago in France, a woman was tried for performing over fifty procedures. I think she was originally from Africa."

Sara shook her head, wondering how a woman could do this to a child.

Nick said, "Hey, what do you already know about this?"

"Infibulation falls under the general heading of F.G.M.," she said, using the acronym for female genital mutilation. "It's sometimes practiced in the Middle East and parts of Africa. It's tied somehow to religion."

"Well, about as much as suicide missions are tied to religion," Nick corrected. "You can make a religious justification for just about anything these days."

Sara made a noise of agreement.

"Mostly, it's a custom passed down from village to village. The more uneducated the group, the more likely they are to do it. There isn't a real good religious argument to justify it, but the men over there like the idea of making sure their women don't stray."

"So they make it impossible for them to enjoy sex. Perfect solution. If this was happening to men over there, Africa and the rest of the Middle East would be an empty crater."

Nick was silent, and Sara felt guilty for painting him with the same brush. "I'm sorry, Nick. It's just—"

"You don't have to explain it to me, Sara," he offered in a soft tone.

She waited a beat, then asked, "What else?"

"Well," he began, and she could hear him shuffling through his notes. "After the procedure, they usually bind the legs together to promote healing." He paused as if to catch his breath. "In a lot of cases, they sew them shut, you know, like your girl was, and leave an opening for her time of the month."

"I read about that," Sara confirmed. She also knew that women in the village who weren't mutilated were not considered marriage material.

"The thread you pulled from the area looks common. I've sent samples to the lab, but they're pretty certain you can find it in any Kmart." He made a thinking noise. "You think whoever did this has some kind of medical experience?"

"Are you looking at the photographs?"

"Yep," he answered. "Looks kind of elementary, but not half-assed."

"I agree," she told him, thinking that whoever had sewn the girl up was probably good with a needle and thread.

"I read this statistic," he said. "A lot of the girls die from shock. They don't exactly anesthetize them, if you know what I mean. Most times they use a piece of broken glass to perform the procedure."

Sara shuddered, but tried to maintain her composure. "Any idea why someone would do this here?"

"You mean someone who's not part of an immigrant population?" he asked, but didn't let her answer. "Over there they do it to make sure a girl stays pure. Usually, the husband opens her up on their wedding night."

"Purity," Sara said, focusing on the word. Jenny Weaver had used it with her mother.

Nick asked, "Was she a virgin?"

"No," Sara answered. "Judging from the size of the vaginal orifice as compared to the urinary meatus, she was sexually active well before the castration. Probably with a number of partners."

"You check her for any STDs?"

"Yes," Sara said. "She came back negative."

"Well, it was worth a shot."

"Anything else?"

Nick was quiet for a few beats, then asked, "You talking to Jeffrey this week?"

Sara felt a bit embarrassed, but said, "Yes."

"Tell him that drawing he sent didn't come up on our computers. We faxed it up to the FBI for a run-through, but you know they'll take their time."

"What's the drawing?" Sara asked.

"Some tattoo. I dunno. He said it was on the webbing between the thumb and pointer finger."

"I'll tell him."

"Over dinner?"

Sara laughed. "What are you getting at, Nick?"

"If you're not busy, I'm gonna be down in your neck of the woods this weekend."

Sara smiled. Nick had asked her out several times before, mostly as a courtesy. He was about six inches shorter than Sara and wore more gold jewelry than any man ought to be allowed. She doubted very seriously that he thought he had a chance in hell with her, but Nick was the kind of man who liked to leave no stone unturned.

She told him, "I guess I'm seeing Jeffrey again."

"You guess?"

"I mean," she paused. "Yes, we're dating again."

He took the refusal good-naturedly, as usual. "Can't blame an old boy for trying."

After they said their good-byes, Sara stayed in her chair, thinking about what Nick had told her. There had to be some connection between Jenny's desire for purity and the castration. She was missing something, probably something very obvious. What would make a girl feel unclean, Sara wondered. Unfortunately, the only thing she could come up with was sex. Jenny Weaver had certainly been active. Maybe the guilt from her sexual promiscuity had been too much for Jenny to bear.

Also, there was the greater question of who had performed the mutilation on Jenny. It wasn't as if the girl could do it to herself. She would pass out from the shock or the pain before it was completed. There had to be another person involved, someone who could do the cutting and sewing. Perhaps Jenny had drunk until she passed out, or bought pain killers or muscle relaxers from someone at the school. A veritable pharmacy existed at the high school. Anyone with the right money could practically stock an operating room.

Nelly slid open the door, saying, "The Patterson kid is here." Then added, "Without the mother," in a hushed whisper.

Sara glanced at her watch. Mark was supposed to have been in yesterday morning. His dropping by today would throw her whole schedule out of whack. "Put him in six," she said. "Tell him he'll have to wait."

"Him?" Nelly asked. "It's Lacey, the girl."

Sara sat up in her chair. "Did she say why she's here?"

"Just that she's not feeling well," Nelly answered, then whispered again, "She doesn't look well, if you ask me."

Sara whispered, "Why are you whispering?"

Nelly allowed a smile, walking into the office. She closed the door, saying, "She's acting strange. She's not with her mother."

Sara felt the hair on the back of her neck rise. "How long has she been waiting?"

"Not long," Nelly answered. "Put her in six?"

Sara nodded, a sinking feeling in her stomach. She picked up the phone to dial Jeffrey's number, then changed her mind. Lacey had come to the clinic because she trusted Sara, and Sara would not betray that confidence. At the very least, the girl needed help. Whatever laws she had broken could be dealt with after Sara made sure she was okay.

Exam six was in the back of the building, at the end of the L-shaped hallway. Normally, it was reserved for very sick children or used as a waiting room for parents while Sara talked to their kids about sex, or birth control, or whatever things they felt they needed to talk to their pediatrician about in private. Sara supposed Molly had stuck Lacey back here to win the girl's trust. Kids did not just show up at the clinic without their parents, even the ones who could drive themselves.

Molly was waiting by the closed exam room door when Sara turned the corner.

She handed Lacey Patterson's chart to Sara outside the exam room, saying, "I'll be in two if you need me."

Sara flipped open the chart to review her notes from Lacey's last visit, even though Sara had looked at the chart just a few days ago. Two months ago, the girl had presented with what appeared to be strep throat. Sara had started her on antibiotics, pending the lab results. Sara thumbed through the chart, but the pink sheet the lab usually sent was not in there. She was about to find Molly when she noticed a noise coming from behind the exam door.

"Lacey?" Sara asked, sliding back the door. "Are you—" She stopped midsentence, thinking that the last time she had seen someone so pale was in the morgue. The girl was sitting in the chair by the exam table, her arms wrapped across her stomach. Despite the weather she was wearing a neon-yellow raincoat. She was doubled over, her arms wrapped around her stomach as if in pain.

Sara put her hand on the girl's back, surprised at how clammy it felt through the coat.

Lacey's teeth were chattering, but she managed to say, "I need to talk to you."

"Come here," Sara said, helping her stand. "Let's get you on the table."

Lacey hesitated, and Sara lifted her up onto the exam table.

"I don't . . . ," Lacey began, but she was shaking too hard to continue. Sara put her hand to the girl's forehead, wondering if Lacey was shaking from fear or from fever. As hot as it was outside, Sara could not tell the difference.

"Let's get this coat off," Sara suggested, but Lacey would not unwrap her arms from her waist.

"What happened?" Sara asked, trying to keep her voice steady. There was an electric charge in the room, as if something really bad had happened.

Lacey tilted forward, and Sara caught her before she fell off the table.

"I'm so sleepy," she said.

"Sit up for me a minute," Sara told her. She raised her voice, calling into the hallway, "Molly?"

"I'm not feeling well," the girl said.

Sara held her hands against Lacey's thin shoulders. "Where do you hurt?"

She opened her mouth to speak, vomiting all over Sara. Of course this had happened to Sara before, and she stepped back, but not in time to keep from getting splattered.

After her sickness subsided, Lacey murmured, "I'm sorry."

"It's okay, sweetie," Sara told her.

"My stomach hurts."

"You're okay," Sara told her. Holding Lacey up with one hand, she stretched toward the paper towel dispenser and gave the girl some cloths.

"I feel sick."

Sara raised her voice again, this time louder than before. "Molly?" she called, knowing that it was futile. Exam two was on the other side of the building.

"Lie back," Sara told Lacey. "If you get sick, turn to the side."

"Don't leave me!" the girl cried, holding on to Sara's hand. "Please, Dr. Linton, I gotta talk to you. I gotta tell you what happened."

Sara could guess what happened, but there were more important things right now than hearing the girl's confession.

"I gotta tell you," the girl repeated.

"About the baby?" Sara guessed. She could tell from Lacey's expression that her guess was right. Sara felt stupid for not having figured it out before. She said, "I know, sweetie. I know. Just lie down and I'll be right back."

The girl's body tensed. "How do you know?"

"Lie down," Sara told her. Thinking this would soothe her, Sara offered, "I'll go call your mom."

Lacey bolted upright. "You can't tell my mom."

"Don't worry about that now."

"You can't tell her," Lacey insisted, tears streaming down her face. "She's sick. She's real sick."

Sara did not understand what the girl meant, but she soothed her anyway. "It's going to be okay."

"Promise me you won't tell her."

Sara said, "Honey, we'll worry about that later."

"No!" she yelled, gripping Sara's arm. "You can't tell my mom. Please. Please don't tell her."

"Stay right here," Sara ordered. "I'll be right back."

She did not wait for an answer. Sara stepped into the

hallway, slipping off her soiled lab coat as she walked toward the nurses' station.

Nelly asked, "What happened?"

"Call an ambulance," Sara said, tossing her coat into the dirty linen bin. She leaned back, looking around the corner to make sure Lacey had not left the room. "Get Molly in six right now, and then call Frank over at the police station."

"Oh, my," Nelly mumbled, picking up the phone.

Elliot came out of one of the exam rooms. "Hey, Sara?" he asked. "I've got a six year old with—"

"Not now," Sara told him, holding up her hand. With a glance down the hallway, she went into her office and dialed Jeffrey's cell phone. She let it ring four times before hanging up. Next, she dialed the station.

Marla Simms answered. "Grant County Police Station. How may I help you?"

"Marla," Sara said. "Find Jeffrey, send him over to the clinic right now."

A banging noise echoed up the hallway, and Sara mumbled a curse as she recognized the sound of the back door popping open.

Marla said, "Sara?"

Sara slammed down the phone and ran out into the hallway, prepared to chase after Lacey. What she saw stopped her cold. Mark Patterson stood at the end of the hall, every muscle in his body tensed. There was a cut across his abdomen that stained his blue shirt to a dark purple, and his jeans were torn at the knee as if he had skidded across asphalt.

"Lacey?" he screamed, sliding open the first door he came to.

Sara heard a shocked gasp from the mother of the patient in the room, followed by the wails of a frightened child.

"Sara?" Nelly asked. She was standing at the nurse's station with the telephone in her hand.

Sara said, "Call the station. Tell them to send whoever they can."

"Lacey?" Mark repeated, his voice vibrating through the hallway. Thankfully, he had not noticed the tail end of the hall and the two exam rooms off to the side.

He came closer, and Sara could see that his clothes were stained and dirty-looking. Flecks of white paint covered everything. His hair looked greasy and was uncombed, as if he had not bathed in a while. Sara had seen Mark many times over the last decade, but she had never seen him looking so unclean.

"Goddamn it!" Mark screamed, throwing his hands into the air. "Where's my fucking sister?"

A couple of doors behind Sara slid open, and she turned, signaling for the parents to stay inside.

Molly stood beside Sara, holding a chart to her chest. It was the first time Sara had ever seen the nurse shocked by anything that happened in the clinic.

"Mark," Sara said, putting some authority into her tone. "What are you doing here?"

"Where's Lacey?" he said, slamming his hand into the next door. The panel shook on its slider, and Sara could hear a child screaming behind it.

Nelly's voice was muffled as she talked to someone on the phone. Sara could not make out the conversation, but she hoped to God they were sending somebody.

"Mark," Sara began, trying to keep her voice calm. "Stop this. She's not here."

"The hell she's not," he countered, taking a step toward her. "Where is that little cunt?" He slammed his hand against the door again, punching an impression into the wood. Nelly screamed and ducked behind the counter.

"Where is she?" he demanded.

Sara purposefully made what she hoped was a nervous glance toward her office. Mark picked up on it immediately.

"Aha," he said. "She in there?"

"No," Sara told him.

He smiled, stepping closer to her. Sara could see that his pupils were as small as pinpricks, and guessed that whatever he was on was not about to dissipate any time soon. Up close, he seemed to be giving off an odor. Sara was not certain, but the smell reminded her of chemicals.

She asked, "What are you on, Mark?"

"I'm about to be on my fucking sister if she doesn't keep her fucking mouth shut."

"She's not here," Sara told him.

"Lace?" Mark said, craning his head around the office door. "You better get the fuck out here right now."

Sara caught movement out of the corner of her eye. She knew from the neon-yellow blur that it was Lacey, trying to make her way out the back door. A cold sweat chilled Sara as she calculated how long it would take for Lacey to make it to the exit. She stared at Mark, willing Lacey to hurry, but the girl was not moving. She was standing stock still as if someone had pinned her to the wall.

"She in there?" Mark asked.

"No," Sara said, looking over his shoulder. "She's behind you."

Lacey's hand went to her mouth as if to stop herself from screaming.

"Right," Mark said, giving Sara a scathing look.

"I want you out of here right now, Mark. You're trespassing."

He ignored her, walking into the office. Sara followed him at a distance, trying to be casual about the fact that she was trapping him in the room. She prayed that Marla had gotten hold of someone, even if it was Brad Stephens.

"Lacey?" Mark said, his voice softer, but in a more menacing way than before. He walked around the desk. "It's only gonna be worse if you don't come out now."

Sara crossed her arms. "What's purity, Mark?"

Mark looked under the desk, cursing when he found it empty. He kicked it, moving the steel desk across the floor a couple of inches.

"Did you make Jenny feel dirty? Is that why she wanted to make herself pure?"

"Get out of my way," he ordered, walking toward Sara.

She put her hand on the door, blocking his exit.

"Get out of the way."

"What's purity?"

He looked like he might answer, but Sara realized too late he was just trying to throw her off guard. The next thing she knew, she was being pushed back, and hard. She fell into the hall, whacking her head on the floor.

"Sara!" Molly said, running around to help her.

"I'm okay," Sara managed, trying to sit up. She looked down the hallway and saw that Lacey was still there about the same time that Mark did.

"Run!" Sara told her. Lacey hesitated, but finally seemed to understand she needed to get out of here. She ran to the door and slammed it open.

"Bitch," Mark yelled, taking after her.

Without thinking, Sara reached out and grabbed at Mark's foot. He tried to yank it away, but she caught the leg of his pants in her fist.

"Stop it," Sara said, trying to hold on.

He reached down, hitting at her hand with his fist. When this did not work, he punched at her face. Sara saw the glint of the red stone in his ring before the first blow caught her on the forehead, and she was so surprised that she let go.

"Oh, my God," Molly breathed, putting her hand to her mouth.

"Crap," Sara hissed, touching her forehead. Mark's ring had caught her right at the temple. She looked at the blood on her fingers, but then thought of Lacey and made herself stand.

Molly began, "Maybe you should—"

Sara took off after Mark and Lacey, shouting, "Where the hell is Jeffrey?" over her shoulder.

Sara stopped outside the back door, trying to get her bearings. The sun was beating down, and Sara shielded her eyes as she tried to spot Lacey in the trees behind the building.

"Did they go around front?" Molly asked, jogging toward the side of the clinic. Sara followed her, bumping into the nurse as she turned the corner.

Molly was pointing to the road. "There she is."

They both took off at the same time, but Sara's stride was longer, and she soon left Molly behind. The road in front of the clinic was hardly a busy thoroughfare, but at lunchtime the professors and students left campus to come into town. Sara watched as Lacey ran into the street, Mark right behind her, screaming at the top of his lungs.

Somehow, they both made it across the road. Lacey ran toward the lake, but Sara watched as another figure, a blur, really, came from the side and tackled Mark to the ground. By the time Sara and Molly crossed the street, Lena Adams was straddling Mark's back like a rodeo rider as she jerked his arms behind him and cuffed his wrists.

"Oh, shit," Lena said, looking up the street.

Lacey was too far away for Sara to recognize her by any other means than the bright yellow raincoat. Sara stood helpless, watching as an old black car stopped beside the girl. The passenger-side door swung open and an arm reached out, grabbing Lacey around the waist and pulling her inside the car.

Sara touched the bandage on her forehead as she got out of the car. Molly had sewn in two sutures, then canceled the rest of Sara's appointments so that she could have some downtime in order to recover from the ordeal at the clinic. Sara's head hurt, and she was hot and irritable. She might as well have stayed at the clinic and seen patients, but Molly had not really given her a choice. Maybe the nurse was right. Every time Sara thought about what had happened at the clinic, she felt as if a band were being tightened around her chest. Knowing another one of her kids was in jeopardy and that there was absolutely nothing she could do made Sara want to put her head on her mother's shoulder and cry.

"Mama?" Sara called, kicking off her shoes as she closed the front door behind her. There was no answer, and Sara walked back to the kitchen, asking, "Mama?" again.

There was still no answer, and Sara felt her heart sink. She filled a glass with water and finished it all in several gulps, then wiped her mouth with the back of her hand.

Sara flopped onto the kitchen stool and picked up the phone, dialing Jeffrey's number. Lena had taken Mark off to the station before Sara had thought to ask her where he was.

"Tolliver," he answered, and she could tell from the hollow echo of his voice that he was in his car.

"Where are you?" she asked.

"I got caught up in Alabama for a while," he told her. "I talked to Lena. She told me about Lacey. You didn't get a look at who was in the car?"

"No," Sara answered. "Did you talk to her parents?"

"Frank's with them now. They don't know anybody who drives a car like that."

"What has Mark said?"

"He won't talk to anybody," Jeffrey told her. "Not even Lena."

"Who would want to kidnap her?"

"I don't know," Jeffrey said. "We've put out an A.P.B. all over the state. I want to talk to Mark and see if we can find anything out."

"I feel like we're missing something big here," she said. "Something right under our noses."

"Yeah." He was quiet, and she could hear the engine rev in his car as he accelerated. He said, "Tell me what happened today. Beginning to end."

Sara took a deep breath, then told him. The part Jeffrey seemed to focus on most was Mark hitting her, probably because it was the only thing he knew he could take care of.

"What did he hit you with?" he asked, his tone sharp.

"His ring," she said, then amended, "His fist, really, but his ring did most of the damage. He wasn't really hitting hard. He just wanted me to turn him loose." She put her fingers to the bandage. "It's not bad."

"Lena wrote him up on assault?"

"Probably," Sara answered, letting him know he should drop it.

He got the hint. "Did it look like Lacey knew the people in the car?"

"It was so far away, Jeffrey. I don't know. I wouldn't have even known it was her except for the bright-yellow coat she was wearing."

"Lena knew the car. Some of the kids from school had seen Jenny Weaver get into it."

Sara played with the cord of the phone as he told her what Lena had learned at the high school. When he was finished, all she could say was, "That doesn't sound like the Jenny I knew."

"I'm beginning to think nobody really knew her."

She said what had been nagging in the back of her mind all along. "Do you think Mark and Lacey are the parents?" she asked. "I mean, I know that's why you wanted the sample on Mark, but it never occurred to me that . . ."

"I know," he said. She could tell from the quick way he answered her that Jeffrey had been thinking about this for a while. "I think it's possible."

She asked, "What was your reading on Teddy Patterson?"

"Possible there, too."

"I doubt he'll submit to a test without an order."

"You got that right."

Sara sighed, wondering how all of this fit together. "Maybe Jenny found out and was jealous?"

"Could be," he said, and she could tell he was concentrating on something else.

"Jeff . . . ," Sara began, not knowing how to broach the subject without making him angry. "Mark was cut across his abdomen. It wasn't bad, but I think someone probably tried to hurt him."

"Good."

"No," she stopped him. "He's a kid. Promise me you won't forget that."

"A kid who may have raped his sister and pimped out her friend," he said. "A kid who punched you in the face."

"Forget about me," Sara told him. "I mean it, Jeffrey. Don't make it about me."

He said something under his breath.

"Jeff?"

He asked, "You didn't get any more information out of her?"

"She seemed disoriented, and terrified."

"Do you think she's seriously ill?"

"I don't know if it's fear or shock or if she's recovering from giving birth. I didn't get to spend much time with her. I . . ."

"What?"

"I feel responsible for not looking out for her. She was in my clinic. If I'd been able to keep her there—"

"She ran away, Sara. You did what you could do."

She pressed her lips together. "I wish that made me feel better."

"I wish it did, too," he said. "I wish I could tell you how to get rid of the guilt, because I sure as hell don't know."

Sara felt tears well into her eyes. She put her hand to her mouth so that Jeffrey could not hear her cry.

"Sara?"

She cleared her throat, wiping under her eyes with her free hand. She sniffed, because her nose was running. "Yes?"

Jeffrey said, "Was there anything else Lacey said? Maybe something about Mark, why he was after her?"

Sara bristled, because asking her the same questions over again wouldn't get them any closer to finding Lacey Patterson. "Stop questioning me. I've had a bad enough day without getting the third degree from you."

He was silent, and she could hear the engine accelerate again.

Sara closed her eyes and leaned her head back against the wall, waiting for him to speak.

"I just . . ." He stopped, then, "I gotta tell you, the idea of somebody hurting you really pisses me off."

She laughed. "Me, too."

"Are you all right?" he asked again.

"Yeah," she said, though she was feeling very unsettled. The clinic had always been a safe place for Sara, and she did not like the fact that her work at the morgue had somehow seeped into her private practice. She felt vulnerable, and she did not like that.

"Nick called," she told Jeffrey, then explained to him what Nick had said.

"Purity?" Jeffrey repeated. "That's what Jenny said."

"Right," Sara agreed. "I think it all goes back to sex. She wanted to be clean again, right?"

"Right."

"So what made her feel unclean?"

"Banging all those guys at the party might have done it."

"She was drunk," Sara reminded him, feeling anger stirring deep inside of her.

"They say she wasn't too drunk to know what she was doing."

"Of course they said that. What else would they say, that they raped her?"

He cleared his throat. "That's a point."

"Why else would she do what she did?" Sara demanded. "Jenny wasn't like that. She was just a little girl, for Christ's sake."

Jeffrey's tone was indulgent. "We don't know exactly what happened, Sara. We probably never will."

Sara changed the subject, knowing she could not have a logical conversation with him about this right now. "Nick sent that tattoo to the FBI. Nothing kicked out on their database."

"That's actually what held me up," Jeffrey told her. "I'll tell you about it tonight."

"No," she said. "Tell me about it tomorrow."

He was silent, then, "I thought you wanted to see me tonight?"

"Yes," Sara assured him. "I do, but not to talk business." She waited a few beats. "I need to not think about this tonight. Okay?"

"Okay," he agreed. "As long as I still get to see you."

"If you can stand it," she said, trying to make light of it. "I've got a big green Band-Aid on my head."

"Does it hurt?"

"Mmm," she mumbled, looking out the window. She saw her mother walking up the steps to Tessa's garage apartment.

"Sara?"

Sara turned back to the conversation. "I'm counting on you to help me take my mind off of it."

He laughed at this, and seemed pleased. "I've got to talk to Mark and do a quick briefing with evening patrol about looking for Lacey. Not that there's much any of us can do tonight. I'll be there as soon as I can, okay?"

"You think it'll be late?"

"Probably," he said. "You want me to let you sleep?"

"No," she told him. "Wake me."

She could almost hear him smiling. "I'll see you then."

"Okay," she answered, then hung up the phone.

Sara got another glass of water before going outside. The pavement was hot as white coals against her bare feet, and she tiptoed the last couple of yards to get to the stairs.

Tessa's apartment was large, with two bedrooms and two baths. She had painted the walls in primary colors and accented these with comfortable chairs and a roomy couch that tended to make the occupant want to take a long nap. Sara had often slept over at Tessa's, especially after the divorce, because she felt safer at the time being here than being in her own home.

"Tessie?" Sara called, trying not to let the screen door slam behind her. Cathy had left the wooden door wide open, which seemed odd since the air was on.

Tessa's voice seemed strained. "Just a minute."

Sara walked back to her sister's bedroom, wondering

what was going on. "Tess?" she said, stopping in the doorway.

Tessa was holding a tissue to her nose, and she did not look up when Sara came into the room. Cathy was beside her, arms crossed over her chest.

"What happened?" Sara asked at the same time Cathy did.

"What?" they both said.

Sara pointed to her sister. "What's wrong with you? Why are you crying?"

Cathy walked over to Sara and put her hand to Sara's head. "Did you hurt yourself?"

"It's a long story," Sara said, waving away her mother's hand. "Tessie, what's wrong?"

Tessa shook her head no, and Sara found herself suddenly feeling dizzy. She sat on the bed, asking, "Is it Daddy?"

Cathy frowned. "Don't be silly. He's healthy as a horse."

Sara put her hand to her chest and let out a puff of air. "Then, what's the matter?"

Tessa walked over to her dresser and picked up a long piece of white plastic. Sara recognized the pregnancy test stick before her sister handed it to her.

Sara could not think what to say, so she said, "You're supposed to do these early in the morning."

"I did," Tessa answered. "Then I did it again at lunch, and then again just now."

"All positive," Cathy said. Then, "I guess we can take her into the city next weekend."

"Into the city?" Sara asked, wondering why they would need to go to Atlanta. She figured it out soon enough, and shook her head no, not accepting this. "You're going to get an abortion?"

Tessa took back the test stick. "I don't really have a choice."

"That's not true," Sara snapped, standing. "Of course you have a choice."

"Sara," Cathy chided.

"Mother," Sara began, then, "Jesus Christ, Tess, you're thirty-three years old, you make a great living, you've got Devon so in love with you he can't see straight."

"What does that have to do with anything?" Tessa asked.

"It has everything to do with it," Sara told her.

"I'm not ready."

Sara felt so shocked that for a moment she could not speak. Finally, she asked, "Do you know what they do, Tessa? Do you know what the procedure entails? Do you know how they—?"

Tessa stopped her. "I know what an abortion is."

"How could you even think—?"

"Think what?" Tessa snapped, "Think that I'm not ready to have a baby? I can think that pretty easily, Sara. I'm not ready."

"Nobody's ever ready," Sara countered, trying not to yell. "How can you be so selfish?"

"Selfish?" Tessa asked, incredulous.

"All you're thinking about is yourself."

"I am not," Tessa shot back.

Sara put her hand over her eyes, not believing she was having this conversation. She dropped her hand, asking, "Do you know what they'll do? Do you know what will happen to the baby?"

Tessa turned away. "It's not even a baby yet."

Sara grabbed her sister's arm and turned her back around. "Look at me."

"Why? So you can try to talk me out of this?" Tessa asked. "This is my choice, Sara."

"What about Devon?" Sara asked. "What does he have to say?"

Tessa pursed her lips. "It's not his decision."

Sara knew what Tessa meant, but asked anyway, "What, you're not sure he's the father?"

"Sara," Cathy warned.

Sara kept her back to her mother. "Is he?"

"Of course he is," Tessa said, indignant.

Sara stared at her sister, trying to find something to say that would stop this. When she opened her mouth to speak, what came out surprised them all. She said, "I'll raise it."

Tessa shook her head no. "I couldn't do that."

"Why?"

"Sara," Tessa said, as if she was being obtuse on purpose. "I couldn't let you raise my child."

Sara tucked her hands into her hips, trying to keep her anger down. "That's just about the most immature thing I've ever heard you say. What, if you can't have it, no one will?"

Tessa's mouth opened and closed. "When did you become so self-righteous? I happen to remember a time when you were pretty pro-abortion."

Sara felt her cheeks turn red. She was very conscious that her mother was in the room. "Stop it."

"Oh, you don't want to tell Mama about the time you thought Steve Mann had knocked you up?"

Cathy kept silent, but Sara could feel that her mother was hurt. Cathy had always made it clear that her daughters could come to her with anything. And, except for this one time, Sara always had.

Sara tried to explain to her mother. "It was a false alarm. I was studying for finals. I was stressed out. My period was late."

Cathy held up her hand, telling Sara to stop.

"I was a teenager," Sara added, her voice weak. "My whole life was ahead of me."

Tessa said, "And the first thing you did was call the women's center in Atlanta to see how fast they could get rid of it."

Sara shook her head, knowing this was not true. The first thing she had done was burst into tears and tear up her acceptance letter from Emory. "That's not how it happened."

Tessa was not finished, and her next remark cut to the bone. "This is so easy for you because you know you'll never get pregnant."

"Tessa," Cathy hissed, but it was too late. The damage was done.

Sara's mouth formed an O but the word would not come out. She felt as if she had been slapped.

Cathy started to say something, but it was Sara's turn to hold up her hand.

"I can't do this right now," she said, because she could not. Sara could not ever remember a time when Tessa had hurt her so much, and she felt as if she had lost her best friend.

Without another word, Sara left Tessa's apartment, letting the screen door slam closed behind her.

11

Marla handed Jeffrey a stack of pink messages before he even had time to take off his jacket. He felt as if he had been gone for three months instead of twenty-four hours.

"This one's important," Marla said, pointing to one of the slips. "And this one, too." She kept going until she had identified all but one of the messages as important. Jeffrey glanced at the unimportant one. There was a man's name he did not recognize, followed by a one–eight hundred number.

"What's this about?"

Marla frowned as she obviously tried to remember. "Either vinyl siding or coffee service. I forget which one." She shrugged apologetically. "He said he'd call back."

Jeffrey balled up the message and tossed it into the trash, asking, "Is Lena around?"

"I'll fetch her," Marla said, backing out of the office.

Jeffrey sat at his desk and the first thing he saw was a missing poster of Lacey Patterson. She was a thin, boyish-looking girl with blonde hair like her mother. The photo was a school picture with an American flag in the background and a globe of the world in front. Her height and weight were under the photo, along with where she was last seen and a number people could call. The flyer had been faxed out to all the precincts in the area and put into the national database that tracked missing children. It would take time for the Georgia Bureau of Investigation to put together a packet to send to law enforcement all around the Southeast. If today was like every other day in America, Lacey Patterson's name had been keyed in along with a hundred other newly missing or abducted children.

Jeffrey picked up the phone and dialed Nick Shelton's number. When Nick answered, Jeffrey was somewhat surprised. The field agent was seldom at his desk.

"Nick? Jeffrey Tolliver."

"Hey, Chief," Nick said, his twangy good-old-boy drawl a bit jarring to Jeffrey's ears. Considering Jeffrey had spent the last twenty-four hours in central Alabama, this said a lot.

Jeffrey asked, "You riding a desk today?"

"Somebody's gotta take care of all this paperwork," Nick told him. "No word yet on your missing girl?"

"No," Jeffrey told him. "Anything on the state-wide alert?"

"Not a peep," Nick said. "It'd help if you had a license plate on that car."

"It was too far away for anyone to see it."

Nick sighed. "Well, I sent it over to the computer lab. Who knows how long it'll take for them to get somebody on it? It's not top priority until something happens one way or the other."

"I know," Jeffrey said. There would need to be a break in the case, some kind of clue to follow or angle to work, before the big guns could be called in. Right now, all they could do was stand around with their hands in their pockets.

Jeffrey asked, "There's no way to move her up on this? Jesus, Nick. Sara and Lena saw the kid being snatched."

"You know how many kids have gone missing in the last twelve hours?"

"Still—"

"Hey, now." Nick lowered his voice. "I made it my business to talk to this old boy used to work in child crimes. He's gonna make a couple of phone calls and see if they can put some kind of priority on it."

"Thanks, Nick."

"Meanwhile, it won't hurt to have some of your boys follow up on those faxes you sent around."

Jeffrey made a note of this, thinking Nick was right. So much trash came through the fax machines at the office that sometimes it took hours before somebody could sort through it.

Nick asked, "Any chance this is just a do-gooder, snatching her up to keep her safe?"

"Hell, Nick," Jeffrey said. "I don't know."

"None of your primaries drives a black Thunderbird?"

"No," Jeffrey said. They'd checked the vehicles of everyone even remotely involved in the case, then spread it out to include all of Grant. No one in the county had an old Ford Thunderbird registered to him.

"In the meantime," Nick said. "What can I do ya for?"

"Purity," Jeffrey said. "Tell me what that means in relation to pedophiles."

"No idea," Nick said. "I can beep it through the computers and let you know."

"I'd appreciate that."

"Your lady was on the phone with me earlier talking about purity," Nick told him. "That castration case, right?"

"Right," Jeffrey said.

"Well, I'll tell you," Nick began, "this castration has a religious angle to it most times. They do it to make sure the girl stays a virgin."

"We know she wasn't that."

"Hell, no," Nick agreed. "From what I heard, she'd been around the block more than a time or two."

Jeffrey tried to let this slide off his back, but Nick's characterization of the child was a little harsh even for him. Law enforcement people tended to be as tough as they could about this kind of thing, and Jeffrey was no exception. Had he not killed the little girl in question, Jeffrey might have laughed. As it was, he could only say, "I've got a name for you to run through the computer."

"Shoot," Nick said.

"Arthur Prynne," Jeffrey said, then spelled out the name of the man he had almost beaten that morning behind Possum's store.

Nick mumbled something, obviously writing down the name. "What is that, Polish, or something?"

"I've got no idea," Jeffrey said. "He's got a tattoo like the one I sent you."

"What am I looking for?"

"He was cruising a day-care center when I happened upon him."

"Can't really arrest him for that," Nick said, though they both knew this was obvious.

"He's got a computer at home. Probably hooks up with other pedophiles that way," Jeffrey said. "Said he was a girl-lover."

"Man," Nick sighed. "I really hate that phrase."

"We could do a search here at the station, but to tell you the truth, Nick, I don't think any of us knows how to find that kind of thing."

"Feds have got a whole squad on it. Having a name makes it a priority. Maybe they can squeeze this guy and get him to flip?"

"Very possible," Jeffrey said. "He didn't have much of a spine when I interviewed him. I can see him turning in some of his friends to save his hide."

"Interviewed him, huh?" Nick chuckled. "He know you were a cop at the time?"

Jeffrey smiled. Nick was a lot of things, but he was not stupid. "Let's say we had a conversation and leave it at that."

Nick laughed again. "How fast you want me to do this?"

"Really fast," Jeffrey said, not wanting the responsibility if Prynne turned out to be less innocent than he seemed.

"I'll put it through to the Alabama boys, pronto," Nick said. Then, "We just caught something over in Augusta that might interest you."

"What's that?"

"Augusta cops busted this guy at his hotel on coke distribution. They kind of stumbled across a bunch of magazines that weren't exactly legal."

"Pornography?" Jeffrey guessed.

"Kiddy porn," Nick confirmed. "There was some freaky shit."

"In Augusta?" Jeffrey asked, surprised that he did not know about this. Augusta was pretty close to Grant, and they tended to swap information with the cops there just to keep everyone in the loop.

"We're sitting on it," Nick said. "Trying to pull down the big guys."

"The perp's turning state's evidence?" Jeffrey asked.

"Flipped faster than a two-dollar whore," Nick told him. "And, before you ask, he doesn't know anything about a black Thunderbird or a missing little girl."

"You sure?"

"Sure as two fists can be."

Jeffrey frowned, though he was hardly in a position to feel superior. "Thanks for checking."

"No offense, Chief, but you better hope she's not with one of these guys. They trade kids like you and me used to trade baseball cards."

"I know that," Jeffrey said, but the truth was, he didn't want to. Thinking about Lacey Patterson being trapped with someone like Prynne made Jeffrey sick.

"Anyway," Nick sighed, "there's supposed to be a delivery tonight or tomorrow. Evidently, Augusta is the distribution point for the Southeast."

"I can't believe they're still printing that shit when you can get it for free on the Internet."

"You can trace through the Internet if you know what you're doing," Nick reminded him. "You want me to give you a holler when it's going down?"

"You've got my cell number, right?"

"Yep," Nick said. "You think this Prynne freak is active?"

"No," Jeffrey said, because his impression had been that Arthur Prynne was the kind of pedophile who was content to look at pictures and not act on his fantasies. "I don't know how long that'll last, though."

Nick asked, "He gonna be expecting a knock on his door?"

"I think he has been all his life," Jeffrey said, looking up to see Lena standing in the doorway. "I've gotta go, Nick. Call me back when you get something on that bust, okay?"

"Will do, Chief."

They hung up, and Jeffrey motioned Lena in, surprised by the way she looked. Her eyes were bloodshot, the way people tend to get when they've been crying for long periods of time. Her nose was red and there were dark circles under her eyes.

"Wanna talk about it?" Jeffrey asked, indicating one of the chairs across from his desk.

She gave him a puzzled look, like she didn't understand. She asked, "Any word on Lacey?"

"Nothing," he said. "Have you set up that appointment we talked about?"

Lena bit her lower lip. "I didn't have time."

"Make time," he told her.

"Yes, sir."

Jeffrey sat back in his chair, staring at her for a few beats. He said, "Tell me what happened when you snatched up Mark. Did he say anything?"

"He's being real tight-lipped all the sudden," she told him. "He won't say anything."

"He lawyer up?"

"Buddy Conford," Lena told him. "Won't that be a conflict of interest?"

Jeffrey considered this. Buddy was the lawyer representing the county if and when Dottie Weaver brought a case against Jeffrey. He asked, "Does Buddy know there's a connection between Mark and what happened with Jenny Weaver?"

"He knows Mark's the one Jenny wanted to shoot. Everybody knows that."

"I mean," Jeffrey said, "does he know we suspect Mark of being the father of the child?"

Lena's eyebrows went up. "Do we?"

"Tell me why he wouldn't be."

"There could be another boy," she suggested.

"With the mother around?"

"She's been sick a lot," Lena said, shrugging. "I get a vibe from the father. He likes to push people around."

"I'll give you that," Jeffrey said, because Patterson had made a sport out of pushing Lena around in the trailer the other day. Jeffrey had been torn between stepping in and seeing if Lena could take care of it herself.

Lena said, "Maybe he molested Mark, and so Mark molested his sister? Kind of like a cause and effect?"

"That's not how pedophiles work," Jeffrey said.

"I don't follow."

"Not all pedophiles were abused as children. You can't make that assumption."

"We're talking theory here, right?" Lena asked. "I mean, it could have happened that way. I don't see Patterson being into boys, though."

"The vibe again?"

"Yeah," Lena nodded. "I don't get that vibe."

"What about Mark?" Jeffrey asked, remembering how Lena had behaved when they first interviewed the kid. "What kind of vibe do you get off of him?"

Lena had the grace to look down. "Well," she began, "he's hypersexual."

"Go on."

"He really seems to work off his appearance, his sexuality." She looked back up. "I think he probably doesn't know how to communicate any other way."

"That tattoo," Jeffrey began. "I found a guy in Alabama who had the same one."

"The hearts?"

"He was watching a day care," Jeffrey said, feeling the same disgust he had felt at Possum's store. "Looking at the kids there."

"Little kids?" Lena asked. "He's a child molester?"

"More like a pedophile," Jeffrey corrected. Sara had given him a lesson on the difference between these two a long time ago during another case, and he told Lena about it now. "Child molesters tend to hate children, and don't want to be around them except to abuse them. Pedophiles think they're doing the kid some good. They think they love them."

"Uh-huh," Lena said, skeptical.

"Pedophilia is considered a mental illness."

"So was homosexuality until the early sixties. I still don't see the difference."

Jeffrey knew that Lena's sister had been gay, so he was surprised to hear her say this. "I suppose the big difference would be that adult-to-adult sexual contact is healthy. Children aren't prepared for that kind of thing." She did not respond, so he continued, "With a child-adult relationship, the balance of power is always going to be on the adult's side. It's not a level playing field. The adult is always going to be the one in control of the kid."

Lena gave him an incredulous look. "It sounds like you're justifying it."

"I'm not doing that at all," Jeffrey said, feeling prickly at her accusation. "I'm just telling you what the mindset is."

"The mindset is pretty fucking perverted."

"I agree with that," Jeffrey told her. "But you can't let your disgust color how you approach this, Lena. If Mark has that tattoo because he's a pedophile or a child molester, you can't let him know that you disapprove. He'll never open up to you." Then, because he had taught her this before, he added, "You know that."

"Well," Lena said. "Which one do you think he is? He's barely older than Lacey."

"Three years at least."

"That's not a huge difference."

"Maybe from thirty to thirty-three it's not, but with kids, that's a pretty big jump when you think about it. That's the difference between being a child and being a young adult."

She was silent, obviously thinking this through.

Jeffrey said, "Look at it this way: A pedophile is more comfortable around children because he's scared of adult relationships. Adults scare him."

"What about Jenny? How did she get sewn up like that? What's the story?"

"That I don't know," Jeffrey said. "Maybe Mark will give it up?"

"He's not talking," Lena told him. "Frank was in with him, and he just stared off into space."

"Is he high?"

She shook her head no. "He was before, but it's worn off by now."

"Is he looking for a fix?"

"He seems okay," she said. "He's not twitching, if that's what you're getting at."

"What about his physical state? Sara said he looked like someone had worked him over."

"Yeah," Lena said. She took some Polaroids out of her breast pocket. "We took some pictures to document it. Dr. Linton said the cut on his belly looks like it was done with a sharp knife. It wasn't deep enough for stitches, though. He's got a bruise coming out on his eye."

Jeffrey looked at the pictures one by one. Mark stared at the camera with a dead look in his eyes. There was one shot where he had his shirt off, and there were grass stains on the waist of his jeans as well as superficial scrapes on his lower abdomen.

"We didn't do any of this?" Jeffrey asked, just to make certain.

"Of course not," Lena said, which was odd, because he had asked her this question on other cases and gotten a straightforward answer with none of the attitude. As if to get a jab in, she said, "Ask your girlfriend. She saw him before I did."

"Someone chased him?" Jeffrey asked, moving along. "Or was he chasing someone else?"

"One or the other," she said. "Defensive wounds on his arms, too."

Jeffrey thought about Arthur Prynne, and how he had covered himself with his arms to keep Jeffrey from hitting his face.

Lena said, "We bagged his clothes. I think Dr. Linton's gonna run the blood on his shirt for the DNA match."

"Did you ask him about his sister?"

"If he cares, he's not showing it. Like I said, he's not talking about anything."

Jeffrey's phone beeped, and he pressed the intercom button.

Marla said, "Pastor Fine is here to see Mark."

Jeffrey and Lena exchanged a look. "In what capacity?"

"He says the parents asked him to act as proxy during your interview." Marla lowered her voice. "Buddy Conford is here with him."

"Thanks," Jeffrey said, pressing the button again. He sat back in his chair, staring at Lena.

She finally asked, "What?"

"You've got this connection with Mark. I don't know what it is, but you need to be careful in there."

"I don't have a connection with him," Lena said, obviously uncomfortable with the thought.

"Maybe he's transferring some emotions on to you because his mother's sick."

Lena gave a half-assed shrug. "Whatever," she said. "Can we just get this over with?"

Buddy Conford had lived a hell of a life. At seventeen, he had lost his right leg from the knee down in a car accident. Later, he lost his left eye to cancer and a kidney to a dissatisfied client with a gun. These losses seemed to have made Buddy stronger rather than weaker. He could fight like a dog with a bone when he put his mind to it. On the other side of that, Buddy was a logical man, and, unlike most lawyers, he was able to recognize right from wrong. He had helped Jeffrey on more than one occasion. Jeffrey approached Mark Patterson's interview hoping this would be such an occasion.

"Chief," Dave Fine said, "I wanted to thank you for letting me be present during this. Mark's mother has taken a turn for the worse, and they wanted me to be here in their stead."

Jeffrey nodded, trying not to point out that he did not really have a choice. Whatever crimes he had committed, Mark was technically still a child. It would be up to the courts to change that designation, if it ever came to that.

Fino asked, "Is there any word on his sister?"

"No," Jeffrey said, staring at Mark, trying to figure out what was going on with the sixteen year old. He looked horrible, and the bruise on his eye was turning blacker by the minute. His lip was cut down the center and his eyes were as bloodshot as Lena's. The orange prison jumpsuit they had given him made the boy look even more pale than he already was. He seemed smaller, too, somehow reduced by his circumstances. His shoulders slouched and he looked slight, even compared to Buddy Conford, who was not exactly tall.

"Mark?" Jeffrey asked.

Mark's lips moved silently, and he kept his gaze on the table, as if he did not want to look up and recognize the situation he was in. There was something pathetic about the boy that made Jeffrey feel something like compassion. Sara was right. No matter what Mark had done, he was still just a kid.

Buddy shuffled through Mark's paperwork. "What are the charges here, Chief?"

"Assault," Jeffrey told him, still staring at Mark. "He hit Sara in the face."

Buddy frowned at his client. "Sara Linton?" he asked, surprise making his voice go up. Buddy had grown up in Grant, and like most natives he considered Sara sort of sacred for the work she did at the clinic.

A jangling noise came from under the table. Mark was handcuffed, and Jeffrey guessed the sound was the cuffs bouncing up and down on his thigh. Jeffrey had heard this sound before in several interviews.

"In front of about ten witnesses," Jeffrey said, talking over the noise. "He was also threatening his sister with bodily harm."

"Uh-huh," Buddy said, stacking the papers. "He get those bruises on his face before or after he was arrested?"

Lena snapped, "Before," with a silent but understood, "*. . . you idiot.*"

Buddy gave her a chastising look. "Witnesses back that up?"

"We took photos," Jeffrey said, pulling the Polaroids Lena had given him out of a folder. He slid them across the table to Buddy. Mark flinched a bit at the movement, and again Jeffrey was struck at how fragile the boy seemed.

Buddy thumbed through them, not looking at Mark until he was finished. "Who did this to him?" he asked Jeffrey.

"You tell us," Jeffrey said.

Mark kept staring down, the cuffs jangling like a metronome.

Buddy slid the photos back to Jeffrey. "Don't look like he wants to talk."

Lena said, "What's going on, Mark?"

Mark looked up, seemingly surprised that Lena was

speaking to him. The noise stopped, and he appeared frozen in time, waiting for Lena to say more.

Lena's voice was softer than Jeffrey had ever heard it, and it felt like Lena and Mark were the only two people in the room when she said, "Tell me what's wrong, Mark."

He continued to stare, and his breathing became more pronounced.

"Who hit you?" she asked, using the same concerned tone. She reached across the table to him, and Mark lifted his hands so that she could touch him. A small sob escaped from his lips when her hand covered his.

Buddy shot Jeffrey a look, and Jeffrey shook his head once, willing the lawyer to stay silent. Dave Fine was silent without prompting, staring at Mark and Lena's hands.

Lena used her thumb to smooth Mark's tattoo. Jeffrey did not need to look at the other men in the room to know that they were a bit uncomfortable with the gesture. The air seemed charged with something unspeakable.

Lena said, "What's going on, Mark? Tell me."

Tears came to his eyes. "You've got to find Lacey."

"We will," Lena told him.

"You've got to find her before something bad happens to her."

"What will happen to her, Mark?"

He shook his head, sobbing, "It's too late. No one can help her now."

"Do you know who could have taken her? Did you recognize the car?"

He shook his head again. "I want to see my mama."

Lena swallowed visibly, and Jeffrey could see that Mark's frailty was getting to her, too.

"I just want to see my mama," Mark repeated, his voice soft.

Dave Fine reached out to the boy, and Mark jerked away so hard that Buddy had to hold his chair to keep Mark from toppling over.

"Don't touch me!" Mark screamed, standing.

Lena stood, too, and half ran around to the other side of the table. She tried to touch Mark's arm, but he jumped away, nearly slamming into the wall. He backed into the corner of the room, putting his head into the angle of the walls. Lena put her hand on his shoulder, whispering something to him.

"Mark," Dave Fine said, holding up his hands. "Settle down, son."

"Why aren't you with my mother?" Mark demanded. "Where's your fucking God when my mother's dying?"

"I'll see her later tonight," Fine said, his voice shaking. "She wanted me to be here for you."

"Who was there for Lacey?" Mark demanded. "Who was there when some freak snatched her off the street?"

Fine looked down, and Jeffrey guessed the man was feeling the same guilt they all did about Lacey Patterson.

"I don't need you," Mark screamed. "Mama does. She needs you, and you're here with me like you can do something."

"Mark—"

"Go help my mother!" Mark screamed.

Fine opened his mouth to say something, then seemed to change his mind.

Mark shook his head, looking away. Lena put her hands on his shoulders and led him back to his chair.

Buddy rapped his knuckles on the table to get Jeffrey's attention, then indicated the door.

Jeffrey stood, indicating that Fine should stand as well. The preacher hesitated, then did as he was told, following Buddy out into the hallway.

"Goddamn," Buddy said, then apologized. "Sorry, Preacher."

Fine nodded, tucking his hands into his pockets. He looked through the small window in the door, watching Lena talk to Mark. He mumbled, "I'll pray for his soul."

Buddy leaned heavily onto his crutch, asking Jeffrey, "What the hell is going on here, Chief?"

Jeffrey did not know how to answer. He asked, "Dave, can you make any sense of this?"

"Me?" Fine asked, surprised. "I have no idea. The last time I saw Mark, he seemed okay. Upset about his mama, but okay."

"When was this?" Jeffrey asked.

"The other night at the hospital. I was praying with Grace."

Jeffrey said, "What happened between you and Jenny Weaver?"

"Jenny Weaver?" Fine asked, genuinely puzzled.

Jeffrey reminded him, "You said you dropped by a couple of times to see her around Christmas."

"Oh, right," Fine agreed. "Brad asked me to see her. She had stopped coming to church and he was worried something was wrong."

"Was there?"

"Yes. At least I think so," Fine answered, frowning. "She wouldn't talk to me. None of them would talk to me about anything."

"None of them meaning who?" Jeffrey asked.

Fine indicated the door. "Mark and Lacey. I talked to Grace about it, but she couldn't do anything with them at that point. Put it down to teenage rebellion, I guess." He shook his head sadly. "A lot of kids drop out of church at that age, but they usually come back when they get older. Grace was worried, though, so I talked to him."

"What did he say?" Jeffrey asked.

Fine colored. "Let's just say he used some words I wouldn't want his mama to hear and leave it at that."

Jeffrey nodded, letting it go. He had heard Mark enough times to know what the boy was capable of. He asked, "What about Grace? How is she doing?"

"She's very sick. I don't think she'll make it to the weekend."

Jeffrey thought about Mark wanting to see his mother. "It's that bad?" he asked.

"Yes," Fine answered. "There's nothing more that they can do for her at this point except try to make her comfortable." He glanced back through the window. "I don't know what this family is going to do without her. It's tearing them apart."

"You weren't on the youth retreat last Christmas, is that right?"

Fine shook his head. "I stayed here. I'm not really involved in the retreats; that's more the youth minister's job. Brad Stephens."

"I've talked to him already."

"He's a fine young man," Fine told them. "I hoped he'd serve as an example for some of the boys."

Jeffrey said, "You counseled Mark some, is that right?"

"A bit," Fine answered. "He didn't really open up. I can look over my notes and let you know if anything came up."

"Do that," Jeffrey told the pastor. "Where will you be tomorrow morning?"

"I suppose at the hospital," Fine told him, glancing at his watch. "As a matter of fact, I'd like to get back over there tonight, unless you have any more questions for me."

"You can go," Jeffrey said. "I'll be at the hospital around ten tomorrow morning. Have your notes."

"I'm sorry I haven't been much help," Fine apologized. He shook Jeffrey's hand, then Buddy's, before leaving.

Buddy watched the preacher go, then turned back to Jeffrey. "I don't much like whatever is going on between your detective and my client."

Jeffrey thought about feigning ignorance, but decided they were past that. "I'll put him on suicide watch tonight."

Buddy didn't buy it. "You still haven't addressed my concern."

Jeffrey looked back into the room. Lena had managed to get Mark to sit down, and she rubbed his back as he cried.

Jeffrey said, "This is connected somehow to the Weaver shooting."

"Aw, shit," Buddy cursed, stamping the floor with his crutch. "Thanks a lot for telling me that, Chief."

"I wasn't sure," Jeffrey lied. "You know he's the kid Weaver wanted to shoot."

"This seemed like a simple assault."

"It is," Jeffrey said. "I mean, it was."

"Wanna speak English with me here?"

Jeffrey looked back into the room. Lena still had her hand on Mark's back, comforting him.

"Honestly, Buddy, I've got no idea what's going on."

"Start from the beginning."

Jeffrey tucked his hands into his pockets. "The baby we found at the skating rink," he said, and Buddy nodded. "We think Mark is the father."

Buddy kept nodding. "Makes sense."

"We think his sister might be the mother."

"One that's been taken?"

Jeffrey nodded. His gut clenched as he thought about Lacey Patterson and what might be happening to her.

Buddy said, "I thought Weaver was the mother."

"No," Jeffrey said. "Sara did the autopsy. Jenny wasn't the mother." He left out what else Sara had found.

"I still haven't heard from Dottie Weaver," Buddy told him. "The mayor's sweating like a whore in church."

"She'll probably wait until the funeral's over," Jeffrey said, wondering when the funeral would be held. He doubted seriously that Sara would be invited, and she had not mentioned anything about it.

"I need to get your deposition in the next day or so, regardless," Buddy ordered. "We need to get it down on paper while it's fresh in your mind."

"I don't think it'll ever not be fresh in my mind, Buddy," Jeffrey said, thinking that he would carry Jenny Weaver's death around with him for the rest of his life.

"What else is going on here?" Buddy asked. "Don't hold back on me."

Jeffrey tucked his hands into his pockets. "Mark has this tattoo on his hand."

"The heart thing?" Buddy asked.

"Yeah," Jeffrey confirmed. "It's a symbol for something."

"Kiddy porn," Buddy supplied, much to Jeffrey's shock. "How do you know that?"

"I've got another client who has the same tattoo," Buddy said. "Some guy a couple of weeks ago over in Augusta. I took the case as a favor to a friend."

"What was the case?"

Buddy glanced around, obviously debating whether or not to answer the question.

Jeffrey pointed out, "I've been more than forthcoming here, Buddy."

Buddy agreed. "Yeah, okay," he said. "He got nailed for coke. Not a lot, but enough to push distribution. He had some information to make the charge go away."

"I've heard this already," Jeffrey said. "He's a distributor, right? For the porn?"

Buddy nodded.

"And he turned state's evidence to keep his ass out of jail."

"Bingo," Buddy said. "How'd you hear about it?"

"The usual way," Jeffrey said, not wanting to give any more information.

"What usual way?" Buddy asked.

Jeffrey tried to divert him. "Where's your leg?" he said, indicating the empty space below Buddy's right knee.

"Shit," Buddy sighed. "My girlfriend took it. Won't give it back."

"What'd you do?"

"That's a cop for you," Buddy said, leaning on his crutch. "Always blame the victim."

Jeffrey laughed. "You want me to talk to her?"

Buddy furrowed his eyebrows. "I'll handle it," he said. "You gonna answer my question about how you know?"

"Nope," Jeffrey said. He looked back into the room. Mark had his head on the table, and Lena sat beside him, holding his hand.

Jeffrey opened the door. "Lena," he said, indicating she should come out into the hall.

Lena opened her mouth, probably to ask him to let her stay, but seemed to think better of it. She stood, not looking at Mark, not touching him, and walked out of the room.

"What did he say?" Jeffrey asked her.

"Nothing," Lena answered. "He wants to go to the hospital and see his mother."

"Go home," Jeffrey told her, and without waiting for her to acknowledge him, he stepped back into the room with Buddy right behind him.

"Mark," Jeffrey began, sitting in the chair Lena had vacated. "We know about the tattoo."

Mark kept his head down. The table shook as he cried.

"We know what it means."

Buddy leaned against the table on the other side of Mark. "Son, it's in your best interest to tell us what's going on here."

Jeffrey said, "Mark, do you have any idea who might have taken your sister?" When there was no answer, he tried, "Mark, we think some bad people have got her. Some people who might hurt her. You need to help us here."

Still, he did not answer.

"Mark," Jeffrey tried again. "Dr. Linton said Lacey seemed sick when she saw her."

Mark sat up, wiping his eyes with his hands. He stared straight ahead at the wall, his body rocking back and forth.

Jeffrey asked, "Was Lacey pregnant? Was that the baby in the skating rink?"

Mark kept rocking back and forth, almost like he was being hypnotized by the wall.

Jeffrey asked, "Were you the father of that baby, Mark?"

Mark continued to stare. Jeffrey waved his hand in front of the boy's eyes, but Mark did not move.

"Mark?" Jeffrey asked, then louder, "Mark?"

Mark did not flinch.

"Mark?" Jeffrey repeated, snapping his fingers.

Buddy put his hand on Mark's shoulder, but the boy did not acknowledge him. Buddy said, "I think we should get him a doctor."

"Sara can—"

"No," Buddy interrupted. "I think he's seen enough of Sara for one day."

* * *

It was ten o'clock by the time Jeffrey left the station. Nearly two hours of his time had been spent calling around the state, making sure other police departments had gotten the flyer on Lacey and knew to be on the lookout for the black Thunderbird. A lot of the cops he spoke with wanted to give him details on open cases they were working. While Jeffrey didn't think he could help some of them, he made all the right noises, hoping the cops on the other end didn't feel like he was giving them lip service. It was more likely some patrol car in Griffin would run across the black Thunderbird than it was for Jeffrey to find a missing wide-screen television that had been stolen out of a police sergeant's mother's house, but he wrote down and repeated back the serial number anyway.

Despite what he had told Nick, Jeffrey wanted to see what he could find on the Internet on his own. With Brad's help, they had found thousands of sites under the general heading of "girl-lovers." Brad's face had turned completely white by the third site they visited, and Jeffrey had dismissed the young patrolman and tried to navigate the Web on his own.

Even with Jeffrey's rudimentary knowledge of the Internet, he was able to find links to site after site containing images of children posed in various compromising positions. By the time he signed off, Jeffrey had felt the need to take a shower just to clean some of the images from his mind. Sara was right. Maybe some distance from the case would give him some perspective. As it stood, Jeffrey did not know where to look next.

Jeffrey tried not to think about what he had seen on the computer as he drove to Sara's house. He had called Sara before he'd left the station to tell her there was still no word on Lacey and that he was on his way over if she still wanted

to see him. Thankfully, she did. He pulled into the driveway, noticing that she had left the lights on for him. When
he got out of the car he could hear a soft, jazzy song playing
in the house. Sara must have been looking out for him, because she opened the door before he had a chance to knock.
Everything that had been troubling him for the last few
days left his mind when he saw her standing there.

"Hi," Sara said, a sly smile at her lips.

Jeffrey was speechless, and all he could do was look at
her. Sara's hair was down around her shoulders, the curls
softer than usual. She was wearing a silky black dress that
wrapped around her body, showing her curves to their best
advantage. A long slit up the side showed a hint of leg. She
was wearing high heels, and they flexed her calf in a way
that made him want to lick it.

She took his hand and led him inside. Jeffrey stopped
her in the hallway, and pulled her close to him. The high
heels added about three inches to her height, and Sara
leaned her hand on his shoulder while she slipped off the
shoes so that she would be back at eye level.

"Better?" she asked. When he did not answer, she leaned
in, brushing her lips across his. He kept his eyes open as
long as he could, watching her kiss him. Her mouth was
sweet, and he tasted wine and a bit of chocolate on her
tongue.

Jeffrey closed the door behind him still watching her. He
could not remember a time when she looked more beautiful, even with the Band-Aid on her forehead.

She said, "I don't want to talk about my day, or your day,
or what's going on."

All he could do was nod.

Sara leaned her arm against the wall, giving him a
quizzical look. "Cat got your tongue?"

Jeffrey put his hand to his chest, trying to articulate how

he felt. "Sometimes," he began, "I forget how beautiful you are, and then I see you . . ." He let his voice trail off, trying to find the right words. "It just takes my breath away."

She raised an eyebrow, as if to ask if he was feeding her some kind of line or not.

"I love you, Sara," he said, taking a step closer to her. "I love you so much."

She seemed to be fighting a smile, and he loved her even more for that. As long as Jeffrey had known her, Sara had never been able to take a compliment.

She said, "I guess this means you like the dress."

"I'd like it even better on the floor."

She stood away from the wall, and he watched as she reached behind her and did something with her hands. She wasn't wearing anything under the dress, so when it fell to the floor she stood completely nude in front of him.

Jeffrey drank her in, craving her in a way that frightened him. He went down on his knees and kissed her until she could not stand anymore.

Wednesday

12

Lena dreamed that she heard a hammer pounding against a nail. When she rolled over in bed, she half expected to see her hand being pinned to the floor, but what she saw instead was Hank, tapping out the hinges to her bedroom door.

Lena sat up in bed, yelling, "What the fuck?"

"I told you things were gonna change," Hank said, still tapping at the pin holding the hinge together.

"Jesus Christ," Lena said, putting her hands to her ears, trying to block out the hammering sound. She looked at the clock on the dresser. "It's not even six o'clock," she yelled. "I don't even have to be at work until nine today."

"Gives us plenty of time," Hank said, sliding the pin from the hinge.

"You're taking off my door?" Lena demanded, pulling the sheet to her chest even though she was wearing a heavy sweatshirt and matching pants. "Who the hell do you think you are?"

Hank ignored her as he started working on the top hinge.

"Stop it," Lena ordered, getting out of bed and taking the sheet with her.

Hank kept tapping, still ignoring her.

He said, "Things are changing, starting today."

"What things?"

He reached into his back pocket and pulled out a folded piece of notebook paper. "Here," he said, handing it to her.

Lena unfolded the paper, but her eyes could not focus on the words. She was reminded of when she was a teenager, and Hank had not approved of a boy Lena was seeing. His solution then had been to nail her bedroom windows shut so that she would not be able to sneak out anymore at night. She had pointed out this was a fire hazard, and Hank had countered that he would rather see her burned alive than hooked up with that trash she was seeing.

Lena tried to take the hammer from him, but he was too strong.

She said, "I'm not a baby, goddamn it."

"You're my baby," Hank said, jerking the hammer back. He tapped out the last pin and the door dropped to the floor. "I held you in these hands," he said, dropping the hammer to show her his hands. "I walked with you at night when you wouldn't stop crying, I made sure you had your lunch when you went to school, and I loaned you the money to make the down payment on this house."

"I paid you back every goddamn penny."

"This here's the interest," he said, wrapping his hands around the edges of the door. He lifted it with a heavy groan.

Lena watched, incredulous, as he carried the door out into the hallway.

"Why are you doing this?" she whined. "Hank, stop it."

"No more secrets in this house," he mumbled, straining to set the door against the wall. He turned to her, saying, "I'm laying down the law here, child."

"I'm not doing any of this," she said, throwing the list at him.

"The hell you say," he countered, catching the paper before it hit the floor. "You're gonna do every goddamn thing on this list every day, or I'll have a talk with your boss. How's that?"

"Don't threaten me," she said, following him back into the bedroom.

"You take it as a threat if you want," Hank said, yanking open one of the drawers in her bureau. He rummaged through her underwear, then slammed the drawer closed and opened the next one.

"What are you doing?"

"Here," he said, pulling out a pair of running shorts and a T-shirt. "Put these on and be downstairs in five minutes."

Lena looked at him, and she noticed for the first time that Hank was not dressed in his usual jeans and loud Hawaiian shirt. He was wearing a white T-shirt with a beer advertisement on it and a pair of shorts that looked so new they still had the creases in them from being folded in the package. Brand new sneakers were on his feet, white socks pulled up to just under his knees. His legs were so white that she had to blink several times to see where his legs stopped and the socks began.

"Downstairs for what?" she asked, crossing her arms.

"We're going running."

"You're going to go running with me?" she asked, not believing this. Hank was about as out of shape as a geriatric in a wheelchair. He did not even like walking to the mailbox.

"Five minutes," he said, leaving the room.

"Bastard," Lena fumed, contemplating whether or not to go after him. She was so mad she couldn't see straight, but still, she took off her pants and slid on the shorts.

"Fucking prick," she mumbled, slipping on the shirt. She had no choice, and that was what was pissing her off. If Hank told Jeffrey half of the stuff he knew about Lena's behavior, Lena would be out on her ass so fast her head would spin.

Lena allowed herself a glance at the list. It started off with "exercise every day," and ended with "eat normal meals for breakfast, lunch, and supper."

From deep inside somewhere, she pulled up every curse word, every expletive, she had ever heard in her ten years as a cop and directed them all toward Hank. She finished with ". . . fucking motherfucker," then grabbed her sneakers and went downstairs.

Lena sat in Jeffrey's office, staring at the clock on his wall. He was ten minutes late, which had never happened as long as Lena could remember. She should probably be glad he wasn't here yet, because Lena needed to sit in order to recover from her morning run with Hank. He was a tough old man, and she had found herself being outpaced by him from their first step outside. Lena had to admit that some of her dogged determination must have come from her uncle, because he seemed to be like Lena: Once he got something in his head that he was going to do, nothing would stop him. Even when Lena had lagged behind, her lungs about to explode, her stomach churning from all the amino acids her muscles were giving up, he had simply jogged in place, his jaw set in an angry line, waiting for her to get over it and get moving.

"Hey," Jeffrey said, rushing into the office. His tie was loose around his neck and he carried his jacket over his arm.

"Hey," Lena said, standing.

He motioned for her to sit down. "Sorry I'm late," he said. "Traffic."

"Where?" Lena asked, because the only traffic in town was around the school, and then only at certain times.

Jeffrey did not answer her. He sat at his desk, buttoning his collar with one hand. Lena was not certain, but she could have sworn she saw a red mark on his neck.

She asked, "No word on Lacey yet?"

"No," he told her, tying his tie. "I talked to Dave Fine on my way in. He's got the notes from his sessions with Mark."

"He's just going to hand them over?" Lena asked, and not for the first time she was glad she had not talked to the pastor about her problems.

"Yeah," Jeffrey said, smoothing down his tie. "I was surprised, too."

Lena crossed her arms, staring at her boss. There was something different about him. She just couldn't place it.

"He's going to meet me at the hospital at ten," Jeffrey said, then looked at his watch. "I'm already late."

"I thought you wanted me to go with you?" Lena asked.

"I want you to get Brad and take Mark to his house," Jeffrey told her. "Get him some clean clothes, let him take a shower, whatever he needs to do, then take him to the hospital."

"Why?"

"His mother took a bad turn last night," Jeffrey said. "Fine thinks she'll probably be gone this morning." He tapped his fingers on his desk. "No matter what he did, I'm not going to keep that boy from seeing his mama one last time before she dies."

Lena was touched by this, but she tried not to let on.

Jeffrey jabbed a finger at her, as if in warning. "I mean it about Brad, Lena. You're not to be with Mark alone. Do you understand me?"

She thought to protest, but he was right. She did not want to be alone with Mark Patterson. There was something about him that was too raw. Perhaps she identified with him too much.

"Lena?" Jeffrey prompted.

She cleared her throat, then answered, "Yes, sir."

As usual, Brad drove through town at exactly the speed limit. Lena tried to quell her impatience at the same time she tried to ignore Mark sitting in the back seat. Without looking, she knew that Mark was staring at her. Both she and Jeffrey had agreed that it would be best to let his father deal with telling the boy his mother would probably be dead before the end of the day, but sitting there in the car with Mark less than two feet behind her, Lena felt like she was doing something wrong. Even with the safety guard between the front and back seats, she felt like Mark might come through the fence and grab her, demanding to know what was going on.

For Mark's part, whatever medication the doctor had given him last night seemed to work. He was back to his usual surly self, standing too close to Lena when she cuffed him, making a suggestive noise as she led him to the car. Lena wondered what had brought the change. Mark had seemed nearly catatonic the day before.

"It sure is hot out," Brad said, taking a left off of Main Street.

"I know," Lena agreed, wanting to keep up the small talk. "It's hotter now than it was last year."

"That's the truth," Brad answered. "I remember when I was little, it didn't seem like it ever got this hot."

"Me, neither," Lena said.

"Didn't even have an air conditioner until I was twelve."

"We got ours when I was fifteen," she told him, allowing a smile at the memory. Lena and Sibyl had stood in front of the little unit until their faces had felt like they were frozen in place.

"We used to beg my daddy to turn the hose on out in the yard," Brad said, giving a little laugh. "I remember once when my cousin Bennie came over—"

Mark kicked at the guard between the seats, saying, "Shut the fuck up."

Brad slammed on the brakes and turned around. "You do that again and we're gonna have to have us a talk."

Lena had never heard Brad threaten anyone, and she was surprised to see that he had it in him. For the first time, she let herself see that Brad actually didn't seem to like Mark Patterson.

"Chill, John Boy," Mark said.

Lena let herself glance back at Mark, and he licked his tongue out suggestively. She turned back around, staring out the front window, trying not to let him know that he had gotten to her.

The car lurched a bit as it moved forward, and Brad was quiet for the rest of the trip. Lena directed him toward the Patterson trailer by pointing with her finger instead of giving him verbal directions. She tried to let herself think that Mark was not in the back seat, but every few minutes she would remember, and it was almost like she could feel his breath on her neck.

"This is it," Lena said, indicating the trailer. She was out of the car before Brad had come to a complete stop. Her thigh muscles protested as she moved, and she cursed Hank again for making her run that morning.

Brad opened the back door, saying, "You gonna behave now?"

Mark took his time getting out of the car. When he stood, he was several inches shorter than Brad. He said something to the young patrolman that Lena could not hear. Whatever it was, it served to embarrass Brad, because his face turned completely red.

"Watch your mouth," Brad said, but there was no real threat to his tone, only what could be called shock. Brad grabbed the handcuffs around Mark's wrists and pulled him toward the trailer.

At the front door, Lena pulled Mark's keys out of her pocket. They had confiscated his things when he was arrested. She guessed that a key to the door would be on the ring.

"It's the third one," Mark said. "The one with the green rim." He smiled at Brad suggestively. "Rim, rimming, rim."

Brad's jaw worked, and he stared at the door as if he could open it with his mind.

Lena found the key and turned it in the lock. A breeze of cold air came from the trailer when she opened the door.

Mark stood in the doorway for just a second, his eyes closed, inhaling the scent of lilacs that greeted them.

"Come on," Brad said, pushing the boy inside.

Lena shot Brad a questioning look, wondering what had gotten into him. Brad was usually the most docile person in the world.

"Take the cuffs off him," Lena said.

Brad shook his head no. "We shouldn't do that."

Lena crossed her arms. "How's he supposed to bathe and get dressed with cuffs on?"

Mark gave Brad a wink. "You could stay with me, officer. Help scrub my back."

Before Lena knew what she was doing, she popped Mark on the back of the head. "Stop that," she told him, angry that he was making Brad so uncomfortable. She told Brad, "Why don't you watch the back of the trailer in case he tries to sneak out?"

Brad seemed relieved by this suggestion, and left without another word.

"What did you say to him?" she demanded.

"Just offered to help him relieve some of that stress he seems to have."

"Jesus Christ," Lena breathed. "Why would you do that to him?"

"Why not?" Mark shrugged.

Lena took out her handcuff key and motioned him over. He put the cuffs tight to his crotch so she would have to touch him to work the key.

"Hands out, Mark," Lena ordered.

He sighed dramatically, but did as he was told. "You like being chained up?" he asked.

"I'll give you ten minutes in the shower," she told him, releasing the cuffs. "If I have to come in after you, I won't be nice about it."

"Mmm . . . ," Mark said, drawing out the sound. "Sounds tasty."

Lena clipped the handcuffs onto the back of her belt. "Ten minutes," she said, wondering if this was how Hank had felt this morning, ordering her around. She walked over to the couch and picked up a magazine before sitting down. Mark stood in the kitchen, watching her for what seemed like a full minute before he went back to his room. A couple of minutes later, she heard water running in the shower. Lena closed the magazine, feeling an overwhelming sense of relief.

She stood from the couch, holding on to the mantel as she stretched out her quads. Her legs hurting this much after what a year ago would have amounted to a light run was beginning to piss her off. She was stronger than this. There was no way she could be so out of shape.

Lena picked up a framed photograph of Mark and Lacey standing in front of a nondescript roller coaster. Both children were smiling, and Mark's arm was thrown around Lacey's shoulders. In turn, she had her hand around his waist. They looked about three years younger than they were now. They looked happy.

"That was at Six Flags," Mark said.

Lena tried not to show he had startled her. Mark was standing about three feet away from her, wearing nothing but a towel around his waist.

"Get dressed," she said.

He pressed his lips together in a lazy smile, and she felt like an idiot for not checking his room first for contraband.

"What are you on?" she asked him.

"Cloud nine," he smiled, dropping onto the couch.

"Mark," Lena said, "Get up. Get dressed."

He stared at her, his lips slightly parted.

She asked, "What?"

He kept staring for just a second more, then asked, "What did it feel like?"

"What did what feel like?"

He looked down at her hands, and she crossed her arms so that he could not see the scars. She shook her head. "No."

"My dad told me what happened."

"I'm sure he took great pleasure in it."

Mark frowned. "He didn't, actually. Teddy doesn't get off on that kind of thing." He must have noticed Lena's surprise, because he said, "Old Ted's a straight arrow, now. Very vanilla."

Lena turned back to the photograph. "Go get dressed, Mark. We don't have time for this."

"You tell me your secrets and I'll tell you mine."

Lena laughed. "You watch too many movies."

"I'm serious."

"I don't think so, Mark."

She heard a lighter click several times, and turned around to see Mark lighting a joint.

"Put that out," she told him.

He inhaled deeply, not obeying.

He said, "Don't you want to know what happened?"

"I want you to get dressed so that you can go see your mother."

He smiled, making himself comfortable on the couch. "I really thought you were going to pull that trigger the other night."

Without thinking, Lena sat at the opposite end of the couch, "You were watching me?" she asked, not feeling violated so much as caught.

He nodded, taking a long hit off the joint.

"Where were you?"

"By the shed," he told her. "I thought you were going to run right over it."

Lena felt a flush of shame.

"That man was beside the house. I thought he saw me, but he was watching you." Mark blew on the tip of the joint. "He's your father?"

"Uncle," she told him.

Mark took another hit on the joint, holding in the smoke for a few beats. He exhaled slowly, then asked, "How'd it feel, holding that gun in your mouth?"

"Wrong," she said, trying to recover. "That's why I didn't do it."

"No. Being raped," he said. "How'd it feel?"

Lena looked around the room, wondering why she was having this conversation with this kid.

"Bad," she said, then shrugged. "Just . . . not good."

He choked on a laugh. "I guess so."

"No," Lena said, then, wanting to get back in charge of the conversation, she said, "Why don't you tell me what happened, Mark?"

"Have you had sex yet?"

She didn't like the way he said "yet" as if it was something inevitable. "That's not really any of your business," she told him, amazed that she was able to talk about it so casually. For the first time in a while, Lena felt in control of herself and her emotions. She felt strong, and capable of handling this kid. In light of the fact that just a day ago she had tried to kill herself, this came as somewhat of a shock to her.

Lena said, "Tell me what's going on."

"My mom's gonna die," he said. "You know that, don't you?"

"Yes," she told him, looking down at her hands because she did not want him to read the truth in her face. "Is that what you want to talk about, your mom?"

He did not respond.

"Mark," Lena said. "Do you know where your sister is?"

He stared at her, his eyes watering. She was struck again by how much of a child he still was.

He said, "We're a lot alike, you know?"

"In what way?"

"In here," he said, putting his hand over his chest. "How did it feel being raped?"

She shook her head, not letting him distract her. "How are we alike, Mark? Has somebody hurt you?"

Something flashed in his eyes, and for just a moment she could see that he was in a tremendous amount of pain. Lena's heart went out to him, and she felt something akin to a maternal urge to take care of Mark Patterson, even if she could not completely take care of herself.

She asked, "Who hurt you, Mark?"

He propped his foot up on the coffee table. "Why are you a cop?"

"Because I want to help people," she told him, though that was no longer entirely true. "Let me help you. Tell me what happened."

He shook his head over this. "How did it feel?" he asked again. "When you were being raped. What did that feel like?"

"Tell me why you want to know and I'll tell you."

He sucked on the joint, finishing it. He looked around for somewhere to put the butt, and Lena slid a plate across the coffee table for him.

He sat up, putting his elbows on his knees. "I wonder sometimes why people do things."

"I do, too," she said. "For instance, why would Jenny want to kill you?"

He waved this off. "She wasn't going to kill me."

"Is that why you pissed yourself?"

He laughed. "Hindsight is twenty-twenty."

"Why'd she do it, Mark?"

"She thought she could stop it."

"Stop what?"

"Stop me?" he asked, as if Lena might actually know the answer.

"Stop you from what?" She waited for him to answer, and when he didn't she tried, "Tell me about that party with Carson and the other boys."

He scowled. "Carson's a pussy."

"Why'd you make Jenny sleep with them?"

"I didn't make her do shit," he spat out. "She wanted to

do that. She was trying to make me jealous, showing me it didn't mean anything."

"Didn't hurt you got her drunk, either."

"Yeah, well," he said, waving her off.

"What did Jenny think she could stop, Mark?" Lena asked. "That night at Skatie's. What did she think she could stop?"

Mark twisted his lips to the side, as if he might tell her, then seemed to change his mind. He asked, "You think you'll find my sister?"

"Do you know where she is?"

He looked down, and she wondered if he knew where Lacey was or if he was feeling guilty for not knowing.

Lena sat back, her arms crossed, waiting for him to say what he needed to say.

"I feel like sometimes I'm not even real," he said. "Like maybe I'm in the room, and maybe I'm breathing the air, but nobody really sees me." He rubbed his eyes. "Then I think maybe if I'm not really here, that I need to be someplace else. Like, maybe I should just go ahead and pull the trigger, you know?"

Lena nodded, because she did know.

"What made you stop?" he asked her. "Why didn't you pull the trigger?"

She told him the truth about the gun, but not about the pills. "I thought about my partner finding me in the morning, and I couldn't do that to him."

"Do you believe in God?"

"I'm not sure," she answered. "Do you?"

He shook his head no.

"Is that why you stopped going to church?"

He looked at her, angry. "Don't be a cop with me."

"I am a cop, Mark." Lena kept her tone even, not matching his anger. She reached out and put her hand on his arm.

"I want to know what happened. Why did Jenny want to kill you?"

He sighed, slouching against the pillows. "She was such a sweet kid," he said. "I really cared about her."

"I know you did."

"Do you?" he asked. "I mean, do you really understand what it means to care about somebody?"

Lena thought of Sibyl when she said, "Yes, I do."

"Not me," he said. "I mean, before Jenny. I just didn't know what it meant to care like that."

"You love your mother."

He laughed, a hollow sound that vibrated in his chest. "She's going to die soon, isn't she?"

Lena pressed her lips together.

"I feel it," he said, putting his hand over his heart. "I felt it this morning, somehow, like she wasn't going to last much longer, like she wanted to let go." He started to cry. "It's this connection, you know? Like, I can feel what she feels." He turned to her suddenly, a bit of desperation in his tone. "Did you know when your sister died?"

"Yes," Lena lied. At the time, she had been on her way back from Macon and had no idea that something bad had happened. "I could feel it here," she said, putting her hand to her chest.

"Then you know," he said. "You know what that emptiness feels like."

Lena nodded, not saying more.

Mark looked away, then closed his eyes. She studied his profile, his sharp nose and squared jaw. Tears rolled down his cheeks and fell onto his chest.

"The first time," Mark began, his voice low, "I guess it was at Thanksgiving."

Lena kept her mouth closed, letting him take his time.

"Lacey and Jenny were down the hall in Lacey's room,

and I wanted to borrow one of her CDs." He sighed, his chest rising and falling with the sound. "She started yelling at me, all mad and shit. I dunno. I guess Mama heard her yelling and came in and told us to stop."

Lena felt her heart rate accelerate, and said a small prayer to whoever was listening that Brad would not pick now to come back into the trailer. She tried to do the math and figure out how much time had passed since he left, but since she dared not look at her watch, Lena wasn't sure.

"Lacey turned up the radio in her room really loud," he said. "Mama let her. It's always been like that. She was always the favorite." He shook his head. "Lacey's sweet underneath, you know? Maybe she's spoiled, but she's sweet underneath. She has a good heart, just like Mama."

Lena waited, counting to twenty-five before Mark started speaking again.

"She came into my room a little later," he said. "I guess she knew I was still pissed off. Wanted to smooth things over. She was always like that, trying to make peace. I guess that's why so many people liked her, because she was good like that." A slight smile came to his lips, but he kept his eyes closed. "She just put her hand around the back of my neck, and then we started kissing for some reason. I mean, just kissing real deep for a long time."

Lena tried to remember what Jeffrey had said about not letting her personal feelings ruin a confession, but the thought of Mark Patterson kissing his baby sister made her stomach roll. She wanted to say something, to stop him so that she would not go through the rest of her life knowing this story, but she knew that she could not.

"I don't know how the rest of it happened," Mark said. "You know, we were kissing, and then she started rubbing me, and it felt so good." He looked at her, asking for her approval. "I know it was wrong, okay? It just felt so good. I didn't want to stop."

Lena nodded, trying to control her expression. She doubted very seriously that Lacey Patterson had seduced her brother. Saying the victim had "asked for it" was a common theme among sexual predators.

"I can tell you don't understand," he said. "But you don't know what it's like. My dad is so fucking hard on me." He slammed his fist into his leg. "He just never lets up on me. Ever."

"I know," Lena told him, reaching out, making herself touch his arm. "I understand that part, Mark. I really do."

His expression softened, and he said, "I didn't make her do it."

"I believe you."

"She came on to me first," he said. "She was the one who came into my room. She was the one who started kissing me, who started touching me."

Lena nodded because that was all that she could do.

"She was so wet for me. I just . . ." He shook his head, squeezing his eyes shut, as if to bring back the memory. "It felt so right being inside of her. And she wanted me. I could tell she wanted me. The way she put her hand on the back of my neck, and pulled me closer to her, deeper."

Lena swallowed back bile.

"Touching her and being with her and inside of her," Mark said. "I just felt complete, you know? Like things were finally right." He put his hand over his eyes. "She was so good at it. I mean, where did she learn to be so damn good at it?"

He seemed to want an honest answer, but Lena could not give him one.

"I mean, I look at my dad," he said, shaking his head. "It's not like he knows anything."

Lena spoke without thinking. "Your dad was sleeping with her, too?"

"Well, duh," he said, as if she were stupid.

Lena put her hand to her stomach, thinking about poor Lacey Patterson, and what hell she must have been through.

She said, "Tell me about Jenny."

Mark gave a humorless laugh. "Yeah, Jenny," he said. "I had been with her a couple of times before, like I told you." He paused. "She was sweet. She was all those things I told you."

"She seemed like a good friend."

"Yeah, well," he said, a bit of derision slipping into his tone. "She was a good friend until she caught us."

"Is that why she pointed the gun at you?"

"I guess part of it was that," he said. "Then, you know, maybe she just wanted it to stop. She said that a lot, that she just wanted it to stop."

"Was she jealous?"

He nodded slowly. "It hurt her to see it."

"She saw you together?"

He nodded again, the same slow movement. "We were in my bed, and she and Lacey came home from school."

Lena felt her heart stop midbeat. She opened her mouth to ask for a clarification, then closed it. She did not want to know. If she could have moved her body, she would have run from the room, covering her ears so that she could not hear any more. She couldn't move, though, and she sat motionless on the couch, watching Mark the way she would watch a car wreck.

"We were together, you know? I guess this was around Christmastime, right before they went on that stupid retreat." He threw his hand into the air. "Mama let me stay home from school. We had the whole day together." He smiled. "She lit some candles, and we took a long bath, and then we made love."

Lena was aware that she had stopped breathing.

"I guess we lost track of time," Mark said, giving a pitiful laugh. "Laccy and Jenny walked right into my room, and that was it."

Lena put her hand to her mouth to keep herself from speaking.

"Jenny loved my mom. I mean, it was complicated. Maybe it's better that Jenny's not around to watch Mama die. I think that would've killed her."

"Right," Lena managed.

"I know what you think, but she loved me, man. It felt so good to know that she loved me. It was like Lacey was always the favorite, but then she came to me, and I was the one. I was the one she loved most." Mark started to cry again. Before Lena knew what was happening, he had buried his face in her neck.

Lena forced the word, "Mark," out of her mouth, trying to push him away from her.

"Don't," he whispered, and his wet lips against her flesh made her want to vomit.

"Mark, no," she said. When he didn't move, Lena pushed him away as hard as she could. "Get away from me!" she yelled.

From the way he was looking at her, she imagined that every ounce of disgust she was feeling was written all over her face.

"Mark—"

"Bitch," he said, standing. "You fucking bitch!"

"Mark—"

The door popped open, and Brad stood there, his hand

on the butt of his gun. Lena motioned him back as Mark stepped toward her.

Mark said, "I thought you would understand."

"I do," she told him, feeling panicked. "I do understand, Mark."

"Fucking bitch," he hissed. "You don't understand shit."

"Mark—"

He closed the distance between them in two steps, grabbing her hand and holding it up between them. "I thought you understood," he said, and she knew he meant her scars. "I thought you knew because you'd been there, man. You know what it's like. I know you do. You just won't fucking admit it because you're a coward."

Lena opened her mouth, but could not speak.

"Hey," Brad said, taking Mark's arm.

"Get away from me, faggot," Mark screamed, yanking his arm out of Brad's grasp. He pointed an accusatory finger at Lena, saying through clenched teeth, "You tricked me. You're all alike, goddamn it. She was right. You're all so weak. You never do the right thing."

Lena cleared her throat, trying, "Mark—"

Mark walked toward the hallway, his footsteps so heavy that the trailer shook.

"What the heck was that about?" Brad asked, his hand still resting on his gun.

Lena shook her head, unable to speak for just a moment.

"Are you okay?" Brad asked, going to the couch. He put his hand on her arm and she did not pull away.

"I can't believe . . ." Lena began, not knowing exactly what to say.

Brad sat beside her, taking her hand. "Lena?" he asked, patting her hand. "Talk to me."

She shook her head, taking back her hand. "He's just a kid," she said.

"A nasty kid," Brad told her. "Sometimes I wonder how they can get that way. When I was his age, I barely even knew what sex was. I thought a good time on a date was getting a kiss at the end."

Lena nodded, zoning out as he talked about his idyllic teen years.

"I just wonder," Brad said. "What makes them like that? What's changed?"

"Their parents," Lena said, but she knew that wasn't right. She pushed her hair back behind her ear, trying to suppress the shock she was still feeling. She looked at her watch, wondering if she should go get Mark. He had been gone a while.

"What did he mean?" Brad asked. "Wasn't that the same stuff Jenny was saying before?"

Lena finally managed to focus on the conversation. "Before when?" she asked.

"In the parking lot," Brad said. "You know, when she said adults never do the right thing."

"Oh, Jesus," Lena breathed, feeling all the air going out of her lungs. She jumped up from the couch and started off down the hall, Brad close behind her.

"Mark?" she yelled, knocking on the only closed door. She tried the handle, but it was locked.

"Dammit," Lena hissed, jamming her shoulder against the door. It would not budge. She motioned to Brad. "Kick it in."

He braced himself against the other side of the hall and punched his foot into the door. Unfortunately, the door was hollow at the center, and Brad's foot stuck in the splintered wood. He used Lena for leverage, pulling his foot out of the hole. She leaned down, looking into the room, trying to find Mark through the narrow opening.

"Oh, God," Lena gasped, stepping back to kick at the

hole Brad had made. He joined in, and between them they managed to enlarge the opening enough for Lena to slip through. The splintered wood tore at her arms and face, but she barely noticed the pain as she tried to get into the room.

"Mark," she said, her voice high with panic. "Hold on, Mark. Hold on."

Brad pushed her from behind, and she fell into the room. Mark had hanged himself from a rod mounted high in the closet. The ceiling of the trailer was not high, and his feet dragged the ground. Still, the belt around his neck seemed to be doing the trick. His face was blue, his tongue protruding slightly. She grabbed his legs, holding him up to take some of the stress off his neck.

"Goddamn it, Brad," she cursed. "Get in here."

Brad finally managed to bust the door open wide enough to squeeze through, and he used his pocket knife to cut the belt while Lena held Mark's legs. It took forever for the knife to cut through the thick leather, and Lena felt her arms start to shake from holding Mark up for so long.

"No, no, no," Lena cried until Mark fell to the ground. She put her ear to his chest, trying to make out a heartbeat. A few seconds passed, then she finally heard a telltale thump, followed by another stronger one.

"Is he okay?" Brad asked, loosening the belt from Mark's neck.

Lena nodded, pulling a blanket off the bed. She wrapped it around Mark's body, saying, "Call an ambulance."

13

"Sara?" Molly asked, then repeated, "Sara?"

"Hmm?" Sara said. Molly, Candy Nelson, and her three children were all staring at her expectantly.

Sara shook her head a little, saying, "Sorry," before she went back to the examination. She had been worrying about Lacey Patterson, wondering what was happening to her.

"Breathe deeply," Sara told Danny Nelson.

"I've been breathing deeply for the last ten minutes," Danny complained.

"Hush up," his mama said.

Sara could feel Molly staring at her, but kept the focus on Danny. "That's good," she told him. "Put your shirt back on and I'll talk to your mother."

Candy Nelson followed her out into the hallway.

Sara said, "I want to send him to a specialist."

The mother put her hand to her heart, as if Sara had just told her Danny only had a couple of months to live.

"It's nothing to be nervous about," she assured her. "I just want you to get his ears checked by someone who knows more about them than I do."

"Are you certain he's okay?"

"I'm certain," Sara said, then, "Molly, could you write a referral for Matt DeAndrea over in Avondale?"

Molly nodded, and Sara walked into her office, dropping her stethoscope on the desk. She sat down in her chair, trying not to sigh. She found herself thinking about Jeffrey. Every part of her body felt alive, if not slightly bruised. Her back was killing her, but that wasn't surprising, considering they had not made it out of the hallway until around three that morning.

"So," Molly said, interrupting Sara's thoughts. "I guess this means we're taking Jeffrey's calls now?"

Sara blushed. "Is it that obvious?"

"Let's just say an ad in the *Grant Observer* would be more subtle."

Sara narrowed her eyes at the nurse.

"That's your last patient," Molly told her, smiling. "Are you going to the morgue?"

Sara opened her mouth to respond, but a banging noise echoed up the hallway, followed by a curse. Sara rolled her eyes at Molly, and trotted up the hall toward the bathroom. Thanks to a six year old with a keen interest in flushing his Matchbox collection down the toilet, the waste pipe had backed up. Sara had actually debated whether or not to call her father, knowing that Tessa would be working with him today. She did not have the proper tools to fix the toilet, however, and since she had taken yesterday afternoon off, she did not have the time to do the job. Besides, her father would have been very hurt if she had not called him to come to her rescue.

"Daddy," Sara whispered, shutting the bathroom door behind her. "This is a children's clinic. You can't cuss like that around here."

He shot her a look over his shoulder. "I cussed around you girls all the time and you turned out okay."

"Dad . . . ," Sara tried again.

"That's right," he said. "I'm your father."

She gave up, sitting on the edge of the tub. As a child, Sara had often watched her father work, and Eddie had put on quite a show for Sara and Tessa, banging pipes, dancing around with a wrench in one hand and a plunger in the other. He wanted to teach his girls to be good with their hands, and comfortable with their abilities. Sara often thought that he had been somewhat disappointed that Sara had not joined the family business when she got out of college, and chose instead to go to medical school. He had picked up the part of her tuition that the scholarships did not pay for, and made sure she had money to live on, but in his heart Sara knew Eddie would have been perfectly happy to have her back living at home, snaking drains and welding pipes alongside him. Some days, Sara was tempted. She certainly would be working fewer hours as a plumber.

Eddie cleared his throat and began, "The old West, right?"

Sara smiled, knowing he was about to tell one of his jokes. "All right."

"This sheriff goes into a saloon and says, 'I'm lookin' for a cowboy wearing a brown paper vest and brown paper pants.' " He waited a beat, making sure Sara was listening. "The bartender says, 'What's he wanted for?' And the sheriff says, 'Rustling.' "

Sara laughed despite herself.

Eddie returned to the job at hand, shoving a toilet auger

down the bowl. The spindle beside him turned slowly, letting out the flexible metal snake with a pointed tip on the end that would hopefully clear the blockage.

He asked, "What'd this kid flush down again?"

"Matchbox car," Sara said. "At least, that's what we think."

"Little bastard," Eddie mumbled, and Sara just shook her head, knowing it was useless to try to censor him. She had learned that lesson nearly thirty years ago at a particularly embarrassing parent-teacher conference. Instead, Sara leaned her elbows on her knees and watched him work. Eddie Linton was not what anyone would call a snappy dresser, even when he tried. He was wearing a Culture Club T-shirt from a concert he had taken Sara and Tessa to when they were in high school. His green shorts were so old that they had strings hanging down. She leaned over and pulled at one.

"Hey," he said.

"You should let me get the scissors," she offered.

"Don't you have patients to see?"

"This is my morgue day," she told him. Even though there was a stack of paperwork waiting for her at the morgue, Sara did not want to deal with it. As a matter of fact, she would be perfectly content to sit here all day with her father. At least until Jeffrey got off work.

Eddie looked at her over his shoulder. "What are you so happy about?"

"Having you here," she said, rubbing his back.

"Yeah, right," he mumbled, shoving the snake in harder. "This is a pain in the ass. You should charge that kid for my time."

"I'll see what his insurance company says."

Eddie sat back on his heels. "Your sister's in the van."

Sara did not respond.

He gave her a serious look. "When I was in the war, I watched men die."

Sara barked a laugh. "You fixed toilets at Fort Gillem, Daddy. You never even left Georgia."

"Well . . ." He waved this off. "There was that corporal from Connecticut who couldn't handle his grits." Eddie crossed his arms and gave her a serious look. "Anyway, what I mean is, life is too short."

"Yes," Sara agreed. She saw evidence of that at the morgue on an almost weekly basis.

"Too short to be mad at your sister."

"Ah," Sara said, getting it. "Did she tell you what we're arguing about?"

"Do you girls ever tell me anything?" he grumbled.

"It's complicated," Sara told him.

"I bet it's not," Eddie countered, pulling the snake out of the toilet, hand over hand. "I bet it's real simple." He rolled the metal snake around a spindle, telling her, "Go get me the power auger."

"I have to get to work," she said.

"Right after you get the auger," he told her, handing her the coiled snake.

Sara hesitated, then took it. "I'm not doing this because you told me to."

He held up his hands. "You haven't done anything I've told you to do since 1979."

She stuck out her tongue at him before leaving the room. Sara took the back door and walked around the clinic so that the patients in the waiting room would not see her. Technically, she was off-duty, but there was always someone who knew her, and Sara did not want to be stopped.

Eddie's work van was backed into a parking space beside Sara's car. LINTON AND DAUGHTERS was painted on the side panels. A drawing of a commode with a roll of pink toilet tissue on the back of the tank served as the logo. As Sara drew near, she could see Tessa sitting behind the wheel, the windows rolled up and the engine on. She had probably been waiting out here for at least thirty minutes.

Sara yanked the passenger's side door open. Tessa did not look up. Obviously, she had seen Sara approach.

"Hey," Sara called over the roar of the air-conditioning, tossing the auger into the back of the van. She got into the van and slammed the door behind her.

Tessa gave a reluctant, "Hey," back, then, "Did they find that kid?"

"Not yet." Sara leaned her back against the door so that she was facing her sister. She slipped off her clogs and hooked her toes onto the edge of Tessa's seat.

"That's my side," Tessa told her, a phrase that had been oft repeated when they took car rides as children.

"So," Sara said, prodding Tessa's leg with her big toe. "What're you gonna do?"

"Stop it," Tessa slapped at her feet. "I'm mad at you."

"I'm mad at you," Sara told her.

Tessa turned back around, resting her hands on the steering wheel. "I'm sorry I said what I said." She paused. "About not having children."

Sara let some time pass. "I'm sorry I asked if Devon's the father."

"Well . . ."—Tessa shrugged—"he is, if you were really wondering."

"I wasn't," she said, though part of her had been.

Tessa turned, leaning her back against the door so she could face Sara. She pulled her feet up under her and the two sisters stared at each other, neither saying anything.

Sara broke the silence. "If you want to do this . . . ," she began, trying to sound like she meant it. "If you really need to do this . . . I'll support you. You know that."

Tessa asked her, "Where did all that come from?"

"I just . . ." Sara began, looking for a way to explain her feelings. "I've just seen so many kids hurt this week, and I . . ." She let her voice trail off. "How I feel about this doesn't matter, Tessie. It's your decision."

"I know that."

"I know it's your choice," Sara repeated. "I know that you're not doing this lightly —"

"It's not that," Tessa stopped her.

"What is it, then?"

Tessa looked out the window, and was silent. After a while, she said, "I'm just really, really scared."

"Tessie." Sara reached out, taking her sister's hand. "What are you scared of?"

"It's Mom and Dad," she said, and she started to cry. "What if I'm not as good as they are? What if I'm a horrible mother?"

"You won't be," Sara assured her, stroking Tessa's hair back.

"You were right before," Tessa told her. "I *am* selfish. I *do* only think of myself."

"I didn't mean that."

"Yes, you did. I know you did, because it's true." Tessa wiped her eyes with the back of her hand. "I know I'm selfish, Sara. I know I'm immature." She laughed with some irony. "I'm thirty-three years old and I still live with my parents."

"Not in the same house."

Tessa laughed, even as she cried. "Oh, God, please, don't stick up for me."

Sara laughed, too. "Tess, you're such a good person. You love kids."

"I know I do. It's just different thinking about having them around twenty-four hours a day." She shook her head. "What if I do something horrible? What if I drop him, or what if it's a girl and I end up dressing her up like that Ramsey kid?"

"Then we'll have you committed."

"I'm serious," Tessa whined, but she laughed as well. "What if I don't know how to do it right?"

"Mama and Daddy will be there to help," Sara reminded her. "I will, too." She let that sink in, then amended, "If that's what you decide to do, I mean. If you want to keep it."

Tessa leaned forward. "You would be a great mother, Sara."

Sara pressed her lips together, not wanting to cry.

"I just don't know what to do."

Sara took a deep breath, then let it go. "You don't have to decide right now," she said. "You could wait a couple of days, just to see how you feel once the shock has worn off."

"Yeah."

"I do think you should tell Devon. He has a right to know."

Tessa nodded slowly. "I know he does," she said. "Maybe I didn't want to tell him because I know what he'll say." She gave a wry smile. "He'll get exactly what he wants."

"You don't have to marry him."

"Oh, and give Dad a heart attack, living in sin?"

"I seriously doubt he'd have a heart attack." Sara smiled. "He might take you over his knee . . ."

"Yeah, well." Tessa took a tissue from the center console. She blew her nose in three short bursts, the way she had done since she was a baby. "Maybe somebody should take me over his knee."

Sara squeezed her hand. "You make this decision, Tess. Whatever you decide, I'm with you."

"Thank you," Tessa mumbled, wiping her nose with another tissue. She sat back against the window again, and took a long look at Sara. After a few beats, a smile broke out on her face.

Sara asked, "What?"

"You look so obvious."

"So obvious what?"

Tessa kept smiling. "So obviously fucked."

Sara laughed, and the sound echoed in the van.

"Was it good?" Tessa asked.

Sara glanced out the window, feeling a bit mischievous. "Which time?"

"You slut," Tessa screamed, throwing the used tissue.

"Hey." Sara deflected the tissue with her hand.

"Don't go all big sister on me," Tessa warned. "Tell me what happened."

Sara felt a blush creeping up her neck. "No way."

"What changed your mind?" she asked. "I mean, last I heard, you didn't even want to date him."

"Mama," Sara answered. "She told me to make up my mind."

"And?"

"We've just been doing this stupid back-and-forth thing for so long." Sara paused, thinking about how to phrase it. "I have to give it another try. I either have to get him out of my system and go on, or keep him in my system and live with it."

Tessa asked, "Was it good?"

"It was nice to feel something new," she said, thinking

about the night before. "It was nice to stop feeling guilty for a while." As an afterthought, she added, "And scared."

"Over that missing girl?"

"Over everything," Sara said, not going into details. She made it a point not to talk about her work at the morgue with her family. This protected Sara as much as it protected them. There had to be a part of her life that wasn't over-shadowed by death and violence. "It was nice to . . ."

"Have a screaming orgasm?"

Sara clicked her tongue, smiling. "It was pretty spectacular." She shook her head, because that wasn't right. "It was amazing. Totally—"

"Oh, shit," Tessa sat up, wiping her eyes. "Dad's coming."

Sara sat up, too, though she did not know why. It was not as if Eddie could send her to her room for sitting in the parking lot too long.

"Where's that auger?" he demanded, throwing open Sara's door. "What're you two talking about in here?" When he did not get an answer, he said, "Do you know how much gas you're wasting, sitting here with the engine running?"

Sara laughed, and he popped her on the leg, asking, "What would your mama say if she saw that look on your face?"

Tessa answered, "Probably, 'It's about damn time.' "

They started giggling, and Eddie gave them both a sharp look before slamming the door closed and walking away.

The morgue was housed in the basement of the Grant Medical Center, and no matter how hot it got outside, it was always cool in the tiled subterranean rooms. Sara felt bumps come out on her skin as she walked back to her office.

"Hey, Dr. Linton," Carlos said in his soft, heavily accented voice. He was dressed in his usual green scrubs, and held a clipboard at an angle against his thick waist. Sara had hired Carlos six years ago, right out of high school. He was short for his age, and wore his hair cut in a bilevel, which did not do much for his round face. Carlos was efficient, though, and he never complained about having to do what amounted to shit work, literal and figurative. Sara could trust him in the morgue to take care of things and keep his mouth shut.

Sara managed a smile for him. "What's up?"

He handed her his clipboard, saying, "That Weaver kid is still here. What do you want me to do with her?"

Sara felt her heart sink as she thought of the baby. Dottie Weaver had no reason to claim the child since Sara had told her it was not Jenny's. Something about that fragile little girl sitting in the freezer broke Sara's heart.

"Dr. Linton?" Carlos asked.

"I'm sorry," Sara apologized. "What did you say?"

"I asked what you wanted to do with the bodies."

Sara shook her head at the plural, thinking she had missed something. She looked down at the chart and saw that Jenny Weaver's name was at the top. Sara thumbed through the paperwork, noting that she had released the body on Sunday. There was no accompanying form from the funeral home to verify that she had been picked up.

"She's still here?" Sara asked.

Carlos nodded, tucking a hand into his hip.

"We haven't gotten a call from Brock?" she asked, referring to the funeral director in town.

"No, ma'am," he said.

Sara glanced back at the paperwork, as if that could offer an explanation. "We haven't heard from the mother?"

"We haven't heard from anybody."

"Let me make some phone calls," she told him, walking into her office.

Sara knew the number to Brock's Funeral Home by heart, and she dialed it into the phone, watching Carlos through the window. He was mopping the floor in slow, deliberate strokes, his back to her.

The phone was picked up on the first ring. "Brock's Funeral Home."

"Brock," Sara said, recognizing the man's voice. Dan Brock was Sara's age, and they had gone to school together from kindergarten on.

"Sara Linton," Brock said, genuine pleasure in his voice. "How you?"

"I'm great, Brock," she answered. "I hate to cut right down to business, but have you gotten a call on a Jennifer Weaver?"

"The one what was shot last weekend?" he asked. "Sure haven't. Gotta say, I was expecting that call."

"Why is that?"

"Well, Dottie goes to my church," he told her. "I just assumed she'd call on me."

"Do you know her well?"

"Well enough to say hi to," he answered. "Plus, that little Jenny was a peach. She was in the children's choir for a while. Sang like an angel."

Sara nodded, remembering that Brock directed the children's choir in his spare time. "Sara?" Brock prompted.

"Sorry," Sara told him, thinking she was too easily distracted lately. "Thanks for the information."

"It hasn't been in the paper, either."

"What's that?"

"The obituaries," Brock said, giving a self-deprecating chuckle. "Tools of the trade. We like to see who's doing who, if you know what I mean."

"And there's been no mention?"

"Nary a peep," he told her. "Maybe they sent her up North? I think that's where her daddy is."

"Still, it would've been in the paper, right?" Sara asked, playing dumb. Brock was generally discreet because of the business he was in, but she did not want to start rumors.

"Maybe," he said. "Or the church bulletin at least. I haven't seen it there, either." He paused, then said, "Heck, Sara, you know how some people are about death. They just don't want to admit it happened, especially with a kid involved. Maybe she handled it quietly just so she could get through it, you know?"

"You're right," Sara told him. "Anyway, thanks for the information."

"I hear Grace Patterson doesn't have much longer," he said, and she imagined business was slow if he was being so chatty. "That's gonna be a hard one."

"You know her, too?"

"She helped me with the choir before she took sick this last time. Wonderful woman."

"I've heard that."

"From what I've gathered, she's just eat up with the cancer," he said. "Those are always the hard ones." His voice had dropped, and he seemed genuinely upset. "Well, hell, Sara, you know what I'm talking about."

Sara did, and she understood his grief. She couldn't imagine having to do Dan Brock's job. He probably felt the same way about hers.

"Guess there's no word on the little girl yet?" he asked.

"No," Sara said. "Not that I know of."

"Jeffrey's a good man," he told her. "If anyone can find her, it's him."

Sara wanted to believe this, but with everything she had learned about the case lately, she wasn't too sure.

Brock lightened his tone. "You take care now," he said. "Best to your mama and them."

Sara wished him the same and hung up the phone. She pressed the button for a new line and called Jeffrey.

14

Lena tried not to make it too obvious that she was listening to Jeffrey's telephone conversation with Sara Linton. This was incredibly difficult to do, as they were both in the front seat of Jeffrey's car. Lena looked out the window, feigning a casualness she did not feel. Part of her was still struck by what had happened with Mark only hours before. Time would only tell if he would make it. Oxygen had been cut off to his brain for some time, and until he woke up from the coma, there was no way to predict how much damage had been done.

Lena glanced at Jeffrey as he told Sara what Mark had said about his relationship with Grace Patterson. Whatever Sara said in response was brief and to the point, because Jeffrey agreed with her immediately.

"I'll see you tonight," Jeffrey said, then replaced the phone in the cradle. He started in on Lena immediately. "I told you not to be alone with Mark," he said.

"I know," Lena responded, and started to tell him again why she had let Brad leave the trailer. He stopped her, holding up his hand.

"I'm only going to say this once, Lena," Jeffrey began, and it seemed like he had been wanting to say this for a while. "You're not the boss here."

"I know that."

"Don't interrupt me," he ordered, cutting his eyes at her. "I've been doing this job a hell of a lot longer than you, and I tell you to do things a certain way because I know what I'm doing."

She opened her mouth to agree, but then thought better of it.

"Being a detective gives you some autonomy, but at the end of the day you take your orders from me." He looked at her, as if anticipating she'd argue. "If I can't trust you to follow simple orders, why should I keep you working for me?"

Obviously, it was her turn to speak, but she couldn't come up with anything to say.

"I want you to think about this, Lena. I know you like your job and I know you're good at it when you decide to be, but after what happened . . ." He shook his head, as if that wasn't right. "Even before what happened. You've got a problem taking orders, and that makes you more dangerous to me than the crooks."

Lena felt the sting from his words and rushed to defend herself. "Mark wouldn't have confided in me if Brad had been there."

"He might not have tried to take his life, either," Jeffrey said. He was quiet, staring out at the road as he drove. He sighed, then said, "That wasn't fair."

Lena was silent.

"Mark probably would've found a way to do something like this. He's a very troubled kid. It wasn't your fault."

She nodded, not knowing whether what he was saying was true or not. At least he was trying to comfort her, which is a hell of a lot more than she had done with him when they had talked about his shooting Jenny Weaver.

"And it's not just Mark. Have you made an appointment with a therapist yet?"

She shook her head.

Jeffrey said, "Lena, I hate to say this now, but there never seems to be a good time." He paused, as if making sure to word this carefully. "You need to think about whether or not you want to be a cop anymore."

She nodded, biting the tip of her tongue so that she wouldn't start crying. How could she not be a cop? If she wasn't a police detective, what was she? Certainly not a sister; barely a woman. Lena wasn't even sure some days if she was a human being.

"You're a good cop," he said.

She nodded again, resting her head against her hand, staring out the side window so he wouldn't see her face. Her throat felt like it was closing up as she strained not to cry. She hated herself for being so weak, and the thought of breaking down in front of Jeffrey was enough to keep her from sobbing like a girl.

"We'll talk when this case is over," Jeffrey told her, and his voice was reassuring, but it didn't help. "I want to help you, Lena, but I can't help you if you don't want to be helped."

It sounded like Hank's A.A. bullshit, and Lena had had enough of that to last her a lifetime. She cleared her throat and said, "Okay," still staring out the window.

Jeffrey was silent as he drove, and she didn't speak again until she noticed that he missed the turnoff heading back into town and the station.

"Where are we going?" she asked.

"Dottie Weaver's house," he said. "She hasn't picked up the body at the morgue."

"It's been a while," Lena said, surreptitiously wiping her eyes with the back of her hand. "Do you think something's wrong with her?"

"I don't know," Jeffrey told her, his jaw working.

"Do you think she's done something?" Lena asked. "Like Mark?"

He gave her a curt nod, and she did not push it.

Jeffrey pointed up the road, saying, "Randolph Street is up here, right?"

"Yes," Lena confirmed, and Jeffrey took the turn onto Randolph. The driveways were few and far between, most of the houses set back from the road and resting on three to four acres each. They were in an older section of Grant, built back before people started throwing cheap houses on top of each other. Jeffrey braked the car in front of a gray mailbox that was open in the front, mail stacked so tight someone would have to use a crowbar to get it out.

"This is it," he said. He backed up the car and turned into a tree-lined driveway. If he noticed the four copies of the *Grant Observer* wrapped in plastic bags at the head of the drive, he did not say.

The Weaver home was farther back from the road than Lena would have guessed, and a few seconds passed before a small ranch house came into view. A second level had been added at some point, and the bottom of the house did not really match the top.

"Do you see a car?" Jeffrey asked, stopping in front of an open carport.

Lena looked around, wondering why he had asked a question with such an obvious answer. "No."

They both got out of the car, and Lena walked around the perimeter of the house, checking every window on the first floor. Either the curtains or the blinds were drawn on each one, and she could not see inside. There was a double door leading to what was probably the basement, but it was locked tight. The small windows around the foundation had been painted black from the inside.

As she circled back around the house, she could hear Jeffrey knocking on the front door, calling, "Mrs. Weaver?"

Lena stood at the bottom of the porch steps, wiping the sweat off her forehead with the back of her arm. "I couldn't see anything. All the curtains are drawn." She told him about the basement and the blackened windows.

Jeffrey glanced around the yard, and she could sense how anxious he was. Dottie Weaver had not bothered to get her newspapers or mail for a while. She was divorced and her daughter had just been killed. Maybe she had felt there wasn't a lot to go on living for.

Jeffrey asked, "Did you check the windows?"

"They're all locked tight," she reported.

"Even that broken one?"

Lena got his meaning. As law officers, they needed a damn good reason to go into Weaver's house without a warrant. A bad feeling was not good enough to go on. A broken window was.

She asked, "You mean the broken one in the basement?"

He gave her a curt nod.

"What if an alarm goes off?"

"Then we'll call the police," he said, walking down the steps.

Lena would have broken the window herself, but she appreciated that Jeffrey was trying to keep her out of this gray area of the law as much as he could. She leaned against the porch railing, waiting for the sound of broken glass. It came about a minute later, and then several more minutes passed with nothing further from Jeffrey. She was about to go around to the back of the house when she heard his foot-steps inside.

He stood in the doorway, one hand on the knob, the other holding a bright yellow raincoat.

"Lacey's?" Lena asked, taking the coat. It was small enough for a child, but the label in the back took away all doubt. Someone had sewn the child's name onto it in case it was lost.

"Jesus," Lena mumbled, then looked back up at Jeffrey. He shook his head no, meaning he had not found her in the house.

He stepped aside so that she could walk in. Heat enveloped her, and the house felt hotter inside than it was outside. The first room was large, and probably was used as a living room. It was hard to tell, though, because all the furniture was gone. Even the carpet had been pulled up from the floor, and the tacking around the perimeter stood out like teeth.

"What the . . . ?" Lena said, walking through the room. She noticed that Jeffrey had his weapon drawn, the muzzle pointed toward the floor. Lena followed suit, kicking herself for being so stupid. She had been so shocked to see Lacey's coat and the state of the house that she had forgotten that someone might still be in the house. With all the noise they had made outside, whoever might be inside was certainly aware there was company.

Jeffrey nodded for her to follow him into the kitchen, which was in the same state as the main room. All the cabinet doors were open, showing empty shelves. Lena walked through the dining room, a den, and a small office, all of them empty, all of them missing carpeting.

The house had a bad feeling to it, and she let herself think what Jeffrey had probably thought when he had found the yellow raincoat. Lacey had been here. She could still be here. At least, her body could.

"Smell that?" Jeffrey whispered.

Lena sniffed the air, and realized that she had been smelling fresh paint with something sharper underneath. "Clorox," she whispered back. "Something else I can't place."

"Those pictures of Mark you took when you arrested him," Jeffrey began. "He had paint on his clothes, right?"

Lena nodded, turning around in the room. She looked around the corner, finding the stairs. "Have you been up yet?" she asked, just as a tapping noise came from upstairs.

They both raised their weapons at the same time, and Lena took point before Jeffrey could. She walked sideways up the stairs, keeping her gun directed up toward the ceiling. She tested her foot on each stair, noting that they, too, had been stripped. Every muscle in her body tensed as adrenaline pumped through her system.

At the top of the stairs, Lena paused before looking down a long hallway. A wall was to her left, a small window that she had not noticed from the outside mounted up high. It was cracked open, and Lena saw some leaves and debris on the floor. Black curtains hung from a rod with weights sewn into the bottom edges. The paint under the window was marked where the weights had hit it, and fresh white paint lined the edge of the material. Lena pointed this out to Jeffrey, thinking it might have caused the noise they heard, and Jeffrey shrugged, as if to say maybe, maybe not.

Lean started to go down the hall, but Jeffrey walked ahead of her, peering into the open doorways of each room. She followed, seeing that the bathroom and two bedrooms had been cleaned out just like the downstairs. She wondered if Jeffrey's gut clenched each time he looked into a room, thinking Lacey Patterson might be in there. Lena had an eerie reminder of this morning with Mark as Jeffrey stopped in front of the only closed door at the end of the hall.

He stood in front of the door, both hands cupping his gun. For some reason, he wasn't moving, and Lena thought to take over, but something about the look on his face stopped her. Was he scared of what he would find? Lena knew she was.

He leaned toward the door, like he heard something.

She mouthed, "What?"

He shook his head, as if to tell her to give him a minute to think. Lena stood beside him, her shoulder to the wall by the door, sweating as she waited for him to make a decision. She hoped he would not wait too long, because stopping to think was taking away some of her resolve.

Finally, he motioned her back behind him, then even farther back. He kept waving her down the hall, then into the stairway. When she was standing on the stair second from the top, her neck craned so she could look around the corner, he seemed satisfied. Lena braced herself for action as he raised his foot and kicked in the door. A flash of light came a split-second later, and somehow the door blew back, pushing Jeffrey down the hallway. A roar came a couple of beats later, and Lena ducked into the stairs as a ball of fire flashed up the hallway.

"Jesus," she whispered, covering herself with her arms as she knelt on the stairs. Lena waited for the heat to envelop her, or flames to eat her alive, but nothing happened. She stood from her crouch and peered around the corner into the hallway. Jeffrey was underneath the door, but he was moving. The top of the door was charred to a crisp. There were black soot marks along the walls, but there was no fire. The heat must have been so intense that it burned itself out.

She heard a crackling to her left and turned quickly. The black curtains were on fire. Lena took off her jacket and beat them until they fell from the rod. She stamped the last embers out on the floor just as Jeffrey pushed the door off of him.

"What the hell happened?" he demanded, touching his face and body, probably to see if he had been burned. He seemed okay from what Lena could tell. Somehow, the door had protected him from the blast.

"I have no idea," she said, dropping her coat and walking over to help him stand.

"I thought I smelled something outside the door," he told her, leaning heavily on her shoulder. "What the hell *was* that?"

She asked, "What did you smell?"

"Gasoline, I guess. I wasn't sure. It was hard to tell with the paint." He brushed his slacks off, but there was really no point. They both looked at his shoes. The soles had melted from the heat.

"Dammit," he muttered. "I just bought these last week."

Lena stared at him, wondering if he had hit his head.

"Are you all right?" he asked, brushing something off her shoulder.

"I'm fine," she told him, and she was, but only because Jeffrey had made her stand in the stairwell.

"Is that out?" he asked, pointing to the window. The heat from the blast had knocked out the panes and busted the sash. There were dark gashes in the wall where the curtains had ignited.

"I think so," Lena said, brushing back her hair. Dust fell out, and she guessed the ends might have been burned.

Jeffrey walked down the hall, stopping just outside the doorway of the room. He was being careful, looking for a second device. Finally, he stepped into the room and turned around. "There was a trigger over the door," he said, his hand over his chest. Lena wondered just for a second how he could be thinking so clearly. He could have easily been killed by the blast.

Jeffrey pointed over the jamb, saying, "There's a wire here that goes . . ." He followed something with his eyes, turning slowly around the room. "Here."

Lena peeked in to see what he was talking about. Three cans of gasoline were stacked in the corner. On top of them was a scorched bath towel and something that looked like it had been a clock radio at one time. The plastic was blown apart, and wires spewed out. The walls and ceiling were scorched and the plastic slats of the blinds in the window looked melted together, but remarkably nothing had ignited.

Lena looked at the device, wondering who could have built something so rudimentary. The metal cans were sealed tight, and the clock had not even been connected to them, as far as she could tell. She touched the towel, then sniffed it. Whoever had arranged the bomb had not even doused the towel in gasoline to help it ignite.

She said, "This was stupid."

"Yeah," Jeffrey agreed. "What exploded, though?"

"I have no idea," she said, looking around the room. For the first time, she noticed that this was the only room in the house that was still furnished. Carpet was on the floor, and posters of boy bands were stuck on the wall. There was a little-girl feel to the room, with its once pink walls, white wicker furniture, and shelves full of stuffed animals. A full-sized bed with a pink blanket over it was against the wall opposite the door. The material was stiff-looking, as if it had been saturated at one point, then air-dried in the heat. Lena touched the blanket, then sniffed her fingers.

She said, "Gasoline."

Jeffrey was looking around the room, too. "Everything

looks like it was soaked in gas," he said. "The windows are locked tight. Maybe the fumes built up, and when the door triggered the clock, the fumes caught fire?" Jeffrey looked down the hallway. "Fire needs oxygen to burn. Maybe the open window at the end of the hall sucked it out?"

"It sure looked that way from where I was standing," Lena told him. "The bomb guys can figure that out."

"Right," he said, and pulled his cell phone out of his breast pocket. He made two calls, one to Frank at the station to get the bomb squad moving, the other to Nick Shelton at the Georgia Bureau of Investigation. He requested that a crime scene team come out to the house and search it with a fine-tooth comb.

"We've got some time before they show up," Jeffrey said, closing the phone.

"Great," Lena mumbled, thinking between the heat and the odor in the house, they might asphyxiate before reinforcements came.

"Why didn't she strip this room, too?" Jeffrey asked.

Lena shrugged. "Maybe it was too hard for her to come in here after Jenny died."

"I guess," he mumbled, wiping something out of his eyes. "But why go to the trouble to strip the house if they thought the bomb would burn it down?"

"Arson inspectors can find just about anything," Lena told him. "You can watch the Discovery channel and know that."

"It's like she hated her," Jeffrey said, not letting it go. "I can understand not stripping the room, but this . . ."—he indicated the gas tanks—"this doesn't make sense."

Lena thought about Mark, and how he might have purposefully rigged the bomb not to explode.

"Who would do this?" he asked. "Grace? Dottie? Was it Mark? None of this makes any sense."

To give herself something to do, she looked around the room. A set of cat figurines was on the dresser alongside some makeup that could only belong to a little girl.

"Maybe she didn't want to be reminded of Jenny?" Lena suggested, and even as she said the words, she got a bad taste in her mouth. "The bomb would have taken out everything."

"Maybe Dottie was abducted," Jeffrey guessed.

"By whom?" Lena asked. "That doesn't jibe. And if she was, how did Lacey's coat get in here? Are you saying that whoever snatched Lacey came after Dottie, too? Then took the time to strip and clean the house?"

Jeffrey asked, "You think Dottie planted the bomb?"

Lena shrugged, even though she was sure in her heart that Mark had planted the bomb. The paint on his clothes, the chemical smell on his body, all pointed to him at the very least being in this house during the last few days. There was no telling what he had been doing.

Jeffrey was obviously thinking the same things as Lena. He said, "Mark had paint on his clothes. We can have the lab check it against the paint on the walls."

"It looked fresh," Lena reluctantly provided.

"Why would Dottie Weaver strip the house this way? Why would she leave without at least burying her daughter?"

Lena wondered again if he'd hit his head. He was repeating the same questions over and over again, as if she might suddenly come up with the answer. She was about to ask him if he wanted to sit down when he turned around and looked at the bed in the middle of the room as if it might start talking to him. After a couple of moments of this, he took his foot and kicked the mattress over.

"What's that?" Lena asked, but she could see well enough for herself. About twenty cheap-looking magazines had been stowed between the mattress and the boxspring. All of them had children on the covers doing the kinds of things that children should never be made to do. They all had the same title, too, *Child-Lovers* in a fancy script with a familiar heart drawing inserted where the "o" in lover should be.

Lena put her hand on the wall, trying to steady herself.

"You okay?" Jeffrey asked, cupping her elbow as if she might faint.

"The design."

"It's the same one Mark has on his hand," he said, pushing through the stack of magazines. He mumbled, "I used to hide shit under my bed, too."

"Why would Mark do that?" Lena asked, not able to move past this point. "Why would he put that on his hand?"

Jeffrey turned back to the bed. "Maybe it's his way of saying he likes younger girls. Maybe that's how those guys operate so they know each other," he suggested, picking up one of the magazines. He leafed through it, then picked up another. His jaw worked as he stopped on a particular page.

"What?" Lena asked, looking over his shoulder. A picture of Mark, probably taken a few years ago, served as the centerfold.

Lena picked up a magazine and skimmed through it until she found another picture of Mark. Jenny was in this one, and they were doing something Lena could not describe. Worse, in the back pages there were photos of Mark with older men and some women. The adults' faces were not shown, but Mark was revealed from head to toe. His expression was pained, and it brought tears to Lena's eyes to see him compromised like this. Seeing what Mark had done and what he had obviously been made to do hurt Lena more than she wanted to admit. She finally understood why he had wanted to know what it felt like for her to be raped. He wanted to compare notes.

Jeffrey examined the magazines, his jaw clenched so tight she had trouble understanding him when he spoke. "These aren't exactly sophisticated. I guess a small press could handle it."

"Probably," she agreed.

"Christ," Jeffrey hissed, scowling at the magazine he was holding. "This guy has on his wedding ring." The disgust in his voice would have peeled paint off the walls. "That's Jenny," he said.

Lena looked at the photograph. Jenny Weaver was pictured, a man's hand firm on the back of her neck as he guided her down. The gold of the man's wedding ring caught the light, and Lena wondered if that was part of the thrill for the perverts who looked at these pictures, thinking that the guy was married and having sex with little girls.

She said, "That's disgusting."

"Here's the same ring in another one," Jeffrey said, but he didn't show her the photo. He continued to flip the pages. "And another one."

Lena asked, "Are you sure it's the same—?"

"Fucking pervert," Jeffrey yelled, then twisted the magazine in his hands and threw it against the wall. "What the fuck is happening here?" he screamed. She could see a vein in his neck throbbing. "How many kids were involved in this thing?"

Lena tucked her hands into her pockets, letting him get it out.

Jeffrey turned, looking out the window at the backyard.

His voice was softer, but she could still hear the anger when he asked, "Do you recognize any of the other kids?"

Lena picked up a magazine, but he stopped her. "I don't want you looking at this shit," he said. "We'll get Nick's people on it." He put his hand to his forehead, like a bad headache was about to strike. "How many kids are involved in this thing?" he repeated. "How many Grant kids were wrapped up in this?"

She didn't have the answer, but he knew that.

He flipped open his phone again. "I'm going to get Nick here to look at this," he said. "I want you to go to the hospital and try to get something out of Grace Patterson."

She shook her head, not understanding.

"She's connected to Mark *and* Jenny. She has to know something," he told her. "I'd do it myself, but I'd probably rip her fucking throat out." She saw his grip tighten around the phone. "Voice mail." He waited a couple of beats, then said, "Nick, Jeff Tolliver. I need you to call me as soon as possible. We've got something new on the Lacey Patterson case." He ended the call, saying to Lena, "There's no way this isn't a priority now."

Lena nodded, thinking she had never seen him this angry, not even at her.

He dialed another number into the phone. While he was waiting for someone to answer, he instructed Lena, "I want you to confront Grace on what you know. I want you to tell her exactly what Mark told you, and I want you to find out what the fuck has been going on."

"Do you think she'll tell me anything?"

"Her daughter is missing," he reminded her. "We found her coat here."

Lena looked down at her hands. "Considering what she was doing to Mark, do you think she cares?"

He flipped the phone closed again, looking her in the eye. "Tell you the truth, Lena, I don't know what the hell to think about anybody involved in this case."

He was about to open his phone again when it rang. Before he answered it, he gave Lena his keys and nodded toward the door, telling her, "Go."

Thursday

15

Jeffrey felt like he had been blown across a hallway with a wooden door plastered to his body. His arms ached, and his knees felt like they would never bend right again. Working at the Weaver house had taken the rest of the day, but when he had called Sara at one in the morning, she had not hesitated to ask him over. Part of him was nervous about the way they had picked up so easily again. He kept waiting for the other shoe to drop, for Sara to say that she could not go through with this. Another part of him was just so damn happy to be back in her life that he wanted to enjoy every minute of it as much as he could. Even sitting in the tub with her, talking about what was probably one of the most horrible cases he had ever worked, he felt at home.

He watched Sara across the tub as she sipped her wine, obviously letting what he had just told her sink in. Jeffrey had forgotten how great the claw-footed tub in her master bathroom was. Six feet long with a center-mounted faucet, it was perfect for two people. They had spent half their marriage in this tub.

Sara rested her glass on her knee. "Where is Lena now?"

"The hospital," Jeffrey told her. "Patterson's still holding on."

"She saying anything?"

"Grace?" Jeffrey asked. Sara nodded, and he said, "She's pretty lucid, but she's got one of those morphine pumps for the pain."

"Breast cancer is an incredibly painful way to die."

"Good," he said, leaning over the tub to pick up his glass of wine. With his parents' shining example, Jeffrey had never taken to alcohol, but after today he needed something to take the edge off. Before he started talking to Sara, he had felt like his mind was spinning, not able to concentrate on one thing at a time like he needed to do. There were so many pieces to the case floating around, and so many questions that had yet to be answered. Somehow, the alcohol was giving him focus.

Sara asked, "Do you really think Grace Patterson will give a deathbed confession?"

"Not really, but you never know. . . ." He paused, measuring his words. "Lena's got this thing about Mark."

"What kind of thing?"

"She kept insisting that he was raped."

"He was," Sara pointed out. "Are you saying he willingly posed for those magazines, that he seduced his mother?"

"Of course not," he said, and he was glad she had made that point. "What I'm really worried about right now is Lena."

"She's doing the best she can," Sara told him. "Give her some time."

"I just can't take that kind of chance with her, Sara." He

rubbed his eyes, still smelling gasoline on his hands even though he had scrubbed himself thoroughly with soap.

He said, "She's too close to the edge. I don't want to be the one standing there watching when she finally goes over. I don't think I could live with myself."

"It's going to take time for her to get past what happened," Sara said in a measured tone. "If she ever does at all."

"She won't even talk to anybody about it."

"You can't force her to do it," Sara countered. "She'll talk about it when she's ready to."

He stared into his glass, not responding.

"So," Sara said, obviously realizing he wanted to move on. "Let's change the subject."

"Okay."

She summarized what they knew, ticking the points off on her fingers. "Mark and Jenny were posing for the magazines at Dottie's house. Grace Patterson was involved with her son."

"Right."

"What about Teddy Patterson?"

"He could be the link here," Jeffrey said. "He's a truck driver. Maybe he picks up the magazines and takes them across the country."

"Where is he now?"

"Either at the hospital or at his trailer. Frank's been tailing him." Jeffrey took a healthy drink from his glass. "He doesn't seem too concerned that one of his kids might be brain dead and the other has been kidnapped."

"What's he doing?"

"Staying by his wife, mostly."

"Maybe he's focusing on one thing at a time?" Sara suggested. "His wife's dying, he's with her. That's something immediate he can do instead of just sitting around feeling helpless."

"Trust me, he's not the kind of guy to feel helpless."

"You think he'll do something?"

"I think he'll leave town as soon as his wife is dead," he told her. "I talked to Nick Shelton. We're thinking Teddy's going to be the contact for his collar over in Augusta."

"The guy Nick arrested who had the child pornography?"

He nodded, debating whether or not to tell Sara the rest, then deciding he should be open with her. "The meeting is being scheduled for tomorrow at noon."

"What meeting?" she asked, and he could see the concern in her eyes.

"Nick's guy, this porn distributor, got a call from a pay phone. A man's voice was on the other end." He paused, trying to gauge Sara's reaction. "I didn't recognize the voice, but they're meeting at the hotel over in Augusta to drop off the magazines."

"And I take it you're going to be there?"

"Yeah," he said. "I take it you've got a problem with that?"

She sighed. "I remember when we were married how I would cringe every time the phone rang and I didn't know exactly where you were."

He drank some wine, letting this sink in. "You never told me that before."

"I know I didn't," she said, then changed the subject again. "So, how does this work? Dottie and Grace do the magazines, Teddy Patterson delivers them, then Nick's guy distributes them around here?"

"Pretty much," Jeffrey confirmed. "We think Patterson probably makes stops all around the Southeast. Nick is going to pull his records from the Department of Transportation as soon as we bust him."

"Why not before?"

"Who knows who'd tip him off?" Jeffrey pointed out.

"Besides, Frank's glued to Teddy. It's not like he's going to be able to get away with anything."

"Why arrest Patterson now? Why not follow him on his route and pick up all the distributors?"

"Nick says they have a phone network. If one of them doesn't call the next with the okay, then they close shop. It's very sophisticated."

"I don't suppose anyone knows anything about where Lacey might be?"

"You don't suppose right."

"How long has the GBI been working on this pornography ring?"

"Years," Jeffrey said. "They just needed to know who was bringing them in."

"Is this where Dottie comes in?"

Jeffrey shrugged, because nothing was clear at this point. "I don't like to think about that woman having some kind of network. It means she's got a safe place to go and hide. It means she's connected to all kinds of people all over the world who are invested in helping her because she keeps supplying them with their sick porn." He felt his anger swelling again, and took a deep breath to calm himself. When that didn't work, he settled on drinking some more wine.

"You know they swap kids," Sara said, her tone measured. "Lacey could be in Canada or Germany by now." She paused, then continued, "Or, Dottie could be abusing Lacey herself. Dottie could be keeping her somewhere, doing God knows what." Sara's voice went up on this last part as the threat seemed to hit her.

Jeffrey rubbed his eyes, like he could wipe this away. "How could a woman, a mother, do that kind of thing to a child?"

"In my experience," Sara began, "women who abuse

children are much more sadistic than men. I think it's because they know they can get away with it. They know no one will believe they're capable of hurting children." She added, "It's especially bad when it's a boy who is being abused. Let's take the incest out of it for a minute. A boy having sex with a woman twice his age is patted on the back. A girl doing the same thing is considered a victim. There's a big disparity there."

Jeffrey said, "I never even suspected his mother."

"Why would you? There was no reason to."

"I didn't have a problem with Teddy Patterson as a suspect."

Sara sat back in the tub and let him talk.

Jeffrey told her, "The crime scene techs are still at Weaver's house, but preliminary results show printer's ink in the basement."

"For magazines?" Sara asked. "I thought they needed a big press."

"They're not exactly slick," Jeffrey said. He drank more wine. "All the articles are about how to meet the right kid."

Sara pressed her lips together.

"I'll tell you what, Sara, I wish to God I hadn't seen any of it."

She stroked his leg with her foot. "Have you found the carpeting from the house?"

"Brad and Frank are going to check the dump at daybreak. Based on what they sampled from the floor, the carpets are coated in fluids."

"Body fluids?" she asked. "They soaked through?"

He nodded, not liking how that sounded, either. "There's also a room in the basement that looks like it was used as a darkroom." He rested his glass on the rim of the tub. "My guess is they used the house to take the pictures, and printed up the magazines there."

"An explosion would have destroyed all of that evidence."

"Yeah," he agreed. "I still can't figure out why she didn't strip Jenny's room."

"She didn't really need anything from Jenny's room, did she?"

"I guess not," he agreed.

"Did you find any evidence in the room?"

"Nothing. The gasoline might have covered semen traces. I don't know how that works."

"But there was nothing obvious?"

"Nothing," he said. "None of the pictures was taken in there. Maybe it was the only room in the house that was clean." He rubbed his eyes, feeling incredibly tired. "I can't believe this was going on in town and nobody knew about it."

Sara picked up the bottle of wine and filled his glass. "Do you remember what she said to me?" she asked. "She asked if I had cut Jenny open. Do you think she meant the castration?"

Jeffrey thought about this for a second. "She could have."

"I keep playing that interview back in my mind, and when I get to that point, I see how Dottie changed. You know what I'm talking about? She was almost relieved."

"I guess," Jeffrey said, though he could not remember. The interview seemed like a lifetime away.

Sara said, "I called the hospital. Mark still hasn't regained consciousness."

"Do they have a prognosis?"

"It's hard to tell with ABIs," she said, then, "anoxic brain injuries." He nodded, and she continued, "There's a lot of swelling in his brain. They won't know how much damage was done until the swelling goes down. The longer it takes, the worse it will be."

"Does he have a chance of being normal?"

She shook her head. "No." She paused, as if to let this sink in. "He'll never be the same again. That is, if he wakes up. There's going to be some damage."

"He just seemed like this punk kid."

Sara finished the wine and set her glass on the floor. "You think Teddy Patterson beat him up before he came to the clinic?"

Jeffrey had forgotten that detail. "I guess it's possible. What about Lacey, though? Why was Mark chasing after her?"

"She could have been threatening to tell."

"We didn't find any pictures of Lacey. Wouldn't Teddy Patterson handle something like that anyway?"

"Possibly," she said. "Maybe he was in the black Thunderbird."

"He was probably at the hospital," Jeffrey pointed out. "I'll have Frank check, but I'm pretty sure."

"If Lacey is the mother of that baby, who do you think the father is?"

"I don't know," he answered, because none of it really made any sense. Jeffrey put his hand over his eyes, trying to understand this. Lately, it seemed like every case he dealt with had some kind of weird twist to it that took a part of him with it. He longed for a simple money-motive or jealous threat gone wrong. He figured that he could take just about anything but knowing a child was in jeopardy.

Sara must have sensed his anguish. She slid toward him, and Jeffrey moved over so that she could put her head on his chest.

"You still smell smoky," she told him.

"Explosions can do that."

She ran her fingers along his chest, but it seemed like she was doing this more to make sure he was really there than to arouse anything in him. She curled a piece of his hair around her finger, saying, "I want you to be careful tomorrow."

"I'm always careful."

Sara sat up a little so that she could look him in the eye. "More careful than usual," she said. "For me, okay?"

"Okay," he nodded, pushing her hair back behind her ear. "What's going on with us?" he asked.

"I dunno," she said.

"It feels good, whatever it is."

She smiled, touching her fingers to his lips. "Yeah."

He opened his mouth to say more, but his cell phone rang, spoiling the moment.

"It's two in the morning," Jeffrey said, as if this made any difference. The phone was on the closed toilet lid, and Sara picked it up and handed it to him. "Maybe it's Nick?"

He checked the caller I.D. "It's the station."

Paul Jennings was a tall, barrel-chested man with a dark beard accentuating his round face. His white dress shirt was wrinkled, as were his brown polyester pants. But for the expectant expression on his face, Jeffrey thought he looked like a high school math teacher.

"Thank you for coming in," he said. "I was going to wait to call you, but I couldn't sleep. I had this feeling."

"It's all right," Jeffrey said, leading the man into his office.

"I know this is a shot in the dark. I just had this feeling," he repeated. "I took the first flight they had."

"I apologize for not returning your call," Jeffrey told him. "My secretary thought you were trying to sell me something."

Paul told him, "I work for a vinyl supply company up in Newark. I guess I should have made it clear why I was calling." He paused. "I've been looking for my daughter for so long, and I've been disappointed so many times." He held his hands up in a shrug. "Part of me couldn't believe they might be here, after all this time."

"I understand," Jeffrey told him, though he really had no idea what kind of pain this man had suffered over the last ten years. "Would you like some coffee?"

"No, no," Paul said, taking the seat Jeffrey indicated.

"We've got a fresh pot in the back," Jeffrey offered, walking around to the opposite side of the desk. He knew who this man was, and what he had to be told. Jeffrey wanted to keep some distance between them. He needed space.

"This is a picture of Wendy when she was three," Paul said, showing Jeffrey a photograph of a happy-looking child. Though it was taken several years ago, Jeffrey was still able to tell that the girl in the photograph had grown up to be Jenny Weaver.

"Was this just before she disappeared?" Jeffrey asked, sliding the photo back across his desk.

The man nodded, showing Jeffrey another picture. "Wanda took her shortly after that."

Jeffrey studied the next photograph, though he knew from first glance that Wanda Jennings was the person he knew as Dottie Weaver. He slid this back across, and watched as Paul stacked them together, putting the picture of Dottie Weaver on the bottom so he would not have to look at her while they talked.

Jeffrey asked, "Can you tell me when it was your wife and daughter disappeared?"

Paul shifted in his chair. "We were living in Canada while I went to graduate school," he said. "Vinyl siding wasn't how I planned to spend my professional career. But when Wendy was taken from me . . ." He paused, a sad smile on his lips. "Wanda was working as a nurse at the hospital. I guess she was there about five months when the allegations started."

"What kind of allegations?"

"She worked in the maternity ward," Paul said. "There were rumors that something wasn't right. That something was going on." He took a deep breath. "I didn't listen to them, of course. We had been married for three years by then. I loved my wife. I would never have thought she was capable of . . . And women don't really do that kind of thing, do they?"

Jeffrey was silent. They both knew the answer to that.

"So," Paul began. "She was put on administrative leave while they investigated the charges. Babies can't really tell you what happens to them, but there were rumors of some physical findings. I still didn't believe what people were saying, until one day there was a knock on the door. Two cops wanted to talk to me."

"Where was your wife?"

"She was out doing the shopping. I suppose they were watching the house, because they knocked on the door ten minutes after she left."

Jeffrey nodded for him to continue.

"They told me about the physical evidence," he said. "They had photographs and . . ." He stopped. "It was graphic."

"You don't have to tell me what they found," Jeffrey told him, and Paul seemed relieved.

"They wanted to check Wendy to see if she had been . . ." He paused. "I still could not accept that Wanda had done these things, let alone that she would ever harm our daughter. Wanda is very good at making people think she's trustworthy."

"Yeah," Jeffrey agreed, because he had seen that first-hand.

"When Wanda got back from the store, I confronted her with what they had said. We argued. Somehow, she convinced me that the police were wrong, that it was another woman at the hospital. A nurse I had met a couple of times and, honestly, did not like."

"People like your wife can be pretty persuasive."

"Yes," Paul said. "A week went by, and it was still in the news. The police actually did investigate this other woman." Tears came to his eyes. "We believe what we want to believe, don't we?"

Jeffrey nodded.

"I suppose it was three weeks later that the police came back. They had a warrant this time, and wanted to search the house." Paul looked at the picture of his child, resting his hand beside it. "They had talked to her the day before. It was an official interview. I guess they had finally found enough evidence to do something." He looked back at Jeffrey. "They came very early, about six in the morning. I was still asleep." He gave a humorless laugh. "I had stayed up late studying for a final. How something like that could have seemed important to me . . ."

"We all cope in different ways."

"Yes, well," he said, obviously not accepting this. "They were gone. Wanda had taken Wendy sometime during the night. I never saw or heard from them again."

"What brought you here?"

"A friend of mine called me," he said. "He runs credit checks for us at work, for the siding, and I had asked him a while back to keep an eye out for their social security numbers. About a week ago, Wendy's came up on a Visa application. The address was a post office box in your town."

Jeffrey nodded, thinking that Dottie Weaver, or whatever the hell her name was, had probably thought it was safe to use her daughter's identity after all of this time. She would have gotten away with it if Paul Jennings had not been so vigilant.

"Do you have the address?" Jeffrey asked, feeling hope for the first time. Dottie obviously wanted that credit card. She would have to come back for it.

Paul Jennings handed him a slip of paper. Jeffrey thought he recognized the address as that of the Mailing Post over in Madison. He copied it down and handed back the paper, hoping they might use this to trace Dottie and maybe find Lacey Patterson.

"I just had to come down and see for myself," Paul said, tucking the page back into his pocket. "To see if she was here."

Paul waited for Jeffrey to speak, but Jeffrey could not think how to tell the man what had happened to his daughter. What's more, Jeffrey was not sure how he could admit to this man, who had been searching for so many years, that the person who had killed Wendy Jennings was sitting across the desk from him.

"Is she here?" Paul repeated, a hopeful tone to his voice that cut Jeffrey in two.

"I don't know how to say this, Paul, but Wanda has disappeared and Wendy's dead."

Jeffrey did not know what he had been expecting the other man to do, but the look Paul Jennings gave him was surprising. For a split second, he seemed almost relieved to finally know for a fact where his daughter was, then it seemed to hit him that after all of this time, all of his searching, she was dead. His face fell, and he covered his eyes with his hands for a moment as he started to cry.

"I'm so sorry," Jeffrey told him.

Paul's voice shook as he asked, "When?"

"Last Saturday," Jeffrey said, then explained to Paul exactly what had happened, leaving out the fact that his daughter had been mutilated. Through the entire story, Paul shook his head, as if he could not accept what he was hearing. When Jeffrey revealed his own involvement in Jenny's death, the father's mouth dropped open.

"I didn't . . ." Jeffrey stopped, because he had been about to say that he did not have a choice. He wasn't so sure about that. Maybe there had been another choice. Maybe Jenny Weaver had not had it in her to pull the trigger. Maybe Jenny Weaver would be alive today.

The two men stared at each other over Jeffrey's desk, neither of them really knowing what to say. Paul's eyes were glazed like he was too shocked by what he had heard to go on.

"With her mother," Paul finally said, "I expected the worst." He pointed to the pictures on Jeffrey's desk. "That's how I think of her, Mr. Tolliver. I think of my little girl. I don't think of what Wanda did to her, the kind of horrible life she must have lived." He stopped, choking on a sob. "I think of my happy little girl."

"That's best," Jeffrey said, picking up on the man's grief. Tears came to his eyes, and when Paul saw this, he seemed to lose his reserve.

"Oh, God," the man said, putting his hand over his mouth. His body shook as he sobbed. "My poor little girl. My baby. My baby." He rocked back and forth to soothe himself.

"Paul," Jeffrey said, his voice thick with his own grief. He reached across the desk to pat the man's arm, but Paul Jennings took Jeffrey's hand in his own. Jeffrey had never held another man's hand before, and it felt odd to be doing so now. Though, if it helped Paul Jennings through his grief, it was the least he could do.

Paul tightened his grip on Jeffrey's hand. "She was such a sweet girl."

"I know she was," Jeffrey agreed, squeezing back. "My wife, Sara, saw her." Jeffrey realized suddenly that he had mis-spoken. "I mean my ex-wife. She's a pediatrician. Sara."

He looked up, hope in his eyes. "She saw Wendy?"

"Yes," Jeffrey told him. "Sara said she was a bright girl. Very intelligent, very sweet. She had a caring heart."

"Was she healthy?"

Jeffrey lied on purpose this time. There was no reason to tell this father what his daughter had been through. "Yes," he said. "She was very healthy."

Paul released Jeffrey's hand and picked up the photograph of his daughter. "She was always sweet, even as a baby. You can just tell with some kids. She had such a good heart."

Jeffrey took out his handkerchief and blew his nose. At the last minute he realized he should have offered it to Paul.

"I'm sorry," Jeffrey said.

"I don't blame you," Paul told him. "I blame her. I blame Wanda. She took my child. She did those horrible things to her." He cleared his throat and wiped his nose with his hand. "She put all of this into motion by being the kind of person she is." He locked eyes with Jeffrey. "I don't blame you," he repeated, his tone vehement. "Don't live with that guilt, Mr. Tolliver. I've lived with guilt my entire life. What if I had never married her? What if I had listened to the rumors? What if I had let the police check my little girl to see if her mother . . . ?" He put his hand to his mouth, and again his body shook as he cried.

Jeffrey felt himself tearing up again, and tried to collect himself. All he could think of was Lacey Patterson's school picture on the flier in his desk drawer. He thought about what Jenny had been through, and what Mark still had ahead of him if he managed to pull out of the coma. He thought of Sara, too, and what she must be going through, the guilt she had to be feeling because these were her kids. Hell, they were Jeffrey's kids, too. Maybe because they didn't have any of their own they felt responsible for the whole town. And look at what Jeffrey had let happen. How many children had been hurt because Jeffrey had been blind to the evil going on in his own backyard?

"You did your job," Paul told Jeffrey, as if reading his mind. "You did what you had to do to protect that boy."

Jeffrey had not helped the girl he knew as Jenny Weaver. He had not rescued Mark or Lacey Patterson. He had not protected anyone but Dottie Weaver, who had sat in this very station house and spoon-fed them her lies.

Paul said, "So much came out after she left town." He looked down at his hands. "She did some baby-sitting on the weekends. Those children were abused, too."

Jeffrey sat up, trying not to let his own grief overshadow Paul's. He asked, "Was a warrant ever issued?"

"No," he said, then gave an ironic smile. "A couple of days later, they issued a warrant to arrest the other woman, but she had left town, too."

Jeffrey felt the hair on the back of his neck rise as he thought about Lacey Patterson. "What was her name?"

"Markson," Paul said, wiping his nose again. "Grace Markson."

16

Lena sat beside Grace Patterson's bed, listening to the slow beeps of the heart monitor beside her. The blind was drawn on the window overlooking the hospital parking lot, but there wasn't much to see at this hour, anyway. Teddy Patterson sat across the bed from Lena in a tall recliner, his head leaned back, his mouth opened as he snored, seeming not to have a care in the world. He had laughed in Lena's face when she suggested Grace had anything to do with what had happened to their children. Patterson was a con, and he had an innate distrust of cops. Of course, if he was involved in this thing up to his eyeballs, he wasn't likely to come clean and tell Lena where his daughter was being held. Teddy had actually demanded Lena leave, but for some reason Grace had requested she be allowed to stay. He had grumbled, but acquiesced. Patterson's wife had her nails dug so deep into his balls he didn't take a shit without getting her permission first. Grace seemed to be the center of Teddy's life and the longer Lena was in the same room with him, the clearer it was to her that Teddy didn't give a shit for either of his children.

Lena looked at Grace Patterson, watching her sleep, wondering at the power the woman seemed to have over her family. She had refused to be put on a ventilator, but a mask gave her oxygen to help her breathe. Pillows were propped around and under her body to keep her comfortable, but there was no mistaking that the woman was dying an extraordinarily painful death. In the few days since Lena had seen her, Grace Patterson had declined rapidly. Maybe it was being in the hospital that had done it to her, but Grace looked as much on her deathbed as she was. Her skin was sallow, her cheeks sunken. Her eyes were rheumy and constantly wept what on a normal person would have been tears.

Lena shifted in her chair, trying to get into a more comfortable position. Her tailbone felt as if it had been beaten with a bat, and her hands and feet were aching like they had after the attack. She had figured out an hour before that this was because she kept clenching her fists and curling her toes. Her body was tight with tension, and just being in the room with the Pattersons made her stomach clench like the rest of her body. She wanted to throttle them both, to remind them that every second ticking by could mean something horrible for Lacey.

Maybe they were being quiet because Lena was in the room. Teddy wasn't exactly acting the part of the grieving husband, as far as Lena could tell. He had watched television while his wife slept, laughing at sitcoms, then narrating for no one in particular the events unfolding during an action movie.

"He's gonna whup his ass," Teddy would tell them. Or, "Give that brother something to think about."

Teddy had fallen asleep during the news and seemed to be a heavy sleeper. Even when the nurse had come in to check Grace's stats, he had not stirred.

All this left Lena with was time to stare at Grace Patterson and think about what had happened in the last few days. Mark was at a different hospital than his mother because the ambulance crew had taken him to the closest emergency room. There was no telling what was going to happen to him, but none of his doctors seemed to think he would ever recover from what he had done to himself.

Lena thought about Mark, who was just like any other boy, just wanting love, wanting his mother's attention, and taking it any way he could. She also remembered herself at that age, and how fucked up she had been. Everything had been so emotional, and she had been desperate for anyone but Hank's approval. She had defined herself by what a small handful of outcasts at school thought of her, and used how she looked to get what in retrospect could only be called the wrong kind of attention.

Lena was fifteen when she first started sleeping with Russ Fleming, and while her body had been ready for the physical side of the relationship, emotionally, she had been a wreck. Russ was twenty-two, something Hank had a really big problem with, but Lena had thought she loved him, and Russ had played her like a pro. Anything he wanted, she gave him. He was a moody asshole, and Lena reacted to him like a thermometer, trying to soothe him one minute and seduce him the next. Her days were constant ups and downs, depending on how Russ was treating her, and if she wasn't crying in her room, she was sitting on the front porch, hands between her knees as she nervously waited for him to show up. She had been so young and so stupid, and Russ had given her what she thought was love.

Looking back now, Lena knew that he was just a paranoid pothead, getting his rocks off screwing a teenage girl, but at the time Lena had thought he was the best thing that had ever happened to her. It was amazing how stupid kids could be, and how desperate they were for love and attention. Mark must have been such an easy target for his mother. He must have felt like an open wound, convinced that only his mother could heal him. And now everything that he had survived had made him want to die. Lena understood the dichotomy all too well.

Grace took a sharp breath, waking up. Her eyes slowly opened. She stared for a while at the ceiling, as if her brain was trying to work out where she was and what was happening. Lena wanted to remind her, to tell her that she was dying, but Grace seemed to make that connection on her own.

The stiff pillowcase crackled as Grace turned her head toward Lena. Her eyes traveled down as far as they could go, past the blood pressure monitor on her arm to the I.V., which she followed to the self-administering morphine pump beside the bed. Lena had had one of these when she was in the hospital. The patient could control the release of morphine by pressing a button attached to the pump. The machine wouldn't let you kill yourself by holding the button down, but it did give the patient some sense of control over her own pain management.

Without being aware of what she was doing, Lena reached over and took the button away from Grace before the woman could press it. Lena had not been alone with Grace since she'd gotten here. Teddy seemed a sound enough sleeper for her to take advantage of the moment.

"Looking for this?" Lena whispered, holding up the device.

Grace's eyes flashed, then darted toward Teddy.

"You want to wake him up so he can hear what I have to say?" Lena asked, still keeping her voice low. "I talked to Mark, Grace. You want Teddy to know just how much you love your little boy?"

She swallowed, but that was all.

"You can talk," Lena said. She had heard Grace ask for ice chips only a few hours before. "I know you can talk."

Slowly, Grace reached up to the mask covering her nose and mouth. She pulled it to the side, panting with the effort. "Give . . . ," she said. "Pump . . ."

Lena tested the weight of the button in her hand. It had felt so much heavier when she had used it for her own pain relief.

She asked, "Hurts, huh?"

Grace nodded, her face contorted in pain.

"You want to trade?" Lena asked, wagging the device like a piece of candy.

Grace had the audacity to smile, and something in her eyes seemed to say that she had underestimated Lena.

"Yeah?" Lena prompted. "Tell me where Lacey is and I'll let you drug yourself to hell and back."

Grace still smiled, but there was a hardness to her eyes now. She turned her head away from Lena to stare back up at the ceiling. Lena could see that the woman's hand shook as she placed it over her chest. The doctor had ordered more powerful narcotics on standby. Why Grace had not called for them earlier was a mystery. It wasn't as if the woman had a chance of getting out of this bed.

Lena said, "I know you want it, Grace. I know you need it."

Grace turned back to her. She inhaled sharply, then breathed out a labored, "No."

Lena stood, clenching her fist around the device. She still kept her voice down so as not to wake Teddy. "I know you raped Mark."

Grace's smile widened, as if this was a fond memory. She closed her eyes, and Lena was under the impression she was recalling a shared moment with her son.

"Tell me about Jenny Weaver," Lena hissed. "What did you do to her?"

"She was . . . ," Grace began, still staring at the ceiling, tears streaming from her eyes. The tears were part of her medical condition, a sign of the physical pain she was in, not an indication that she felt any grief.

The mask was still pushed to the side, and Grace put her hand on it to move it back, but not before saying, "Such . . . a . . . sweet . . ."

Her voice trailed off, and Lena stood there, waiting for her to finish the sentence. When nothing came, she prompted, "Sweet what?"

Grace gave an almost angelic smile behind the mask. "Sweet . . . fuck."

"You bitch," Lena whispered, grabbing the pillow at Grace's side. She moved the mask off the woman's face and pressed the pillow down over her. Grace did not struggle under Lena, who was keeping her eye on Teddy as she tried to smother his wife. Grace's legs twitched slightly, and Lena stopped—made herself stop—pulling back the pillow. She fumbled, putting the mask back onto Grace's face, making sure she got the oxygen. What seemed like minutes but could have only been seconds passed before Grace opened her eyes again. She seemed surprised, then angry. Lena knew that killing her would have been a mercy. Grace Patterson only had a few hours at most left in this world. Lena would not hasten them.

Grace was panting angrily as she glared at Lena. Her mouth worked, and she whispered, "Coward."

Mark had called Lena this before, and maybe it was true, but not for the reason Grace was thinking.

Lena countered, "Not as cowardly as raping a child."

Grace shook her head, either denying that Mark was a child or that what she had done to him was rape.

"He tried to kill himself," Lena told her. "Did you know that?"

She could tell from Grace's reaction that she did not.

"Hanged himself in his closet, right after he told me you'd fucked him," she clarified. "He didn't want to live anymore, knowing what you'd done to him."

Grace stared back at the ceiling. The tears still came, but Lena could not tell if they were from grief or pain.

"He's in a coma. Probably won't wake up."

Grace whispered something, but Lena could not make out what she was saying. Lena leaned down, putting her ear close to the woman's mouth, her hand on the side of the bed. Without warning, Grace reached out, grabbing Lena's hand. The woman was weak from the labor of dying, and Lena was able to pull her hand away, but not before she felt Grace's thumb brush across the scar on Lena's hand. The touch was tender, almost sexual, and Lena could see the charge Grace got out of it.

"You sick bitch," Lena said, rubbing her hand as if she could wipe off the sensation. "You're going to rot in hell."

It seemed to take all of her energy, but the mother said in one smooth line, "I'll see you there."

Lena backed away until she was standing against the wall, feeling an eerie sense of déjà vu. Mark and Jenny had said almost the exact same thing to each other the night Jenny had died.

Lena stood there for a moment, watching Grace Patterson, then checking on Teddy. He was still sound asleep. She checked her watch. There were three more hours until sunrise, when the nurse would be back to check on Grace. Lena clipped the morphine button to the railing, well out of Grace's reach. She sat down in the chair, ignoring her own shaking hands as she waited for Grace Patterson to die.

17

Jeffrey was sweating under his bulletproof vest. The August heat combined with the weight of the Teflon vest would have felled an elephant by now. He had lost enough water from sweating to make the back of his throat feel like it had been rubbed with sandpaper.

"Good times," Nick said, using his handkerchief to wipe the back of his neck.

Jeffrey bit back a cutting remark, asking instead, "What time is it?"

Nick checked his watch. "Ten after," he said. "Don't sweat it, Chief. Criminals got their own sense of time."

"Yeah," Joe Stewart piped up. He was Nick's perp who had flipped, and from the way he was acting, Jeffrey imagined Nick had let the man do a little blow to keep the edge off. He was as wired as a Las Vegas street corner.

Jeffrey said, "You're sure you don't know anything about a missing girl?"

"How young is she?" Joe licked his lips. "You gotta picture of her?"

"Sit down," Nick ordered, kicking at Joe's shins with his pointy cowboy boots. Nick had gone all out for the part of a pedophile, and was wearing a pressed black shirt tucked into the tightest pair of blue jeans Jeffrey had ever seen on a man. Nick had even taken off his gold necklace and trimmed his beard for the occasion. Jeffrey imagined Nick lived for this kind of action. Truthfully, so did every cop Jeffrey knew, including himself.

"I tole you to sit," Nick reminded Joe.

Joe slumped on the bed, scratching his arms as he mumbled something under his breath. He was a skinny kid, probably in his late twenties. Pimples littered his face like spots on a dog, and he had picked at some of them, bringing blood.

Jeffrey looked at Nick. "Did you have to get him pumped up like this?"

"You want him pissing in his pants?" Nick asked.

"Wouldn't be much of a difference," Jeffrey pointed out. Joe smelled almost as bad as the musty thirty-dollar-a-night hotel room they were standing in.

Jeffrey asked, "Are you sure the air conditioner isn't working?"

"We turn it on, we won't be able to pick up the audio," Nick reminded him. "Settle down, Chief. It'll be over soon."

"What about Atlanta?" Jeffrey asked.

Nick's eyes darted to Joe. The post office box in Grant that Dottie had used for the credit card was a dummy drop. A forwarding address had been given so that all mail sent to Grant would automatically be forwarded on to a different post office box in Atlanta. Jeffrey had asked Nick to set up a surveillance, hoping Dottie would show up.

"It's in place," Nick told him. "As soon as I know something, you'll know something."

Jeffrey's phone vibrated at his side, and he clipped it off his belt. "Yeah?"

"Hey," Frank said. "Patterson's been in his trailer since his wife died this morning."

Jeffrey felt the tension drain from his body. Maybe Patterson had canceled the meeting. "Are you sure?"

"Of course I'm sure," Frank bristled. "He didn't even go to the hospital to see his kid."

"All right," Jeffrey said. He snapped the phone shut and reported the news to Nick.

"Maybe we'll be seeing Dottie?" Nick suggested. "Patterson's no fool. He knows he's being watched."

As if on cue, two knocks came at the door, followed by a pause, then another knock.

Jeffrey slipped into the bathroom, leaving the door slightly open so as not to draw attention to it. He grimaced at the smell in the tiny room, which probably had not been ventilated since the Nixon administration.

Joe said, "Hey, man," and the door squeaked open.

"Who's this?" a man asked. Jeffrey strained to place the voice. The only thing he was certain of was that it did not belong to Dottie Weaver.

"Friend of mine," Joe said. "He likes little girls."

"Little, little girls," Nick chimed in. "Know what I mean, hoss?"

"Let's just get this over with," the man said in a terse voice. "I got the van pulled up on the side of the building. Let's go."

Jeffrey waited until they had left the room before walking out of the bathroom. He kept playing the man's voice in his mind, trying to place it, but no epiphany came. What did come was more sweat, and Jeffrey loosened the belt on his vest, wishing he hadn't worn it. Sara had asked him to, though, and he had told her that he would. Maybe if she had considered that he might pass out from heat exhaustion, she would not have insisted.

The door was too dirty to lean against, so Jeffrey just stood beside it, sweating his ass off, waiting for Nick to give him the all-clear. To make the case stick, they had to get delivery, and that meant making sure the truck outside was filled with magazines.

To pass the time, Jeffrey counted to a slow one hundred in his head. He was around sixty-five when he heard Nick yelling, "Get down! Get down!"

Jeffrey pushed the door open, his weapon drawn. Nick had already taken down the suspect, and a lanky looking man in a black suit was facedown on the ground with his hands on the back of his head.

"Don't move, you perverted motherfucker," Nick told him, frisking for weapons. "Am I gonna find anything that'll cut me?" he asked.

The man mumbled something, and Nick kicked him. "Am I?" he repeated.

A firm "No" came this time.

There were three other GBI agents covering the perp, so Jeffrey tucked his gun back into his holster as he walked toward the scene.

Nick was still so pumped full of adrenaline from the arrest that when he spoke to Jeffrey he was still yelling. "This your man?" he asked. "This the scumbag motherfucker?"

Jeffrey could tell from the back that it wasn't Teddy Patterson, never mind the fact that Teddy would have had to have been Superman to get from Grant to Augusta this fast.

"Turn him over," Jeffrey said, resting his hand on the butt of his gun.

Nick grabbed the guy by his cuffed hands and yanked

him around so hard that Jeffrey thought he heard the man's shoulder popping.

"Hold on," the man yelled. He gave Nick a dirty look, and started to give one to Jeffrey before recognition came. All the color drained from the man's face, and his lips parted slightly in surprise.

Jeffrey imagined he looked just as shocked.

Nick asked, "I guess you know him?"

Jeffrey couldn't find his voice. He cleared his throat a couple of times before he could tell Nick, "His name is Dave Fine."

18

Brock's Funeral Home was housed in one of the oldest houses in Grant. The man who had been in charge of the railroad maintenance depot had built the Victorian castle, complete with turrets, before his bosses in Atlanta thought to question where he was getting all the money to build such a prestigious home. John Brock had purchased the house at auction for a ridiculously low sum and started a funeral home out of the first floor and basement shortly after. The family lived above the business, and Dan Brock had suffered endless taunts from other kids, starting when the bus picked him up in front of the house every morning and only ending at the end of the day when he was dropped off. Brock had learned to fight back at an early age, and threatened to touch them all with his dead-man hands if they did not leave him alone. All of them but Sara, that is. She had never been part of the boisterous crowd, and spent most of the ride studying for class. Dan usually shared a seat with

Sara on the bus, because everyone else was too scared he would give them cooties.

Inside the funeral home, the first floor of the house was decorated with rich velvet curtains and heavy green carpeting. Chandeliers dating back to the early 1900s hung at opposite ends of the long hall that divided the house. Long benches were against the wall, interspersed with tables containing boxes of Kleenex and trays with water pitchers and fresh glasses. Two large viewing rooms were at the front of the hall, with a smaller one in back, opposite the casket showroom. The house's original kitchen served as an office. Sara stood outside the heavy oak door in front of the office, giving it two soft knocks. When no one answered, she opened the door and peered in. Audra Brock, Dan's mother, had her head down on the desk. Sara listened quietly, picking out the older woman's muffled snores. A plate of half-finished barbecue was by Audra's arm, and Sara assumed the old woman was taking an after-lunch nap.

Sara had attended many viewings at Brock's, and she was familiar enough with the layout to find her way to the basement, where the embalming room was. She held on to the railing lining the narrow stairway, stepping carefully on the bare wooden steps. A long time ago Sara had slipped on these stairs and it had taken her bruised tailbone three weeks to heal.

At the bottom of the steps, she took a left, going past the casket storage room and into a large open space that served as the embalming area. A pump had been turned on, and Sara could feel the noise vibrating through the walls. Dan Brock sat by the body of Grace Patterson, reading a newspaper as the embalming machine removed her blood and replaced it with chemicals.

Sara said, "Dan," to get his attention.

Brock jumped, dropping his newspaper. "Oh, me," he laughed. "I thought that came from her."

"I know the feeling," she told him, because despite the fact that she had worked for the county going on ten years, Sara still got spooked sometimes late at night when she was alone in the morgue.

He stood from the chair and offered her his hand. "To what do I owe this pleasure, Dr. Linton?"

Sara took his hand, wrapping it in both of her own. "I've got a really strange request," she began. "And you may throw me out for asking."

He cocked his head, giving her a puzzled look. "I can't imagine anything you could say that would make me do that, Sara."

"Well," she said, still holding onto his hand. "Let me ask you, then you can decide."

The clinic was humming with activity when Sara opened the back door. She walked to the nurses' station, and without even saying hello asked Nelly, "Has Jeffrey called?"

Nelly gave a tight smile. "And how was your lunch, Dr. Linton?"

"I had to postpone," Sara told her, leaving out why. Nelly had made it clear that she wasn't exactly comfortable with the work Sara did at the morgue.

Sara asked, "Has he called?"

Nelly shook her head. "I did hear something about Dottie Weaver, though."

Sara raised an eyebrow. "What, exactly?"

Nelly lowered her voice. "Deanie Phillips lives next door to her," she said. "She heard a loud boom yesterday and walked over to see what was happening."

"What was happening?"

"Well," Nelly said, leaning her elbows on the counter. "According to Deanie, she heard some of the cops talking about Dottie being involved in something to do with Lacey Patterson's disappearance."

Sara tried not to groan. Despite the fact that she had lived in Grant almost all of her life, Sara was still amazed at how fast gossip got around town. "Don't believe everything you hear," Sara told Nelly, though the fact that the gossip was closer to the truth than not was a little startling. There was no telling what the town would do when they found out that Dottie Weaver was really Wanda Jennings. Sara was having a hard time reconciling that fact herself, not to mention that her exam at the funeral home pointed to the fact that Grace Patterson had recently given birth to a child.

"Yes, ma'am," Nelly said, a coy smile at her lips. She could read Sara almost as well as Cathy Linton could.

"Anyone call while I was out?"

"You've got three achy-grumpies," Nelly said, handing her the messages.

Sara glanced through them, asking, "When's my next appointment?"

"The Jordans in about five minutes," Nelly said. "They're scheduled for one-thirty, but you know Gillian's always late."

Sara looked at her watch, wondering why Jeffrey had not called. Surely it didn't take as long as an hour to process Teddy Patterson, especially considering it was still technically Nick's case. For just a second, she thought about calling him, but then reconsidered. Jeffrey probably would not appreciate her checking up on him, even if she had a good reason.

"I'm gonna grab a Coke," she told Nelly. "I'll be right back."

Sara looked at her watch again as she walked down the

hallway. She did the math in her head, thinking Jeffrey should not take longer than an hour to get back to Grant.

She walked into exam room seven and flipped on the lights. Over the past ten years, they had used this room for storage, and it looked like it. Rows of shelves ran the length of the room like bookshelves in a library. Sara could not even remember half the things that were in here.

She opened the refrigerator and let out a curse when she saw that all the Diet Cokes were gone. "Elliot," she muttered, because he was always stealing things from the fridge. She opened the freezer and was not too surprised to see that her Dove Bars and a couple of frozen dinners were gone. Well, not technically gone. With his usual sensitivity, Elliot had thought to leave the empty boxes and wrappers in the freezer.

"I'm gonna kill him," she said, slamming the fridge shut.

Sara walked up the hallway, feeling all the anger that had been welling up for the last week coming to a head. She stopped herself outside her office, thinking it wasn't fair to Elliot to let him take the brunt of this, even if he was a Dove-Bar-stealing ferret.

"Give me a minute," she said, holding up her hand to Nelly, who was approaching with an armful of charts.

Sara walked into her office and slid the door closed behind her. She looked around the small room, taking in all the pictures stuck on the wall, until she got to Laccy Patterson's. The photo had been taken a few years ago, and the girl's hair was shorter than Sara remembered. Compared to the school picture in the missing-person flier, Lacey could be a different girl. That was the thing with children at this age—in a couple of years, there was no telling what she would look like. She could put on weight or lose weight. Her hair might get darker or lighter. Her cheekbones might become pronounced, her jaw softer. Dottie Weaver, or whoever she was, had this huge advantage going for her: Lacey would grow up. Of course, after a certain amount of time, this would become a liability for someone in the business of exploiting young children. What would happen to Lacey when she was too old for the game? Would she end up like her mother, abusing other children? Would she find a way to get out from Dottie's clutches?

"Dr. Linton?" Nelly knocked on the door. "Chief's on line four."

Sara leaned over her desk, snatching up the phone. "Jeff?" she asked, aware of the hope in her voice.

"We haven't found her," he said, sounding defeated.

Sara tried to hide her disappointment. The more time that passed the less likely they would be to find the girl. "I'm just glad you're okay," she said. "Did Teddy come without a fight?"

"It wasn't Teddy," he said, then told her who it was.

Sara was sure she had heard wrong. "The preacher?"

"I'll call you later, okay?"

"Yeah," she said, hanging up the phone.

Sara looked around the office. She found pictures of Dave Fine's two kids to the left of Lacey's, then let her eyes travel over the others: girls who had been in the church choir Dave helped out with, or who had been coached by him on the softball team. There was no telling how many kids Dave Fine had been trusted with, and no telling how many kids there were whose trust he had betrayed.

19

Dave Fine had asked for a Bible, and the preacher rested his right hand on top of the book as he stared blankly at Nick Shelton. He seemed almost perplexed as to why he was here.

"I love children," Fine said. "I've always loved children."

Nick leaned back in his chair, balancing it on the back legs. "Sure you do, Preacher."

Jeffrey kept his mouth closed, because Dave Fine was Nick's collar. His fists were itching to do some real damage to the preacher, and there was a buzzing in the back of Jeffrey's mind, telling him that Dottie was still out there, doing God only knows what to Lacey Patterson, and the asshole pervert across the table from him was one of the people who had helped her get away.

"Well," Nick said, holding his arms out in a big shrug. "Tell me your story."

Fine stared at the Bible, as if he felt he could get strength from the book. His hands were sweating, and Jeffrey could see a darker streak on the black cover where perspiration had rubbed off his palm.

"I've worked at the church for going on fifteen years," Fine said. "I grew up in Grant. I was baptized in that very chapel."

Nick bounced the chair slightly, waiting him out.

"I married my wife there," he continued. "I baptized my two little boys there."

Silence filled the room, and Jeffrey let himself look at Dave Fine. He was the type of man who served as a living example of the phrase "pillar of his community." Fine volunteered with the seniors' program down at the Y, delivering meals to the elderly every weekend. His children played softball on the peewee league, and Fine coached the girls' team.

Jeffrey loosened his collar, thinking about all the young girls Fine came in contact with on a daily basis. His fists clenched again.

"I never touched any of them," Fine said, as if he could read Jeffrey's mind. "I know it's wrong. I know that." He ran his thumb along the spine of the Bible. "I prayed for strength, and God gave it to me."

Nick crossed his arms, and Jeffrey could sense that this was getting to the other man. Nick wasn't overtly religious, but Jeffrey knew that he attended church every Sunday. One of the clunky gold charms around his neck was a cross with a diamond embedded at the center.

"I never touched my children," Fine insisted. "I never hurt my boys."

Nick said, "You understand we can't take your word for that."

Fine seemed shocked that someone would not trust him. "I would never touch my sons," he said. "I would never do that."

"We know you're not into little boys," Nick told him. "But, you gotta understand, Preacher, we gotta check it out."

Fine stared at the Bible. "I would never have acted on my feelings if she hadn't approached me."

"Dottie Weaver?" Nick clarified.

"Jenny was such a sweet child. She had a light in her. A true light that God put there." Fine's lips curved up in a smile. "She sang like an angel. She really did. You could hear God coming through her voice."

"Yeah," Nick said. "I bet you could."

Fine gave him a sharp look, as if he deserved more respect than this. The man seemed not to realize that he was in a police station, about to be sent to jail for a long time.

Jeffrey said, "How did Dottie approach you?"

Fine seemed relieved that Jeffrey was taking over. "She didn't exactly approach me so much as lure me," he said. "Adam never thought to eat of the forbidden fruit until Eve tempted him."

Nick said, "Seems to me Adam's snake had something to do with that."

Fine frowned. "It wasn't like that. It was never about sex for me."

"But, you did have sex with her," Nick said.

Fine chewed his lip. "Not at first," he said. "I just wanted to spend some time with her." He paused, and took a deep breath. "Dottie let me take her to the movies, and sometimes we would go into Macon to get her some clothes." He looked up at Jeffrey and Nick, obviously needing their approval. "Her father had abandoned her," he told them. "I was just trying to fill in, to make her feel loved and wanted."

Nick was silent, but Jeffrey could see the muscles in his arms tense.

"I just wanted to nurture her, to give her some guidance."

"Did you?" Nick asked, not bothering to hide his hostility.

"I know what you're thinking, and it's not like that, it's not like that at all."

Jeffrey tried to remain calm, asking, "What's it like?"

"It's like . . ."—Fine made a wide gesture with his hands—"it's about love. It's about listening to children, and trying to understand their wants and their needs."

"Did she want sex from you?" Nick asked.

Fine dropped his hands. "I never would have touched her that way. I was content just to have her company."

Jeffrey asked, "What changed that?"

"Dottie." He spit the word out of his mouth as if it was poison. "I had always thought about it, always. Not with Jenny, but with other girls. Some girls that I saw just around town." He blinked his eyes several times, and Jeffrey was struck by how easily these men cried for themselves. They never seemed to cry for the children they hurt.

Fine said, "But I've always been content with my fantasies. That's always been enough for me." His voice rose. "I'm a happily married man," he told them. "I love my wife and my sons."

"Sure you do," Nick said, the flippant tone back.

Fine shook his head. "You don't understand."

Jeffrey leaned over the table. "Explain it to me, Dave. I want to understand."

"She was such a smart girl, and so well-spoken." He picked up the Bible. "She read the Book with me. We prayed. We understood each other."

Jeffrey glanced at the Bible. While at some level Jeffrey had always believed in the presence of good and evil, he had never really attached a biblical significance to it. Seeing Dave Fine's hand on the Bible, hearing his tale of seducing Jenny Weaver through prayer, struck him as the highest form of blasphemy.

Nick said, "Okay, you prayed with her. What happened to change that?"

Fine set the book back on the table. "Dottie changed that," he said. "She called me in the middle of the night."

"When was this?"

"Around Thanksgiving," he said. "This past Thanksgiving."

"Then what?" Jeffrey asked, thinking the bastard was probably lying.

"I went to her house, because she said that Jenny wasn't doing well. She said she was upset, and that she needed to talk to me." His eyes filled with tears again. "I was her friend. I couldn't ignore a plea for help."

Jeffrey nodded for him to continue, trying to block the image that came to his mind of Sara pointing out the pelvic fracture in Jenny Weaver's X ray. The girl had been brutally raped. Dave Fine could have been the man who did it.

Dave cleared his throat. "I had never really been inside the house before. Jenny always waited for me on the front steps." He wiped his eyes with the back of his hand. "When I got there, Dottie led me upstairs. Upstairs to Jenny's room."

Fine fell silent, and neither Jeffrey nor Nick prompted him to continue. After what seemed like a long while, he picked back up where he had left off.

"We did things," he said, his voice low. "I'm ashamed to say that we did things."

"*You* did things," Jeffrey told him, wanting to make that point.

"Yes," Fine agreed. "I did things."

"Did the acts only take place in Jenny's room?" Jeffrey asked, thinking that this would explain why Dottie would risk not stripping Jenny's room. The only evidence they found would point back to Dave Fine.

"Yes." He swallowed hard. "Only in her room."

The men were silent as Fine seemed to get his thoughts together. He was certainly good at painting himself as a helpless victim. A thirteen-year-old girl might have bought his act, but the more excuses Fine made for his actions, the more Jeffrey wanted to kill him.

Finally, Fine said, "Dottie took pictures. I didn't know until later." He gave a humorless chuckle. "She brought them to the church the next day, and threatened to expose me if I didn't do what she said."

"What did she want you to do?"

"Make those deliveries," he said. "I used the church van." He put his hand over his mouth. "God forgive me, I used the church van."

Jeffrey crossed his arms, willing himself to calm down. Nick Shelton was so angry there was almost a heat coming off of him. How this sick fuck could cry for himself was beyond him. Dave Fine felt sorrier for himself than he did for the kid he raped.

Jeffrey asked, "Where's Dottie now?"

"I have no idea," Fine said, tapping his palm on the Bible for emphasis. "That's the God's truth."

"When did you see her last?" Jeffrey asked, knowing he could not trust the answer.

"Monday. She had Mark at the house. They stripped everything. They painted the walls, they moved the printing press."

"Where did they move it to?"

"I don't know," he said, and he seemed to be telling the truth. "They put it in a truck, an unmarked truck."

"And then?"

"She told me that I still had to make this last delivery or she would send the pictures to the police station."

"What about Lacey Patterson?"

Jeffrey wasn't sure whether or not something registered in Fine's eyes. The man said, "I have no idea. Dottie wouldn't tell me something like that. I wasn't involved in that end of things. I only did what she said to protect my family. Our lives."

Jeffrey crossed his arms, asking, "When did you get the magazines?"

"That night," he answered. "I put them in the basement of the church until this morning."

"You already knew about the meeting in Augusta?"

"No," he shook his head, vehement. "She called me last night. It sounded like she was on a cell phone."

"You said the last time you saw her was Monday," Jeffrey reminded him.

"It *was* the last time," Fine countered. "You said the last time I saw her, not the last time I spoke with her."

Jeffrey let this pass. "What did she say?"

"She told me about the hotel, when to meet Joe, what the code word was for the next pickup." Fine paused. "She said she was still around, watching me."

"Do you believe that?" Nick asked. "You think she's still in town?"

Fine shrugged. "She's capable of anything," he said.

"Capable of what, for instance?" Jeffrey asked. When Fine did not answer, he asked, "What do you think she's going to do to Lacey Patterson?"

Fine looked away. "I don't know what she does. I was only involved with Jenny."

Jeffrey stared at the other man, trying to understand him. Fine was so good at justifying his actions, he could probably pass a lie detector test. Jeffrey seriously doubted the man even believed what he had done to Jenny Weaver was wrong.

Fine volunteered, "I know Dottie needs money. She told me she had to wait around for the next payoff." His voice rose as he tried to defend himself. "I was being blackmailed. I had no choice."

Jeffrey ignored the excuse, instead thinking about Dottie's post office box in Atlanta. Dottie had no way of knowing that they knew about the drop. She would think she was safe. They might have a chance of catching her before she had time to rape another kid, or sell off Lacey Patterson.

"So," Nick said. "You packed the magazines in the church van this morning and toddled on over to Augusta?"

"I had a bad feeling about it," he said, picking at the pages of the Bible. "I guess I wanted to get caught. I couldn't go on with this hanging over me."

Jeffrey said, "Mark felt the same way."

Fine snorted. "Mark," he said, as if he were talking about the devil himself.

Nick exchanged a glance with Jeffrey.

"You know why Jenny wanted to shoot him?" Fine asked them, a slight grimace on his face. "Because he was going to end up doing the same thing."

"Doing what?"

"He enjoyed it," Fine told them. "Mark didn't have any qualms about what he was doing."

"And you did?" Nick shot back.

Fine ignored the question.

"You're saying Mark liked posing for the pictures?" Jeffrey asked, and in his mind he saw Mark's pained expression in the magazines they had found. This was not the face of a kid who was enjoying himself.

"He didn't just like it. He wanted to do it." Fine tapped

his finger on the table. "If you ask me, it was just a matter of time before he started in on his sister. Jenny knew that. As cruel as that family was to her, she knew what Mark had become. She knew he would end up abusing Lacey." He sniffed, as if holding back tears. "Jenny was trying to protect Lacey from that animal."

"You have proof of this?" Jeffrey demanded.

"Grace had him in the game since he was six," Fine told them. "It was only a matter of time. Jenny knew this."

"You have no way of knowing what Mark would've ended up doing," Jeffrey said. "If every kid who was raped by some freak like you grew up to molest children—"

Fine interrupted him. "You don't know Mark very well, Chief Tolliver. Trust me, he would've been hurting kids, just like his mother." He shook his head, giving a snort. "He learned from the master."

Jeffrey countered, "He was just a kid himself."

Fine held up his finger, as if he was making a good point. "He was a grown man. He could've stopped."

Nick barked, "So could you."

The comment cut, and Fine showed it by looking down at the Bible, his lips pursed in a classic pout, like he had been falsely accused.

The room was quiet as they all seemed to take a deep breath.

Jeffrey tried to keep his tone even, asking, "Did you tell Jenny your theory about Mark? Is that why she wanted to shoot him?"

Fine stared at the Bible.

Jeffrey took his silence as a confirmation. "What else did Dottie have you do?"

"Just the deliveries."

"No, before that."

"She made me come over when she was taking the pictures," he said. "I didn't want to, but she held my life in her hands." He held out his hands to illustrate the point. "If those pictures ever got out," he said, "it would have ruined me. My wife, my children . . ." Tears welled into his eyes. "I have responsibilities."

"You posed for more pictures?" Jeffrey asked, wondering at anyone who could be so stupid. Or, maybe he wasn't stupid, maybe he enjoyed it.

Fine nodded. "I didn't want to. She . . ."—he looked for the right word—"she liked to humiliate people. She got something out of that."

"How did she humiliate you?"

"She knew I didn't like boys, and she made me do things."

"Things with Mark Patterson?"

He gave a tight nod, and for the first time, he actually showed shame. "What Jenny and I had was . . . special. I know you don't understand that, but there was something between us. Something that bonded us." He put his hand over his eyes. "She was my first. I loved her so much."

Jeffrey cut him off. "Shut up about that part of it, Dave, or I swear to God I'll beat the ever loving shit out of you."

Fine looked up, and he seemed hurt that they did not understand.

Jeffrey said, "Why did you stop? With Jenny, I mean. What stopped the sexual contact?"

"She rejected me," he told them, tears welling into his eyes. "She said she didn't want anything more to do with me." He sniffed loudly. "After the pictures . . . I don't know. It was as if Dottie was proving something to Jenny, my showing up that night."

"Proving you were all alike," Jeffrey provided, thinking this was just the kind of thing a woman like Dottie Weaver would do.

"That's not true," Fine insisted. "I loved Jenny. I cared about her deeply."

"That's why you tried to visit her after the church retreat?"

"She looked sick," Fine told them. "I didn't know what was wrong with her and Dottie wouldn't let me near her. I even posed for more of her pictures just to get into the house, just to see if Jenny was all right, but Grace kept her at the trailer when I was there."

Jeffrey clenched his teeth together knowing Fine had willingly gone to Dottie's so he could molest more children. The fact that Fine truly believed he loved Jenny Weaver was just as obvious as the fact that there was something seriously wrong with his mind.

Nick asked, "What about Grace Patterson? What was her involvement in this?"

Fine scowled at the name. "She was worse than Dottie. She was disgusting."

"How so?"

"The things she came up with," he said, his voice coarse. "May she rot in hell for her sins."

Jeffrey did not point out the obvious. "Dottie and Grace were together on this?"

He nodded. "Grace directed most of the photo shoots. Dottie took care of the business end of things." He waited a beat. "All the poses were Grace's idea. She liked to get in on them, touch some of the children. The more sadistic it could be the better."

"Dottie never did this, too?"

"She knew how to make the ones that looked real. The romantic ones. Dottie worked the softer stuff and Grace worked the hard core." He licked his lips nervously, as if by default the women were more guilty than he was. "They knew each other from way back."

"They told you this?"

"No," he said. "Jenny did. Jenny said that she and her mother moved around a lot. Wherever they went, Grace would visit them at least once a month."

Jeffrey asked, "What about Teddy Patterson?"

Fine shook his head. "He would have killed us all if he had known."

Nick showed his surprise. "He didn't know?"

"Of course not," Fine snapped. "We never did anything unless he was out of town on business. He drove a truck."

Nick sounded as skeptical as Jeffrey felt. "He never delivered any of the magazines?"

"Grace kept him out of it," Fine said. "He wasn't that kind of man."

"What kind of man is that?" Nick asked.

Fine stared at the Bible again. "A man like me, I guess. A man who would be with children."

"A man who would hurt children," Nick corrected.

"I didn't hurt her."

"You didn't?" Jeffrey asked, leaning across the table. "You wanna tell me how a thirteen-year-old girl gets a pelvic fracture?"

"There were other men she was with," Fine countered, yet he did not seem surprised by the information.

"Other men who weren't gentle like you?" Jeffrey goaded.

"It wasn't like that."

"Really?" Jeffrey said, incredulous. "How big are you, Dave? You want me to look up in Jenny's autopsy records how much smaller she is than you?"

Fine cleared his throat, but he did not answer. He took the Bible off the table and held it to his chest. Jeffrey stared at the man, thinking there was something he was missing. He saw it then—the wedding ring on Dave's left hand. His mind flashed on the image he had seen earlier in the magazine: the hand firmly behind Jenny Weaver's head, pushing her down so that she gagged on him.

"You son of a bitch," Jeffrey said, lunging across the table. His knee caught the edge, but he didn't care as his hands wrapped around the Bible.

"Jeffrey," Nick yelled, halfheartedly trying to pull Jeffrey back.

Jeffrey let the anger take hold of him, saying, "You sick son of a bitch," as he ripped the Bible from the preacher's hands. Fine had been holding on so tightly that he fell back in his chair. "I saw the pictures, asshole. I saw what you did to her. I saw how you raped her."

Jeffrey stood, looking at him over the table. "You don't deserve this," he said, indicating the Book. "What you did to those kids . . . what you did to her . . ."

"It was just Jenny," Fine insisted, sitting up.

Jeffrey started to go around the table, then stopped himself, thinking Fine wasn't worth it.

Fine repeated, "It was just Jenny."

"You left your fucking wedding ring on in those pictures," Jeffrey told him, putting the Bible down. "I saw it in at least ten different pictures with ten different kids." He walked around the table, groaning at the pain in his knee. "You fucking idiot."

"You can't talk to me that way," Fine snapped.

Jeffrey grabbed his arm, yanking him up off the floor. "You'd better be glad I'm talking and not beating the shit out of you."

"This is police brutality," Fine said, brushing off his pants. "I want a lawyer."

Jeffrey said, "Buddy Conford wouldn't touch you with a ten-foot pole."

"I've got someone else," Dave said, tucking his shirt into his pants. "Someone from Atlanta."

Nick provided, "Someone who defends perverts like him all the time. Probably takes his fee in pictures."

Fine smiled, and for the first time, he appeared to be on the outside what he was on the inside. "Or little girls."

Jeffrey felt his shoulders tighten, and the animal desire to rip Fine's throat out was only quelled by the possibility that Fine knew more than he was saying.

"You're going to jail," Jeffrey told the preacher. "You know what they do to people like you in jail?"

"Right," Fine said. "I watch television. I know you're just talking crap."

"Crap?" Nick said. "You mean that bloody stuff you're gonna find in your underwear every morning?"

Fine had the gall to look smug. "I don't think I'm going to jail."

Nick asked, "What makes you think that?"

"I've got a bargaining chip," Fine said, smiling.

"What bargaining chip," Jeffrey shot back, trying not to sound eager. If Fine thought he had power here he would never tell them what he knew.

"Let's just wait for my lawyer to get here," Fine said, holding out his hands to be cuffed. "I don't have anything to say without my lawyer."

"Think about that in general lockup," Jeffrey said, pulling out his handcuffs.

"Goodness me," Nick breathed. "General lockup."

"What's that?" Fine asked, something close to panic in his voice.

Jeffrey tightened the cuffs on Fine's wrists. "Just jail."

"Funny thing about jail, though," Nick began. "Lots of fellas in there had someone just like you in their lives when they were growing up."

Fine turned around. "What does that mean?"

Jeffrey smiled, turning Fine toward the door. "Means while you're waiting for your fancy lawyer to drive here all the way from Atlanta, you'll have plenty of time to explain to your fellow inmates how it's all about love."

"Wait a minute." Fine stood where he was, even as Jeffrey tried to push him. "I'll have my own cell," he said as if he was certain this would happen.

"No you won't, you sick fuck," Jeffrey said, pushing him so hard that Nick had to catch him before he fell.

"It's the law," Fine insisted. "You can't put me in with other inmates."

"I can do whatever I want," Jeffrey told him.

"Wait a minute," Fine repeated, his voice shrill and panicked. "You can't do that."

"Why not?" Jeffrey asked, grabbing the preacher by the collar and forcing him out of the room.

"No," Fine said, reaching for the door but missing. His fingernails trailed across the wood as he grabbed for anything to hold on to.

"You got something to tell me, Dave?" Jeffrey asked, pushing him down the hall.

"Help me," Fine said, reaching for a patrolman who happened to be coming out of the bathroom. The cop looked at Fine, then Jeffrey, then walked on as if he hadn't seen anything.

"Move," Jeffrey said, still holding him up by his collar.

"Somebody help me!" Fine screamed, bending his knees until he was on the floor. Jeffrey still dragged him down the hallway by his shirt collar.

"Help!" Fine screamed.

"Help you like you helped Jenny?" Nick asked, walking beside him. "Help you like you're helping Lacey?"

"I don't know where she is!" Fine screamed, putting his hands on the floor to give more resistance.

Jeffrey saw Marla stick her head around the corner. She looked at Fine, then turned back around.

"Help me!" Fine cried, his voice hoarse from the effort. "Oh, Lord, please help me."

Jeffrey's hand was cramping. He let go, and Fine dropped to the floor, sobbing. "Oh, Lord, please deliver me from these men," he prayed.

Nick bent down in front of him. "The Lord helps those who help themselves," he suggested.

"But you can keep on praying, Dave," Jeffrey told him. "You can pray the papers don't print how you died from having your asshole ripped open."

Nick put his hand on Fine's shoulder. "Hate to have your wife and kids read about that, Dave. It's a bad way to have to go."

Fine looked up, tears streaming down his face. "Okay," he said. "Okay, okay."

"Okay what?" Jeffrey asked.

"Okay," he repeated. "I might know where she is."

Jeffrey drove while Nick sat in the back seat alongside Fine. Behind them, an unmarked car with four GBI officers drove at a safe distance.

"You better not be fucking with us, Dave," Jeffrey said, making a right turn to circle the block for the third time.

"I told you I'm not sure what the address is," Fine insisted. "Dottie only took me here once."

"What'd she take you here for?" Nick asked.

"Nothing," he mumbled, looking out the window.

Jeffrey looked at him in the rearview mirror. "This better not be just you postponing the inevitable."

"I'm not, okay?" Fine snapped. "I told you this was where she did some business."

"What kind of business?" Jeffrey asked.

Fine looked like he wasn't going to answer, but for some reason he did. Jeffrey liked to think it was guilt that made Fine tell them things, but he had been a cop long enough to know it was plain and simple stupidity.

Fine said, "This guy, he keeps kids here sometimes."

"You sure it's just him alone there?" Jeffrey asked.

"Yes," Fine insisted. "It's mostly used as a safe house."

"Safe for who?" Nick asked.

"Who do you think?" Fine snapped. "He keeps pictures mostly, but a couple of times I saw some kids and a couple of cameras."

"And out of the goodness of your heart you reported him to the police," Nick suggested.

Fine stared out the window, probably feeling sorry for himself. They had spent an hour driving to Macon, then another two hours driving around different subdivisions looking for this house that Dave Fine said he would recognize only by sight. Jeffrey looked in the rearview mirror, wondering how much longer they had before somebody called the Macon cops about two suspicious-looking cars in the neighborhood.

They were on tricky ground here. Technically, the Georgia Bureau of Investigation had jurisdiction over the state, but as a courtesy, they should have notified the Macon Police Department that they were conducting surveillance on their turf. As Jeffrey and Nick weren't even sure Dave Fine had ever been here, let alone whether or not Lacey Patterson was being held in Macon, there wasn't much they could tell the Macon Police Department. They couldn't get a warrant without a street address, but Nick was counting on imminent jeopardy to cut through that red tape. They could always say later that they saw something suspicious in the house. With a child involved, and time being of the essence, neither one of them was worried about getting slapped on the wrist for this.

"Turn here," Fine said. "Left up here. This street looks familiar."

Jeffrey did as he was told, thinking it was pointless because they'd already been down this road.

"Then up here on the right," Fine told him, excitement in his voice.

Jeffrey took the right, going down a new street. He exchanged a look with Nick.

"There it is," Fine told them. "It's the one on the right with the gate."

Jeffrey didn't slow the car, but he had enough time to see that all the windows had the blinds drawn. The outside security lights were also on even though it was the middle of the day. The gate had a large padlock on it. Whether or not this was to keep people out or keep them in remained to be seen.

Jeffrey stopped the car at the end of the street and waited for the other car to catch up with them. He could hear cars from the interstate, which was less than thirty feet from where they had parked. Jeffrey guessed the people who lived around here got used to the noise, but right now, every car was like fingernails against a blackboard.

Agent Wallace got out of the car, leaving two men and one woman inside. He adjusted his belt, even though he was wearing a shoulder harness. He was a beefy young guy who worked out enough to make the material around the short sleeves of his shirt look about ready to break. His cheeks were so close-shaven that Jeffrey could almost make out the razor marks.

"That the house with the gate?" he asked, taking off his sunglasses.

"That's what our guy says," Jeffrey told him.

Wallace looked back at the car, meeting Dave Fine's glare. He spit on the road, crossing his arms across his broad chest. "Motherless piece of shit," he mumbled.

Nick had been on the other side of the car, calling the Macon Police Department. "He's not happy," Nick said.

"Didn't think he would be," Jeffrey answered, knowing that if someone from the GBI had called Jeffrey to say an operation was going down in Grant that Jeffrey knew nothing about, he'd be pissed, too.

Nick said, "It'll take 'em a while to get their heads out of their asses and get over here."

"Did you tell them the house?"

Nick smiled. "Hell, I couldn't even remember the street."

Jeffrey laughed, glad he was here instead of back at the Macon police department.

Nick opened the back door and grabbed Dave Fine's hands. Before the preacher could protest, Nick had cuffed him to the strap over the door. "That'll hold him."

Fine said, "You can't leave me here."

"If I were you," Nick said, "I'd relish this time alone."

Fine colored. "You said I'd get my own cell back at the station."

"Yeah," Jeffrey agreed. "That's the station, though. I've got no control over what happens to you in prison."

Nick chuckled, knocking on the hood of the car. "Don't worry, Davey boy. I'm sure you'll meet yourself some quality folk in prison."

"You can't do that," Fine insisted.

Nick smiled. "Don't worry there, preacher. Near about all of 'em already found God. You can pray with them till your heart's content."

Fine shot Jeffrey a panicked look. "You promised!"

"I promised about my jail, Dave," Jeffrey reminded him. "I've got no control over what happens in the big jail. That's up to you and the state."

"You said we'd work out a deal."

Jeffrey said, "A deal for reduced sentence, but you're still going to jail."

Fine started to say more, but Nick slammed the door in the man's face.

"Pussy," Nick said.

"He will be to somebody," Jeffrey agreed, using the remote to lock the car doors.

"Goddamn," Nick said, his eyes lighting up as he checked his revolver. "Can't believe I'm getting to do this twice in one day."

"We'll take junior, here." Jeffrey indicated Wallace, who looked about ready to jump out of his skin. Jeffrey probably looked the same way. There was enough adrenaline in his blood to give a lesser man a heart attack.

Nick bounced on the balls of his feet as he walked toward the other car and told the three agents inside they were in charge of the back.

"Let's give 'em a couple, three minutes head start," Nick said, checking his watch. Time could either stand still or fly during a situation like this.

Nick looked back at the car, where Dave Fine was pouting. He said, "I wouldn't leave a dog trapped in that car in this heat."

"Me, neither," Jeffrey said, making no move to roll down the windows.

They were quiet, staring out at the busy interstate while they waited for Nick's signal.

Finally, Nick looked at his watch and said, "Let's go."

Jeffrey tucked his gun into his shoulder holster as they

walked. He had worn his ankle holster as well. Normally, Jeffrey would feel uncomfortable armed this way, but for the moment he felt ready for anything the small house might have to offer.

Trees and high shrubs had obscured a lot of the house from the street. Up close, Jeffrey could see it was mostly brick with vinyl siding on the trim and overhangs. The gutters were painted a bright white to match the trim. The house was small, probably two bedrooms with one bath and a kitchen–living room combination. There were houses like this all over Grant, built cheap just after the war, meant to be starter homes for returning veterans. Cement blocks served as the foundation with vents to let the house breathe.

"No basement," Nick said.

Jeffrey nodded, pointing to the roofline. There did not appear to be a second story, either, but someone could definitely hide in the attic.

Wallace went first, easily scaling the five-foot-tall chain-link fence from the side that was most concealed by the shrubs. Nick had a little more difficulty, and groaned quietly as he lost his footing on the other side, his butt hitting the ground. Jeffrey followed them, wondering why his knee was giving him trouble, then remembering how he had hurt it lunging for Fine.

When they were all safe on the other side, Nick took a small walkie-talkie out of his pocket and said, "We're inside the perimeter."

There was a faint "Check," as the others got into position.

Jeffrey took out his gun indicating they should head toward the front door. As they got closer, they could hear soft music coming from the house. Jeffrey recognized a boy group, but couldn't put a name to them.

Wallace stopped at the front door, his gun held up beside his head. He counted off to three then kicked at the door.

Nothing happened.

"Shit," Wallace cursed, shaking his leg out. For just a moment, Jeffrey considered that they might have the wrong house. Then he thought about the fact that someone could be waiting behind that locked front door with a double-barreled shotgun, ready to blow off their heads. He thought of Sara for a split second, and how she said she worried about him, then he thought about Lacey Patterson and pushed everything else from his mind.

Jeffrey indicated to Wallace that they would kick together this time. He counted off to three, and this time the door didn't hold.

"Police!" Nick yelled, storming in after them. There was no man standing inside with a shotgun. Instead there was a young girl wearing a short pink T-shirt and matching underwear. She could have just woken up from a nap.

Jeffrey pointed his gun up to the ceiling. He was about to ask her if she was okay when the little girl pointed silently down a hallway.

Jeffrey took off his jacket and put it around the girl while Nick and Wallace checked the other side of the house. He ushered her to the front porch, telling her to wait for him inside the front of the gate. He wanted to say something to her, to put his arm around her and tell her that she was okay now, but there was something so vacant about the child he could not bring himself to do it. She seemed beyond any kind of comfort.

Nick and Wallace came back, shaking their heads that no one was in the other side of the house. Nick tilted his chin up, indicating he would go first down the hall. Jeffrey was eerily reminded of Dottie Weaver's house as they walked in. The setup was similar, but the feeling was different. A dirty strip of carpeting muffled the sound of their feet on the hardwood floor. There were framed pictures of children's art on the wall.

Ahead, Nick flattened himself against the wall beside a closed door. This was where the music was coming from, and Jeffrey could make out the chorus now, "I love you, love you, my sweet baby."

Nick reached down and opened the door, crouching in the entrance in one swift motion. Something unreadable passed on his face, and he stood, walking into the room with his gun still drawn. Jeffrey followed him, seeing a king-size bed with mirrors all around it. The sheets were messed up, as if there had been recent activity, and there was a smell in the room that Jeffrey did not want to put a name to. The stereo was propped up on the box it came in, sickly sweet music still pouring out from the speakers. Two video cameras on tripods were pointed at the bed, the mirrors on the walls reflecting the scene back to Jeffrey. He stood there, wanting nothing more than to get out of this room, as Nick checked under the bed, then opened the door to one of the closets.

Wallace made a noise to get their attention then nodded down the hallway. Jeffrey backed outside the room as Nick checked the last closet, then followed.

Wallace put his mouth close to Jeffrey's ear and whispered, "I saw a boy go in there," indicating a closed door on the opposite side of the hall.

Nick pointed to a cord hanging down from the ceiling where the retractable stairs to the attic were. The cord wasn't moving, but that was no guarantee no one was up there.

Jeffrey passed the bathroom, which was small and dirty. Toys were stacked on the counter and in the empty tub. There was no shower curtain or closet in there, but some cabinets were built into the wall along the hallway. Jeffrey opened the first cabinet, but all it contained were the items you would expect: towels, wash rags, some diapers. The diapers got to him for some reason, and for the first time that day, he lost what little hope he had that they would find Lacey Patterson alive.

Nick put his hand on Jeffrey's shoulder, and Jeffrey got the feeling he was thinking the same thing.

There was one last room in the small house, and Jeffrey took the lead this time, pressing himself to the closed door just as Nick had. He threw the door open, crouching around the corner with his gun drawn, but the room appeared empty.

Three twin beds were shoved into the corner, dirty-looking sheets bunched up on them. There were no frames or box springs, just the mattresses flat on the floor. Sheets were nailed tightly to the windows like canvas over a frame. There was only one closet in the room, and Jeffrey walked over to it, expecting to see the worst behind it. He stood to the side and opened it, only to find shelves packed tight with boxes. Red numbers labeled the boxes, and Jeffrey pulled one of them out, frowning when he saw it was full of pictures. He looked at the other boxes and realized the numbers were probably the age of the kids in the pictures. The top row contained a few that were labeled "0–1."

He remembered the boy Wallace had seen, and bent down on one knee. A couple of boxes on the bottom of the closet looked crooked, and Jeffrey pulled them out. He leaned down and saw a frightened little boy, not more than six years old, with his head between his knees. The boy saw Jeffrey, then reached out to pull the boxes back around him. He was so frightened that the boxes shook from his touch.

Jeffrey stood, thinking he would see the fear in that kid's eyes for as long as he lived. He wanted to pull the boy out from his hiding place and tell him that it was over, but Jeffrey wasn't sure that it was. The adult or adults who had done this were still in this house somewhere. It was better to leave the kid where he was safe rather than put him in more danger.

Jeffrey heard Nick's boots on the floor and turned to see him walking out the door. He watched as Nick lowered the attic stairs, the springs squeaking loud enough to vibrate in Jeffrey's ears. He unfolded the steps, which made a hollow thunking noise against the floor. Nick took out a mini flashlight, holding it between his teeth as he used one hand to climb the stairs and held his service revolver in the other. Jeffrey held his breath as Nick poked his head into the attic space. After a quick look around, Nick shook his head, taking the flashlight out of his mouth.

"Empty," Nick said. He took the radio out of his pocket and asked, "Did anyone come out the back?"

Crackling came, then a woman's voice said, "That's a negative, sir. We've got the back and the sides."

Nick sighed heavily, disappointment coming off him like sweat. "Let Robbins stay back there. I need you and Peters inside to help us do another check."

"You think we missed anything?" Wallace asked.

"Hell, I don't know," Nick said. He picked up the stairs to fold them back up, but his hand slipped, and the stairs thunked to the ground again. He started to try again, but Jeffrey stopped him, pointing to the floor.

Nick shook his head, but then he seemed to play it back in his mind and realized what Jeffrey had. The stairs hadn't sounded right when they hit the floor. Nick finally nodded, and he leaned down, pointing to a line of dirt where the rug had been raised then dropped back down.

Jeffrey pulled the stairs up and tucked them back into the attic. He holstered his gun and picked up the carpet. There was an outline of a trap door underneath it, about three feet square with a small, hinged pull in the center. Jeffrey indicated for Wallace to stand on the back side of the door, straddling the sides, and open it. Nick and Jeffrey stood on the other side, their guns drawn.

Time moved slowly, and Jeffrey could hear the stupid song that had been playing since they'd come in switch to another equally drippy ballad as the trap door creaked open. He could feel sweat dripping down his face, and tasted blood in his mouth as he bit the inside of his lip. Then the door was open, and about three feet down he saw a very scared-looking Lacey Patterson lying curled up on the ground under the house. She was filthy, and her hair had been cut close to her scalp. There was a bruise on her forehead, and her eyes were barely open. She had either been drugged or beaten or both.

"Holy Jesus," Wallace muttered.

Jeffrey got down on his stomach so that he could see her better, asking, "Lacey?"

The child did not respond, though at this distance, he could see there was something white at the corners of her mouth.

"Lacey?" he tried again, putting his gun beside him on the floor so he could reach in and touch her forehead. She felt clammy and there was something gritty on her skin.

Jeffrey told Wallace, "Hold my feet," as he reached into the hole. He managed to hook his hands under her arms and get a good grip on her. Wallace kept him from sliding in as Jeffrey started to pull Lacey out. She was small, but her body was deadweight. He asked Nick for help, and between the three of them they managed to get her out of the hole.

"You're okay," Nick said, setting her down on the floor inside the bedroom.

Jeffrey sat back on his heels, wiping the dust from his forehead. The crawl space was filthy, red Georgia clay like powder from the heat.

Suddenly, there was a scratching noise from underneath the house as if someone was moving. Without thinking, Jeffrey dove into the hole, catching himself with his hands so he wouldn't fall on his face. It was dark under the house, low-hanging pipes giving it the appearance of a maze. Jeffrey blinked several times, trying to acclimate himself, when a flash of light came from the far end of the house.

"Nick!" he yelled, taking off, using his elbows and feet to propel himself through the small space. From above, he heard footsteps running through the house, and prayed Nick's man in the back would act quickly.

Up ahead, he saw a pair of feet slipping through a narrow vent opening. Jeffrey followed as fast as he could, banging his head on a gas line. He kept going toward the light, turning at the last minute and using his feet to kick at the hole. The mortar was weak in the old house, and bricks flew out from the force. Jeffrey turned back around, pushing himself through the opening, feeling intense pain as his pants tore on the jagged brick.

"Stop!" Robbins screamed. He was just a kid, his feet out wide, his gun in front of him, pointing at the figure running toward him.

Jeffrey knew what was going to happen and it did. The runner smacked right into Robbins, who dropped his gun. Jeffrey stood, unable to move as he recognized the runner.

"Dottie!" Jeffrey yelled.

Dottie stood, their eyes locking. She raised her hands like she meant to surrender, then took off running toward the backyard. Jeffrey knelt, pulling out his ankle gun in one swift movement as he lined up to take the shot. He stopped as Dottie jumped the fence and ran into the neighbor's backyard, which was full of kids playing on a swing set.

Jeffrey took off after her, pumping his arms as he ran. He

hurdled the fence without breaking stride, running around kids like an obstacle course. He saw Dottie run into the house, slamming the door behind her. Jeffrey took the steps two at a time, busting the door open with his shoulder, breaking into the hallway and nearly smacking into a line of kids. The first one barely came up to Jeffrey's waist, and he sidestepped to miss the boy, slamming full force into the wall. His arm felt like it was on fire, and Jeffrey dropped his gun.

"Sir?" a young woman asked. She was probably around twenty, and her dark brown hair was pulled back into a ponytail. She looked terrified.

Jeffrey sat up, pressing his fingers into his arm to see if he had broken anything. He realized he was panting from running. There were at least ten kids around, all of them looking at Jeffrey with the same fear in their eyes as the young woman had. His heart stopped as he realized he was in a day-care center. All of these kids, so close to Dottie; he could not fathom the implications.

"Sir?" the woman repeated, pulling some of the kids close to her.

Jeffrey pulled his badge out of his back pocket, showing it to her. He tried to catch his breath so he could speak. "Where . . . ?" he began. "The woman . . . ?"

"Wendy?" the girl asked. "Wendy James?"

Jeffrey shook his head, thinking she did not understand.

"She just left," the girl told him. "She ran through the house and—"

Jeffrey jumped up, scattering the kids as he retrieved his gun. He ran out the open front door, into the yard and to the street. He could see a car ahead, taking a right to merge onto the busy interstate. It could have been white or tan or gray. It could have been a four door or a coupe or a hatchback. He did not know what kind of car it was. All he knew was that it was gone.

20

Jeffrey walked around to the dock behind Sara's house. The moon was high above the trees, and a breeze was coming in off the lake. Jeffrey stood in the grass, watching Sara, feeling some of the stress start to drain out of him. She sat in one of the two deck chairs on the dock, her legs crossed at the ankle in front of her. In the moonlight, Jeffrey could see she was staring out at the rocks in the water. The greyhounds were with her and she rested her hand on Bob's head. She was wearing a pair of shorts and one of his old shirts. Jeffrey stared at her, thinking that she looked even better now than she did the night before.

She turned in her chair when she heard his footsteps on the dock. Billy and Bob kept their heads down, staring out at the water.

"Don't let them scare you," Sara teased.

"They're so ferocious," Jeffrey said. He went on one knee to pet Bob on the head. The dog rolled over, kicking his left leg into the air as Jeffrey scratched his belly.

Sara put her hand on Jeffrey's shoulder. "How's Lacey?"

He sighed. "Better. The sleeping pills are wearing off, but she's still groggy."

"Did they find anything?"

"There was no evidence of recent abuse," Jeffrey said.

"Just recent?"

He nodded. "There were signs that something happened before."

Sara seemed to sense he did not want to give specifics right now. She asked, "What did her father say?"

Jeffrey kept scratching Bob's belly, enjoying the simple pleasure. "He said he's glad to have her back."

"Does he have a problem with me talking to her tomorrow?"

"Not last I checked," Jeffrey said. "He still thinks it was all Dottie."

She stroked his hair back behind his ear. "Have they identified the kids yet?"

"They're running the fingerprints now. Who knows what will come up? One of them sounded Canadian. This boy . . ." He let his voice trail off, not sure he could tell Sara what they found in that house. It was like a cancer, rotting his brain every time he thought about it.

"What about the day care behind the house?"

"She had just started working there," Jeffrey said. "Maybe a week or so. All the kids are being checked out, but they're thinking she didn't have time."

Sara asked the question that had kept him up at night, "Do you think you'll ever find Dottie?"

"We're hoping she doesn't know we picked up on Jenny's social security number," he said, giving Billy equal time behind the ears and on his belly. "She's picked up mail there before, according to one of the workers. She's been renting the box about a year now. Mail from two other boxes has been forwarded there."

Sara pressed her lips together. "Sounds like she knows what she's doing."

"We're coordinating with the credit card company. They're mailing it out tomorrow. It should be in the box in a couple of days." He shrugged. "From there, we just sit and wait. She shouldn't take long to get it. I'm sure she needs the money to set up shop, wherever she is."

"You think that's what she's doing?"

He gave her a sad smile. "The guy at the post office says there's another card from a different company in the box right now."

"What's with all the cooperation?" Sara asked. She knew better than anyone that people were reluctant to assist the police these days. "Didn't they ask for a subpoena?"

"No," Jeffrey told her. "It's amazing how helpful people are when you tell them that children are involved."

"So," Sara began. "What next?

"We're going to have to coordinate with the school, find out how many kids were involved in this thing."

"I want to check every file at the clinic."

"Will Molly help you?"

Sara nodded. "I already talked with her. We need to be careful about this. The hard part is going to be dealing with the hysterics whose kids never had contact with Dave Fine or Dottie or Grace."

"You think people will do that?"

"Yes," Sara answered. "You can't blame them, but we're going to have to find a way to screen out the real cases from the bogus ones. We're lucky in a way that this was happening to older kids who can talk about what happened."

"They didn't look that old in the pictures."

"The FBI will have someone assign ages to the kids. They'll use the Tanner scale. There are certain markers that tell you how old a kid is."

"I hate that there's even such a thing."

"Do you want me to go to the school with you?"

Jeffrey sighed, thinking about how hard the next few days were going to be. Of course, it wasn't her job to talk to Lacey Patterson, either. He said, "I know you don't have to, Sara, but do you mind?"

"No," she told him. "Of course not."

"What I want to know is why do the kids protect these people?" Jeffrey asked, because that was the one thing that he could not understand. "Why didn't Lacey or Jenny talk to one of their teachers, or go to you?"

"It's hard for them," Sara explained. "Their parents are all they have, all they know. It's not like they can move out and get jobs. A lot of times parents convince them that it's normal, or that they don't have an alternative."

"Like Stockholm syndrome," he said. "Where the victim falls in love with the abductor."

"That's a good analogy," Sara told him. "Their parents set up this pattern where they abuse them, then buy them ice cream. Or they guilt them into doing what they want, or trick them. Kids don't know that it's not supposed to be that way." Sara sighed. "And the fact is, the kids love their parents. They want to please them. They don't want to get their parents in trouble. They want the behavior to stop, but they don't want to lose their mother and father." She paused. "There's a real dependency there. The parents cause the pain, but they're also the ones who take it away."

She continued, "I've also been thinking about the baby."

He didn't look at her, but said, "Yeah?"

"Grace's baby was a girl. Maybe Jenny thought she was

protecting the baby. Maybe that's why she helped Grace get rid of the baby."

He thought it over, thinking that Jenny was so afraid of Grace she would've done anything to avoid her wrath. Jeffrey finally said, "It's possible."

"I really think that's why she did it," Sara said with conviction. "I think Grace made her help kill the baby and Jenny was so upset all she could think to do was kill Mark, the father." She sounded so sure of herself that Jeffrey looked up at her. He could see how this was eating her up inside as much as it was him.

Jeffrey stood and stretched his arms up to the sky. He did not want to think about this anymore. He did not want to know that there were other kids like Jenny and Mark out there, being abused by their parents. He did not want to think about Dottie Weaver holding on to Lacey Patterson so she could exploit the child. Something had to give. Jeffrey did not think he could go on knowing that Dottie Weaver was out there doing whatever she wanted to children. He did not want to think about her preying on another small town somewhere.

He said, "It's almost cool out here."

"Isn't the breeze nice? I'd forgotten what it was like."

"It doesn't bother you to be out here in the dark?"

"Why would it?" she asked.

He looked at her. "Sometimes I think you're the strongest person I know."

She smiled, indicating that he should sit beside her.

He sat in the chair with a groan. Jeffrey had not realized until that moment just how tired he was. He leaned his head back, looking up at the night sky. Clouds obscured the stars, and it looked like August was releasing its stranglehold on the thermometer. Fall would come soon, and the leaves would drop from the trees and the air would turn colder and Jenny Weaver would still be dead.

Jeffrey asked, "Did you release the body?"

"Yes," she answered.

"What about the baby?"

"I talked to Brock. He's donating the service. There's a plot in the Roanoke Cemetery."

"I'll pay for it."

"I already took care of it," she said. "Will you go to the service with me?"

"Yeah," he answered, feeling it was the least he could do.

"Paul Jennings said to tell you to remember what he said."

Jeffrey was silent.

"What did he say?"

"That I shouldn't blame myself for what happened," he told her. "That I shouldn't make myself live with that guilt."

She reached over and squeezed his arm. "He's right."

"He said I should blame Dottie."

"Maybe you should."

"Dave Fine blames Dottie, too."

"It's not the same thing," she told him, sitting up in her chair. "Jeffrey, look at me. . . ." She waited until he did. "You did what you had to do."

"I stopped Jenny from killing Mark so that he could turn around and hang himself," Jeffrey told her. "He still hasn't regained consciousness. He might never."

"And that's your fault?" she asked him. "I never knew you were so powerful, Jeffrey." She listed things out: "You made Jenny Weaver point a gun at Mark, you made Mark hang himself. Did you bring Dottie here, too? Did you make her abduct Lacey? Did you make Dottie work with Grace Patterson at that hospital? Did you make her do those things she did to children?"

"I'm not saying that."

"But, you are," she insisted. "If you want to blame somebody, blame me."

He shook his head, saying, "No."

"I saw all of them," Sara pointed out. "I saw Mark and Lacey practically from the time they were born. Jenny was a patient of mine. Is it my fault?"

"Of course it's not."

"Then how is it yours?"

Jeffery leaned his head on his hand, not wanting Sara to see how upset he was. "You didn't pull the trigger," he said. "You didn't kill her."

Sara got out of her chair and knelt in front of him. She took his hands in hers and said, "You know how I told you I worry about you when I don't know where you are and the phone rings?"

He nodded.

"I worry because I know you," she said, squeezing his hands for emphasis. "I know what kind of cop you are, and what kind of man you are."

"What kind of man am I?" he asked.

Her voice took on a softer tone. "The kind of man who wouldn't hesitate to be the one to kick in that door instead of Lena. The kind of man who risks his life every day to make sure that other people are safe. I love that about you," she insisted. "I love that you're strong, and that you think things through, and that you don't just react." Sara put her hand to his cheek. "I love that you're gentle, and that you worry about Lena, and that you feel responsible for everything that happens in town."

He started to speak, but she pressed her finger to his lips so that he would not interrupt her. "I love you because you know how to comfort me and how to drive me crazy, and how to make my dad want to beat you to a pulp." She lowered her voice. "I love how you touch me, and how safe I feel when I'm with you." She kissed his hands. "You're a good man, Jeffrey," she told him. "Listen to Paul Jennings. Listen to me. You did the right thing." She held his hands to her lips and kissed his fingers.

She said, "It's okay to question yourself, Jeffrey. You did that, and now you have to move on."

He looked out at the rocks jutting from the lake, and wondered if there would ever be a day in his life when he did not think of Jenny Weaver, and the role he had played in her death.

Sara told him, "You're a good man, Jeffrey."

He did not believe her. Maybe if he still didn't feel pain in his knee from jumping Dave Fine, or remember how good it felt to kick Arthur Prynne in the gut, it would be easier. Maybe if he didn't still see that set of frightened eyes from the back of the closet in Macon.

"Jeffrey," Sara repeated. "You're a good man."

"I know," he lied.

"Know it in here," she told him, pressing her fingers to his chest.

Jeffrey brushed Sara's hair back behind her ear, and all he could think to say was, "You're so beautiful."

Sara rolled her eyes at the compliment. "Is that all you've got to say?"

He offered, "Why don't we go inside, and I'll answer you in greater detail?"

Sara leaned back on her hands, a smile playing at her lips. "Why do we have to go inside?"

Friday

21

Lena gritted her teeth, pounding her feet into the pavement. She could hear Hank's heavy footsteps behind her, his cheap Wal-Mart sneakers popping against the ground like a stick on an oil drum.

"That all you got?" he asked, pulling ahead of her. She let him take the lead for a while, watching him from behind. The sun did not agree with him, and rather than tanning, his pasty skin had taken on a reddish tone. The track marks on his forearms stood in a burgundy relief against this, and the back of his neck was as red as fire.

His breathing was more like a wheeze, but he held his own against her as she sped up to run beside him. His yellowish-gray hair was pasted to his head with sweat, and the turkey giblet hanging down from his neck bounced with each step he took. Still, Lena couldn't help but think he wasn't in bad shape for an old man. She had certainly seen worse.

"This way," he said.

Lena followed him as he took a sharp turn off the road, and jogged along a path through the woods. The soft ground underfoot brought some relief to her aching knees, and her thighs started to feel like they might not ignite from the heat in her muscles as her second wind kicked in. Before, this was what she had lived for: the intense pain, then overcoming it. Pushing herself past the physical through sheer force of will, making herself finish the course. Her body felt strong and powerful, invincible, like she could do anything she wanted. Like she was the old Lena again.

She knew in the back of her mind where he was going, but she was still surprised when they reached the cemetery. They jogged through the rows of stones, both of them keeping their eyes straight ahead, not stopping until they got to Sibyl's marker.

Lena put her hand on top of the gravestone, using it to steady herself as she stretched her legs. The black marble stone was cool to the touch, and it felt good against her hand. Touching it was like touching part of Sibyl.

Hank stood beside her, lifting his T-shirt to wipe the sweat out of his eyes.

"Jesus, Hank," Lena said, shielding her eyes from the glare off his white belly. There were track marks there, too, but she did not comment on them.

"It's a warm day," Hank said. "I think the heat's about to break, though. Don't you?"

Lena took a minute to realize that he was talking to her and not Sibyl. "Yeah," she mumbled.

Hank continued to talk about the weather, and Lena stood there, trying not to show how awkward she felt.

She looked at Sibyl's gravestone. Hank had taken care of the arrangements, and chosen the words on the stone. Above the dates, chiseled into the stone, were the words

SIBYL MARIE ADAMS, NIECE, SISTER, FRIEND. Lena was surprised he had not put "lover" for Nan's benefit. That would have been just like him.

"Look at this," Hank mumbled, bending down in front of the stone. Someone had placed a small vase with a single white rose at the base, and it was starting to wilt in the morning heat. "Isn't this pretty?"

"Yeah," Lena said, but she could tell from the startled look Hank gave her that he had been talking to Sibyl.

He said, "I bet Nan left this for her. Sibby always liked roses."

Lena was silent. Nan had probably left the flower here that morning. She must have always done this early in the morning, because Lena had never run into her. Not that Lena made a habit out of visiting Sibyl's grave. At first, she had been incapable of making the trip because it was difficult to walk, let alone sit in the car for the ride from the house. Then, she had been embarrassed, thinking that Sibyl knew what had happened, that Lena had somehow been changed, compromised. Lately, it just felt eerie, visiting her dead sister. And the way Hank talked to Sibyl, as if she were still there, made Lena feel uncomfortable.

Hank said, "White looks pretty against the black, don't you think?"

"Yeah."

They both stood there, Lena with her arms crossed, Hank with his hands in his pockets, staring at the stone. The single rose did look pretty against the black marble. Lena had never understood people sending flowers to a funeral home, but she finally realized that the flowers were something for the living to enjoy, a reminder that there was still life in the world, that people could go on.

Hank turned to her, waiting for her attention. "I guess I'm going back to Reece," he said. "Maybe tomorrow."

Lena nodded, swallowing past the lump in her throat. "Yeah," she said, "that's probably a good idea." She had not told him that Jeffrey had given her an ultimatum: either take the time to get some help, or don't bother coming back at all. Partly, she had kept this secret because she did not want Hank to make the choice for her. He would easily take her back to Reece, give her a job in his bar, so that she could live her life under his watchful eye. That wouldn't really work, though, because one day Hank would be gone. He was an old man. He would not be there forever, and then what would Lena do?

For some reason, the thought that one day Hank would be dead brought tears to her eyes. She looked away from him, trying to gain her composure. Silently, he took his handkerchief out of his back pocket and handed it to her. The cloth was wet from his sweat, and hot, but she used it to blow her nose with anyway.

"I can postpone it," he offered.

"No," she said. "It's probably better."

"I'll sell the bar," he offered. "I can find a job here." He added, "You could come with me, back home."

She shook her head no, feeling the tears coming again. There was no way to tell Hank that she wasn't upset about his leaving so much as about knowing that one day he would be dead. It was all too morbid, and what she really wanted from him, needed from him, was to know that she could always pick up the phone and he would be there. That was all Lena had ever wanted from Hank. That was actually the one thing he had always given her.

Hank cleared his throat and said, "You've always been the strong one, Lee."

She laughed, because she had never felt so weak and helpless in her life.

"With Sibby, I knew I had to be there, had to hold her hand every step of the way." He paused, staring back at the tent from the recent funeral. "With you, it was harder. You didn't want me. Need me."

"I don't know if that's true."

"Hell, yes, it is," he countered. "You always did everything on your own. Skipped college, joined the police academy, moved here, didn't tell me about it until after it was all done."

Lena felt there was something she should say, but could not think what.

"Anyway," he said, taking back the handkerchief. She watched as he folded it. "I guess I'll take off tomorrow."

"Okay," she nodded, turning back to Sibyl's grave.

"They'll probably need you here for a while, anyway," Hank said. "What with that girl being found. I'm sure there's a lot more kids around here who went through the same thing. Those people don't tend to be as isolated as you'd think."

"No," Lena agreed. "They don't."

"Good that girl's back, though," Hank added. "That your chief found her."

"Yes," Lena said, but she wondered about that. What kind of things had been done to Lacey Patterson in that house? What memories would she carry with her for the rest of her life? Would she even be able to carry them, or would she take the easy way out, like her brother? Lena knew from her own experience that the lure of not having to think about the things that happened was seductive. Even after all she had been through, she was not sure that tomorrow she might decide that it wasn't worth it to keep on going.

Hank said, "I'm sorry about pushing Preacher Fine on you. I guess it's hard to see something like that."

Lena took the apology in stride. "Brad's a cop and he didn't see it either," she told him, though if Hank knew Brad, he would know that wasn't much of a consolation.

Hank tucked the handkerchief back into his pocket. He dropped his hands to his sides, the back of his hand brushing against hers for just a moment. Like Lena, he was sweaty, and she could feel the heat coming off his skin.

After a while, he said, "You know if you need me you can call me, right? You know I'll be there."

Lena smiled, and she really felt it this time. "Yeah, Hank," she said. "I know."

Lena walked through the hospice, trying to breathe through her mouth so that the smell didn't overwhelm her. The building had a certain odor that reminded her of piss and alcohol. It kind of reminded her of Hank's bar.

She jabbed at the button on the elevator, feeling claustrophobic as it slowly climbed to the third floor. Her neck felt gritty, and she used her hand to wipe it. After her run with Hank, she had taken a long shower, but she was already sweating again from the heat.

Lena sighed with relief as the doors opened and the smell of urine did not assault her nostrils. Most of the residents on Mark's floor were catheterized and somewhat sterile compared to their more active counterparts on the lower floors. The stench was controlled because of this.

She stepped into the hall, looking out the window across from the elevator. The clouds were dark and fluffy, filled with rain that seemed on the verge of falling. She was reminded of the morning Grace Patterson had died, and how she had stood behind Teddy Patterson while he slept, watching the sun come up and relishing the thought that the monster lying in the bed would never be able to feel the sun on her face again. Lena never questioned herself about making sure Grace did not go peacefully. She knew she had done the right thing. There was no doubt in her mind.

"Can I help you?" a woman asked as she walked in front of the nurses' station.

"I'm looking for Mark Patterson's room," Lena told her.

"Oh," the woman said, obviously surprised. "He hasn't had any visitors."

Lena could have guessed that Teddy Patterson would not want to see his son, but she still felt surprised.

Even though Lena knew the answer, she had to ask, "Has he regained consciousness?"

The woman shook her head, saying, "No," as she pointed down the hallway. "Three-ten," she told Lena. "Right, then left, across from the linen storage."

Lena thanked her and followed the directions. She traced her fingers along the railing lining the hall as she walked, purposely taking her time. There was no reason for Lena to see Mark. She wasn't working the case. Hell, she wasn't even sure if she was a cop anymore.

Even though Mark was not about to tell her to come in, Lena knocked on the door marked 310. She waited outside, then pushed the door open. The lights were out, and no one had opened the blinds to let the sun in. Mark lay in bed, tubes running in and out of him, looking paler than she had ever seen him. Machines beat softly in the background, and a bag filled with urine hung off the railing around the bed. The room was stark and institutional. There were no flowers on the bed table, and the single chair pushed against the wall had not been used. The television was off, the dark screen looking almost sinister.

"Let's let some light in," Lena said, not knowing what else to do. She twisted the wand on the blinds and the slats opened, pouring in light. She turned back to Mark, and adjusted the blinds so that he wasn't getting the full force of the sun.

There was a tube in his mouth helping him breathe, and saliva had built up around it. Lena went into the bathroom and wet a washcloth with warm water. At the bed, she wiped Mark's mouth. Then, because she had appreciated this when she was in the hospital, she folded the cloth and ran it along his face and neck, then along his arms. Next, she got some lotion out of the unopened patient-care kit in the stand beside the bed. She warmed it in her hands before rubbing it on his arms and neck, then patting some on his face. Lena wasn't sure, but his skin seemed to have more color to it when she was finished.

"Looks like they're treating you okay here," Lena said, though she didn't think that was necessarily true. "I, uh . . . ," Lena began, then stopped. She looked at the door, feeling foolish for talking to Mark when he obviously could not hear her, thinking this was about as stupid as Hank talking to Sibyl's grave.

Despite this, she took his hand. "Lacey's okay," she told him. "Well, she's back. They found her over in Macon and she's . . ."

Lena looked around the room not knowing how to do this.

"They're watching the post office," she told him. "The chief thinks Dottie will show up soon." Lena took a deep breath and held it awhile before exhaling. "We'll catch her, Mark. She won't get away with this."

She was silent, listening to the in and out of his breath as the machine pushed air into his lungs. Of course Mark did not respond to her, and again she felt foolish. Why did Hank do this with Sibyl? What did it accomplish, telling her things? It was like talking to the wind. It was really just talking to yourself.

Lena laughed, realizing that of course this was why Hank did it. Talking to someone who could not answer you, who could not voice concern or disapproval or anger or hatred, was the ultimate freedom. You could say anything you wanted without fear of repercussion.

"I'm not sure I'm going to be a cop anymore," she told Mark, feeling a little giddy as she spoke the words aloud. Her mind had been playing around with this thought for a while, like a marble spinning through a maze in a child's game, but she had not let herself accept the possibility until just this moment.

"I've got to talk to my boss in a couple of days." She paused, looking at the tattoo on Mark's hand. She wondered briefly what she could do to have the tattoo removed. There were procedures that could take them off. She had seen them advertised on television.

"I don't know what I'm going to tell Jeffrey," Lena said, still feeling silly. "I talked to Hank, and I know I could move back to Reece with him." She stopped. "I don't know, though. I don't know if I can go back."

Lena noticed that his blanket had come undone, and she walked around the bed to tuck it back in. She smoothed the material with her hand, saying, "Anyway, I don't want to leave Sibyl here alone. I know she's got Nan to look after her, but, still . . ."

Lena walked around the room, trying to think of what to say. The sound of her voice in the room was making her self-conscious, but it felt better to say these things, to speak the words that had been jumbled up in her head for so long.

The chair screeched across the floor as she moved it to the bed. She sat, and took Mark's hand again. "I wanted to say," she began, but could not go on. She finally forced herself to speak. "I wanted to say that I'm sorry for the way I reacted when you told me what happened. . . ." She paused, as if waiting for a response, then clarified, "About you and your mom."

Lena looked at his face, wondering if he could hear any of this.

She said, "I wanted to let you know that I understand. I mean, I understand as much as I can." She shook her head. "I mean . . . ," she began, then stopped again. "I know what it took, Mark. I know what it took for you to tell me your secret." She paused, trying to remember to breathe. "You were right when you said I'd been through the same thing, that I knew what you were talking about."

She looked at him again, and still he was mute. His chest rose and fell with the pump that forced him to breathe. The heart monitor beeped with his heart.

"I didn't think this would be so hard," she whispered. "I thought I was being strong. . . ." She stopped again. "You were right, though. I was a coward. I *am* a coward."

Lena took a deep breath, holding it in until she thought her lungs might burst. She felt the room closing in on her, and suddenly, she was back in that dark place, splayed to the floor, with *him* somewhere in the house, ignoring her. The worst part was when the drugs started to wear off, and she realized where she was and what was being done to her, and that she was powerless. She would feel a pressure in her chest, as if someone had carved her out and filled her with a liquid-black loneliness. When she got to this place, this stripped-down, empty place, the light under the door became her salvation, and she would find herself wanting to see him, wanting to hear his voice, no matter what the cost.

"I was so scared," she told Mark. "I didn't know where I was, or how much time had passed, or what was going on."

She felt her throat tighten as the memory overwhelmed her. "He nailed me down to the floor," she told him, though surely Mark knew this. "He nailed me down, and I couldn't move away. I didn't have a choice. There was nothing I could do except wait, and let him do to me what he did."

Lena's breath came in pants, and she could feel herself going back to that room again, feeling trapped and helpless. "The drugs . . . ," she said, then stopped herself. Mark had obviously used drugs to dull his pain, too. Only, Lena had not been given a choice about what she would take, or when.

"He gave me these drugs," she said. "They made me feel . . ." She tried to find words. "Free," she said. "Like I was floating, like I was above everything. And Greg, my boyfriend—ex-boyfriend— was there." She stopped again, thinking about the Greg from her drugged dreams, not the Greg she had actually known. In her dreams, Greg was much more sure of himself, more in control of their love-making. He pushed her in her dreams, pushed her to the edge where she did not know the difference between pain and pleasure, and did not *want* to know. All she wanted when she was in this state was to have him inside of her, to have him touching her, and filling her up from the inside, pushing deeper into her, until she thought she might explode. Then, when he took her to this point, the release was almost ethereal. She had never known such pleasure in her life as her body opened up to him completely.

She told Mark, "Greg was never like that. I knew that. I knew that in my mind." She squeezed Mark's hand. "I knew it somewhere, and I didn't care. I just wanted to be with him. I wanted to feel him."

She put her hand to her mouth, but there was no turning back now. "Then, the drugs would wear off," she said, feeling like she was describing something that had happened to someone else. "And I would start to feel things. I would start to realize what was going on, who I really was." She swallowed hard. "What I had done with him." Lena felt her stomach turn in disgust. "The noises I had made," she whispered, remembering them now, how she had talked back to him, how she had pleaded with him the way she would plead with a lover.

Her hand dropped to her chest, and she could feel her heart pounding. "And then I would cry," she said, tears streaming down her face. "I would cry, because I was so disgusted with myself, and then I would cry because I felt so alone." She wiped her eyes with the back of her hand. "I would cry because I didn't want to be alone, didn't want to know what had happened.

"And when he came to me . . . ," she whispered. "When he came back into the room, and I wasn't alone anymore . . ."

Lena had to stop, because she was going to hyperventilate if she did not get her breathing under control. She looked at Mark's hand, rubbing her fingers across the tattoo.

Mark's confession came back to Lena in a flood, and she could hear now what she could not let herself hear in that trailer. He had talked about the crime against him like a lover recalling a particularly passionate moment. As Lena played his words in her head over and over again, she finally knew why he had branded himself with the tattoo. She knew the guilt Mark carried around with him like an anvil tied to his heart. Part of him would always be his mother's son. Part of him would always be back in that trailer, listening to a CD, when his mother came into his room and raped him. Part of him would always remember how good it felt, if only for the moment, to be inside of her, to fuck her. No matter where he went or what he did, Mark would carry that brand inside of him. The tattoo only made it so that other people could see. The tattoo was Mark's way of telling people that he did not belong to them, that he would always belong to his mother. What she had done had marked him inside the way no needle and ink could ever mark his skin.

For the rest of his life, maybe even right now, trapped in his body as he was, Mark would carry with him the knowledge that he had enjoyed it. Just for that moment in time, he had been his mother's favorite, he had experienced what he thought of as love for maybe the first time in his life. In her sick, twisted way, Grace Patterson had made her son feel wanted, and he had loved her back for it, even as he had hated her for doing something so wrong.

The room was silent but for the machines and the blood pounding in Lena's ears. She heard a high-pitched whining noise, but knew it was only in her head. She wanted to stand up, to let go of Mark, to leave him in this bed to die because he would do that with or without her.

Still, she had come this far. There was no one stopping her, no one questioning the insanity of her revelations. There was just Lena in the room, and if Mark was there, if he was really there with her, hearing what she was saying, then he was probably the only other person in the world who could understand what she was saying.

"I was so lonely when he left me there," Lena began, her voice a hoarse whisper as she made herself go back to that horrible place. She clenched her teeth, not sure she could go on. It was this part that killed her every time, the reason she would never go into therapy or tell anyone what had really happened in that room four months ago.

"When he came back—back into the room—and I wasn't alone anymore . . ." Lena stopped, choking on a sob. She could not say this. She could not make herself admit this to anyone, not even Mark, not even this lifeless shell who wasn't even Mark anymore. She was not strong enough. She could not overcome this.

"Shit," Lena cried, trying to keep herself from breaking

down. Her body shook, and soon she was wracked with sobbing. If Mark could still feel things, he would be able to feel
her hands shaking, sense the fear that held her body like a
steel trap. He would understand the pain that touched her
deep inside the way no one ever would be able to again. No
pills would take this away. Even a bullet passing through her
brain would not push out the knowledge, and Lena knew
that even if she did manage to do it, to pull that trigger or
take all of those pills, her last thoughts would still be of *him*.

"No," Lena said, shaking her head violently side to side.
"No, no, no," she insisted, thinking about what Nan had
said, knowing what Sibyl would say if she were here.

"Be strong," Lena said, speaking for Sibyl. "Be stronger
than this."

Lena thought of Hank, too, sitting on the floor in her
bathroom, weeping openly, just as she wept now.

"When he came back into the room with me," Lena began, forcing herself to speak, pushing herself to say *his*
name. "When he came back to me," she repeated, "part of
me was relieved." She stopped, knowing that was still not
right. She could tell Mark this, because Mark understood.
He knew what it was like to be so empty that you took
whatever people gave you. She knew the loneliness of being locked in a pitch-black room with nothing to do but
wait. She knew that there came a point when your mind told
you everything was wrong, but your body betrayed you
anyway, reaching out for whatever comfort was offered.

She swallowed, starting again. "When he came back
into the room," she began, "part of me was . . . happy."

22

Sara sat on the floor across from Lacey Patterson in the back room of the children's clinic. Just a few days ago, Lacey had come here seeking help. Now she was back, having gone through unspeakable things, and all Sara could do was wait for the girl to talk.

"Dottie just left you at Wayne's house?" Sara asked.

"Yeah," Lacey said, looking down at her shoes. She had asked to sit on the floor for some reason, and Sara had obliged, wanting to make the girl as comfortable as possible. She did not want Sara close, and so they had decided Sara would sit a foot away with her back against the closed door. Lacey sat in the middle of the room.

Lacey said, "The pills made me sleepy."

"And you don't remember anything that went on until you woke up in the hospital?"

She nodded, then started to bite her fingernails. Time passed, and the little girl was down to the cuticle on her thumb, and working on her pinky finger when Sara reached out and stopped her.

"You'll hurt yourself," Sara said, then realized from Lacey's expression how silly the warning was.

Lacey chewed at her cuticle, asking, "Is Mark going to be okay?"

"I don't know, sweetie."

Lacey teared up, but she did not cry. "I didn't mean to hurt him," she said.

"How did you hurt him?"

"He was coming after me again, and I just grabbed the knife."

"You're the one who cut him?"

She nodded, chewing another nail. "They were at Dottie's, taking things out of the house and painting. I was hiding, but Mark found me. I kicked him in the head with my foot." She took her fingers out of her mouth. "Mark didn't want me to come here to see you. I wanted to say goodbye, and then I was so scared I got sick. I'm sorry."

"That's okay," Sara assured her. "So you came here and then Mark showed up? And then you ran and Dottie picked you up in the black car?"

Lacey nodded, but she still would not say who had been driving the car. She asked, "You don't think that's why he tried to kill himself, do you? Because I hit him?"

"No," Sara assured her. "I think that Mark had a lot of other problems that led him to think that was his only choice."

"Can I see him?" she asked in a small voice.

"If you want to."

"I want to."

Sara sat back, watching the girl chew her fingers. Lacey's hair had been cut almost in a buzz cut. Dottie had probably planned to disguise her as a boy until she could sell her off to the highest bidder.

"Is my daddy coming back soon?" Lacey asked.

"Do you want to see him?"

"He didn't know," she said, as if she could read Sara's mind. "I knew about Mark and Mama, but Daddy didn't know."

"Are you sure?"

She nodded. "If he found out, he would've killed Mark."

"How about you, honey?" Sara asked. "Did Mark ever touch you?"

She looked away.

"Lacey?"

She shook her head vehemently, but Sara did not believe her. She was still torn on the subject of Mark Patterson. On the one hand, he had been a victim, and on the other, he had obviously been an abuser.

Lacey said, "Mark was nice to me."

Sara let this pass. "Did Dottie ever make you sit for pictures?"

"No," she said. "Mark and Jenny did, though. They got their pictures taken, and sometimes they were in movies. I saw them doing it."

"But you never did?"

Lacey put her hand back in her mouth. "Mark said if he ever caught me doing any of that he would tell Daddy."

"Mark didn't want you to do it?"

"I wanted to," she countered, taking on a petulant child's tone. "Jenny was doing it, and she went to a party and did it with lots of boys."

"Do you think Jenny enjoyed doing that?"

"I tried it once, and Mark found out." She dropped her hand into her lap. "That's when he hit me."

Sara let this sink in. She had never even dreamed that Mark was trying to protect his sister.

"This was when Mark got arrested, right?"

Lacey seemed surprised that Sara knew this. "Yeah."

"But, he didn't tell your father?"

"I told him if he did that I would tell about him and Mama."

She said "him and Mama" in a singsong way, as if the phrase had been practiced over and over. Sara imagined that Lacey had used this as a threat on more than one occasion. She was still a child at heart, and most children would do anything they could to get their way.

"I didn't like it anyway," Lacey said. "I told him I wouldn't do it anymore. I didn't like it." She frowned. "Dottie was mean when she was like that. Not like she was when we were playing."

"You played with her?"

"She would baby-sit us sometimes." Lacey smiled. "She had this game we would play, where we would get all dressed up, and she would take us to the movies and let us stay dressed up."

"That sounds nice."

"She wasn't like that all the time, though." Lacey started to pick at a scab on her leg. "She was mean sometimes. I didn't like her then."

"I don't blame you," Sara told her. "Was she the one who talked about purity?"

Lacey jerked her head up. "Where did you hear that?"

Sara decided to lie. "Mark told me."

Lacey shook her head. "He wouldn't have told you about that."

"Are you sure?"

She shrugged, but Sara could see that she wasn't. "Dottic got mad at Jenny because she said she was obsessed with it."

"Obsessed with what?"

"What they do to little girls over there," she mumbled. "Jenny had this report in school last year about Africa, and different tribes. She said that the women were lucky because they belonged to people. To their daddies, or their husbands, and as long as they did right they were safe."

"Do you believe that, Lacey?"

She ignored Sara's question. "Dottie was mad. Jenny wouldn't drop it. Even when Mama came over and told her to stop." She turned her head to the side. "Mama can usually make people do things that maybe they don't want to do. She's good at that."

Sara took a deep breath, trying to get her head around what the child was revealing. She asked, "So your mom and Dottie told Jenny to stop talking about the mutilation?"

"They were worried she'd get in trouble at school. They had to move before because of it. A guidance counselor came to the house. Dottie said he was gonna call the police because of what Jenny said."

"About girls being cut like that?" Sara asked, wondering at a girl obsessed with self-mutilation.

"Jenny said women over there didn't have to worry about stuff. . . ." She paused, then, "Like, sex stuff. And like what Dottie was doing. They don't have that over there, because children are sacred. Girls are protected."

"Why would Dottie cut her, Lacey?"

"She didn't," Lacey said. "After the Christmas trip, Jenny decided to do it to herself."

Sara shook her head, not accepting this. "There's no way she could have done that to herself, sweetie."

"But, she did," Lacey insisted. "She used a razor, only

she started screaming, and Dottie ran upstairs and started screaming, too."

"You were in the house?"

"I was downstairs with Mama because it was payday."

Sara knew she should not have been surprised that these women had a regular payday, but it made sense that they ran their sick little publication like a business. They had been doing this for at least thirteen years, and knew what they were doing.

"Jenny yelled so loud, like she was dying," Lacey said. "And then Mama came back downstairs and told me what Jenny had done to herself."

Sara nodded for her to continue, because that was all she could do.

"They couldn't take her to the hospital, so Mama said the best thing they could do was finish what she started. . . ." Lacey paused. "So, they did."

"Did they anesthetize her?" Sara asked.

"Mama gave her some of her pills so she wouldn't get an infection."

"That's not what I meant," Sara told her. "Did they knock her out before they finished cutting her? Or make her go to sleep so she wouldn't feel it?"

"I think she fell asleep on her own when they started," Lacey provided. "At least, she stopped screaming after a while."

Sara chewed her bottom lip, trying to think of a response. She asked, "What made Jenny do that to herself?"

"Carson and Rory were making fun of her when we went skiing, like she would go with them, and she wouldn't."

"Go with them, meaning sex?"

She nodded. "She said she wouldn't, that they weren't clean, and they got mad at her and called her a whore, and she didn't know why, but when Cooper told her that she had before, this time she went over to their house with Mark." She shrugged. "Mark put something in her drink to make her act funny and not remember."

"Do you know what it was?"

"Something that makes you feel really bad the next day," Lacey answered. "She got sick to her stomach and had to stay home from school for two days, and Dottie said she had the flu."

Rohypnol, Sara thought. The date rape drug.

Lacey continued, "She did what she did, you know. Mark says that drugs just make you do the things you want to do anyway."

"That's not true," Sara told her. "Especially with the drug he probably gave her."

Lacey shrugged as if it didn't matter. "She liked Cooper Barrett anyway."

"Was he on the ski retreat?" Sara asked.

"Him and Rory and Carson," she said. "They slipped notes under the door at the hotel, and when we got up one morning, there was a sign over the room number that said some mean things." She looked up at Sara. "I guess they were the ones who stole stuff out of her locker at school."

"What kinds of stuff?"

"Pictures and things. They tore them up, so she had to stop keeping stuff in there except for books."

"I guess that upset her a lot."

Lacey shrugged, but Sara could tell it had bothered her.

"Why did Mark do that to her, do you think?" Sara asked. "Did Dottie ask him to take her to the party?"

Lacey nodded, and Sara put her hand to her stomach, thinking about Mark pimping out Jenny Weaver to recruit more kids for Dottie.

"Jenny was upset about them bothering her," Lacey said.

"And Dottie told Jenny just to go with them again and that would make them stop, but Jenny didn't want to. She said she wanted to be pure."

"So, that's what made her cut herself between the legs?" Sara asked.

Lacey said, "She started it, but Dottie had to finish it."

Lacey returned to the scab, and Sara watched as she picked it until it started to bleed.

Sara took a tissue out of her pocket and dabbed the blood off the girl's leg. She asked, "Did you ever see what Dottie did to Jenny that night?"

Again, she shook her head. "I wasn't allowed to talk to her anymore."

"Why?"

"Because Mama told me not to," she said, looking back down at the scab as she picked it. "Mama told me if I talked to Jenny, then she would let Dottie do me the same way." She indicated her lap. "Down there."

"Was your mother mad at Jenny, too?"

With her head down, Lacey's voice was muffled. Sara had to strain to hear her say, "Mama said Mark had been with Jenny, and that wasn't right. It made Jenny crazy, and that's why she did that to herself." She paused. "Children should only be with adults, because adults know what they're doing, and kids don't."

"Are you sure your daddy didn't know about this?"

She shook her head again, her lips pressed together in a straight line. "He would've killed Mark."

"Don't you think he would have been mad at your mother, too?" Sara decided to push her a little further. "Don't you think he would have been upset that your mother was pregnant?"

Lacey's head jerked up. "How did you know?"

"I know a lot of things," Sara told the girl.

"It was Mark's fault she got pregnant," Lacey said, and again, Sara was struck by the practiced tone. Obviously, this was something the child had been taught. "Mama told Daddy she couldn't be with him when she got sick again. That's how she knew it was Mark's."

Again, Sara took a deep breath. She doubted very seriously whether or not they would ever know who the real father of that baby was.

"Last Saturday," Sara began. "What happened?"

"Mama went up to Skatie's to find Mark, and she got sick."

"Sick how?" Sara asked.

Lacey looked back down at her leg. "She drove us up there, looking for Mark, and she got real sick and had to go to the bathroom."

Sara tried to remember how tall Grace Patterson was. She was a small woman, and Tessa could have easily mistaken her for a teenage girl.

Sara asked, "Did you go with her into the bathroom?"

Lacey nodded.

"And then did Jenny come?"

"She saw us go in."

"What happened then?"

Lacey gave a long sigh. "The baby came out from between her legs, and there was a lot of blood. . . ." She paused, still not looking up at Sara. "Mama said it was sick from the cancer medicine she took, and they had to take care of it."

Sara swallowed hard.

"She told me to go wait in the car while she and Jenny took care of it."

"Why did she make Jenny stay?"

"To punish her. It was Jenny's fault all of this happened. If she hadn't been with Mark to begin with, then Mama wouldn't have had to do what she did."

Sara leaned her head against the door, trying to think of something to say. She was amazed at the power Grace Patterson and Dottie Weaver had over these children. That Sara had been in their presence and not noticed how horrible they were was something for which she would never forgive herself.

Lacey made sure she had Sara's attention, then told her, "Mama told Jenny if she didn't stay and help, then she'd tell you what Jenny had been doing."

"Me?" Sara asked, unable to hide her shock.

"Jenny wanted to be a doctor for kids like you are," the girl said. "She didn't think you'd help her if you knew she was having sex with all those people." The practiced tone came back to her voice as she said, " 'If you don't do this, I'm gonna tell Dr. Linton what a whore you are.' "

Sara felt horrified her name had been used to threaten a child. "That's not true," Sara told her vehemently. "That's not true at all."

Lacey shrugged as if it didn't matter.

Sara wanted to shake her. "I would have done everything I could to help her, Lacey. Just like I'll do whatever I can to help you."

"I don't need help now," Lacey said, her tone implying that it was too late.

Sara was so angry that tears welled into her eyes. She had autopsied the baby. She knew exactly what Grace and Jenny had done to the poor creature. To think Jenny complied in the mutilation for fear of being exposed to Sara made bile rise into her throat.

"Mama said that a lot," Lacey told her. "Jenny wanted you to think she was a good person."

Sara put her hand to her throat. "She *was* a good person."

Lacey looked down at the floor. "Whatever."

"What happened to Jenny was horrible. It wasn't her fault."

Again, Lacey shrugged.

"Sweetheart," Sara said, trying to sound reassuring. She reached for Lacey's hand, but the girl pulled away.

Sara let a minute pass before asking, "Why do you think Jenny threatened to kill Mark?"

Lacey shrugged, but Sara could tell she knew the answer.

"Do you think she wanted it to stop?"

She shrugged.

"Do you think this was the only way she thought she could stop it, by pointing that gun at Mark? By ending up in . . ." Sara stopped, feeling a heavy weight settle on her chest. Jenny had known that she would end up on a table in the morgue. Making Jeffrey pull that trigger was her way of forcing Sara to see what was happening to her.

Lacey looked up, her face completely devoid of emotion. "Jenny knew better than that," she said. "She knew it could never be stopped."

Sara reached for a response, more afraid than anything that what the girl said was true. "We'll catch Dottie before she does this again, Lacey. I promise we'll do everything we can to stop her."

"Yeah, well . . ." She shrugged, as if Sara had just told her an impossible fantasy. She asked, "Is my daddy gonna be here soon? I wanna go home."

"Lacey," Sara began, not knowing what else to say.

The girl looked up, tears in her eyes. The past few days had aged her. She no longer looked like a carefree little girl with nothing more to worry about than whether or not she would make the cheerleading squad. The people who had abused her were gone, but she would always carry around what they did to her in her heart. Looking at her, Sara had never felt so helpless in her life. She wanted to do something, to help, but she knew it was much too late for that. She also knew that there were more kids like Lacey out there, more children who had fallen victim to Dottie Weaver—and many more who still could.

Lacey wiped her nose with the back of her hand, sniffing loudly. She managed a smile for Sara, repeating, "Is my daddy gonna be here soon? I wanna go home."

Sunday

One Week Later

23

Tessa flopped into the chair opposite Sara at the dining room table. "Am I going to be throwing up like this for the rest of my life?"

"I hope not," Sara mumbled, not really paying attention. She was reading through a chart, trying to make sense of her own handwriting. "What does this say?" she asked, sliding the chart across to Tessa.

Tessa studied the scribble. "Permanent apples?" she guessed.

"That's what I got, too," Sara mumbled, taking back the file. She stared at the words, willing them to make sense.

Tessa reached into Sara's briefcase and took out a magazine.

"That's a journal," Sara told her.

"I may not be a doctor, but I *do* know how to read," Tessa shot back, flipping through the pages. After a couple of beats, she closed it, saying, "There aren't any pictures."

"There're some in the back," Sara told her, reaching

across the table to show her sister a close-up of a very red, very enlarged appendix. She flipped the page to the companion shot, which showed the organ dissected in all of its bleeding glory.

"Oh, Jesus," Tessa groaned, clamping her hand over her mouth as she stood from the table. She nearly knocked Cathy over as she ran out of the room.

Cathy asked, "What's wrong with her?" as she put a plate of deviled eggs on the table.

"Dunno," Sara said, staring at the chart. "Oh," she said, finally figuring it out. "Palpated appendix."

Cathy frowned. "Do you have to do that at the dining room table?"

Sara stacked the charts together. "Not anymore," she said. "That was the last one."

Cathy sat across from her, taking a sip of Sara's iced tea. "How's that going?" she asked, indicating the charts.

"Slowly," Sara told her. "But, better than I thought. I mean, better for Grant. She kept a low profile here."

"As your father would say, don't shit where you eat."

"Exactly," Sara answered, her smile feeling tight across her face.

"Speaking of which," Cathy said. "I heard Dave Fine is going to trial."

Sara nodded. "He thinks he can stay out of jail."

"I think jail might be the only safe place for him," Cathy said, taking another sip of tea. "Did you talk to Lacey's father about her helping out at the clinic after school?"

Sara nodded, tucking the charts into her briefcase. "He's going to think about it."

"I don't imagine he'll stick around town long," Cathy said, giving Sara a careful look. "No matter what he's saying, people think he knew."

Sara shrugged, not comfortable talking about this with her mother.

Cathy said, "I heard his tires got slashed outside the Piggly Wiggly the other day."

Sara studied her mother, trying to figure out what she was getting at.

"I just don't want you to get hurt," Cathy finally said. "I don't want to see you get close to this girl, then have her father take her away."

Sara busied herself arranging her briefcase. Jeffrey had said the same thing to her the other night.

"You know," Cathy began, "you could always adopt a child."

Sara felt a tight smile on her face. She took off her glasses and set them on the table. "I, uh . . ." She stopped, giving a humorless laugh. It was so much more complicated than that.

Cathy waited for Sara to speak.

"I really don't want to talk about that right now, Mama."

Cathy reached over and took Sara's hands in hers. "I'm here when you want to."

"I know."

Tessa walked back into the room and popped Sara on the back of the head, muttering, "Bitch."

Sara laughed, and Tessa stuck out her tongue.

Cathy raised an eyebrow as she stood from the table, but did not comment. She asked Tessa, "You feeling okay, baby?"

"Yes, Mama," Tessa answered, but she did not look it. Sara felt a flash of guilt for showing her the photograph.

"You sure?" Sara asked.

"Oh, I'm just peachy," Tessa snapped back. "My hair is oily, my skin feels scritchy, my pants are too tight." She stopped on this, tugging at the legs of her shorts. "They keep crawling up my crotch."

"Nature abhors a vacuum," Sara told her, laughing.

"Sara," Cathy warned, but she was laughing as she walked back into the kitchen.

Tessa sat down again, taking one of the deviled eggs. "Where's Jeffrey? He's half an hour late."

"I don't know," Sara said, watching her sister suck down the egg. "I thought you were sick to your stomach."

"I was," Tessa said, taking another egg. "Now . . . not so much."

Sara started to say something, then stopped when she heard a car pull up in the driveway. "That's Jeffrey," she said, standing up from the table so quickly that her chair fell back. She caught it before it hit the ground, and gave Tessa a nasty look, hoping to cut off the comment her sister obviously wanted to make.

Sara purposefully took her time walking to the front door. Jeffrey was about to knock when she opened the door. She leaned in to kiss him, but stopped when she saw the expression on his face. "What is it?"

He held up a videotape as his answer.

She shook her head, asking, "What?"

"Let's go into the den," he said, leading the way down the stairs. She could tell from the way Jeffrey held his shoulders as he walked that he was angry. His posture was rigid, his jaw set in a firm line.

Sara sat on the couch, watching Jeffrey put the tape in the VCR. He took a seat beside her, working the remote control until the picture came up. Sara recognized the black-and-white format as a surveillance tape.

"The post office in Atlanta," she said.

Jeffrey leaned back on the couch, and Sara pressed herself against him as they watched the tape. The scene was pretty ordinary, a room full of post office boxes with a table in the center of it. Jeffrey fast-forwarded the tape, playing it when a slim-looking young man came into the frame.

"He could be Mark Patterson," Sara whispered, watching the kid walk to the back of the room. As he came closer to the camera, the similarity between the boy and Mark was amazing. They had the same lanky build and insolent look about them. The way his clothes hung on his body conveyed the same androgynous sexuality.

Jeffrey said, "He looks just like him."

On screen, the boy had a suspicious walk as he crossed the room. He stopped, furtively looking around before opening a box. His back was to the camera, blocking the view, as he took out the contents of the box, looked around again, then shoved the envelopes into the waist of his pants. He tucked his shirt in as he walked toward the exit and past the camera

Jeffrey paused the tape, freezing the image of the boy on the screen.

"She sent someone else," Sara guessed.

"He walked out into the parking lot, got into a black Thunderbird, and drove to a local mall," Jeffrey said. "No one showed up to meet him. He waited a couple of hours, then used a pay phone."

"To call whom?"

"Nick traced the number to a cell phone. No one answered it."

"What about the kid?"

"David Ross, a.k.a. Ross Davis," he told her. "Nick ran his prints. He was abducted ten years ago from his home in broad daylight. Missing, presumed dead."

Sara felt her heart sink in her chest. "Ten years?"

"Yeah," Jeffrey said, anger in his tone. "He was playing outside with his older brother. Dottie came up in her car.

They think it was Dottie. Wanda. Whoever the fuck she is. It was a woman. Ross Davis went with her and never came home."

Sara put her hand to her heart. "His poor parents."

"He's not their kid anymore, Sara. He's just like Mark. He won't talk. Nick grilled him for six hours, and the kid wouldn't say a word. Wouldn't even acknowledge that he knew Dottie. He just said he was there picking up some of his mail."

"Did he have a tattoo like Mark?"

Jeffrey shook his head.

"How old is he?"

"Seventeen."

"He was taken when he was seven?" she asked.

"He's legally an adult now," Jeffrey said, and there was such an air of defeat to him that Sara took his hand in hers.

She asked, "Did you notify his parents?"

"Nick did," Jeffrey said. "He couldn't hold the kid, though. It's not illegal to check a post office box, and the car is legally registered to him."

"Nick put a tail on him, right?" Sara asked. "At least he can tell the parents where he is."

Jeffrey nodded, his eyes on the frozen image of the boy. "Watch," he said, pointing the remote at the VCR again. He pressed play, and the boy left.

The tape showed the empty room for the next few seconds. Sara was about to ask what she was supposed to be looking for when another figure came on screen. A woman wearing a baseball cap and glasses walked purposefully into the camera's range. She went directly to the back of the room and opened the same box the boy had just checked minutes ago. She took out a couple of envelopes, then tucked them into her purse. When she turned, Sara gasped, even though she should not have been surprised.

"Is that Dottie Weaver?" Sara asked, but she knew that it was. There was no mistaking the woman on screen for anyone else. Then, as if she knew that they would one day be watching her, Dottie lifted up her sunglasses, stared right into the camera, and raised her middle finger at them.

Jeffrey paused the tape.

"Where was everybody?" Sara demanded, sitting up on the edge of the couch. "Where was the tail?"

"They followed the boy," Jeffrey told her. "Nick found a bunch of junk mail on him. The credit cards were left in the box."

"She can't possibly use them," Sara countered, still incredulous. "As soon as the numbers come up in the computer, they'll know where she is."

"She knows that," Jeffrey assured her. "She gave you and Lena all those clues when you interviewed her. It's all a game. She's just fucking with us."

"Why?"

"Because she can," he said caustically. "God damn her."

Sara put her hand on his shoulder. "Jeff." She tried to help, pointing out, "Dave Fine will never get out of jail. Lacey is home. Grace is dead."

"Don't comfort me, Sara," he said, his voice tight in his throat. "Please."

She dropped her hand, and he leaned forward, putting his elbows on his knees, his head in his hands.

Jeffrey said, "She's out there, Sara. She's out there doing this again."

"Someone will catch her," Sara told him, but she wasn't sure of this herself. Jeffrey must have sensed the hesitancy in her tone, because he turned to look at her. There was so much pain in his eyes that Sara had to look away.

Sara stared instead at the television, at Dottie Weaver telling them in no uncertain terms that she was not only free from the law, she was free to do whatever she wanted to children like Mark and Lacey Patterson. She was probably doing it right now.

"How could this happen?" Sara asked, but there was no answer to the question. She thought of Lacey, and what the child had been through, and the things that Lacey had experienced but was still incapable of talking about. The thirteen-year-old girl had been through more pain and suffering than anyone should be expected to bear, yet she was still getting up for school in the mornings, going to church with her father on Sundays, as if she were still a child, and not aged by circumstance.

Jeffrey sat back on the couch, taking Sara's hand in his, holding it too tight. They sat like that, neither of them talking, both of them incapable of expressing how they felt, until Cathy stood at the top of the stairs and called them up for dinner.

ACKNOWLEDGMENTS

First thanks as always goes to my agent, Victoria Sanders. It would take three people to fill her shoes. Meaghan Dowling, my editor at Morrow, gave me focus and spot-on advice. Kate Elton at Century was great help as well. The marketing and publicity people at Morrow and Century have been fabulous. Juliette Shapland is worth her weight in Tim Tams.

Medical information again came from Michael A. Rolnick, M.D., and Carol Barbier Rolnick. Captain Jo Ann Cain fielded procedural questions. Ric Brandt offered firearms advice. Melissa Cary told me how to snake a drain. Jatha Slaughter answered my drug questions with honesty and aplomb. Fellow authors Jane Haddam, Keith Snyder, Ellen Conford, and Eileen Moushey were there for moral support. Writer Sal Towse walked with me across the Golden Gate Bridge, an experience I will never forget. Laura "Slim" Lippman was a good sounding board. Any mistakes I've made are entirely her own.

My daddy has been a constant support throughout my life and I feel lucky to have him. Judy Jordan is a cherished friend. As for D.A.—whatever our souls are made of, yours and mine are the same.

I will always owe a debt of gratitude to Billie Bennett Ward, my ninth-grade English teacher. I am just one of the few people I know who owe their careers if not their lives to a teacher. They should all be praised for the good they do.

Lastly, thanks to the little scamps who go over the posted thirty-minute time limit at my local Y; I have conjured many a violent murder waiting in line for a treadmill.

Turn the page
to enter the dark and twisted world of

KARIN SLAUGHTER

Heartsdale, Georgia, is a small town with a seriously dark side. It's up to Dr. Sara Linton, the town's pediatrician and coroner; Jeffrey Tolliver, her wayward ex-husband and chief of police; and Lena Adams, the county's only female detective, to keep everyone safe.

Blindsighted

A small Georgia town erupts in panic when a young college professor is found brutally mutilated in the local diner. But it's only when town pediatrician and coroner Sara Linton does the autopsy that the full extent of the killer's twisted work becomes clear.

Sara's ex-husband, police chief Jeffrey Tolliver, leads the investigation—a trail of terror that grows increasingly macabre when another local woman is found crucified a few days later. But he's got more than a sadistic serial killer on his hands, for the county's sole female detective, Lena Adams—the first victim's sister—wants to serve her own justice.

But it is Sara who holds the key to finding the killer. A secret from her past could unmask the brilliantly malevolent psychopath . . . or mean her death.

———— -- ————

Sara Linton leaned back in her chair, mumbling a soft "Yes, Mama" into the telephone. She wondered briefly if there would ever come a point in time when she would be too old to be taken over her mother's knee.

"Yes, Mama," Sara repeated, tapping her pen on the desk. She felt heat coming off her cheeks, and an overwhelming sense of embarrassment took hold.

A soft knock came at the office door, followed by a tentative "Dr. Linton?"

Sara suppressed her relief. "I need to go," she said to her mother, who shot off one last admonishment before hanging up the phone.

Nelly Morgan slid open the door, giving Sara a hard look. As office manager for the Heartsdale Children's Clinic, Nelly was the closest thing Sara had to a secretary. Nelly had been running the place for as long as Sara could remember, even as far back as when Sara was herself a patient here.

Nelly said, "Your cheeks are on fire."

"I just got yelled at by my mother."

Nelly raised an eyebrow. "I assume with good reason."

"Well," Sara said, hoping that would end it.

"The labs on Jimmy Powell came in," Nelly said, still eyeing Sara. "And the mail," she added, dropping a stack of letters on top of the in-basket. The plastic bowed under the added weight.

Sara sighed as she read over the fax. On a good day, she diagnosed earaches and sore throats. Today, she would have to tell the parents of a twelve-year-old boy that he had acute myeloblastic leukemia.

"Not good," Nelly guessed. She had worked at the clinic long enough to know how to read a lab report.

"No," Sara agreed, rubbing her eyes. "Not good at all." She sat back in her chair, asking, "The Powells are at Disney World, right?"

"For his birthday," Nelly said. "They should be back tonight."

Sara felt a sadness come over her. She had never gotten used to delivering this kind of news.

Nelly offered, "I can schedule them for first thing in the morning."

"Thanks," Sara answered, tucking the report into Jimmy Powell's chart. She glanced at the clock on the wall as she did this and let out an audible gasp. "Is that right?" she asked, checking the time against her watch. "I was supposed to meet Tessa at lunch fifteen minutes ago."

Nelly checked her own watch. "This late in the day? It's closer to suppertime."

"It was the only time I could make it," Sara said, gathering charts together. She bumped the in-box and papers fell onto the floor in a heap, cracking the plastic tray.

"Crap," Sara hissed.

Nelly started to help, but Sara stopped her. Aside from the fact that Sara did not like other people cleaning up her messes, if Nelly somehow managed to get down on her knees, it was doubtful she would be able to get back up without considerable assistance.

"I've got it," Sara told her, scooping up the whole pile and dropping it on her desk. "Was there anything else?"

Nelly flashed a smile. "Chief Tolliver's holding on line three."

Sara sat back on her heels, a feeling of dread washing over her. She did double duty as the town's pediatrician and coroner. Jeffrey Tolliver, her ex-husband, was the chief of police. There were only two reasons for him to be calling Sara in the middle of the day, neither of them particularly pleasant.

Sara stood and picked up the phone, giving him the benefit of the doubt. "Somebody better be dead."

Kisscut

Saturday night dates at the skating rink have been a tradition in the small southern town of Heartsdale for as long as anyone can remember, but when a teenage quarrel explodes into a deadly shoot-out, Sara Linton—the town's pediatrician and medical examiner—finds herself entangled in a terrible tragedy.

What seemed at first to be a horrific but individual catastrophe proves to have wider implications. The autopsy reveals evidence of long-term abuse and ritualistic self-mutilation, but when Sara and police chief Jeffrey Tolliver start to investigate, they are frustrated at every turn.

The children surrounding the victim close ranks. The families turn their backs. Then a young girl is abducted, and it becomes clear that the first death is linked to an even more brutal crime, one far more shocking than anyone could have imagined. Meanwhile, detective Lena Adams, still recovering from her sister's death and her own brutal attack, finds herself drawn to a young man who might hold the answers. But unless Lena, Sara, and Jeffrey can uncover the deadly secrets the children hide, it's going to happen again . . .

"Dancing Queen," Sara Linton mumbled with the music as she made her way around the skating rink. "Young and sweet, only seventeen."

She heard a furious clicking of wheels to her left and turned just in time to catch a small child before he crashed into her.

"Justin?" she asked, recognizing the seven year old. She held him up by the back of his shirt as his ankles wobbled over his in-line skates.

"Hey, Dr. Linton," Justin managed around gasps for breath. His helmet was too big for his head, and he pushed it back several times as he tried to look up at her.

Sara returned his smile, trying not to laugh. "Hello, Justin."

"I guess you like this music, huh? My mom likes it, too." He stared at her openly, his lips slightly parted. Like most of Sara's patients, Justin seemed a bit shocked to see her outside of the clinic. Sometimes she wondered if they thought she lived in the basement there, waiting for them to get colds or fevers so she could see them.

"Anyway," Justin pushed back his helmet again, knocking himself in the nose with his elbow pad. "I saw you singing it."

"Here," Sara offered, leaning down to adjust the chin strap. The music in the rink was so loud that Sara could feel the bass vibrating through the plastic buckle as she tightened it under his chin.

"Thanks," Justin yelled, then for some reason he put both his hands on top of the helmet, as if to rest them. The motion threw him off balance, and he stumbled, clamping on to Sara's leg.

Sara grabbed his shirt again and led them both over to the safety railing lining the rink. After trying on a pair of in-line skates herself, Sara had asked for the old four-wheel kind, not wanting to fall on her ass in front of half the town.

"Wow." Justin giggled, throwing his arms over the railing for support. He was looking down at her skates. "Your feet are so huge!"

Sara looked down at her skates, feeling a flush of embarrassment. She had been teased about her large feet since she was seven years old. After nearly thirty years of hearing it, Sara still felt the urge to hide under the bed with a bowl of chocolate-fudge ice cream.

"You're wearing boy's skates!" Justin screeched, letting go of the rail so that he could point at her black skates. Sara caught him just before he hit the ground.

"Sweety," Sara whispered politely into his ear. "Remember this when you're due for your booster shots."

Justin managed a smile for his pediatrician. "I think my mom wants me," he mumbled, edging along the rail, hand over hand, casting a wary eye over his shoulder to make sure Sara was not following him.

She crossed her arms, leaning against the railing as she watched him go. Sara loved kids, a characteristic most pediatricians shared, but there was something to be said for not spending her Saturday night surrounded by them.

"That your date?" Tessa asked, coming to a stop beside her.

Sara gave her sister a hard look. "Remind me how I got roped into this."

Tessa tried to smile. "Because you love me?"

"Right," Sara returned caustically. Across the rink, Sara picked out Devon Lockwood, Tessa's latest boyfriend, who also worked in the Linton family's plumbing business. Devon was leading his nephew around the kiddy rink while his brother watched.

"His mother hates me," Tessa mumbled. "She gives me nasty looks every time I get near him."

"Daddy's the same way about us," Sara reminded her.

Devon noticed them staring and waved.

"He's good with children," Sara noted, returning his wave.

"He's good with his hands," Tessa said in a low voice, almost to herself. She turned back to Sara. "Speaking of which, where's Jeffrey?"

Sara looked back at the front entrance, wondering that herself. Wondering, too, why she cared whether or not her ex-husband showed up. "I don't know," she answered. "When did this place get so packed?"

"It's Saturday night and football season hasn't started; what else are people going to do?" Tessa asked, but did not let Sara change the subject. "Where's Jeffrey?"

"Maybe he won't come."

Tessa smiled in a way that let Sara know she was holding back a snide comment.

"Go ahead and say it."

"I wasn't going to say anything," Tessa said, and Sara could not tell if she was lying or not.

"We're just dating." Sara paused, wondering whom she was trying to convince, Tessa or herself. She added, "It's not even serious."

"I know."

"We've barely even kissed."

Tessa held up her palms in resignation. "I know," she repeated, a smirk on her lips.

"Just a few dates. That's all."

"You don't have to convince me."

Sara groaned as she leaned back against the railing. She felt stupid, like a teenager instead of a grown woman. She had divorced Jeffrey two years ago after catching him with the woman who owned the sign shop in town. Why she had started seeing him again was as much a mystery to Sara as it was to her family.

A Faint Cold Fear

Sara Linton, medical examiner in the small town of Heartsdale, Georgia, is called out to an apparent suicide on the local college campus. The mutilated body provides little in the way of clues—and the college authorities are eager to avoid a scandal—but for Sara and police chief Jeffrey Tolliver, things don't add up.

Two more suspicious suicides follow, and a young woman is brutally attacked. For Sara, the violence strikes far too close to home. And as Jeffrey pursues the sadistic killer, he discovers that ex-police detective Lena Adams, now a security guard on campus, may be in possession of crucial information. But, bruised and angered by her expulsion from the force, Lena seems to be barely capable of protecting herself, let alone saving the next victim.

Sara Linton stared at the entrance to the Dairy Queen, watching her very pregnant sister walk out with a cup of chocolate-covered ice cream in each hand. As Tessa crossed the parking lot, the wind picked up, and her purple dress rose above her knees. She struggled to keep the jumper down without spilling the ice cream, and Sara could hear her cursing as she got closer to the car.

Sara tried not to laugh as she leaned over to open the door, asking, "Need help?"

"No," Tessa said, wedging her body into the car. She settled in, handing Sara her ice cream. "And you can shut up laughing at me."

Sara winced as her sister kicked off her sandals and propped her bare feet on the dashboard. The BMW 330i was less than two weeks old, and Tessa had already left a bag of Goobers to melt in the backseat and spilled an orange Fanta on the carpet in the front. Had Tessa not been nearly eight months pregnant, Sara would have strangled her.

Sara asked, "What took you so long?"

"I had to pee."

"Again?"

"No, I just like being in the bathroom at the damn Dairy Queen," Tessa snapped. She fanned her hand in front of her face. "Jesus, it's hot."

Sara kept her mouth shut as she turned up the air-conditioning. As a doctor, she knew that Tessa was merely a victim of her own hormones, but there were times when Sara thought that the best thing for all concerned would be to lock Tessa in a box and not open it until they heard a baby crying.

"That place was packed," Tessa managed around a mouth-ful of chocolate syrup. "Goddamn, shouldn't all those people be at church or something?"

"Hm," Sara said.

"The whole place was filthy. Look at this parking lot," Tessa said, swooping her spoon in the air. "People just dump their trash here and don't even care about who has to pick it up. Like they think the trash fairy's gonna do it or something."

Sara murmured some words of agreement, eating her ice cream as Tessa continued a litany of complaints about everyone in the Dairy Queen, from the man who was talking on his cell phone to the woman who waited in line for ten minutes and then couldn't decide what she wanted when she got to the counter. After a while Sara zoned out, staring at the parking lot, thinking about the busy week she had ahead of her.

Several years ago Sara had taken on the part-time job of county coroner to help buy out her retiring partner at the Heartsdale Children's Clinic, and lately Sara's work at the morgue was playing havoc with her schedule at the clinic. Nor-mally the county job did not require much of Sara's time, but a court appearance had taken her out of the clinic for two days last week, and she was going to have to make up for it this week by putting in overtime.

Increasingly, Sara's work at the morgue was infringing on clinic time, and she knew that in a couple of years she would have to make a choice between the two. When the time came, the decision would be a hard one. The medical examiner's job was a challenge, one Sara had sorely needed thirteen years ago when she had left Atlanta and moved back to Grant County. Part of her thought her brain would atrophy without the constant obstacles presented by forensic medicine. Still, there was something restorative about treating children, and Sara, who could not have children of her own, knew that she would miss the contact. She vacillated daily on which job was better. Generally, a bad day at one made the other look ideal.

"Getting on up there!" Tessa screeched, loud enough to get Sara's attention. "I'm thirty-four, not fifty. What the hell kind of thing is that for a nurse to say to a pregnant woman?"

Sara stared at her sister. "What?"

"Have you heard a word I've said?"

She tried to sound convincing. "Yes. Of course I have."

Tessa frowned. "You're thinking about Jeffrey, aren't you?"

Sara was surprised by the question. For once her ex-husband had been the last thing on her mind. "No."

"Sara, don't lie to me," Tessa countered. "Everybody in town saw that sign girl up at the station Friday."

"She was lettering the new police car," Sara answered, feeling a warm flush come to her cheeks.

Tessa gave a disbelieving look. "Wasn't that his excuse the last time?"

Sara did not answer. She could still remember the day she'd come home early from work to find Jeffrey in bed with the owner of the local sign shop. The whole Linton family was both amazed and irritated that Sara was dating Jeffrey again, and while Sara for the most part shared their sentiments, she felt incapable of making a clean break. Logic eluded her where Jeffrey was concerned.

Tessa warned, "You just need to be careful with him. Don't let him get too comfortable."

Indelible

An officer is shot point-blank in the Grant County police station and police chief Jeffrey Tolliver is wounded, setting off a terrifying hostage situation with medical examiner Sara Linton at the center. Working outside the station, Lena Adams, newly reinstated to the force, and Frank Wallace, Jeffrey's second in command, must try to piece together who the shooter is and how to rescue their friends before Jeffrey dies. For the sins of the past have caught up with Sara and Jeffrey—with a vengeance . . .

Well, look what the cat dragged in," Marla Simms bellowed, giving Sara a pointed look over her silver-rimmed bifocals. The secretary for the police station held a magazine in her arthritic hands, but she set it aside, indicating she had plenty of time to talk.

Sara forced some cheer into her voice, though she had purposefully timed her visit for Marla's coffee break. "Hey, Marla. How're you doing?"

The old woman stared for a beat, a tinge of disapproval putting a crease in her naturally down-turned lips. Sara forced herself not to squirm. Marla had taught the children's Sunday school class at the Primitive Baptist from the day they opened the front doors, and she could still put the fear of God into anyone in town who'd been born after 1952.

She kept her eyes locked on Sara. "Haven't seen you around here in a while."

"Hm," Sara offered, glancing over Marla's shoulder, trying to see into Jeffrey's office. His door was open but he was not behind his desk. The squad room was empty, which meant he was probably in the back. Sara knew she should just walk behind the counter and find him herself—she had done it hundreds of times before—but survivor's instinct kept her from crossing that bridge without first paying the troll.

Marla sat back in her chair, her arms folded. "Nice day out," she said, her tone still casual.

Sara glanced out the door at Main Street, where heat made the asphalt look wavy. The air this morning was humid enough to open every pore on her body. "Sure is."

"And don't you look pretty this morning," Marla continued, indicating the linen dress Sara had chosen after going through nearly every item of clothing in her closet. "What's the occasion?"

"Nothing special," Sara lied. Before she knew what she was doing, she started to fidget with her briefcase, shifting from one foot to the other like she was four instead of nearly forty.

A glimmer of victory flashed in the older woman's eyes. She drew out the silence a bit more before asking, "How's your mama and them?"

"Good," Sara answered, trying not to sound too circumspect. She wasn't naive enough to believe that her private life was no one else's business—in a county as small as Grant, Sara could barely sneeze without the phone ringing from up the street with a helpful "Bless you"—but she would be damned if she'd make it easy for them to gather their information.

"And your sister?"

Sara was about to respond when Brad Stephens saved her by tripping through the front door. The young patrolman caught himself before he fell flat on his face, but the momentum popped his hat off his head and onto the floor at Sara's feet. His gun belt and nightstick flopped under his arms like extra appendages. Behind him, a gaggle of prepubescent children squawked with laughter at his less-than-graceful entrance.

"Oh," Brad said, looking at Sara, then back to the kids, then at Sara again. He picked up his hat, brushing it off with more care than was warranted. She imagined he could not decide which was more embarrassing: eight 10-year-olds laughing at his clumsiness or his former pediatrician fighting an obvious smile of amusement.

Apparently, the latter was worse. He turned back to the group, his voice deeper than usual as if to assert some authority. "This, of course, is the station house, where we do business. Police business. Uh, and we're in the lobby now." Brad glanced at Sara. To call the area where they stood a lobby was a bit of a stretch. The room was barely ten feet by eight, with a cement block wall opposite the glass door at the entrance. A row of photographs showing various squads in the Grant County police force lined the wall to Sara's right, a large portrait in the center showing Mac Anders, the only police officer in the history of the force who had been killed in the line of duty.

Across from the portrait gallery, Marla stood sentry behind a tall beige laminate counter that separated visitors from the squad room. She was not a naturally short woman, but age had made her so by crooking her body into a nearly perfect question mark. Her glasses were usually halfway down the bridge of her nose, and Sara, who wore glasses to read, was always tempted to push them back up. Not that Sara would ever do such a thing. For all Marla knew about everybody and their neighbor—and their dog—in town, not much was known about her. She was a widow with no children. Her husband had died in the Second World War. She had always lived on Hemlock, which was two streets over from Sara's parents. She knitted and she taught Sunday school and worked full-time at the station answering phones and trying to make sense of the mountains of paperwork. These facts hardly offered great insight into Marla Simms. Still, Sara always thought there had to be more to the life of a woman who had lived some eighty-odd years, even if she'd lived all of them in the same house where she had been born.

Brad continued his tour of the station, pointing to the large, open room behind Marla. "Back there's where the detectives and patrol officers like myself conduct their business . . . calls and whatnot. Talking to witnesses, writing reports, typing stuff into the computer, and, uh . . ." His voice trailed off as he finally noticed he was losing his audience. Most of the children could barely see over the counter. Even if they could, thirty empty desks spread out in rows of five with various sizes of filing cabinets between them were hardly attention grabbing. Sara imagined the kids were wishing they had stayed in school today.